P9-EMP-858

# ACCOLADES FOR *THE SNIPER'S WIFE* AND ARCHER MAYOR

★ ★ ★ ★

"The unfamiliar setting brings out a new, edge-of-the-knife side of Kunkle's incisive descriptive powers."
—**Marilyn Stasio,** *New York Times Book Review*

"The writing is strong, with sharp social observations throughout....Gunther grows on you from novel to novel."
—*Washington Post Book World*

"As always in a Mayor novel, the investigation is detailed and authoritative."
—*Philadelphia Inquirer*

"Mayor keeps getting better with age....Few writers deliver such well-rounded novels of such consistently high quality."
—*Arizona Daily Star*

"Here, Mayor does for New York what he has done for Vermont: He takes a longer, more careful look at the odd parts of a city we thought we knew all about."
—*Hartford Courant*

"Mayor's understanding of human behavior makes his tortured protagonist an unforgettable character. His powers of description not confined to Vermont, the author imbues well-known and obscure New York neighborhoods with a sparkling sense of place."
—*Publishers Weekly* (starred review)

*more . . .*

"One of the best contemporary American mystery writers."
—*Providence Sunday Journal*

"Mayor, a master of the slow-paced, small-town mystery, proves equally capable here of tightening his grip around the neck of the hard-boiled novel—without losing his feel for the subtlety of human interaction."

—*Booklist*

"A must read....Kunkle is a complex character....The early police procedural takes off into an action-packed crescendo."
—**www.bookloons.com**

"Deserves to move [Mayor] onto the A-list of mystery authors....The plot is flawless, the writing is smooth, and, like all good mysteries, we care about the characters as much as the story....Mayor has written one of the better mysteries of the year."

—**www.MyShelf.com**

"Strong...a powerful police procedural not so much because of the three seemingly separate parallel investigations but on account of the deep insight into what makes Willy what he is today."

—**www.bookbrowser.com**

"One of the sharpest writers of police procedurals."
—*Midwest Book Review*

"A great storyteller."
—*Maine Sunday Telegram*

"Lead a cheer for Archer Mayor and his ability not only to understand human relationships, but to convey them to his readers."
—*Washington Sunday Times*

"Mayor's major strength is his ability to etch personalities in their settings so that they are as vivid as a video."
—*St. Petersburg Times*

"Mayor's strength lies in his dedication to the old-fashioned puzzle, brought to a reasonable conclusion."
—*San Jose Mercury News*

"Mayor knows how to keep you turning pages."
—*Trenton Times*

"One of Mayor's strongest points is his detailed knowledge and application of police procedure."
—*Southbridge Evening News* (MA)

## Other Books by Archer Mayor

*Tucker Peak*

*The Marble Mask*

*Occam's Razor*

*The Disposable Man*

*Bellows Falls*

*The Ragman's Memory*

*The Dark Root*

*Fruits of the Poisonous Tree*

*The Skeleton's Knee*

*Scent of Evil*

*Borderlines*

*Open Season*

# THE
# SNIPER'S
# WIFE

---

# ARCHER MAYOR

**WARNER BOOKS**

NEW YORK   BOSTON

This is a work of fiction. Names, characters, places, and incidents are the product of the author's imagination or are used fictitiously. Any resemblance to actual events, locales, or persons, living or dead, is coincidental.

If you purchase this book without a cover you should be aware that this book may have been stolen property and reported as "unsold and destroyed" to the publisher. In such case neither the author nor the publisher has received any payment for this "stripped book."

WARNER BOOKS EDITION

Copyright © 2002 by Archer Mayor
Excerpt from *Gatekeeper* copyright © 2003 by Archer Mayor
All rights reserved. No part of this book may be reproduced in any form or by any electronic or mechanical means, including information storage and retrieval systems, without permission in writing from the publisher, except by a reviewer who may quote brief passages in a review.

*Cover design and art by Robert Santora*

Warner Books, Inc.
1271 Avenue of the Americas
New York, NY 10020

Visit our Web site at www.twbookmark.com

 An AOL Time Warner Company

Printed in the United States of America

Originally published in hardcover by The Mysterious Press

First Paperback Printing: October 2003

10  9  8  7  6  5  4  3

ATTENTION: CORPORATIONS AND ORGANIZATIONS:
Most WARNER books are available at quantity discounts with bulk purchase for educational, business, or sales promotional use. For information, please call or write: Special Markets Department, Warner Books, Inc. 135 W. 50th Street, New York, NY. 10020-1393.
Telephone: 1-800-222-6747  Fax: 1-800-477-5925.

To **Bob** Maas, for letting me glance over his shoulder from the front row seat.

# Acknowledgments

Seasoned veterans of the Joe Gunther series will note a change of approach in this book, not only with the narrative viewpoint, but with the setting as well. *The Sniper's Wife* is placed in New York City for the most part. This onetime change of locale is just that—I will not be abandoning the places and people that I and my readers have come to call our own over the years. But I do hope I will be forever exploring new ideas and concepts as I've done in the past, and that you will all continue to enjoy the ride.

That having been said, I owe a big debt of thanks to a great many people who helped me get as good a grip on New York and the workings of its police and corrections departments as possible. I hope I have not let them down—a more generous and encouraging group I have rarely met—but if I have, the fault is mine. I have nothing but gratitude to those listed below and to the many others who lent me a hand along the way.

The New York City Police Department, in particular Commissioner (retired) Bernard Kerick; Deputy Chief Joe Reznick; Detective Walter Burnes; Officer Mel Maurice; Sergeant (retired) Bob Maas; and Deputy Chief Jane Perlov (NYPD retired, currently Chief of Police, Raleigh, North Carolina, Police Department).

The New York City Department of Correction, in particular Commander William Fraser; Captain William Burgos; Officer Richard De Jesus; and Officer Edward "Ray" Raymond.

The Portsmouth, New Hampshire, Police Department, in particular Lieutenant Janet Champlin.

The Department of Alcohol, Tobacco, and Firearms, in particular Joe Green.

And also:
Phil Sarcione
Frank Thornton
Ana Mayor
Caroline and Tim Scully
Nick Bernstein
Dick Flynn
Fred Gardy
Colleen Mohyde
Michael J. and Sandra Lewis Smith
John McDonough, a true "dinosaur" from Massachusetts

To all of you, my deepest appreciation.

# Chapter 1

Willy Kunkle dipped his large right hand into the sink and scooped a splash of warm water onto his face, washing away the last of the shaving soap. He straightened, used the edge of a towel hanging to the right of the mirror to mop his cheeks and chin with the same hand, and studied his reflection in the harsh fluorescent light.

He wasn't looking for flaws in his shaving. And, God knows, there was no narcissism taking place. Willy was the first to acknowledge his was a purely functional appearance. He had what was necessary: a nose, two eyes, a mouth, none of it particularly remarkable. As far as it went, it was just a face.

And yet he studied it every morning the same way, carefully, warily, especially watching the eyes for any deepening of the intensity which even he found disturbing. Had he seen them on somebody else, they were eyes that would have given him pause—eyes which troubled him all the more that they were his. They were what made of the whole truly something to remember, and although he didn't know it, they were the one feature almost everyone remembered about his face.

His scrutiny drifted lower, again as usual, to his neck, to his collarbone, and finally to his left shoulder and the useless arm below it. He'd been symmetrical once—at the very least that. Now he was someone who carried an arm as an eccentric might perpetually lug around a heavy stuffed animal.

Except that his burden wasn't that interesting. It was just an arm, withered, pale, splotchy with poor circulation—something straight out of Dachau but pinned to his otherwise healthy body—put there by a rifle bullet in a police shootout years ago. In fact, the scar marked the dividing line between the alive and the dead of his body the way a ragged and permanent tear identifies where a sleeve has been torn from a shirt.

It did draw attention away from the eyes, though. People overlooked them altogether when describing him as "the cop with one arm." Which was an advantage, as far as Willy was concerned. He appreciated that a lesser but adequately flamboyant deformity covered for a far more telling one. It suited his personality. And his need. As he'd watched those eyes every morning—those windows into the workings of his head—he'd actually become grateful for the arm. It was his own built-in red herring.

He reached up and turned off the light. Time to go to work.

Winter had passed by at last, even mud season was nearing an end. A year's worth of weather in Vermont has been called nine months of winter and three more of damned poor sledding, but a quantity of subtleties is lost there. In fact, to those brought up in its midst, Vermont offers as many temperature and mood swings as any moderately complicated marriage, which is also how many natives view their relationship with the state.

Willy Kunkle was not a native. A "flatlander" by birth, transplanted from New York almost twenty years before, he didn't much care about the local fondness for climatology. It was either hot or cold to him, dry or wet. And discussing it wasn't going to change anything. Still, this was a very pleasant morning, and despite himself, he enjoyed the almost uncomfortably cold air drifting in through the open car window on his drive downtown.

Willy lived in Brattleboro, Vermont, a topsy-turvy, nineteenth century, postindustrial town of some twelve thousand residents squeezed into the state's southeast corner, hard by the Connecticut River and straddling three of Interstate 91's first exits out of Massachusetts.

This was a significant geographical detail. It made of Brattleboro the first taste of small-town Vermont to all those high-speed travelers coming out of the south, which is why a multimillion-dollar, high-tech welcome center had just been erected below Exit 1, and helped explain the town's financial survival when other historical mementos, like Springfield, Bellows Falls, and Windsor farther north, complete with similarly picturesque redbrick hearts, had faded to become mere economic ghosts of their former selves.

More specific credit for Brattleboro's stamina came from another unlikely flatlander source: back during the sixties, a small army of disaffected social dropouts, dizzy with blurry images of sylvan splendor and a thirst for isolation, barely crossed the state line to set up communes, natural food restaurants, and back-to-the-earth farms. Eventually, once the spiritual glow had either faded or aged, these erstwhile hippies amended enough of their more doctrinaire enthusiasms to become an integral part of an interestingly quirky, often contentious social fabric.

To the local police, however, Brattleboro's proximity to New Hampshire, Massachusetts, and the interstate had been slowly transforming the town from what the chamber of commerce called the gateway to Vermont into its doormat, a magnet for all the ills leaking out of the urban south—a cynical and narrow view, no doubt, but allowable given the source.

It also helped explain Willy Kunkle's presence here.

An ex–New York City patrolman, a Vietnam vet, and a dedicated alcoholic, Willy had ended up in Brattleboro first because he'd needed gas on his way to someplace—anyplace—he hadn't been to before, perhaps Canada. It hadn't been love at first sight or like having a revelation, but the double discovery of Brattleboro's busy downtown and a poster advertising openings at the police department had conspired to make him stay.

He'd begun by walking the streets, shunning patrol cars in exchange for the traditional beat, and had honed a talent for making contacts and connections in those parts of town few upstanding citizens cared to acknowledge. In the process, he'd become the one cop who most reliably could extract information where others came up empty-handed.

Thus, a serendipitous stop for gas and a job had led to a personal and professional progression he'd tried since to forget. Marching less to his own drummer and more as if on autopilot, Willy went through the standard evolutionary motions, watching himself like a spectator at a private parade. He met a local girl more confused than he, married her without much thought from either one of them, got transferred to the detective bureau in reward for his good work, and began hitting the bottle as never before.

Over a long, slow, agonizing period of years, he became like a gambler, his stake eroding to nothing, fully aware that his chances of winning were nil, but unwilling to change strategies and unable to leave the table. The alcohol abuse and disillusion led to self-loathing and anger, to wife abuse and a preordained divorce. He was crippled by a bullet in the line of duty, transferred off the police force, and came within half a step of joining the people he'd once been paid to arrest.

Then, in defiance of the gravitational pull he should have followed straight to the bottom, and with much the same disappointed bewilderment experienced by a drowner miraculously pulled back from a death finally become soothingly seductive, he was put back on the police payroll, told to fill in the proper paperwork, and accepted as a member of a newly created, statewide investigative agency called the Vermont Bureau of Investigation, with five regional offices, including one in Brattleboro.

Thus encouraged—almost cajoled—he'd gone from the edge of oblivion to getting on the wagon by his own sheer willpower, finding himself romantically involved with a female co-worker, and being regarded as one of the elite in his profession.

A roller-coaster ride of mixed and paradoxical emotions, and a happy, bittersweet end result entirely due—as he saw it in a typically angry dismissal of his own personal efforts—to a man named Joe Gunther.

Willy frowned and sighed heavily at the thought, cresting the top of High Street as it descended to intersect Main downtown, nearby Mount Wantastiquet in neighboring New Hampshire looming over a wall of buildings directly before him like a sleeping giant.

Joe Gunther hung on Willy's mind almost as much as the dead arm now resting in his lap.

Willy had read somewhere—unless he'd seen it at the movies—that in certain cultures, if you saved someone's life, that poor bastard was stuck having to return the debt and therefore keep you company until the day he could make good. If ever.

Well, much as he hated to admit it, Willy probably owed his life to Joe Gunther. Joe had been his boss on the police department's detective squad, had hovered sympathetically when he'd wrestled with booze and the divorce. He'd threatened to invoke the Americans with Disabilities Act and sue the town to get Willy back on the force after his injury. He'd cut him slack time and again, hadn't taken offense when Willy did his damnedest to give it, and had acted as a go-between when Willy had fallen in love with Sammie Martens—the other detective who'd made the move from the PD to the Bureau. Finally, after the legislature had created the VBI and the commissioner of public safety had tapped Joe as its field force commander, he'd made it clear that he wouldn't take the job unless Willy's application was given a fair review, after which he'd persuaded Willy to apply.

Why? Because Joe was a decent guy who acted the same way with everyone, and because, while he might not have been the life of any party, he was like a dog with a bone when it came to doing the right thing.

There were times, lots of times, when Willy raged at this man.

He waited at the stoplight, preparing to turn left up

Main. There was a shorter route to the office, but driving through downtown every morning had become a ritual.

The pedestrian walk sign began flashing, accompanied by an obnoxious chirping sound designed to help the blind cross safely. Willy shook his head. Only in Brattleboro, capital city of granola heads, where nothing ever happened without everyone worrying about how everyone else *felt* about it. There was enough hot air in this town to pop the *Titanic* back to the surface like a cork.

This cynicism belied Willy's years of service to this community, and his caring for its vital signs the way a doctor would a patient's every ache and pain.

He drove north, up Main toward the new, modern courthouse, perched on a grassy knoll like a shiny anchored ship, forcing the street to split around it like a current. Across the way, balanced on a second hill, was a complete architectural contrast: the ancient municipal building. A remodeled nineteenth century school, all bricks and spires and wrought-iron knickknacks, it was where Willy used to work as a cop and still did as a special agent, since the VBI had a small office located on the monstrosity's second floor.

His morning rounds completed, Willy circled the courthouse, cut around the block, and parked in the lot behind the municipal building.

Upstairs, Sammie Martens paused by the window at the end of the central hallway just outside the ladies' room, holding a pitcher of water intended for the office coffee machine. She saw Willy get out of his car, cross the parking lot, and vanish from view as he entered the building.

She waited to greet him, knowing he'd come straight

up, as usual. She preferred seeing him first in private, if possible, especially if they hadn't spent the previous night together. It helped prepare her for whatever mood he might be in. Dark to middling was the standard she'd grown used to before they'd become intimate, although nowadays, she was happy to note, there was the occasional suggestion that he was lightening up.

She listened in vain for his footsteps coming up the stairs, eventually resting the pitcher on the windowsill. It seemed he'd run into someone in the lobby.

She glanced out the window again, attracted by a sudden movement below, and saw Willy running back to his car, fumbling for his keys.

Surprised, she returned to the office, placed the water beside the coffeemaker, and addressed the older man sitting behind one of the four corner desks.

"Joe, did we just have a call come in? My pager didn't go off."

Joe Gunther looked up from what he'd been reading and gave her a thoughtful look before answering. "Not that I know of."

"I just saw Willy go running back out of the building to his car."

Her boss sat back in his chair and pursed his lips. "Maybe he forgot something at home."

She wasn't convinced. "Maybe. It didn't look like that. I saw him drive up like usual and waited for him at the top of the stairs for almost five minutes. He never made it."

Sam was suddenly struck by her own odd choice of words.

Gunther was used to Willy's ways. In the past, it had usually paid to give him a little leeway, and sometimes much more than a little. Whether Willy was the son Joe had never had or merely possessed by a spirit Joe found perversely irresistible, the bottom line remained that Willy Kunkle was one of the most instinctive police officers Joe had ever worked with, and therefore worth a little more than the usual slack.

"Give him half an hour, Sam. That'll allow for a round trip home and then some. After that, we can start shaking the bushes. If he's on to something, the first thing he'll want is to be left alone."

Sammie Martens went back to making coffee, unsatisfied and faintly apprehensive.

Exactly one-half hour later, she glanced at Gunther again, who merely caught her eye and nodded without comment. Sammie picked up the phone and called Willy's house.

There was no answer.

Frustrated, she rose and headed for the door. "I'm going downstairs—see if I can find out what set him off."

She turned into the radio dispatch area on the first floor and rapped on the bulletproof glass separating the dispatchers from the public. A woman half rose in her seat to peer over the console between them. "Hey, Sam." Her voice was made metallic by the two-way intercom. "What's happenin'?"

"I'm looking for Willy. You see him this morning?"

The woman's expression registered surprise, then confusion. "He didn't tell you guys?" She gestured to the side. "Come around to the door."

Sammie moved down the hallway to a locked door that opened almost as soon as she reached it. The dispatcher took her through the patrol officer's room to an empty office normally used by the PD's parking enforcement division, calling through the door of her own office as she did so, "Wayne, cover for me a sec, will you?"

"It was kinda funny," she explained to Sammie. "We got a call from a New York City detective asking if we could send an officer to locate someone named William Kunkle, who supposedly lived in Brattleboro. I started laughing and told him no one went out of their way to dig up Willy if they could avoid it. The guy was dead quiet, so I explained that Willy was a cop who worked upstairs. Which was exactly when Willy walked by the window. So I shouted to him to take the call on the wall phone. I was watching when he answered. He looked really intense for a couple of minutes, and then he hung up and vanished, just like that." She snapped her fingers. "I figured he was booking it upstairs to see you."

Sammie Martens shook her head. "I saw him through the window, running back to his car. What was the name of the New York cop?"

"Hang on." The woman crossed the narrow hallway into the dispatch area and retrieved a pad from her console desk. "Detective Ogden." She handed the pad over. "That's the number."

Sammie placed her hand on a nearby phone. "This okay?"

The woman nodded before resuming her seat at the console.

Sammie dialed and heard a deep, clear, almost radioquality male voice pick up on the other end. "Detective squad—Ogden."

"Detective Ogden, this is Special Agent Samantha Martens of the Vermont Bureau of Investigation in Brattleboro. You just talked to a colleague of mine, Willy Kunkle?"

"That I did."

"I don't want to step on any toes here, but could I ask what you talked about? He took out of here like a jackrabbit and didn't tell us what was up."

There was a long hesitation.

Sammie tried to help the man out. "I could have my supervisor call you. Or you can call him, so you'd know for sure I am who I say I am. VBI's in the phone book."

Ogden relented. "It's nothing that confidential. We were looking for a next-of-kin for a DOA we have down here."

Sammie was stunned and increasingly confused, having had to make a few calls like that herself. "Oh, my God. One of his family? But why call him? He has relatives right in New York that could act as next-of-kin."

"It's not that easy. The woman we have isn't strictly family. In fact, we don't know who she's related to. All we found in her apartment were her divorce papers from Mr. Kunkle. That's why I called him. I was looking for a blood relation and thought he could help. I didn't realize he took it so hard. That didn't come across in his voice."

Sammie nodded at the familiarity of that. "Did he give you a name?"

"Her mother's, but he said it would be a waste of time. And he was right. I just hung up on her. Told me her daughter had been dead to her for years already—that she didn't want anything to do with her. Actually, I'm kind of glad you called, 'cause we need a definite ID on this woman—"

"Mary," Sammie interrupted. "That was her name."

Ogden was caught off guard. "What? Oh, right. Sorry. Did you know her?"

"We met once, a long time ago. Department picnic."

"Okay. Well, anyway, we really need someone to ID Mary, and it's looking like William might be it, if he's willing. Mary's mother said that would suit her fine."

Sammie was filled with sadness, anxiety, even a perverse pinch of jealousy. She'd only met Mary Kunkle that single time, true enough, but she knew of their history as a couple, and the guilt that Willy carried for having beaten her once in a drunken rage and bringing the marriage to ruin. Never an emotional brick at the best of times, Willy was going to take this hard.

"What did she die of?"

"We're looking good for an accidental overdose. You think you could help me out?" Ogden asked.

Oh, Christ, Sammie thought, the word "overdose" rising like a snake from hiding. Now she knew for sure what channel Willy was on, which made her all the more fearful. "I don't think I need to," she answered. "He's already on his way."

# Chapter 2

It was nearing dark when Willy Kunkle approached the city. It shouldn't have been that late. It normally took under five hours to drive from Brattleboro to New York, and he'd gotten the call from Ogden first thing in the morning. The traffic wasn't to blame, however. It had been the turmoil in his head that had slowed him down and finally forced him off the road somewhere in Connecticut. He'd ended up going for a long, aimless walk before finding himself at a diner, drinking countless cups of coffee and pushing something slimy and uneaten around a plate with his fork.

None of it had helped. If he'd been more focused, he would have recognized the dangers of reverting to old, destructive, brooding habits, and moved to avoid feeding them. Increasingly, Willy had found that his best chance for peace of mind was in simply getting things done. He didn't talk about most issues, large or small. He definitely didn't ask how other people felt about them. He avoided even thinking about them. He just set himself a task, from cooking dinner to running an investigation to making love with Sammie, and then he did it. The trick was to get down that corridor between conception and goal without wasting time, without opening doors along the way, and without suffering fools who might try to make him do so. That's how he'd finally dealt with the nightmares after 'Nam, how he'd beaten off the alcohol, and how he'd learned to cope with the crippled arm. It's how he'd partitioned off what he'd done to Mary and what the attending loss of self-respect had cost him.

He'd finally concluded at the diner that he would therefore cut his ties to Vermont and to Joe Gunther, Sammie Martens, and the hope they represented. That way, if he didn't survive this trip down memory lane, if he slipped and was dragged under as was already beginning to happen, at least he'd have gone down alone, leaving behind only the memory of the world's most irascible colleague, friend, and lover.

And there was a hardheaded correctness to this that he willed himself to believe: He'd be goddamned if he was going to be the kind of excess emotional baggage for others that he'd always claimed others were for him.

However, as he crossed the Harlem River on the Henry Hudson Bridge with his pager off, and passed the very neighborhood he grew up in and where his mother still lived, he knew in his gut there would be enough baggage to go around for everybody.

And it wouldn't be long in coming.

The visit to Bellevue only aggravated the roiling anxieties Willy was trying so hard to tamp down. Even with a recent and extensive remodeling, the huge hospital and the familiar journey to the morgue reached up like a stifling fog to constrict his throat. As a rookie New York cop so many years before, he'd made this trip a half dozen times, collecting paperwork or dropping things off to help in some busy detective's investigation. He'd enjoyed being part of something outside a patrolman's routine and had found the morgue's forensics aspects interesting and stimulating: all those racked bodies offering entire biographies to those clever and motivated enough to decipher them. These visits had helped him to believe that although at the bottom of the ladder police work left something to be desired, the promises it held justified sticking it out for the long run.

Of course, that was before he'd drowned all such thinking in the bottom of a bottle.

The white-coated attendant greeted him at the reception area with little more than a grunt, and he followed him down a long, windowless, antiseptically white hallway, through a pair of double doors. There they entered a huge enhancement of Willy Kunkle's memory of the place: a tall room, shimmering with fluorescence and equipped with two opposing walls of square, shiny floor-to-ceiling steel doors. The sight of it made him stop in his tracks, struck by the image of a storage room full of high-end dormitory refrigerators, stacked and ready for shipment, gleaming and new.

The attendant glanced over his shoulder. "You are all right?" he asked in broken English.

Willy sensed the man's concern was purely self-interested. He didn't want to deal with a hysterical next-of-kin and miss more than he already had of the television program he'd been enjoying out front.

"Yeah." Kunkle joined him almost halfway down the row of cold cubicles.

The attendant consulted the clipboard in his hand one

last time and pulled open the drawer directly before him with one powerful, practiced gesture.

Like a ghost appearing through a solid barrier, the white-draped shape of a supine woman suddenly materialized between them, hovering as if suspended in midair.

The attendant flipped back the sheet from the body's face. "This is her?"

Willy watched the other man's face for a moment, looking for anything besides boredom. He thought he might be Indian, but in truth, he had no idea. He'd recently heard that forty percent of New York's population was foreign-born, now as in 1910.

The man scowled at him, suspicious of Willy's expression. "You see?"

Willy dropped his eyes to the woman floating by his waist, looking down at her as if she were asleep on the berth of a spaceship and they were about to share a voyage to eternity.

He studied her features, feeling as cold as she seemed, his heart as still as hers. A numbness filled him from his feet to his head, as if he were a vessel into which ice water had been poured.

Romantics would have the dead appear as marble or snow sculptures. The reality was far less remote and pleasant. Whatever blemishes the deceased once had were enhanced by death's yellow cast, and the tiny amount of shapeliness the musculature had maintained even in sleep was lacking, allowing the cheeks to pull back the smallest bit and the entire face to strain against the boniness of the skull beneath. This was truly a corpse, and little else.

He reached out slowly, but stopped short of touching her, struck by the vitality of his large, powerful right hand next to her drained, thin, mottled face, the same face he'd reduced to tears a dozen times over. She looked tired, as if the sleep she was engaged in now were of no use to her whatsoever. For some reason, that made him saddest of all. Surely she'd wished for some peace and quiet when she'd opted for this state. It almost broke his heart to think she hadn't been successful.

The attendant sighed. "It is Mary Kunkle?"

He'd butchered the last name. Willy glanced down the length of her shrouded body and noticed a toe tag ludicrously sticking out from under the far end of the sheet. It made her seem as if she were for sale.

He moved down to read the tag. It had her name and an address in Manhattan's Lower East Side, just south of the Williamsburg Bridge.

That small detail triggered the dormant analytical part of his brain and made him lift the sheet off her left arm. The detective on the phone had said she'd died of an overdose, and there, as stark evidence, was not only the single fresh wound of a needle mark in the pale, skinny crook of her arm, but ancient signs of similar abuse clustered about it like memories refusing to disappear.

"Yes, that's her," he finally answered, stepping back, allowing the attendant to flip the sheet back over Mary's face with all the detached flair of a custodian covering a sofa.


Willy stepped out into the city at night—huge, enveloping, teeming with life, extending for miles beyond reason. He looked around at the vaulting, gloomy, light-studded buildings looming over him like haphazardly placed monoliths, their black profiles outlined against a sky whose stars had been blotted out by the dull ocher stain of the city's reflected glow. He knew it was a cliché, but he couldn't shake the feeling of being just one of a million insects lost in an enormous ant farm, each a part of something whole, and yet, perhaps precisely because of that, utterly isolated. Mary had been one of them, and now lay dead, unnoticed and unmourned, for all he knew. He'd been one of them, too, and was feeling the ambivalence of being back in the fold. He wondered if erstwhile prisoners of Alcatraz felt the same way when they returned as ancient tourists.

The air had turned cooler and felt good against his forehead. He was hot and slightly dizzy, still teetering over the abyss between his past—exemplified by this city and the body in the morgue—and what he'd once thought was his future, but which all of a sudden was feeling impossibly remote. He stood on the sidewalk struggling to make sense of this time warp, worrying that the weight of the past would prove too heavy to shake off.

The smart thing would have been to get back in his car then and there and return to Vermont. He'd signed the morgue's paperwork on the way out. The police and other authorities would be satisfied with his service and would know where to find him in any case. He could even make arrangements for Mary's disposal long-distance, perhaps shipping her to her mother as a small poetic gesture.

But he knew he wouldn't be doing any of that. He'd known it on the drive down. Mary's death had made clear the need to settle issues he'd tried to abandon by escaping New York, but which had continued to cripple him as surely as any rifle bullet.

The real question, therefore, wasn't whether he would stay in the city to discover what had pushed Mary to vir-

tual suicide. It was whether the small glimmerings of
hopefulness he'd recently been acquiring in Vermont
would be strong enough to fight the undertow he could
already feel tugging at his ankles.

He shivered and pulled his light coat tighter around his
neck. The twilight season between winter and summer
was hard to call spring in a world of concrete and steel.
The days were pleasantly warm, but the nights still held
a snow-sharpened edge. Burying his hands in his pockets,
he set off toward the Lower East Side, some thirty blocks
to the south.

The decision to walk had immediate benefits. It put
him in motion, it let him blow off steam, and it took him
outside of his own head, a place he knew wasn't the
healthiest of environments. In a telling paradox, however,
walking these streets helped resurrect memories he'd
been struggling to suppress since hitting the city limits.

He'd grown up in New York, near the George Washington Bridge at the north end of Manhattan. He knew
these urban sounds and moods in particular, and was familiar with the almost organic energy that seeped from
the city's pavements like a steady pulse, twenty-four
hours a day. Alone in the middle of a darkened street, you
knew you were amid a huge number of people. You could
almost hear their collective breathing.

And despite the sterility implied in the "concrete
canyons" of lore, there were as many smells to this world
as might linger in any rain forest. As he strode along,
reacquainting himself with the rhythm of the evenly
spaced city blocks, ignoring the metronomically regular
pedestrian crosswalk signs in favor of what the traffic
was really doing, Willy Kunkle picked up dozens of
odors, some sour, some surprisingly sweet, most reminis-

cent of food, cooking or rotting, depending on his proximity to restaurant or alleyway. Most surprising was the occasional whiff of grass or silage, a furtive gift from an elusive Mother Nature.

Willy had walked such streets as a beat cop, fresh out of the academy, both proud and nervous to be in uniform, conscious of the heavy .38 bumping his hip, and honing the sarcastic, tough-guy demeanor he'd used defensively at home and which would become his trademark. He instinctively sought the company of the rougher crowd at the precinct, the guys who bent the rules and made sure the law was enforced to their own best advantage—the bullies and braggarts who in later years would turn his stomach and rank among his favorite targets.

It seemed so long ago now, before he went to Vietnam, before the booze he began sharing with those same men became more than a social habit, before he fled to Vermont, got married, and hit bottom.

There had been good times during his short stint as a New York cop, times of redemption and grace when his actions had benefited others. Why those moments hadn't guided him instead of being mere oases, he didn't know. Nor did he fully remember why he'd left to enlist, although there was a typical perverseness to joining a wrongheaded war everybody knew was a defeat in the making, and which even the right-wingers were hard-pressed to defend. When Willy landed in Vietnam, the fall of Saigon was barely a year away.

But there were other reasons pushing him to leave, too. Not just his own tension-filled family dynamics, but larger, cultural ones. New York in the late thirties, when his parents arrived from Europe, was the most powerful, influential city on Earth. Then, over the next forty years, hundreds of neighborhoods were gutted by expressways and gargantuan building projects. The autocratic Robert Moses and his urban renewal cronies sacrificed a city of people to a future devoted to the automobile, disturbing the intricacy of a living human tapestry and encapsulating huge numbers of displaced poor inside towering clusters of bland, geographically marginalized housing units that served as thinly disguised penitentiaries. The postwar economic expansion challenged the concept of centralized urban powerhouses like New York, and with startling speed the city went broke, garbage piled up in the streets, and the fuse began to burn. It became a city to abandon, and Willy took the hint.

He was in the East Village section by now, going strong, no longer mindful of the night air, watching how both the architecture and the mood had changed from that of just a few blocks earlier. This was the fringe of old New York, where numbered streets became names, and the strict grid pattern slowly yielded to the quirky remnants of an agrarian past, where waterways and farm-to-market paths marked the way people traveled hundreds of years ago. The city of neighborhoods began opening before him, the buildings becoming lower, older, more eccentric in design, their ground floors occupied by a bazaar of mom-and-pop outlets selling everything and anything. This was where the opposition to Moses and his road builders had finally succeeded, and made of New York one of the few big cities in the U.S. without a freeway splitting the downtown in two.

There was the inevitable dark side, of course, and ample evidence of decay. As he neared the Lower East Side—a slum virtually from its inception—where Mary had last lived, this transition grew exponentially, until at last all that was left, up and down her actual street, was a grimy, silent, commerce-free backwater of urban depression: a home for rats, cockroaches, and humanity's rejects.

Willy stood across from his late ex-wife's address and thought back to how often he'd gone to buildings similar to this, both here and in Vermont's grittiest corners, knowing that all he would find would be hopelessness personified.

For a man who pretended he'd lost the habit, this was way too much thinking. Willy took a deep breath and crossed the street.

# Chapter 3

The security in Mary's building was poor, no great surprise. Willy punched ten of the call buttons above the row of dented, graffiti-decorated mailboxes, got an atonal chorus of mixed replies over the loudspeakers, and at least one person who merely hit the buzzer opening the front door lock.

He decided to reconnoiter first, climbing to the third floor to find the apartment number he'd seen in the lobby under Mary's name, reacquainting himself with the familiar smell of poverty that clung to the walls like fresh paint. One flight up, however, he was stopped by an elderly woman who stepped out from behind her door.

"You ring downstairs?" she asked, her voice sharp and her jaundiced eyes narrowed. "Somebody rang."

He put on a surprised expression. "Me? No. Why?"

She ignored the question. "I don't know you."

He reached into his back pocket with feigned boredom and flashed his Vermont badge too fast for her to read it. It didn't actually look much like a New York detective's gold shield, but it was the right color, and he had the right attitude.

"Believe me, lady, the pleasure's all mine."

Her faced reddened and she slammed the door. He continued upstairs.

On the third floor, he caught sight of the yellow crime scene sticker down the hall to the left. The apartment was halfway to the end, the telltale sticker carefully applied to span where the door met the jamb. He studied the door briefly—old, battered, in need of paint, but undamaged—and gave the knob a tentative twist.

That would have been too lucky.

He checked out the rest of the floor, getting a feel for the place, before retreating back downstairs, past the lobby, and descending to the basement. There, he found a door labeled, "Super," just as he'd hoped.

A small, dark-skinned man with a thick mustache opened the door at the second knock. Willy already had his pad out, opened to a blank page.

"What?" the man asked.

Willy glanced at the pad. "Mr. Martinez? Detective Murphy. I need to get into apartment 318." Seemingly as an afterthought, he did the same dismissive badge flash he'd pulled on the old woman.

The super didn't even glance at it. "My name is José Rivera. I don't know Martinez."

Willy flipped back a couple of pages. "Jerks. Somebody screwed up—has you as Martinez in one place, Rivera in another. Typical. You got the key?"

Rivera looked disgusted. "Yeah, I got the key. Why, I don't know. Somebody dies and I lose the place for a year. You watch. What good's a key for a place I can't rent? You people need to fix that. The system stinks, and the apartment stinks, too. All the shit that's in there, and nobody to clean it up. The neighbors bitch and I can't do nothing about it. I had a guy die two years ago and rot for a week before I found out. I lost three places that time—the people next to him moved out 'cause of the smell. Three places I was out." He held up three fingers.

Willy nodded. "Key?"

Rivera stared at him a moment. "You guys," he muttered disgustedly, before unhooking a key from the wall just inside the door. "Here." He pointed to an old-fashioned mail slot cut into his front door. "When you're done with it, put it back here."

Back upstairs, Willy paused before Mary's door, again listening to the murmurs of life around him, and more specifically to how well he could hear them. It was a reflex born of years of practice. His pilgrimage here was emotionally stimulated. He wasn't running an investigation. But habits, good and bad, were hard to break, and this one told his subconscious that the walls in this building were as thin as might be expected—and, as the woman downstairs had demonstrated, not without ears.

He carefully slit the police label at its crease, fitted the key to the lock, and pushed the door open.

The smell that swept out to envelop him wasn't staggering, but it wasn't good, either: cloying, sweet, with an overripe pungency that caught in his throat. He began breathing through his mouth and closed the door softly behind him.

He didn't turn on any lights at first. He just stood there, looking around, letting his eyes adapt to the darkness. He could see from the faint glimmer seeping in through the far door facing him that he was already in a small, narrow kitchen. He'd noticed earlier that the building easily dated back a hundred and fifty years, maybe more. The kitchens had probably all been afterthoughts, put in where entryways had once allowed visitors to take off their coats.

Moving slowly, he passed by a counter, sink, and stove to his left, a closet and a shallow pantry on his right. At the doorway opposite, he stopped again.

Light through a dirty window on the right wall etched a glowing rectangle across the floor and partially up the wall beside him, brightly enough that he could see most of the room's details. There was a dark, caved-in couch before him facing the window, a narrow coffee table in front of it, and some shelves lining the wall opposite, bracketing both sides of the window. In the corner across from him was an armchair, covered with a shawl. Hard to his right, doubling back and paralleling the kitchen, was a tiny bathroom, and just beyond its open door was a wooden crate, also draped, supporting a small, ancient television set. A little incongruously, given the cool temperature, there was a plastic electric fan balanced on top of the set.

On the far side of the living room was another open door.

He studied the gore and debris spread across the couch and the floor before it—the bodily fluids showing black, and the gloves and other discarded medical paraphernalia looking like bits of bleached wreckage in the gloom. Overlying it all, quivering and moving with a barely perceptible clicking, a carpet of cockroaches was feasting.

His heart rate didn't increase, he made no gesture or comment, he showed no emotion whatsoever as he recreated in his head the scene that had left such a signature. He could almost see Mary's body sprawled across the couch, and the paramedics doing whatever they routinely did to bodies they had no real intention of reviving.

He'd seen too much of this kind of thing to do anything other than look at it clinically.

He crossed over to the last room in the apartment, noticing as he did that the window overlooked a fire escape and a dark alleyway below, and that the light seeping through it came from an assortment of apartments across the way.

He was now looking into a small bedroom, the darkest corner yet, especially with him filling the doorway. Its one narrow window had been blocked with a colorful poster and jammed shut with a wad of old subway Metro cards. But the lingering odor in here, even tainted by what was behind him, was fresher, cleaner, and faintly scented by intimate memories of a bright-eyed, smiling, happy young woman.

He returned to the living room window, drew down the paper shade for privacy, and began turning on lights.

This should have resulted in a jarring contrast: a place of misery cloaked in darkness, revealed in brittle brightness as even worse than imagined. Instead, the reverse proved true. What Willy discovered was a poor, rundown, seedy little apartment enhanced by paint and colorful fabrics, highlighted by fake flowers and cheerful calendar pictures. The mask couldn't hide the reality of the setting, but the attempt had been heartfelt and thorough, and by and large successful. The mess covering the couch stood out not as confirmation of the lifestyle echoed throughout the rest of the building and the neighborhood, but in gruesome contrast to Mary's concerted efforts to make this hole a home.

Willy made a second survey, still not touching anything, carefully placing his feet. The apartment was far from tidy, although the mess had clearly been made by others: the bedroom drawers had been rifled, the nearby desktop pawed over, the closets opened and their contents disturbed. All signs of a typical police search. Somewhere in here, the detectives who'd caught this case had found Mary and Willy's divorce papers in their pursuit of a next-of-kin, and, he assumed, had removed them and any other relevant records and items of value for safe-keeping. What they'd left behind was the miniature version of a passing army's pillaging.

But as with any army, what had been taken were things of specific worth, here relating to identity and research and to closing a case quickly. Left behind was the rest, details of a life interrupted in midcourse, and the very items Willy Kunkle most wanted to peruse.

He returned to the kitchen, scattering all but the most brazen of the roaches, and began reacquainting himself with his ex-wife from the outside in, starting with her eating habits. Using his pocketknife or grabbing things by their edges, he opened drawers, doors, and cabinets and took inventory.

What he found didn't fit the usual profile of a junkie. The standard binge items heavy in sugar or fat were missing, the lopsidedness of a larder composed solely of canned soup and frozen dinners was also absent. Instead, he was left with an economical and healthily varied assortment, neatly sorted and arranged. He closed the last cabinet softly, leaned up against the doorjamb, and gazed out into the living room again for a moment's careful reflection. A process born of instinct but without particular purpose now shifted gears with this finding. He began thinking like an investigator.

He crossed over to the bedroom, knowing the living room would hold the least, although perhaps the most subtle, information.

He started with the bed. It was disturbed, but only slightly, as if the person sleeping in it had just gotten up. Otherwise, its bottom corners and far side were tucked in, indicating the habitual tidiness he remembered of Mary in her prime, and he could tell from the single pillow and the way the night table and reading light were arranged that she was used to sleeping alone. Pushing his nose against the sheets to close off the odor from the room next door, Willy found they were also clean, and smelled faintly of detergent.

He checked beneath the bed. The floor was free of dust, and all he saw was a small, empty suitcase and a pair of well-worn slippers, neatly arranged.

Next came the closet. Again, he was struck by the same sense of order that had ruled the kitchen. There were no clothes on the floor, the few shoes were lined up, the odds and ends found in every closet were either stacked on the overhead shelf or hidden away in several small cardboard boxes. He checked their contents and found only belts, gloves, rolled-up pantyhose, hair clips, and an assortment of other mundane items. He went through the two purses he also unearthed and the pockets of every coat, jacket, and pair of pants. All he located were a few neighborhood grocery receipts, an old movie stub, and several more expired Metro cards, which he placed in a small stack along with the other Metro stubs he now extracted from the window jamb.

He moved to the desk, knowing the most obviously useful material had already been removed. Still, as he went through what was left—mostly old bills—he was once more struck by the sense of a life under control, rudely interrupted.

The desk doubled as a makeup table, and after looking through its one deep drawer, Willy sat back and studied the boxes, bottles, and paraphernalia spread before him, again mentally subtracting from them what had obviously been disturbed in the search. What it revealed to him was a woman concerned with her appearance, whose aids in caring for it were new or well maintained. All the containers of lipstick or powder or mascara were capped, carefully arranged, and out for ready use.

Willy paused thoughtfully. Now that his professional interest had been called up, he regretted the thoroughness of those preceding him. They'd taken almost everything of value. Mary had used a date book in the old days. It was missing. She'd always kept personal letters. There were none around. No phone records were in the desk, no bank statements. Oddly, touchingly, tucked into the mirror's edge was a small snapshot of Willy and Mary on a ferryboat crossing Lake Champlain, with Burlington in the background.

He reached out and plucked it from its niche. On the back, in pencil, was the year they were married. He stared at it for a while, studying both their faces, watching his own eyes for any signs of what lay ahead, thinking he saw it all clearly, and wondering why she hadn't. He also looked at his then-functional left arm, draped casually across her shoulders. The guy who'd taken the picture had asked him to do that, saying it would look friendlier. Willy had told her later he'd thought the guy was an asshole. She'd merely looked at him sadly. In his mind's eye, he could again feel the warmth of her shoulders through the fabric of his shirt.

He tossed the picture onto the tabletop and got up. So far, he hadn't found any sign of her being involved with another man.

He went to the small bathroom beside the kitchen. There was a shower curtain running around the inside of an old claw-foot tub, a pedestal sink facing a wall cabinet with a mirrored door, and a toilet. It was all ancient and battered, but built to withstand the average artillery assault—heavy porcelain, cast iron, a tile floor. What Mary had been able to make clean, she had. The rest was either chipped, cracked, or stained beyond the help of minor surgery. It was standard New York fare, and made him think back to his own bathroom as a boy, or at least the one he'd shared with the rest of the family. He'd hated that bathroom—the constant interruptions when he'd hoped to be alone, the presence of so many other people's personal items, from Kotex pads in the pail by the toilet, to mangled toothbrushes and mysterious smears of who-knew-what around the sink. And his mother used to leave her underwear hanging off the shower nozzle overnight, after washing it in the sink. Drove him nuts.

Not Mary, though. Here, nothing was out of place. That had driven him nuts, too.

He opened the cabinet door: aspirin, brush, comb, a headband to hold back her hair, cotton balls in a dish, a variety of lotions and creams, toothbrush and paste, a backup bar of soap, still in its wrapper.

And a birth control dispenser, its dated slots empty up to the day she died.

He held the plastic clamshell in his hand, reading the prescription on its cover. These were sometimes taken medicinally, he thought, not just for practical purposes. Other times, they were merely wishful thinking in pill form, and didn't actually indicate any active sexuality. Given the lack of romantic evidence elsewhere in the apartment, Willy was left to wonder.

Finally, ignoring the stench, he returned to the living room and tried imagining the life it had once contained. Here, books were read, conversations held on the phone by the couch, the TV was watched. Sometimes, the walls were studied during daydreams or in thought—or in despair. Frugality spoke for itself. Everything was threadbare, worn, or cheaply made. But there was pride as well. The place was clean, the colorful accents he'd noticed earlier had been strategically placed to either please the eye or cover a defect, or both.

He approached the pine-board-and-brick bookshelves next to the window and studied their contents. Romantic novels, a few standard reference works, carefully piled-up fashion and travel magazines. Gaps between volumes were filled with plastic figurines or a cheerful piece of inexpensive pottery. He recognized an odd-looking rock she'd collected when they'd been walking together near the river back in Brattleboro, and which he'd told her was a stupid thing to lug around. There were other familiar odds and ends he saw from their time together.

A few pictures stood among the books, either framed and free-standing on a pop-out cardboard leg or simply propped up and slightly curling. He recognized the mother who would have nothing to do with her—a hardbitten woman with cold, judgmental eyes. There was a sunset photograph of some Vermont mountain, probably Jay Peak. And a group shot of Mary surrounded by five others, all laughing at the camera, their arms interlaced. Willy brought this last off the shelf and held it under the light, studying the faces before him, his eyes lingering over Mary's. She looked absolutely, totally happy. In the background was a sign mounted against a gritty, urban brick wall, which he assumed belonged in this city. It read, "The Re-Coop." There was nothing written on the back of the photograph, but tucked into the corner of the actual image was a burned-in date. The picture has been taken only two months before. Willy slipped it into his breast pocket.

He continued his search, carefully riffling through the books, checking the magazines for earmarks or stray pages or notes. He looked under the small rug, checked under the pillows of the couch and armchair. Other than some change, a couple of paper clips, and a petrified pretzel, he found nothing.

Finished at last, he was left standing beside the coffee table, almost absentmindedly staring at the one utterly discordant note in the whole place: the clotted, fetid remains of what Mary's body had left behind, and the reemboldened army of cockroaches that had taken his ignoring them as encouragement to resume their meal.

After a pause, Willy moved to the kitchen, retrieved what he needed, and set to work cleaning up the mess, double bagging what he could collect using a sponge, and scrubbing the remaining stains with disinfectant and cleaning fluid. It took him over an hour, and when he was done, the damp spots he'd created looked worse than what had been there before. But he knew they would dry and disappear, and already the air smelled better. It wasn't as good as Mary could have done, but it returned the apartment to being a more suitable monument. As for the scene's integrity, Willy didn't even want to think what the cops would say of his handiwork. Assuming it mattered. He knew this police department. He knew this city.

He even knew how he would have dealt with this situation had he caught the case. This wasn't a crime scene, as far as the NYPD was concerned. It was just an apartment caught in the limbo of a ponderous bureaucracy which would take six months or more to decide that nothing unusual had happened here.

And maybe they were right, although Willy now had some questions.

He gathered his refuse together, added to it the increasingly odorous garbage from under the kitchen sink, and dumped it all down the chute he found partway down the third-floor corridor.

Afterward, he neatened the disarray the cops had created in their search, killed most of the lights, lifted the window shade, settled into the dry corner of the couch, and watched the play of lights and shadows in the windows across the alleyway.

Eventually, without intending to, he finally yielded to the anxiety and adrenaline that had fueled him most of the day and drifted off to sleep.

# Chapter 4

NYPD precinct houses generally come in two basic models: old, dating back to before Teddy Roosevelt and awkwardly retrofitted for almost everything, including electricity; and modern, meaning circa 1970, implying some up-to-date conveniences, but only in exchange for an architectural style as lacking in taste as the clothing of the same era. When Willy Kunkle had worked for the department, he'd been stationed at one of the old-timers, which, despite its many drawbacks, had appealed to him for its sheer sense of place. The huge, elaborately carved golden oak sergeant's desk in the entrance lobby, the wrought-iron and brass details throughout the building, and its solid stone appearance had all reminded him of the history and traditions that helped see the department through its rough times—and occasionally led it straight into them.

The Seventh Precinct house, however, had none of that. Of the modern era, made of red brick, and sharing its roof with a fire department ladder company, it was bland-ness personified, as creatively and sensitively designed as a security-minded high school or a low-profile prison. It was spacious, though, or a least bigger than many of its ancient brethren, and so had more room for its occupants to complain about.

One detail all these buildings shared, however, came back to Willy's memory before he was a half block from the front door: The parking was lousy. For some reason, none of the precincts were equipped with more than a minuscule number of designated spots, which meant anyone who wasn't in management double-parked on the street, pulled up onto the sidewalks, or otherwise caused enough of a problem that the precinct commander was constantly in meetings with irate neighborhood representatives.

Willy walked past car after haphazardly parked car with special plates thrown onto their dashboards before finally passing through the Seventh Precinct's front door. He was greeted with a familiar chorus of sights, sounds, and smells he doubted was much different from any one of the other seventy-five houses sprinkled across the city's five boroughs. The ringing phones, general milling population, and the institutional decor consisting of framed portraits of department leaders and motivational posters all brought him back to the very first day he'd entered this world, feeling awkward in his bulky new uniform. It was early enough in the day, in fact, that the morning patrol shift was still in the muster room across from the long, battered, pressed-wood sergeant's desk. Willy could see, through its broad doors, the uniformed assemblage facing the duty sergeant at his podium, taking notes as he read from a binder and pointed from time to time at a collection of glassed-in wall maps covered with variously colored pins—crime maps indicating current trends in the precinct.

"May I help you?" the receptionist asked him from her school-style desk.

He looked down at her as if she'd interrupted him in mid-dream. "I'm here to see Detective Ogden. My name's Kunkle."

She glanced at his left arm, its hand as usual stuffed into his trousers pocket. "Upstairs, second floor, third door on the right."

He glanced over her head at the activity at the long front desk, manned by an oversized, avuncular sergeant and his frazzled-looking aide. These were the precinct's air traffic controllers. They knew which prisoners were in holding, who was out on patrol and where, what weapons had been logged in for safekeeping, and a multitude of other details that helped keep the place running. They took messages, handled phone calls, assigned tasks throughout the building, and acted as human bulletin boards, all amid a din of colliding human voices. They were the keepers of the *Patrol Guide,* the bible of the uniformed cop, and knew its contents the way they knew their own family members, dispensing advice whenever called upon. The flow of officers and civilians alike in front of this desk, picking up or dropping off paperwork or just chatting briefly, was nonstop.

Upstairs, the noise was less of a commingled babble, being segregated into a series of offices extending off to both sides of the landing. He counted three doors on his right, walked past several stacks of old boxed case files, and stepped into an office with a cardboard sign labeled, "Detectives."

There he stopped, observing the scene before him. The room was moderately large, with a mismatched scattering of dented and scarred desks. The lighting was fluorescent, accompanied by some daylight through a row of high, smudged windows. The floors were damaged and worn linoleum, the painted cinderblock walls plastered with charts, rows of clipboards, more framed photographs and posters, and multiple bulletin boards, all attempting to hide a paint job of queasy industrial green. The air was filled with ringing phones, general conversation, and, in an almost incongruous throwback to a previous era, the sound of typewriters. As in the hallway outside, there were boxes piled everywhere: along the walls, under the windows, between doors. The place looked like a moving company on a lunch break, except he knew from past experience that few of these boxes had been moved in years.

There were five men sitting at the odd assortment of desks in the middle of the floor, none of whom paid him any attention.

"Help you?" a voice asked from his right.

He turned and saw a civilian employee sitting at a workstation equipped with the room's most modern computer.

"Yeah. I'm looking for Detective Ogden."

The computer operator called out to a man working near one of the windows—tall, broad-shouldered, with close-cropped gray hair, looking comfortable enough that the entire precinct house might have been built around him. Ogden was speaking quietly on the phone, reading from an open file before him. He glanced up, saw the assistant point to Willy with raised eyebrows, and waved Willy over, gesturing to the wooden chair beside his desk. One of its slats was missing.

"Thanks," Willy muttered, and crossed the room,

noticing as he did so the flickered glances of the men he passed, taking inventory.

A tiny glimmer of gold from Ogden's sport coat caught Willy's eye as he sat down: a small lapel pin in the shape of a brontosaurus. Willy studied the other officer more carefully, thinking back to Joe Gunther in Vermont.

That pin identified Ward Ogden as a "dinosaur," one of an elite few, the NYPD version of a Knight of the Round Table—skilled, battle-scarred, savvy, with an elephantine memory and enviable contacts. Dinosaurs were career detectives, classified First Grade and thus pulling down a lieutenant's salary, but preferring to stay on the streets, catching cases, and given those rare pins by their respectful peers. For the most part, they were older, nearing retirement, had often gone to the academy with people who were now chiefs and sometimes even the commissioner, and were the most seasoned of what the detective bureau could offer. But they were more than that. It wasn't just age that made a dinosaur. There was a mystique behind the lapel pin. These people had true bearing within the department. They'd successfully closed headline cases, sometimes several of them, with dignity and grace, paying homage to all who'd helped them, and avoiding the publicity that their more politically minded, upwardly mobile brethren so eagerly courted. Dinosaurs, like the brontosauruses chosen to symbolize them, were quiet giants.

More cynically, Willy also knew, a helpful dinosaur was worth money in the bank, while the pissed-off version would make staying in New York a waste of time.

Ogden hung up the phone and stuck out his hand to shake Willy's. "Detective Kunkle?"

Willy was surprised. "How'd you know?"

Ogden laughed. "Lucky guess. I'm Ward Ogden. Thanks for coming by. I'm sorry for your loss. Would you like a cup of coffee?"

Willy shook his head. "No, thanks. Had one already."

Ogden pointed his chin at the mug on his desk. "Smart man. I drink way too much of the stuff. My wife, Maria, says it'll be the end of me in the long run. Probably right, too, although I tell her she hangs around doctors too much. She's a nurse. When did you get in?"

Willy proceeded carefully. "Last night. I didn't want to waste time."

Ogden understood. "So, you've been by Bellevue already?"

Willy watched the other man's eyes, looking for what he might be after. In this kind of conversation, a man with Ogden's experience didn't ask questions he didn't have the answers to, especially when they were already part of the record somewhere. No more than he had to rely on any "lucky guess" to know who Willy was. Willy decided to call him on it and establish a bit of his own credibility.

"Just like it says in their report."

Ogden smiled slightly. "What's it like being a cop in Vermont?"

"Not so intense. We get to spend more time on our cases. The press covers each and every one, though, the money's lousy, and turf's still a big deal."

Ogden nodded. "Yeah. I guess every homicide is front page news—everybody wants a piece of it."

"Every homicide, every robbery, damn near every fender bender." Willy had questions, too, and he dearly wanted the answers, but for once in his life, he was going to let the other party lead the dance.

Ogden sat back in his chair. "Well, more to the point,

I was sorry to be the one to break the news of your ex-wife's death. That must have been a shock."

Willy kept it short and honest. "Yes, it was."

"Had you two kept in touch at all?"

"No. It wasn't the friendliest of breakups." He wondered why he'd volunteered that bit. It was none of Ogden's business.

"That's too bad. Marriage and cops are a tough mix."

"You been divorced?"

The older man looked at him before responding, and Willy realized he'd broken an unstated ground rule. This was not a level playing field, despite the professional courtesy.

"How long ago was that?" Ogden asked.

Willy felt himself bristling on the inside, and felt doubly angry. Ever so gently, Ogden was pushing him around. Successfully.

He tried the same approach of a minute ago. "Like it says in the divorce papers you have: twelve years."

Ogden looked solicitous. "I apologize, Detective Kunkle. Is this a sore subject?"

Normally, Willy would have called the man an asshole and walked out of the room. But that was partly the point of the question. Ogden was taking his measure.

Willy took a deep breath and admitted, "I was a drunk back then. I hit her once. And that was the end of it. She was right to leave. I was a loser."

Ogden shook his head gently. "You've quit drinking, you were wounded on duty, and now you're on a top-notch squad. Could be you're being a little tough on yourself."

It was meant as a compliment, even though it confirmed that Ogden had checked him out. But there was more to Willy's past than what was available through a computer check and some phone calls. And that gap made Willy think resentfully of Joe Gunther again, the man who'd had more to do with Willy's upward mobility than he believed he had himself.

"Could be Vermont's like a cop version of kindergarten," he blurted out resentfully. "Doesn't take a wizard to get ahead. Even a gimpy drunk can do it."

Ogden's expression didn't change, but his eyes stayed on Willy's, and Willy felt all the more foolish for his outburst. He wished he could go back outside and at least take a walk around the block to clear his head. Back home, he routinely took people apart during interrogations, while never laying a hand on them. He'd humiliate them, cajole them, embarrass them, almost pummel them with language. And here he was, rising to every bait Ogden put before him, including the ones Ogden wasn't aware of.

"What d'you have on Mary's death?" Willy finally asked, as much to move on as to get an answer.

Ogden's face softened. "The ME left a message for me. I got it this morning. They did the autopsy right after you ID'd the body. There's a detailed final protocol and a tox report that won't come through for weeks, but absent any signs of criminality there, they're confirming what we've thought all along: apparent heroin overdose."

Willy's jaw tightened. That wasn't enough for him—a couple of cops poking around, a late-night off-the-cuff one-liner from a medical examiner. It didn't fit what he'd found at the apartment, or, more importantly, what he'd felt spending the night there. But that wasn't anything he could admit, nor did he want anyone to know of his misgivings, for fear of being thrown out.

Still, if he didn't show at least part of his hand, he'd never get Ogden to do the same with what they'd collected. And that was something Willy really wanted to see.

"I saw her track marks," he said, trying to sound purely professional. "Except for the one that killed her, they all looked pretty old."

Ogden's eyebrows furrowed slightly. "That's not too surprising, is it? A lot of addicts overdose because they shoot the same load they did when they were regulars. Only their systems aren't used to it anymore."

That ran against Willy's professional instinct to always "think dirty." Even knowing what this man's workload must be, he found the comment conveniently pat. "I suppose."

Ogden sighed slightly. "The door was locked from the inside, the window, too. There was no sign of violence and nothing obvious missing. I know this is hard to face, but I think what we see here is what we got."

After a pause, still studying Willy's face, he added, "What're your plans?"

Willy didn't want to lie outright, but he hedged his bets with his phrasing. "I want to find out more about her life down here—what led her to it."

Ogden hesitated before asking, "There anything going on I should know about?"

"I don't know," Willy answered truthfully. "I need to talk to some of the people who knew her—if I can find out who they were." He then steered for safer waters, adding blandly, "I'm not arguing with your conclusions. She was a user. I just . . . well, you know . . . I feel pretty responsible."

That was truer than Ogden could know, but his choice

of words had been kept simple for their manipulative effect. One thing about dinosaurs: In exchange for their experience and wisdom, they often lost the knee-jerk judgmental hard edge they might have had early on. Having seen damn near everything there was to see, they viewed their fellow humans in a more tolerant light. Willy was counting on Ward Ogden's sharing that outlook, and perhaps on his cutting him a little slack.

Ogden was apparently having the same internal debate. "You don't know any of her friends down here?" he asked.

"Nobody."

After another thoughtful pause, Ogden reached a conclusion. He stood up, motioning Willy to stay. "I have to go use the men's room for about fifteen minutes." He tapped on a closed file with his fingertip. "That's what we got on your wife. Make sure you don't give it a quick read while I'm gone."

He leaned forward slightly, resting one hand on the desktop so his face was inches from Willy's. "Don't do me dirt here, okay? This is cop-to-cop."

Willy matched his gaze. "You got it."

He waited until Ogden had left the room before reaching out and swiveling the file around right side up. No one else in the room was paying any attention, so he flipped it open and began to read.

First on top was the responding patrol officer's UF-61 complaint report. In dry, unimaginative prose, it told of Mary's ailing, elderly neighbor's calling to say that Mary hadn't knocked on her door in several days to share their ritual cup of morning coffee. Additionally, the super, Mr. Rivera, when told of the same concern, had pounded on Mary's door to no response, but had noticed a foul odor coming from the apartment. It was the super using his master key who let the officer in, where he found the decedent, an apparent overdose, dressed in her nightgown, lying on the couch, the needle she'd used still in her arm.

Beneath the UF-61 was Ogden's own DD-5, or follow-up report, commonly called a "pink" for its color.

Willy skimmed the pink before moving quickly on to the scene photos and sketches, feeling his face tighten as he saw Mary from every angle, harshly lit, grotesquely exposed, rendered disgusting and foul by her body's own reactions to the poison she'd injected. General shots of the apartment showed him most of what he'd seen last night, except that the shade was drawn in front of the window and the entire apartment looked neat and tidy, since the pictures predated the search.

Of the close-ups, he studied the shots of the locked window and door, the syringe dangling from her arm just below the rubber tubing she'd wrapped around her biceps, and the photograph of the plastic bag containing the heroin she'd used. Crudely stamped on its surface in red ink was a simple cartoon drawing of a devil, complete with horns, tail, pitchfork, and leering expression: the dealer's trademark, as relevant in the competitive urban drug world as any other advertisement. Willy didn't doubt that if he asked the right people about Little Devil or Red Devil or whatever name went with this symbol, he'd be directed to the proper outlet. He also knew that was about all he'd gain from the experience. Nevertheless, he pocketed one of the pictures of the bag.

Next in the file came the papers he'd been looking for: the divorce decree, tax forms, pay stubs, various bills, personal letters, and Mary's bank account. In fact, there

wasn't much there. If the sum total of such documenta-
tion was any reflection of a person's standing in society,
then Mary Kunkle barely had a toehold. There were only
three letters, all recent, all from friends telling her about
things of no interest to Willy. Her back account revealed
that she had $228.34 in checking, her tax records showed
her below the poverty level, and her pay stubs for a miserable amount came from the same place he'd seen in the
background of the group photograph back in her apartment: the Re-Coop. There was no address book anywhere
in the file, nor was there a date book or journal. And she
had always had both in the past.

The phone bill was the last item and was just two
pages long, largely made up of the arcane and slippery-
sounding fees and extra charges that always seemed to be
there.

Willy glanced at it with no great care, mostly looking
for an unusual prefix, either to someplace far away or to
a 900 number that might indicate an interesting wrinkle
in Mary's lifestyle.

Instead, he found several calls to a number in southern
Westchester County—a number he didn't need to cross-
reference.

It belonged to his brother, Bob.

Ward Ogden returned from checking some files down the
hall—and using the bathroom so as not to be a total liar—
and found the file where he'd left it. Willy Kunkle was
gone.

"You see where the guy went who was sitting here?"
he asked one of his colleagues.

The other man looked up from his paperwork, a phone

wedged under his chin. "He left," he said vaguely, "not two minutes ago. Said to say thanks."

Ogden resumed his seat and tapped on the file with his fingertips. "Yeah, I bet," he said softly.

The phone next to him rang. "Ogden—detective squad."

"Detective, this is Joe Gunther." The voice on the other end was hollow and tinny-sounding, clearly on a speakerphone. "Special Agent Sammie Martens is on the line with me. We're with the Vermont Bureau of Investigation."

Ward Ogden knew where this was heading. "You looking for your boy Willy?"

The woman's voice he recognized from the day before. "Have you seen him?" she asked, clearly on edge.

"He just left," Ogden answered, his interest piqued. For an accidental overdose, Mary Kunkle was raising more dust than he was used to. Of course, most such victims weren't ex-wives of out-of-towner cops.

"What's he up to?" Gunther asked with a directness that made Ogden smile.

"Not sure I know. He ID'd his wife's remains last night and dropped by this morning to ask me what we had on her." He resisted saying more. Two things you learned in this department in particular: Never say, "I don't know," and never volunteer any more information than is strictly necessary.

"And what do you have, if that's okay to ask?"

"Same as I told you yesterday. Her apartment was locked from the inside and she was found with a needle in her arm. We're treating it as a ground ball."

The woman's voice came back on. "So, he's heading back?"

Ogden chose his phrasing carefully. "Could be. He was here and then he left. I didn't ask and he didn't say."

There was a long silence on the other end of the line, which made Ogden show some pity. He was a little torn here, on one hand understanding their concern for a colleague, and on the other wondering why it was such a big deal.

"I got the feeling," he volunteered, "that he was at least going to talk to a few of her friends. He told me he wanted to find out why she'd done what she did."

"You make it sound like a suicide," Gunther suggested.

"There was no note," Ogden countered. "But you could say any overdose is a suicide. That's how I look at them."

"I see what you mean," Gunther agreed. "One last question: Do you know which friends Willy may be contacting?"

Ogden shook his head, even though no one could see it. "Not the slightest clue." He then asked what he thought would be an obvious question: "Why don't you ask him?"

Sammie Martens didn't make a sound, but Gunther actually laughed. "Detective, if you knew him better, you'd know the answer there. You want to find out anything about Willy Kunkle, he's the last one you ask. Thanks for your help."

"No problem," Ogden answered, and slowly replaced the receiver, seriously doubting this would be the last he'd hear about Mr. Kunkle.

\*          \*          \*

Joe Gunther pushed the off button on the side of the speakerphone and looked up at his younger colleague. Sammie Martens was scowling and staring at the floor.

"It's a natural reaction, Sam. He needs to talk to a few people. Find out what was going on in her life."

"I know that," she answered almost angrily. "It's just frustrating not knowing."

Gunther mulled that over a moment, carefully considering the person they were discussing before asking, "Not knowing what he's doing? Or what he will do?"

The questions were purely rhetorical, since they both knew the answers would not only defy convention, but possibly dictate Willy's survival.

# Chapter 5

Willy Kunkle emerged from the subway as from a slightly faulty time machine. He was in New York's Washington Heights section, far to Manhattan's northern tip, near the George Washington Bridge, just one of dozens of distinct neighborhoods spread across the five boroughs. To outsiders, the whole city was simply New York, but to its residents, it wasn't even fragmented into Brooklyn or Manhattan. Instead, it was minutely parsed into Canarsie or Greenwich Village or Green Point—communities as finite and defining to their inhabitants as the famed "hollers" of West Virginia or the hundreds of towns and villages in Vermont.

That's how it had been for young Willy Kunkle, growing up. Washington Heights had been his entire world, what had helped form him as a human being. Midtown Manhattan, just a subway ride away, had remained as foreign to him as if he'd lived in Germany.

And the comparison was relevant, since Willy's own roots were German. His parents had emigrated before he was born, part of a huge exodus stimulated by Hitler's ascent. The world where he'd begun his childhood had been highlighted by the sights of Hasidic Jews in the streets, the sounds of German and Yiddish in countless stores and apartments. One of his early struggles within the family had been his refusal to speak in anything other than English and his insistence that his parents wake up to the realities around them. Not only was Washington Heights not the Germany they'd left, now so long ago, but it wasn't even the neighborhood they'd created by sheer force of numbers after stepping off the boat. For one thing could be said about Washington Heights without doubt: It was a community in constant cultural flux.

Once a retreat for the city's mega-rich, famous for its sprawling nineteenth century estates and sweeping views of the two rivers bordering it, it had again and again undergone radical changes, influenced variously by urban expansion, the arrival of the subway line, the ebb and flow of foreign immigrants, and the spread of affordable housing. In 1965, the little piece of the Old Fatherland was where Malcolm X was assassinated before a local rally of African Americans, and where, just a few decades later, the Dominican community here and in next-door Inwood was recognized as the largest of its kind in the entire United States.

Washington Heights had seen race riots, poverty, overcrowding, rampant crime, and drug dealing, and yet, through it all, had maintained a thriving business section, kept its many parks from being paved over, and had managed to sustain a definable, if transient, sense of identity.

Stepping forth from the subway, Willy Kunkle, the erstwhile child of these streets, both warmed to the familiarity of it all and was swamped once again by the sense of suffocation it revived in him. He had fought with his family for independence and freedom, had broken away from this world he linked to his early despair, and yet, enveloped by its embrace once more, he couldn't deny the influence it had on him still.

But he didn't like it, and it soured his mood.

He was here to meet his brother, Bob. He'd called him earlier, using the Westchester number on Mary's phone bill, but Bob's wife had told Willy, not bothering to hide her displeasure at hearing his voice, that Bob was in the city, visiting their mother.

He'd received the news with mixed emotions. His mother and he hadn't spoken in years, not because of the sort of vitriol and disappointment that had soured Mary's link to her mother, but instead to keep a door shut he never wanted reopened. It didn't matter to him that such an act merely emulated his father's abandoning the family when Willy was a child, compounding the pain inflicted on his mother. For much of his adult life, and subliminally before then, Willy had been in survival mode—not a great place to breed empathy for others.

So, he'd called the house, grateful that Bob had answered, and arranged to meet him in Wright Park, at West 175th, cautioning him to keep their get-together to himself.

Not that Bob would have instinctively shared the news with their mother. He was the protective son, who'd trod the straight and narrow. He hadn't known their father as Willy had, hadn't felt the loss and witnessed the fallout. By the time Bob had become conscious of the world around him, Mom was back in the saddle with a vengeance, guaranteeing she'd have at least one bond in the family that would stick. And stick it had.

Willy wasn't complaining. It had worked for those two, and had allowed him to absorb a little less guilt in the process, although not enough to want to look his mother in the eyes.

He saw Bob just outside the small park, ordering up a hot dog from a sidewalk vendor across from the public school, paying no attention to his surroundings and giving Willy a few unobserved moments to reacquaint himself with his sibling.

Although Willy's junior by ten years, Bob didn't look it. Prematurely bald, with a soft middle and a permanently pale complexion, he looked much like the men's clothing store manager he was. He spent his days dressed in a fine suit, dividing his time between well-heeled customers in a fake Victorian decor and working the books in a windowless, concrete-walled office jammed with filing cabinets and a desk bought cheap at a fire sale. He had a wife, two kids, a dog and a cat, an aboveground swimming pool, and a ten-year-old car, and was utterly convinced he'd grabbed hold of the gold ring. Willy, despite a natural tendency to dismiss such notions, thought that in Bob's case it might be the truth.

He came at him from an oblique angle, noticing how his brother was ogling the hot dog just handed to him.

"Hey."

Bob turned, his round face open and smiling. "Willy. Hey, yourself. Gosh, it's good to see you."

He moved to give Willy a hug, discovered the hot dog still in his left hand, laughed with embarrassment, and settled for a quick handshake followed by a pat of Willy's left shoulder, which his face then showed he instantly regretted.

"It's okay, Bob," Willy told him. "It won't break."

Bob's face reddened. "I know. I'm sorry. Would you like a dog? My treat."

Willy looked at the multihued mess he was being offered and shook his head. "I'll pass."

Suddenly self-conscious, Bob stared down at his meal. "Yeah, I guess this isn't too appetizing. I can only eat the stuff when Junie's not around. She gives me hell otherwise. I'll buy you something else, though. What would you like?"

Two minutes into the conversation, and Willy was already getting restless. "Give it a rest. I'm not hungry."

Bob looked crestfallen. "Okay. Sorry. Well, let's sit down, at least."

He led the way into the park, giving his hot dog a tentative bite and dropping a glob of fluorescent mustard onto the sidewalk. Willy walked around it in disgust. As with Ward Ogden earlier, he was going to have to mind his manners to get what he was after, but with Bob, he wasn't so sure he'd be able to pull it off. The older brother's impulse to slap the younger one down was going to be hard to resist. He'd had so many years of practice before leaving home—something Bob should have remembered and resented, as Willy would have in his place, but never had.

Bob took them through the playground nearest the street, filled with screaming, running kids, past several benches lining the curving walkway, and up a flight of steps onto a broad, paved observation platform at the back of the park. This had been built expressly for its commanding view of the George Washington Bridge, which spanned at an oblique angle the width of the Hudson River into New Jersey.

Bob settled onto a bench facing the view, patting the seat next to him as if inviting a pet to jump up. Willy remained standing, slightly off to one side, so they were looking at the same scenery.

Bob was now holding his meal as if wondering how it had appeared in his hand. He glanced quickly at Willy. "I was really surprised to hear your voice on the phone. I couldn't believe you were back in town."

"In town, or that I called you up?"

Bob looked away. "Both, I guess. It's been a while."

Willy snorted. "No shit."

"You been okay?"

"Yeah. Terrific. You been seeing Mary?"

Bob's head jerked up. "What?"

"Mary. You know. I was married to her."

"No. I mean, yeah. I was just surprised is all. I mean, you and Mary. That was so long ago."

"So, you've been seeing her?"

"Talking to her, really. Junie, too. She'd call up, just to chat. Didn't seem to matter which one of us answered the phone. Why? What's up?"

Willy ignored the question. "What did she talk about?"

"I don't know. Nothing in particular. She asked about you a few times. She was happy you were doing better."

"Not a drunk, you mean?"

"Yeah. Well, that and getting the new job."

"You told her about that?"

"Sure. It wasn't a secret, was it?"

"How did she seem? Up, down? What?"

Bob thought a moment. "Pretty much up, I'd say. Junie told me that wasn't always true. Maybe she was more honest woman-to-woman. But it seemed like her biggest trouble was money. Things were tight. She was getting along otherwise, though. She liked her job, she'd kicked her habit, she was talking about finding a new place to live when she'd saved up enough."

"Tell me about the job."

Bob hesitated. "What's going on, Willy?"

"Later. The job."

As if in protest, Bob took a large bite of his hot dog instead of answering, forcing his older brother to stew in silence for several minutes.

"It was at a place called the Re-Coop," he finally said. "A drug rehab center run by some nonprofit setup. I don't know who. Anyhow, she'd gone there to straighten up, and did well enough that they offered her a job. Nothing fancy, but she was pretty proud of it."

"She ever talk about her social life? A boyfriend, maybe?"

Bob shook his head. "Not to me. At least not recently. Last boyfriend I knew about was Andy, but that was a few years ago."

"Andy Liptak?"

"Sure. You keep up with him?"

Willy didn't answer. Andy Liptak and he had been in 'Nam together. Both from New York, both from working-class families. Liptak had done well for himself later. Willy thought he lived in Brooklyn somewhere, near his old neighborhood. He'd known Andy and Mary had hooked up years ago, after the divorce and Mary's moving to New York. Hell, Willy had introduced them at a party she and Willy had attended in the city, what seemed like a lifetime ago, and Andy had dropped by their house in Vermont a couple of times on skiing trips. Mary had always liked him, which Willy had written off to his high-roller city ways and Mary's hunger for something bigger and better than the rural life she'd been born to.

"What was between them?"

Bob was looking increasingly confused. "Geez, Willy. They were boyfriend/girlfriend—for years. She lived with him. You know how it goes."

"How'd they break up?"

"Same as always, I guess. I don't know the details. She wasn't calling us back then. Well, she did early on, after the divorce, but then she stopped for a long time. I suppose they weren't compatible, finally. She was still on dope in those days, you know? That must've made it tough. I don't think it was anything he did, though. He sounded like a decent enough guy."

"When did she start calling?"

Bob shrugged, resigning himself to never hearing the reason for this grilling. "The second time? About six months ago, after she got the job at the Re-Coop."

"Out of the blue?"

"Yeah. She told us, now that she was putting her life back together, she wanted to reopen some of the doors she'd shut behind her, or something like that. I didn't care about her reasons. It was just nice to hear from her again. Oh, yeah, she also said something about our being almost the only family she had, since she and her mom don't talk and you were out of the picture. I just figured it was a nostalgia thing."

"And you last talked pretty recently?"

Bob looked at him wide-eyed. "How'd you know that? If you've seen her, why all the questions, Willy? Just ask her this stuff yourself."

"Would if I could. She's dead."

Bob's mouth dropped open. "What?"

Willy's voice was a monotone. "Overdose. They found her with a needle in her arm."

"My God," Bob murmured. He caught sight of the partially eaten hot dog still in his hand and dropped it into the trash barrel beside the bench.

"I'm just trying to figure what she was up to," Willy added.

Bob finally stood up and faced his brother. His pale features were splotchy with anger, but as he spoke, his words were almost calm, barring a slight tremor. "That's really big of you. You are one son-of-a-bitch, you know that? You walk through life with your own little black cloud, like you were the only one who had it tough, and you treat people like shit as if we all owed you something. Well, we don't. In fact, we deserve a little courtesy for putting up with your crap. You threw Mary away. You beat her, climbed into your bottle, and pulled the cork in after you."

He smiled bitterly at Willy's slight grimace. "Oh? You didn't know we knew that you smacked her? Sure. She told us about it, and about a lot more, too. You were a total bastard, and she still loved you anyway. That's why she was calling us lately: not so much because we were the only family she had, but because we were your family, and she wanted to know how you were doing."

He sat back down, his elbows on his knees, and shook his head sorrowfully. "And then you come around like Dick Tracy, playing twenty questions and not even telling me she'd died. You are some piece of work."

Willy didn't respond at first. He stayed rooted in place, his exterior rigidly placid. In all their years as brothers, Bob had maybe spoken to him like that three times—and that was probably an exaggeration. Willy had always lorded over Bob, using his powerful personality to cut him off even if he had no reason to.

The sad thing was that Willy admired his brother for keeping his life together, for not letting the factors that had derailed Willy affect him. Bob's wasn't an exciting life. He hadn't done anything that would merit comment on a plaque or stimulate a rousing memorial speech. But he'd been stalwart and honest and faithful and responsible and had created a life Willy could only envy.

Not that Willy would ever tell him even part of that.

He did sit beside him on the bench, though, and lightly punched his shoulder as he said, "Some speech, Bobby."

Bob swung his head around to glance at him and give him a sour smile. "You are such an asshole."

Willy laughed. "Don't I know it. How's Mom?"

Bob straightened and sat back, sighing deeply, his hands in his lap. " 'How's Mom?' he asks. You called her house to talk to me. You could have asked her yourself, you know? There's another woman you abuse and who still thinks you're the perfect son. I visit her every week, bring Junie and the kids by on a regular basis, have her up to the house for weekends during the summer. All she talks about is you. What the hell is it about you that makes people care so much?"

Willy had been staring straight ahead, waiting for Bob to finish, until he noticed his brother was looking right at him, actually expecting an answer.

"Give me a break, Bob," he said.

After a telling pause, Bob let out a small laugh of defeat. "Who am I kidding? You have no idea what I'm talking about. Even I love you, and you're probably the most unpleasant person I know."

"Thanks," Willy responded. "So, how's Mom?"

"She's got emphysema, a bad ticker, and her hip hurts so bad she can hardly walk, but she won't go for replacement surgery. Other than that, she's great. She's still as domineering, short-tempered, and impatient as ever, and still knows everything about everything, even when she's dead wrong. You ought to drop by and see her. The two of you might kill each other and let the rest of us get on with our lives."

Willy smiled. "Gee, Bob, you've become quite the sentimentalist in your old age."

"Yeah."

They sat side by side for several minutes in silence, staring at the enormous bridge and its steady burden of anonymous humanity, surrounded by the muted sounds of the city enveloping them.

Finally, Bob asked, "Why'd she do it? She talked like life was getting better."

Willy thought back to some of the things his brother had accused him of, and of how it had never occurred to him to deny them.

"I don't know, but I intend to find out. It may be too little, too late, but that much I can do."

# Chapter 6

The Re-Coop didn't open until midafternoon, which, given most of its clientele, was still probably early. When Willy appeared across the street from its entrance, recognizing it not just from the sign but from the photograph he'd removed from Mary's apartment, it looked empty.

Of course, all the other buildings on the block looked empty, too. The Lower East Side was distinctive that way, one block being a bustling bazaar, merchandise spilling out onto crowded sidewalks already festooned with clothes and fabrics hanging from overhead signs, while the very next street was silent, closed up, and virtually lifeless.

Unlike Willy's old Washington Heights stomping grounds, though, the Lower East Side had been a catchment area for the poor and the dispossessed since its birth. And yet, perhaps for that very reason, it had also once thrived with life and creativity, with thousands of families jammed into single blocks, fomenting radical thinkers, social activists, and talents like the Gershwin and Marx brothers, Jimmy Durante, and Al Jolson.

But not lately. Nowadays, minus the spark of sheer

numbers, that contradictory clash of creativity and despair had melted into something more numbing. While the occasional bustling street still flourished, especially on weekends, the overall neighborhood seemed locked in a permanent funk of poverty, drug abuse, and hopelessness.

The Re-Coop, in other words, was truly a product of its environment.

Willy crossed the street and walked through the door under the brightly painted sign—the only thing distinguishing this entrance from any of its equally dark and brooding neighbors.

That, thankfully, was where all comparisons stopped, however. Once inside, Willy was pleasantly surprised at the light and cheerful atmosphere that greeted him. The walls were colorfully painted and decorated, plants and flowers plentiful, and toys and children's books piled in the corners. It reminded him of an upbeat day-care center in some well-heeled suburb.

"How can I help?" a young woman asked from behind a reception counter. The only doors in the room, other than the one he'd just used, were located behind her on either side, and the front windows, so blank from the street, he saw now had been painted in, further ensuring privacy.

"Yeah. I'd like to talk to someone about Mary Kunkle." He did the routine with the quick flip of the badge.

"What was that supposed to be?" she asked, just as quickly.

He went to Plan B without a pause, pulling the badge back out of his pocket with a feigned sigh of exasperation and laying it on the counter before her. "It's a badge—Vermont Bureau of Investigation. No one's ever heard of us. I usually don't even bother showing it, but I thought you'd like to know who I was."

She peered at it carefully, patently unimpressed. "I bet. Looks real flashy. Why don't you wait over there?" She pointed to a chair near the front door. "I'll get somebody to talk with you."

She slid off her chair and disappeared through one of the back doors. Willy sat down and studied the room carefully, eventually finding the small surveillance camera he'd been expecting. Drug rehab centers came in all shapes and sizes, from the dreary dumps that made shooting up seem like a friendly alternative, to the cold, clinical, hospital look-alikes that reduced everyone in them to the status of a lab rat.

This place was the happy medium, had obviously been set up with serious cash, and would logically have a security system to protect itself. Willy waved at the camera.

Five minutes later, a black woman in her fifties with her hair pulled back in a bun appeared behind the counter. She was solidly built, dressed in no-nonsense, practical clothes, and didn't look as though she appreciated having her time wasted. Willy recognized her as one of the smiling people in the photograph—the one standing in the group's center.

"You were asking about Mary Kunkle?" she asked.

He stood up. "Yes. I used to be her husband."

She studied him silently for a few moments. Suddenly the front door opened and a pale, scrawny young man stepped in, stopped nervously in his tracks, and looked at them both. The older woman's face broke into a wide smile. "Hey, Tommy, good you could make it. Let me tell Dave you're here."

She then gave Willy a hard look, although she kept her voice artificially bright. "Why don't you come with me?"

Willy followed her through to a back hallway lined with closed doors and muted lighting. She stopped at one of the doors, stuck her head in, and said, "Tommy's here," before leading Willy to what was apparently her own office halfway down the corridor. Again, the environment was soothing, upbeat, pleasant, and well paid for.

"You guys must be pretty good fund-raisers," Willy commented.

The woman pointed at a comfortable armchair facing her desk. "Sit."

She circled the desk, settled behind it, and steepled her fingers just below her chin, so that she was looking at Willy as if he'd been pinned under glass.

"One call to the police department about that little trick with the badge and I could have you arrested."

"It's real," he said without emotion.

"It's also irrelevant, and it was used to intimidate. I don't like that."

"Okay."

"What do you want?"

"I wouldn't mind knowing who you are, for starters," he said.

She made no apologies. "I'm Rosalie Coven, the center's director."

She left it at that, letting the ensuing pause suggest that her question had been left unanswered.

He got the hint. "I'm trying to find out why Mary killed herself."

Coven's eyes narrowed slightly. "I was told it was accidental."

"Might have been. She still killed herself."

"Point taken. Why do you care?"

"Because I was married to her. Because I'm the only one they could find to identify her at the morgue."

"You also abused her when she was most vulnerable."

Was there anybody in this city who didn't know about that? he wondered. "Most vulnerable compared to what?" he asked instead. "I'm not asking for forgiveness, but I was pretty messed up, too."

"The devil made you do it?" she suggested sarcastically.

He saw where this was going, and knew he'd get nothing in return if he continued. "No," he conceded. "I did it all by myself, and while it sounds pretty lame right now, I've lived with it ever since."

Rosalie Coven stared at him for a few moments before asking, "What happened to the arm?"

"Job-related. I was shot."

"Long ago?"

"About ten years."

"Soon after you two broke up, if my memory's right."

"It's right."

For some reason she wasn't about to reveal, that seemed to thaw Rosalie Coven ever so slightly. The hands unsteepled and she pointed to a metal carafe and some cups on a filing cabinet by his side. "Pour yourself some coffee. It should be pretty hot."

He took her up on the offer, dexterously manipulating the process with his one hand. Coven watched him work, as if grading a test.

"You have doubts about how Mary died?" she finally asked.

"Don't you?" he countered. "So far, people I've talked to said she was on the mend."

Coven shook her head. "I've been doing this way too long to think that means much. You're an alcoholic. You should know."

"Still," he insisted.

She yielded. "I was surprised. I thought she was further along."

He felt the blood rise slowly to his neck and cheeks. "That's it? You had her on the wrong place on the graph? Too bad, but shit happens?"

The woman opposite him leaned forward and rested her forearms on the desk, staring at him intently. "Don't give me that, you little toad. You helped put her on that graph. You don't *ever* get to be self-righteous."

He held up his hand as if to stop her coming over the tabletop at him. "Okay, okay. Enough with the who's holier crap. Maybe I sent her down this road, and maybe you missed the signs and let her hit the ditch. So, we're both feeling guilty. Who cares? I just want to find out if it's true."

To pay Rosalie Coven her due, she took Willy's dismissal of her outburst in stride and seriously considered his last comment.

"She was one of the few I thought would make it."

"Were there any signs at all she was heading downhill?" he asked.

Coven shook her head. "Nothing. Everything was pointing in the opposite direction."

"Was there anyone here she was tight with? Someone besides you she might have confided in?"

"Louisa Obregon, everyone calls her Loui. They were very close. But I asked her about Mary, and she was as stunned as the rest of us." Coven looked at him sourly before adding, "Not that that'll stop you from pestering her anyhow."

He merely smiled back at her. "What's her address?"

"She lives in the neighborhood, like most of us." She scribbled the location on a piece of paper and handed it to him. "Here. It's probably a waste of time telling a cop this, but go easy with her, okay? She took this hard. She left work right after we heard and hasn't been back since."

Willy glanced at the address and slipped the note into his breast pocket.

Coven gave him a stern look. "I've done you a favor I normally never do, giving you that. You better not disappoint me."

Willy rose to his feet and crossed to the door. "Little late now, isn't it?"

The address Rosalie Coven gave Willy Kunkle led him to a slightly improved version of Mary's building: more modern, less run-down, and on a street that didn't look so much like a depopulated, hundred-year-old daguerreotype. In fact, just standing in the lobby with his finger on Louisa Obregon's doorbell, Willy found the surrounding sounds of kids shouting and the smell of food on the stove a crucial vital sign, and a big difference from the stale silence of Mary's place.

"Yes? Who is it?"

"Is this Louisa Obregon?"

The slightly accented voice dropped a note into wariness. "Who is this, please?"

Willy chose his wording carefully, knowing he probably had only one shot at gaining entry. "I'm a police officer, Ms. Obregon. Rosalie Coven at the Re-Coop gave me your address. It's in connection to the death of Mary Kunkle."

There was no response, but the door lock buzzed him through.

He took the elevator to the fifth floor, stepped into the corridor, and heard the same voice call out, "Turn right. About halfway down."

He walked up to a barely open door and saw through the crack both a thick, taut chain and the dark, suspicious eye of a woman checking him out.

"You have identification?"

He put on his best manners while he reached into his pocket. "Yes, ma'am. I should warn you, though, I'm from Vermont. That's where I'm a cop." He held out his identity card and shield so she could read it, keeping one fingertip over his last name.

"The Vermont Bureau of Investigation?" she asked. "What do you have to do with Mary's death?"

"She was from there, as I'm sure you know. The nature of how she died has raised some questions we'd like to have answered."

As implausible as that sounded to him, it seemed to work for her. The door closed briefly, the chain was taken off, and Louisa Obregon let Willy in.

"What do you think happened?" she asked. "We were told it was an overdose."

"Nobody I've talked to seems to think she was back on drugs. I'm not saying it couldn't have been that way, but it does make you wonder."

A little girl in a flowered dress and bunny slippers appeared from around the corner and hugged her mother's knee. Obregon spoke to her quickly in Spanish and the child disappeared. Moments later, they heard the sounds of music leaking in from farther back in the apartment.

"Mrs. Obregon," Willy said. "Could we sit down someplace? I'd like to ask you a few questions about Mary."

But Louisa Obregon stood her ground. "It is Miss Obregon, and there is nothing I can tell you. Mary was fine up to the last time I saw her. She was happy and normal."

"I understand her finances were pretty tight."

Obregon laughed harshly. "Everybody's finances are tight. She wasn't in worse shape than anybody else, and things were going to get better soon."

"How so?" Willy asked, remembering Bob's comment that Mary had been hoping to move soon.

But Obregon wasn't very helpful. "I don't know. Maybe it wasn't true. I say the same thing all the time, too. But she liked her job, and she said she wanted to go back to school to become a drug counselor."

Willy sensed a softness welling up behind her resistant exterior and worked to expand it. "I can see why. It sounds like the Re-Coop saved her life."

It was an educated shot in the dark, but a lucky one. Obregon's eyes glistened suddenly at his words and she nodded vigorously. "Hers and mine both. And by saving mine, Teresa's, too." She pointed to where the music could still be heard in the background. "Mary and I couldn't have made it without Rosalie and the others."

Willy smiled sympathetically. "Rosalie told me everyone calls you Loui. Is that okay? Could you tell me a little about Mary before she turned herself around? What she was up to, who she hung out with? Anything would help."

Louisa Obregon gave in finally and half turned on her heel. "Would you like to sit down in the living room? Sorry I was a little suspicious at first. I don't have a great history with cops, and they don't cut people like me a lot of slack."

Willy followed her into a small, cluttered, but pleasantly decorated room. The childish music they'd been listening to was coming from a next-door bedroom. "I'm an alcoholic, Loui, sober nine years now. I'm not most cops."

She glanced at him over her shoulder, observing the crippled arm. "I noticed that. Have a seat."

They settled down in opposite corners of a sofa, their legs crossed. Loui folded her hands in her lap and looked up at the ceiling briefly. "Okay: Mary before she turned things around . . ." She stopped, sighed, wiped under one eye, and faced him with a wan smile. "It's tough, you know? I've lost so many friends this way, to drugs, or AIDS, or that whole world. You try to go on, count yourself lucky, think back over that friendship, and make it less than it was. You try to make the hurt go away. But it doesn't really work. It all kind of piles up inside."

Willy nodded, but kept quiet, trusting Loui to get where he'd asked her to go in her own good time.

She did after taking a deep breath. "I don't know too much. We met when we were being treated at the Re-Coop. But she told me things, kind of now and then. Maybe that'll help."

"Give it a shot," he encouraged her.

"Well, you know she was from Vermont, of course, somewhere way up north. She didn't talk much about that, but she did tell me her family and her had stopped talking, and that she'd had a shitty marriage to some guy who abused her. He was a drunk, too," she added brightly, little knowing the accuracy of the comparison. "It was after she got divorced that she came down here."

"Why?" Willy interjected quickly.

"Why come here? I don't know. Bright city lights? She said she wanted to get away, make something of herself. I don't know too much else."

"There wasn't a guy?"

Loui Obregon smiled sadly. "There's always a guy, right?"

Willy retreated slightly. "Well, I didn't mean—"

But she cut him off with a wave of her hand. "No, no. You're right. I meant it. There always is a guy with women like us. We're like sheep. Rosalie tells us that all the time. Tells us to stand up on our own two feet."

Her eyes lost their focus as she stared off across the room. "But, you know, it's hard. Sleeping alone, sometimes with just a kid in your life. You get lonely. You want someone to put your arms around."

Willy compressed his lips slightly, uncomfortable with where this was heading. Gunther was good with shit like this, and Willy could hold his own, but he hated it.

"What was the guy's name?" he asked.

She blinked once and looked at him. "His name? I don't know. I mean, there were a lot of them. I guess there were. She was a pretty lady. And fun, too."

"You met some of them?"

"Oh. Well. I met one . . . no, two men. I don't know if they were, you know, intimate or anything. After Mary started going to the Re-Coop, her life changed, see? So there was less of that. That's what I meant about Rosalie talking to us. It wasn't encouraged, like they say."

"You catch the names of these two men?"

But she shook her head. "No. It was something like Bill or Dave or Paul or something. Not a name to remember."

"How about Andy Liptak?" he asked, thinking back not only to his talk with Bob, but to how his brother's name fit the short, bland coterie she'd just recited. "He ever come up?"

"Not that I remember."

He tried steering her back on track, disappointed. "Okay. So, she's moved to the city to live her dream. She sees a lot of guys. What else? What does she do for a job?"

"Not much that I know. She said it was like back home, but worse: waitress jobs, counter work, taking shit from other people all day and getting paid pennies."

"Where was she living then?"

"Brooklyn, mostly. Beats me where, exactly. She said she liked Brooklyn best, and that's why she lived there, so that's how I know."

"How'd she get into drugs?"

Loui's laugh was short and hard. "How'd you get into booze? Life stinks, you look for some relief. One thing leads to another."

Willy was growing irritated with the vagueness of her answers. Not a patient man by nature, he had to fight the constant urge to hurry things along, as if tarrying over a subject, or with another person, might get him caught out in the open.

"Specifically, though, do you have any names you can give me?"

She shook her head, suddenly angry, sensing his restlessness. "Cops. You don't care about Mary or me or anybody else. It's all about who your contact is. Making a bust. You treat us just like the people selling us junk."

Willy fought back the urge to agree with her. "Loui," he said instead, laying on the sincerity, "I know what it's like to be where you are. That's what drives me nuts. You fought your way back just like I did. I just want to keep going—getting the bastards that're feeding off people like us. We all do what we can to hang on to something. You've got Teresa, Mary wanted to be a counselor. I go after the scumbags."

He paused, judging her reaction, pondering his actual motivations at the same time, as if standing outside himself and watching two strangers.

Loui apparently bought his line, because she confessed, "That's not how it works, at least not in this city. You know your own dealer, but you don't brag about him. They're like a secret you got to keep to yourself or it'll go away. And they do sometimes. If I got busted and they squeezed me for my supplier, if I had somebody else's name, I'd give them that, not my own guy. You protect your source, and you don't risk it by talking about it."

Willy couldn't argue the logic, but he was still getting nowhere. He decided to help himself out by changing subjects slightly, defusing his own tension. "The Re-Coop. They find you or you find them?"

"Both, kind of. They have ads around and people refer you to them. I got told about them by my priest."

"Fancy place, though. Doesn't look like the standard city services fare. They charge you anything?"

"No, no. It's privately supported—some foundation."

Willy was surprised. "One foundation? What's it called?"

"Like the place itself: the Re-Coop Foundation."

"You ever met anyone from it?"

"No. You'd have to ask Rosalie. She's the only one who deals with them."

Willy scratched his head. "Aren't they swamped, though? An upscale free clinic in a pisshole area like this? What's the catch?"

She shrugged. "I only volunteer there a few hours a week, sort of to pay back, you know? I couldn't tell you. There is an interview process. I don't think a ton of people make it through that."

Willy couldn't repress a sneer. "Right, and then they probably brag about how good their numbers are, since they screen their patients from the start. What a scam."

Once again, Louisa Obregon's face darkened. "What do you know? I was real sick when I went there, and so was Mary. They helped us out. Who cares if they don't take everybody? They work real hard on everybody they do take. Would you want to run a place like that and have to deal with all the psychos and slashers just because you let everybody in? Then nobody would be saved. They're good people and you don't know what you're talking about."

Perhaps lured by the tone of her mother's voice, young Teresa appeared in the doorway.

"Mama?" she asked.

Loui rose from her seat and comforted the child with a hug and some murmured comments Willy couldn't hear. From where she was squatting, Loui looked over her shoulder. "You should leave now. I told you all I know."

Willy got up also, feeling he'd dropped the ball. "I'm

sorry," he admitted. "I lose sight of the good things sometimes. Maybe I've been at this too long."

Louisa straightened, sending her comforted daughter back to her room and escorting Willy back into the hallway. "It's okay. I wouldn't want to do what you do."

Willy tried one last question at the front door. "The reason I asked about the dealer earlier is that there was a bag of heroin next to Mary's body. It had a mark on it, a red devil. I was hoping you might know who sold that brand."

A crease appeared between her eyes. "I don't know about the brand, but you're wrong about it being heroin. Mary shot up speedballs last."

Willy looked her straight in the eyes. "You're sure of that? No chance she changed or decided to experiment?"

But Louisa Obregon stood her ground. "No, she wouldn't. She used to shoot heroin, back in the old days, but before she kicked everything, she only did speedballs. It was a thing with her, cutting the heroin with coke. She said she'd never do straight horse again."

Which made Willy wonder if in fact she had.

# Chapter 7

Willy Kunkle hadn't spoken with or seen Andy Liptak in over a decade. Close friends once, having met fresh off the plane in Vietnam, they'd actually been an unlikely pair from the start. For one thing, unusual in a military friendship, they weren't in the same unit. They'd bumped into one another purely by chance, had immediately discovered their mutual New York backgrounds, and had hit it off before being pipelined to their final assignments: Andy to a supply company, and Willy to the closest thing that bizarre war ever had resembling a front line—or, in his case, beyond it. During their time in country, they kept in touch, spent their off-duty time together, and bonded over the standard fare of overpriced alcohol and underage women. The fact that they endured utterly different experiences in the war both helped keep their connection alive while they served and explained its erosion afterward. What to Willy turned out to be a crucible of cruelty, violence, fear, and loss had amounted to little more than an interesting stint in an overseas warehouse to Andy, even though all this occurred during the war's chaotic waning days. The contrasting aftereffects were predictably undermining to a relationship based primarily on escapism.

And that didn't even factor in Mary.

Willy had brought Mary to the city shortly after their marriage, largely as a gift to her. It had been her first trip outside of Vermont, not counting a few quick illegal border crossings into Canada to get booze during her youth, and she'd been predictably overwhelmed by both New York's vast, flat expanse and the millions of people inhabiting it. Beginning the trip shy and intimidated, she'd ended up loving the twenty-four-hour vitality and diversity of the place.

Meeting Andy Liptak had merely been part of the schedule, and at the time not something of any great significance. Andy had been gregarious as always, but with a newfound man-on-the-make charmer's sheen that had encouraged Willy in his belief that some memories, and most people, were best left in the past. Liptak had hit the ground running back in New York, using his contacts and entrepreneurial savvy to start up a variety of businesses, and he'd developed into the sort of man Willy had come to loathe, all the more so in this case since Andy had survived Vietnam without a scratch, while Willy, as in a psychological dress rehearsal to the eventual loss of his left arm, had been crippled forever.

After Mary and Willy had returned home, therefore, he'd been disappointed by how impressed she'd been by the very man he'd wished they hadn't visited. As he saw it, she'd fallen prey to all the superficial trappings and mannerisms that merely advertise such people as flagrant phonies.

Not that he was qualified to pass judgment. In the end, drinking hard, increasingly abusive, and hanging on to his job only through Gunther's resented good graces, Willy Kunkle eventually understood that he was functioning as deviously as he'd ever done in the jungle, but with only a fraction of his former skill. His earlier, short-lived pretense in showing an interest in Mary, in what she was doing, and in sharing a life with her, all fell prey to his own toboggan ride straight to the bottom of self-indulgent despair.

Before the final crash, however, he'd acceded to their seeing Andy Liptak again during a couple of the latter's ski vacations to Vermont. It didn't go well. Mary betrayed how taken she was with Andy's world and its trappings, and Willy was all but incapable of hiding his contempt. Traditional jealousy never played a part, and in fact Andy was perfectly behaved throughout, but it didn't matter, given the rift following the last of Andy's visits. Later, after the divorce, Willy had heard that his ex-wife and Andy had linked up in New York, and in a rare moment of lucidity he'd conceded both the logic and the suitability of the match. At the time, he'd thought that Mary might have even found happiness at last.

Which now served to remind him of how wrong he could be.

On the phone, Andy had sounded only surprised and pleased to hear that Willy was in town, and quickly suggested they meet over dinner at Peter Luger's, in the Williamsburg section of Brooklyn. Mary's name didn't come up.

Luger's is tucked away in a typically eccentric Brooklyn corner, close to the looming Erector Set span of the Williamsburg Bridge, and right across the East River from Manhattan's Lower East Side, the Seventh Precinct, and Mary's apartment. Willy knew that Andy lived somewhere near Brooklyn Heights, across the sprawling old Brooklyn Navy Yard from Williamsburg, but the coincidence was curious.

He got off the Marcy Avenue subway stop, having stashed his car earlier in an open-air lot near Bellevue Hospital, and doubled back, heading toward the riverbank and the darker, grittier buildings there.

Despite the buffed, shiny, man-made glory of Manhattan's skyline, poking up above the run-down buildings before him, Willy had always been attracted to New York's older, seamier neighborhoods, many of which lined the rivers that had once functioned as commercial arteries and made of the city a world-class port.

New York was still a large port, of course, but not to the standard of its heyday, when every inch of its almost six hundred miles of shoreline was lined with a pier, a dock, a warehouse, or some other shipping facility. As he neared the restaurant, he noticed, here as in so many other places, that the streets were often paved over cobblestones, and sported traces of the short rail lines that had once run between the loading docks and the storage houses.

Now most of that muscle was atrophied—empty, soiled, quiet, and awaiting someone or something with enough money to either destroy it, turn it into condos, or revitalize it commercially. Huge deserted lots lay pinned between the water and the metal fencing put up to hide them from view, and grimy, hulking, factory-style buildings, incongruously detailed here and there with quaint architectural flourishes, sat as if in suspended animation, pending the proper financial kiss to bring them back to life.

Or maybe not.

Willy crossed the intersection, noting a cluster of SUVs, limos, and high-priced cars parked like a circling of frightened upper-class wagons, and entered Peter Luger's front door, blinking to adjust his eyes as he walked straight into the long, crowded bar. The smell of food and beer commingled with a steady rumble of conversation, adding warmth to a setting that he found surprisingly lacking in decor. Aside from the finely worked pressed-tin ceiling overhead, the rest of the place was almost drab.

A shadow separated itself from the crowd before him, still looking like a wrestler in shape and size, but gone adrift around the middle. "Holy Christ. If it ain't the Sniper."

Andy Liptak shook his hand, both smiling and solicitous. "I heard about the arm. I couldn't believe it, after all you went through in 'Nam. Some raw deal. You want a drink?"

His eyes now focused, Willy looked into the face of his old friend, wondering about the depth—or the truth—of his ignorance. "I'm on the wagon," he answered, reflecting also on the use of his old nickname—the Sniper. Serving as such had been just one of his official functions in Vietnam. But his machinelike technique, his remote demeanor, and the way others treated him had all earned him the title. Snipers were outsiders, despised by the enemy and usually shunned as cold killers by their own. At the time, he'd enjoyed the distinction. Now it embarrassed him.

Andy didn't falter, giving Willy's good arm a squeeze. "That's really great. I wish I had the discipline. Come on back. I got a nice table reserved."

He led the way through the back of the bar and around

a corner to a large, open dining room sprinkled with a haphazard collection of tables and chairs. He took Willy to a corner near the windows where the noise seemed less and the mood more intimate.

"Here we are," he said, the affable host. "Have a seat."

Willy slid into his chair, thinking back to when the two of them, dressed in sweat-stained tropical khakis, their faces sheening in the heat, would share beer after beer in noisy, hot dives with names they couldn't pronounce or remember, hoping to find in each other's company some touchstone of a home far away in time and place.

That necessity now having been removed, Willy wondered what he'd ever seen in this man.

Andy seemed to pick up on his thoughts, cupping his cheek in his hand and staring at Willy with a faint smile on his face. "Asking yourself how we got here?"

Willy hesitated before answering. Since the moment he'd returned to this city, he'd been tiptoeing through a minefield of other people's good graces. He'd kept his true nature from Mary's apartment superintendent, Ward Ogden, Rosalie Coven, Louisa Obregon, even his brother, Bob, presenting to them all a measured, even muted front.

Doing so had bordered on agony. Ever since he'd begun his recovery from alcoholism, he'd gotten used to using honesty with surgical precision, regardless of how it was received. Total candor had been the Stateside equivalent of his Vietnam-born contempt of adversity—a showy conviction that he had nothing left to lose. He'd known even then it was merely a mask, of course. His chilling aloofness in combat was mostly self-loathing and despair, and his plain speaking nowadays was largely to stave people off, but there was no denying the advantages the mask had over the reality. There were times, in fact, when his self-deception was running strong or his confidence hitting bottom, when even he believed that his crippled arm and verbal bluntness were somehow things to be proud of.

Which was why right now, with his entire past overtaking him, he so urgently wanted to speak honestly—truly—and tell Andy Liptak of all the anger, contempt, nostalgia, even love and confusion that he felt welling up inside him as he watched his friend smiling from across the table.

But once more, he kept his guard.

"It's been a long time," he said blandly instead.

Andy gestured to the waiter, an older man with an apron tied around his waist. "Give me a Brooklyn Lager, and a . . ."

"Coke," Willy finished for him.

The waiter disappeared as Andy shook his head. "Yeah, long time. Who would've thought way back that we'd end up where we are? The Sniper and me, after all these years. Jesus. How's life in Vermont? Didn't I hear through the grapevine you got a new job?"

Now that the conversation had begun, especially along such superficial lines, Willy felt more comfortable biding his time about his true purpose for being here. The brief emotional flurry of a moment ago was snuffed out by the hard, cool veneer he called on so often.

"Yup. Kind of a crazy deal. It's like a statewide detective unit, except nobody knows about us and no local cop wants us around stealing his cases. Typical bureaucratic bullshit."

"Sounds fancy, though."

"Till they pull the plug on it," Willy admitted. "We're

so new, no one would notice. Things going okay with you?"

Andy made an expansive gesture, like a lord displaying his acreage. "Pretty good. Got a lot of irons in the fire. Never could resist a deal, and this town's full of 'em. Real estate around here is like trading pork bellies: it's fun and a little scary and when it pays off, it's like knocking off a bank. So, I do some of that, and I own a few businesses I don't even know what they do, and a bunch of other stuff. When we were in 'Nam and I was wrestling palletloads of condoms and shit like that, I never figured I'd be swimming these waters. But I've gotten into it, and I can't complain. It's almost like a sport, like rock climbing or white-water canoeing or something—full of unpredictables. No day's like the last."

Their drinks came, and after that the traditional Peter Luger meal of porterhouse steak, onion and tomato salad, and creamed spinach. Willy didn't have to do much to keep Andy going, especially as the beers kept pace. Like most self-made social scramblers, Andy Liptak loved talking about himself, and the more he did, the more Willy learned, and the less he had to worry that the tables might be turned.

But the substance, and eventually the point of it all, finally became elusive. The more Andy rambled on, the less Willy paid attention, until he finally realized he'd been subliminally avoiding the very reason he'd contacted this man. The purpose here was Mary, as it had been when he'd arranged this reunion. But seeing Andy again, and being hit by a wall of meaningless chatter, Willy felt hunkered down as in a trench. He became loath to break cover by asking questions that would only speed up his revisiting the past. He had expended such effort in closing off those years, and had lost so much in his blind, enraged fumbling, it felt like leaping off a cliff merely to ask a simple leading question.

But ask it he finally did.

It wasn't out of context. Andy by now was expounding on family values and the benefits of settling down. He apparently had a wife who preferred their Long Island beach house to the city place he favored and used as an office. He was bragging about yet a third home in Portsmouth, New Hampshire—a huge, blue-blooded estate, reminiscent of the Astors summering by the sea— that he'd picked up in a roundabout way, and implying he might have a girlfriend or two on the side, when Willy casually asked, "Did you ever keep up with Mary after you two split up?"

That brought on a pause, and an expression touched with both sorrow and guilt. Finally, Andy chewed his lower lip briefly and leaned forward, his elbows on either side of his after-dinner coffee.

"Did Bob or anybody give you the scoop on Mary and me?" he asked.

Willy wasn't about to suggest they had, and he was surprised that Bob's name had cropped up. He didn't realize they knew one another, although he now remembered Bob saying Andy "sounded" like a decent guy.

"Just that you'd gone separate ways," Willy said.

"You didn't keep up with her?"

He shook his head. "Too many ghosts."

Andy nodded sympathetically. "I know the feeling. She told me you two had it pretty rough toward the end."

Willy couldn't stop himself. "What'd she say?"

"That you fought a lot, that you had a drinking problem

and a lot of anger. That you kept obsessing about 'Nam. I hope this doesn't sound wrong, but she really loved you. She brought that up so much, I kinda got sick of it. That might've had something to do with why her and me didn't work out. She was still stuck on what happened between you."

Willy regretted having broached the subject, and tried to get back on track. "Why did you break up, though? You said that was only part of it."

Andy put on a philosophical look. "Part of it, all of it. Hard to tell, when you think back. I mean, I'm no shrink, and she had a lot of issues, probably before you ever met her, so who knows where all that crap comes from? And I wasn't in such a great place, either—a super bad choice for her, looking back. But you know how she was: all that energy . . . hard to resist. And I don't resist too well any-how."

He toyed with his coffee cup a little before adding, "I always felt weird about that, you know? Her being your ex. I hope that never pissed you off too much."

Here, at least, Willy could be perfectly honest. "Never did. I thought you'd be a good match."

Andy smiled ruefully. "So did I. We might have been, if she'd gotten you out of her system. And even with that, the first two or three years were great, after she finally moved in with me." Suddenly he laughed with embarrassment. "That's pretty good, huh? Turns out I was more ticked off at you than you were at me, and I was the one living with her. Boy."

After a moment's stilted silence, Willy asked, "How'd she get hooked?"

Andy looked pained. "Know what I said about my being a bad choice for her? That was no lie. I didn't see it coming . . . I guess that's nothing new. What with the divorce and living with me and her mom rejecting her, I should've known better. But I was too busy doin' deals and living hard. By then, I'd taken her for granted, too. She was just sort of there all the time."

He was having trouble forming his words. He passed a hand across his face as if to clear it of cobwebs. Willy thought the beer might be having both a liberating and a fogging effect by now.

Finally, Andy sat up straight and admitted, "Look, you got good reason to punch me out for this, but I guess I got her into that shit. I was doing a little myself then—pills and some heroin, and the booze like always. I hate to admit it, but that's what got her started. She didn't want to be left out more than she already was, and since I was doin' it anyhow, I didn't see any harm. I know it sounds bad—I mean, it is bad—but we were clueless. It was fun, felt good, the money was startin' to roll in. By the time I woke up, she was pretty far gone. Heroin's a hard habit to break."

He didn't add anything for a while, concentrating on the empty coffee cup as if it contained nitroglycerin.

Willy prodded him in a quiet voice. "What happened, finally?"

Andy didn't meet his eyes. "Well, we did break up, of course. Her talking about you, me bitching that she was either zoned all the time or out trying to score. It got pretty ugly, and I didn't have the patience for it. I never been too good with that, either."

"You threw her out," Willy suggested, paying him back a little for the you-broke-her-heart refrain.

Andy looked at him then, an almost pleading expression on his face. "No. I mean, she did move out and we did have one last big fight. But I was too screwed up to be that decisive. It just sort of fell apart. I guess, though," he added after a pause, "that I didn't stop her, either. And I didn't go after her."

"How long ago was this?"

Andy rubbed his eyes with his fingertips. "Years. A few years. Shit, I don't remember."

"You ever keep up with her?"

He shook his head. "Nah. Damn, this sure doesn't look good, does it?"

Willy pursed his lips, thinking, it's not about you, but said instead, "When she was out trying to score, do you know who she dealt with?"

Andy was obviously confused by the question. "Who she got her stuff from?" He scratched his head. "Jesus . . . I don't . . . she started with people I introduced her to, but after things got crazy, I put the word out to shut her down. I don't know who she used after that. It doesn't matter anyway—even my old dealers are all dead, gone, or in the joint by now. Why all the questions?"

"You heard she'd cleaned up, though, right?" Willy persisted, ignoring him. "You said you'd talked to Bob. You knew about my new job."

Andy squirmed in his seat. "Damn, you really are a cop, aren't you?" He smiled guiltily. "Okay, yeah. I did hear. I mean, I asked and Bob told me. I was curious, you know? You reach a certain age, you get married, settle down, begin to think back—you and me, 'Nam, Mary . . . I started to wonder. The stuff you did when you were young starts to mean more."

"You called Bob out of the blue?"

"I had his number from when Mary was still around. She used to call him to find out about you. Pissed me off, actually. I told her to cut it out, but I kept the number. He was surprised to hear from me—I think even a little embarrassed—but he sort of gave me the condensed version of what was going on. I felt bad about putting him on the spot."

Which explained why Bob hadn't admitted to the phone call, Willy thought.

He noticed Andy was looking at him with a pointed seriousness all of a sudden, his drunkenness apparently evaporated.

"Enough, Willy. Why the third degree?"

Willy hesitated, pondering the value of his information and when its release could serve him best. Now seemed as good a time as any.

"She's dead. That's why I'm down here."

Andy stared at him in silence for a moment, his mouth half open, his hands tight around the coffee cup.

"Jesus," he finally murmured, barely audible amid the noise around them.

"They found her with a needle in her arm," Willy added for effect, wondering why, right after the words left his mouth. Andy had been helpful and straightforward, undeserving of such brutality. But by his own admission, he'd also taken a fragile woman, introduced her to drugs, and then tossed her out. Regardless of his sensitivity now, he'd been as bad as Willy on this score, if in a different manner, and Willy didn't see treating him any more lightly than he treated himself.

Andy sat back in his seat and swallowed hard. After taking a shuddering breath, he said softly, "That's pretty cold, Sniper. Just like the old days."

"I didn't introduce her to the shit in that needle," Willy said.

Andy's face turned dark red. He awkwardly rose to his feet and glared down at him. "The hell you didn't. You don't know the basket case I inherited. You fucked with her head so good not even the heroin had any effect. Shit . . . I was just the poor dumb slob standing between what you did to her and where she ended up. She was like on autopilot all the way." He leaned forward, his anger climbing. "Don't you lay that shit on me, you goddamn cripple. You don't get off the hook that easy."

He stood there breathing hard for a moment, before finally straightening and adding as he left, "The meal's on you, jerk. I hope it wipes you out."

Willy sat at the table for a long while afterward, almost motionless, trying to do what he'd done so well for years: batten the hatches and bottle up the turmoil.

But as he'd suspected they might even before he'd arrived in this city, certain survival techniques were beginning to fail.

# Chapter 8

Sammie Martens parked in the narrow driveway behind Joe Gunther's car and killed the engine. Gunther lived in a converted carriage house tucked behind a huge Victorian pile on one of Brattleboro's residential streets. The town was littered with such ornate buildings, in both the high-and low-rent districts—remnants of a past industrial age when New England and its dozens of sooty redbrick communities pumped their commodities into a growing, hungry, affluent society. Now the former showpiece homes of bosses and middle managers ran the gamut from private residences to run-down apartment buildings, depending on how the town's neighborhoods had settled out.

It was late, and Sammie knew she had no real reason for being here, that nothing could be gained from it, but the lights showing through Gunther's windows encouraged her nevertheless. After all, it was the nature of Joe's character, and of how he'd encouraged them all to speak freely with him, that had prompted her to come here in the first place.

She swung out of the car into the sharp evening air and

closed the door softly behind her. The carriage house was small enough that it reminded her of a toy railroad model, or something designed for dolls—seemingly an odd kind of place for an old cop to live, unless you knew him.

Gunther wasn't cut from the Marine Corps model of square-jawed law enforcement, although he had that military experience in his past, including time in combat. If anything, given her aggressive style, Sammie fit that image better. Instead, Gunther could almost be fatherly: quiet, thoughtful, slow to anger or to rebuke, and unusually attentive to his people's personal dilemmas. He had periodically gone to extremes to keep Willy out of trouble, but he'd also watched out for Sammie's well-being over the years, as he had most of the people who'd ever worked with him.

Willy had groused to her occasionally that the "Old Man," in his words, was compensating for having no kids or wife, and that he should mind his own business. Sammie not only disagreed, but knew the comment had more to do with Willy's shortcomings than with Gunther's. Joe didn't have kids or a wife, true enough, but he had been married long ago to a woman who'd died of cancer, and was involved with another, for well over a decade now, with whom he had a devoted if quirky relationship—including not only separate residences, but also absences lasting for weeks on end when she was working at her lobbyist job up in Montpelier. Their alliance was obviously something only the two of them fully understood, but it seemed to work quite well.

Sammie could only envy them there. Her love life had been as turbulent and dreary as Joe's had been placid, and her present involvement with Willy hardly seemed proof of a cure.

The front door opened to her knock and Joe Gunther stood before her with a plane in his hand and wood shavings sprinkled across the front of his pants. "Hi, Sam," he said, unperturbed by the late hour. "Come on in. I was just goofing off in the shop."

He'd converted a small barn off the back of the house into a woodworking shop. It was a newfound hobby for a man who used to only read and listen to classical music on those rare evenings he wasn't working late. Sammie found it endearing, imagining her boss as a late-blooming elf, priming his talents to make toys for Santa. Except that she also knew it was largely a front. For all his soft-spoken ways and seeming imperturbability, Joe Gunther was actually more of a Clydesdale: an unstoppable force who compensated for a lack of genius with a doggedness second to none. Sammie had seen him plow through adversity, pain, and personal loss with stamina and courage she could only imagine.

"You want a cup of coffee?" he asked, ushering her in.

"No. I'm okay."

He took her jacket and hung it on a nearby hook and invited her into the small living room around the corner, whose back door, standing ajar, led directly into the wood shop. He gestured to her to take a seat and, placing the plane on the coffee table between them, settled into an old armchair, scattering a few wood shavings onto the rug.

"You heard from Willy yet?" he asked.

"No," she admitted.

"Which is why you're here," he suggested gently.

She looked at him ruefully. "Yeah. I'm sorry to be a pain. I'm just worried."

"So am I," he admitted, which surprised and comforted her. "I even called Detective Ogden again to see if he knew anything. Which he didn't," he added in response to her hopeful expression.

"So, what're we supposed to do?" she asked.

Gunther shrugged. "There are options. Technically, he's AWOL, so we could act on that. For the moment, I've just put him on bereavement leave, which is stretching things a bit for an ex-spouse. But we're not too busy right now, and the rest of us can handle his caseload, so I don't see the harm, and I sure don't see blowing the whistle on him."

"And in the meantime, we wait?" she asked, her voice rich with impatience and frustration.

He nodded. "Yup. He's got to work this out."

Sammie slapped her leg with her hand. "Work what out? I understand he feels guilty about messing up their marriage, but that was years ago. From what he told me, she wasn't the most stable person in the world to start with, and he wasn't the one who put her on drugs. I mean, Christ knows he's no saint, but it takes two to tango. What's he doing down there?"

Gunther smiled softly. "Seeking absolution, I would guess. He's a man driven by devils. By guilt now, anger when he went to Vietnam, self-loathing when he hit the bottle. Right now, I figure he's hoping he can get himself off the hook somehow, even if he's convinced he'll never succeed. If we're lucky, he'll come home when he runs out of gas."

Sammie stared at him in silence. He laughed and held up a hand. "All right. That's a little too easy, but don't you forget how you felt about him in the old days. I'm really happy you two are together, but our Willy is a handful. You should remember that and protect yourself a little."

Sammie didn't answer, choosing to fix her eyes on the dark fireplace across from her.

"Right?" he repeated.

She glanced at him, slightly irritated. But she knew him well, having worked under him for more than ten years, first at the Brattleboro PD with Willy and then for this new outfit, and she knew he didn't say such things without reason. She swallowed her defensive first reaction and considered what he'd said. It was true that when she and Willy were first on Joe's detective squad, they'd fought like dogs, protecting their turf and taking swipes at each other at the slightest provocation. They laughed a little edgily about that now, when they were feeling sure of each other, but it was hard sometimes not to believe that their current affection was merely the same old passion with a twist. Willy was sometimes hard to love.

That thought process finally made her nod in response to Joe's question. "I guess so. You've known him a long time. Did he ever tell you about Vietnam?"

Gunther thought awhile. "Sort of. I was able to fill in some of the blanks from my own time in combat. He did a lot of long-range recon work, deep into the enemy's back pocket. It got pretty ugly sometimes—guys making up their own rules as they went and not saying much when they got back. I know his nickname was the Sniper, if that tells you anything. I guess it described his attitude as much as any specialty he had. And he wasn't alone there. The war had fallen apart, the American public was sick of it, the rest of the world thought we were the pits. The Kennedys and Malcolm X and Martin Luther King had been assassinated one by one. Urban riots were the norm. You're young enough that it all looks kind of quaint and antiseptic now. But there were serious doubts we'd survive as a nation. When Willy went off to fight, returning vets were already being met at the airports by protesters spitting on them and calling them baby killers. Those were very tough years."

"Why did he go, then?" she asked.

"I always thought it was because he was ready to kill somebody—he just had sense enough to want to do it legally."

Sammie stared at him wide-eyed. "He told you that?"

Gunther shook his head. "No. He had a tough time growing up. I don't know all the details, but by his late teens, I guess he was a basket case. He tried the cops first. Apparently, that wasn't enough. The military suited his needs better anyway. It was a post-World War Two army, transfixed by the Great Red Menace—basically the same bunch who'd trained me earlier. They weren't the sensitive guys who let you enlist to 'Be all that You Can Be.' Back then, it was kill the gook. Simple.

"Willy allowed himself to be turned into the equivalent of a human knife blade, probably hoping for some sort of cathartic release. Except that it only complicated things and added to the baggage he was already carrying."

"He is pretty certifiable sometimes," Sammie said.

But Joe shook his head. "My back pocket psychology is that we're all giving him the support today he craved growing up, but since he's literally been to the wars and back, he doesn't know how to accept it. He needs it, wants it, and hangs around to receive it, but he'll flip you the finger when you pony it up because he sees all dependence as a sign of weakness."

Sammie pondered that for a while, a frown growing across her face. "Sounds like I got stuck with another Froot Loop." She smacked her forehead with the heel of her hand in mock penitence. "Stupid, stupid, stupid."

Gunther laughed, but his eyes were serious. "You really believe that?"

"What's not to believe?" she asked him. "You're describing a guy who needs help but who kicks whoever's helping him in the teeth so he can maintain his self-image. That sound like a pick of the litter to you?"

"It wouldn't be if it weren't a work in progress. He is improving."

She wanted to argue the point, but she couldn't. It was true. Willy had learned to control his alcoholism through sheer willpower. His more flagrantly self-destructive behavior was largely a thing of the past. When they were alone together, he'd exhibited tenderness and warmth she'd never thought him capable of in the old days. And, as naive as it sounded even to her, there was the art—the pencil sketches he did, often while on stakeout, quickly and efficiently with that powerful, dexterous right hand, turning out images of subtle beauty.

Still, it pissed her off. "Why can't I fall for a normal guy?"

Joe Gunther gazed at her affectionately. "Because you're not a normal woman."

"Perfect. I really wanted to hear that. What was Mary like?" she asked after a pause.

He thought a moment before answering, "There's a danger right now of just seeing her as a junkie loser. But when I met her, she was naive and shy and damaged and a real sweetheart. And she worshiped Willy, probably for all the wrong reasons. The way that marriage ended burned both of them terribly—her because of the betrayal she'd suffered, and him because it was the latest and biggest example of his failure as a human being. I don't know what Mary was up to in New York, but it was more than just being a victim. 'Cause she was smart, too, and, after Willy, good and angry. Whatever she was planning by going down there, you can bet that getting even was part of it."

Sammie shook her head. "I just hope he's not the target, even from the grave."

At around the same moment, back in New York's Lower East Side, Willy Kunkle stood quietly in the shadows of an empty warehouse, hidden behind a concrete buttress, watching a small piece of urban theater play out at the end of the block. There, along a darker stretch of East Broadway, a young man paced the sidewalk, a quirky combination of self-confidence and nervousness. Dressed in the quasi-uniform of baggy pants, sneakers, watch cap, and loose logo jacket, he bounced back and forth like an eager dog prowling a dock, awaiting the return of its owner's boat. But the boats, in this case passing cars, went back and forth in a blur, seemingly ignoring him.

Until one slowed, veered slightly to get out of traffic, and then stopped. The young man's body language instantly changed. Now diffident, almost surly, he reluctantly approached the car as if it had a bad odor, and condescended to bend ever so slightly at the waist to address the driver through the passenger-side window. There was a short conversation, after which the young man—a drug dealer's so-called steerer—straightened dismissively and gestured to the driver to pull over to the entrance of an alleyway directly across from Willy's observation post. His role fulfilled, the steerer returned to keeping a lookout for both customers and cops.

Willy continued watching as a small boy suddenly appeared on a bike, despite the late hour and poor visibility, and rode up and down the street without apparent purpose—the mobile perimeter sentry, activated by the driver emerging from his car. This man, white, conservatively dressed, clearly on edge, looked up and down the sidewalk before crossing to the alleyway and pausing at its opening. Willy extracted a small, inexpensive telescope he kept in his coat pocket for such occasions, and focused on the dimly lit scene.

Barely visible, the outline of a man appeared from the gloom beyond the buyer. The two conferred briefly, the dealer taking something from the buyer, after which he reached above his head to one of the upper support brackets of the roll-down metal curtain protecting a shop window next to him, and retrieved a small package—all in a gesture as smooth and fast as a hummingbird sipping from a flower.

The buyer took the drugs, quickly broke away, returned to his car, and joined his brethren in the flow of traffic. The whole thing took about two minutes.

As a final sign of returning normalcy, the underage bicyclist rolled to a stop opposite his perch barely within sight of the steerer, and waited for the next heads up.

Willy smiled and pocketed the telescope, having found what he was after. He separated himself from his hiding spot, walked down the side street, crossed East Broadway, and approached the steerer at an angle that put the young man between him and the opening to the alleyway.

Like any midrange occupant of the urban food chain,

the steerer noticed Willy early and warily, stopped his restless weaving, and turned to face the threat, while balancing on the balls of his sneakered feet, ready for flight. One hand drifted toward the right-hand pocket of his jacket.

Willy shook his head from a distance. "Don't do that."

The steerer hesitated. Close up, he couldn't have been older than sixteen, all the hardness he could muster twitching around his mouth and nostrils, but only fleeting in his eyes. He could clearly see that the strange-looking, asymmetrical man coming toward him was no one to bluff.

"You the man?" he asked.

Willy smiled slightly. "You want to find out?"

"I didn't do nuthin'."

"Then we're just having a conversation." Willy extracted a photograph from his pocket and showed it to the steerer. "Tell me about this."

It was the evidence picture of the package of drugs found next to Mary's body, labeled with the caricature of the red devil.

"I don't know about that shit."

"Maybe your main man does in the alleyway."

The steerer's eyes widened slightly. "What're you talkin' about?"

"You pull 'em in, you and the kid on the bike keep an eye out, and the third guy does the deal. Why're we talkin' about this? Eyeball the picture and tell me about the red devil. Then I'm gone and you're back in business."

The steerer pressed his lips together in thought. "That's it?"

Willy pretended to be losing patience. "I'm being polite here, showing you respect. I coulda gone straight to your man in the alley, shined a light in his face, grabbed his goods from above the security gate, and showed him you can't do your job, but I didn't do that, did I? You wanna screw that up?"

The youngster showed his age by clenching his fists and stamping one foot. "Shit, man. You fuckin' with me?"

Willy held out the picture again. "Tell me about the red devil. That's it."

The steerer finally made up his mind with a quick glance over his shoulder. "We don't do that shit."

"We talkin' in circles here?" Willy asked menacingly.

"No, man. I mean it ain't ours. That comes from up-town. Diablo."

"That's what they call it? Where uptown?"

"A hundred and fifty-fifth. The Old Polo Grounds."

That caught Willy by surprise. The Polo Grounds were only twenty blocks south of where he'd met Bob earlier that day. The old neighborhood.

"Who sells it?"

The young man took a step backward, shaking his head vigorously. "No way, man. You asked what I know. That's it. I ain't tellin' you more."

Willy didn't care. If the kid had given him a name, it might well have been wrong or a street alias of little value. The key was to know where Diablo called home. From there, Willy could track it back to its maker.

And he knew just the man to consult.

He slipped the photograph back into his pocket. "You've been a scholar and a gentleman. I will go to the oracle."

The kid stared at him suspiciously. "What is that?"

Willy paused and smiled as he turned away. "Good question. I hope it's the other shoe dropping."

# Chapter 9

Nathan Lee had lived in Washington Heights all his life, and had done almost everything within reach to make a living. He wasn't a major player, just one of thousands on the hustle, a discreet man with a professionally short memory, who never forgot anything or anyone, knew how and where to get things done, and whose comfort level with things legal and illegal had finally reached an even keel. Just as he would never hold a nine-to-five job, he would also never touch anything that might cost him more than a night's detention.

That hadn't always been true, and his coming to terms with moderation owed a lot to Willy Kunkle.

All those years ago, before Willy left for Vietnam and while still a rookie on the NYPD, he stopped Nate Lee on a drug possession charge. The circumstances weren't egregious. It was a routine piece of business, but the laws were such, and Nate's record long enough, that had Willy actually arrested him, Nate, no spring chicken even back then, would have spent the rest of his life in prison.

That hadn't happened. For reasons neither man was likely to be able to explain, an odd connection was made that night between the troubled patrol officer who, unbeknownst to himself, was already in freefall, and the penny-ante street hustler one step away from a life sentence. Like one failing relay racer tossing the baton to the next man up, Willy spontaneously granted Nate absolution, with no strings attached. He merely poured the drugs into a storm drain, told Nate to nurture the gift he'd just been granted, and walked away.

The two never met again.

To Willy, the experience was like a passing inspiration, unsought at the time, inexplicable later, and finally all but forgotten. To Nate, however, it had more significance. He pondered the chances of being as lucky as he'd been with Willy, and found them slim enough to warrant his paying attention. Not that he then joined the church or found redemption. But he started thinking before he acted, considering his own survival, and never again put himself in such peril. After a couple of years practicing this new habit, he then thought a show of thanks might be in order, so he wrote a letter to Patrol Officer Kunkle, care of the NYPD, reminding him of that night without going into detail, expressing his gratitude, and hoping that everything in Kunkle's life was equally on the upswing.

He never heard back, never expected he would, but was content to have made the gesture.

Kunkle actually got that letter, a long time after it was sent. The police department forwarded it to Vietnam, where Willy opened it in an alcoholic stupor one night, and injected into its mundane wording an intangible significance. Some act of grace that he'd practiced without thought a seeming lifetime ago had been brought back to his attention in the middle of a hell on earth like some elusive sign. Willy kept the letter almost as a talisman, rereading it occasionally until it finally became lost in the wake of his turbulent travels.

When the young steerer mentioned Washington Heights, however, forcing Willy to think back not just to his childhood, but to when he'd walked the beat in exactly that neighborhood, the memory of Nate's letter came back to mind with abrupt and total clarity. That's why he'd referred to the second shoe dropping.

In fact, such a historic connection was by now becoming the norm. Since crossing the Harlem River, he'd been traveling backward in time like a man walking into freezing cold water. Mary's death, the fact that he'd been the one called to identify her, its happening in New York, seeing Bob and Andy, and finally his sudden recall of Nathan Lee's innocuous letter in relation to Washington Heights, were all part of a progressive pattern.

As Willy rode the subway north into Harlem late that night, he couldn't help but wonder whether—even hope that—the journey he was on might clarify more than just the questions surrounding Mary's death.

Because he was feeling the need for a whole lot of answers.


Nathan Lee swung out the door and stepped lightly down the stairs of the apartment building fronting Amsterdam Avenue, a wad of cash tight in his back pocket. He'd known a man who needed a job done, and knew another man who could do it. That was largely the nature of Nate's existence nowadays, hovering in the middle of as much action as possible, like a party balloon being swatted from one table to another—he made it his business to pass between disparate people, and made sure that with each swat, he got a small percentage.

He looked up and down the sidewalk with a smile. It was long after midnight, which for him was mid-work-day, and he was in the mood to see if he couldn't hit two scores in one night.

He turned south toward 155th Street and headed for his office, an all-night, pocket-sized general store selling everything from cigarettes to playing cards to soda and candy bars, and whose owner, Riley Cox, he'd known since Riley was a kid.

Nate had been a street hustler even back then. Part of his success now, in fact, lay in how old he was. White-haired, bandy-legged, and skinny as a pole, he was the epitome of the elderly black caricature, watching life passing by on the stoop of a brownstone. Except that he had too much energy for that. The combination of his appearance and his natural enthusiasm made him hard to resist and, more importantly, harder to target as a fall guy when things went awry. The tough people he often dealt with either protected him or dismissed him, but they rarely held him to blame. It was a blessing he nurtured and never took for granted.

He entered 155th and walked west, his feet moving to a tune that kept echoing in his head, something he'd heard on the radio last week. He saw Riley's sign in the distance, a yellow beacon offering friendship, comfort, and maybe a hot lead.

Now snapping his fingers to the tune, he rounded the newspaper rack outside and pulled open the glass door into a wall of warm, aromatic air, as embracing to him as a home kitchen on a winter day, even though the odors were of dust, cigarette smoke, and stale humanity.

Nate caught Riley's eye as he stepped inside and felt his opening one-liner die on his lips. There was nothing amiss about the tiny store. It was as busy as always, and even Riley looked almost normal. But you didn't know someone for decades without sensing that single element's being out of place. Nate stopped in his tracks, the door still open in his hand, and readied himself for a fast retreat.

"Hey, Riley. How's it keepin'?"

In response, Riley shifted his gaze to the nearest of the two aisles inside the store, the one that was just out of Nate's line of sight. Nate silently leaned to his left in order to get a better view, his hand still on the doorknob. Slowly, the aisle came into view, revealing a thin, hatchet-faced man with intense dark eyes and a shriveled left arm.

Nate, whose business was faces, didn't hesitate, even after all the years. He broke into a wide smile and released the door. Riley visibly relaxed. "Why, if it ain't Officer Kunkle."

"Long time, Nate," Willy answered.

Nate approached him with an appraising eye. "Not to be rude, but you're lookin' a little rough, if that's all right to say."

Willy let out a small snort. "Can't argue with the truth."

"What happened to you?"

"Took a ride along the bottom a few years back."

Nate stuck out his hand and Willy shook it, enjoying the warm, smooth feel of it.

"And the arm?"

"Bullet wound," Willy answered shortly.

Nate nodded sympathetically. "Oh, my lord. So, you're not with the police anymore."

Willy smiled thinly and gave an indirect answer. "You don't get that lucky. They can't fire you if you can still do the job."

Nate tried to hide his skepticism. "Hell, given some of your brothers, they're not even that picky. Why're you back, after all this time?"

They were looking at one another straight in the eyes, as if reading the real dialogue between them.

"Favor for a favor?" Willy suggested.

Nate chuckled. "I didn't forget. That's why I'm still here to talk to you. What're you after?"

Someone squeezed by them to pay at Riley's counter.

"You up for a walk around the block?" Willy asked.

Nate glanced over his shoulder at Riley and raised his eyebrows.

"It'll keep," Riley answered enigmatically.

That put Nate back in his good mood. He was intrigued by Kunkle's reappearance, but he doubted it would fatten his wallet. Riley's comment, however, implied the night might still be young, as he'd been hoping.

Nate patted Willy's right elbow. "Follow me. I got just the place."

He led the way down the block and up a side street. Before a dilapidated brownstone with the front door connected to the sidewalk by a set of broad steps, Nate ducked to the right and climbed down a narrow metal staircase to what had once been the service entrance. It was so dark at the bottom of this trench that Willy could barely see the back of the man before him.

Nate gave the door a coded knock and waited. A small, weak light went on overhead for no more than two seconds, before the door swung back just wide enough to let them both into a small, quiet antechamber that reminded Willy of an air lock. A huge, barrel-chested man with no hair and a goatee gave Nate a broad smile and a pat on the shoulder. "How're tricks, Nate? Keepin' busy?"

"You know it, Jesse. How's your sister?"

"Much better. I'll tell her you asked."

The man's voice was friendly and relaxed, but his eyes hadn't left Willy's face since the moment he'd come into view.

Nate laid a protective hand on Willy's shoulder. "This is Willy, Jesse. An old friend who did me a big favor a long time back."

"And the man," Jesse said simply, his smile only half in place.

"That's true," Nate agreed. "You got the eye. But he's still okay."

Jesse weighed that in his mind for a moment, and then gave a single nod with his large head. "Well, then I guess he's okay with me, too."

He took one step toward the rear of the small room and pushed a button Willy didn't see. A back door opened with a click, and they were instantly met with the sounds of laughter and music and ice chinking against glass. Nate had taken them to an after-hours bar, the new century's equivalent of a flapper-era speakeasy, and as big a business during the predawn hours now as any of its predecessors had been all through the 1920s. New York prided itself on being a twenty-four-hour town, and it wasn't going to let any arbitrary bar curfew stand in its way.

Nate exchanged greetings with half a dozen people as

he led the way around a pool table and down a row of booths to a bar at the far end of the room.

There the bartender instructed them, "Place your orders, gentlemen," as if they'd just arrived at the Ritz. The place wasn't that fancy, but it wasn't a dive. Dimly lit and simply but tastefully decorated, it could have held its own against any of its legitimate brethren. There was also a decent CD player leaking out good jazz, and since almost everyone present was over fifty, there was the mellow feeling of an old-fashioned men's club.

Nate ordered a rum, Willy merely bought an overpriced tonic water and was handed a warm bottle without a glass.

"Over here," Nate said, indicating a tiny table wedged against the far wall near a back door labeled, "Outhouse."

They settled down, comfortably far from the music, and sat almost knee to knee.

Nate had the contented look of a man watching an old home movie. He shook his head, took a sip of his drink, sighed with a contented smile, and said, "Officer Kunkle. Man, oh, man. I wasn't sure I'd ever see you again. I thought maybe you were like the nomad in the desert or somethin'—the righteous man who delivers the word of truth and then vanishes forever." He pointed at the arm and added, "And I guess if you'd been standing a few inches in the wrong direction, that'd be the fact of it, too. You ever get my letter?"

"I got it." Willy didn't detail its effect on him.

"Well, I meant every word in it, and I still do. That was an act of grace in an ungenerous world. You did yourself proud that night."

"That's just because it was your bacon I spared. You

would've called me a patsy if I'd cut someone else the same slack."

Nate laughed and took another drink. "I am disappointed at the depth of your cynicism, but I can't deny your point. In any case, you did me the big favor, and I will always be grateful."

Willy removed the evidence photo he'd stolen from Ogden and laid it on the table before Nathan Lee. "You know where this stuff comes from? It's called Diablo."

Nate looked at the picture without touching it, his face suddenly grim. Narcotics were what got him in touch with Kunkle the first time, and he'd never dabbled in them again. The fact that the same man was back discussing the same topic didn't bode well.

"I know what it's called," he said shortly.

"Comes from around here, right?"

"Why you want to know?"

Willy hesitated. A cop's first impulse in a conversation is to never volunteer anything. Every word you say is to get the other guy talking. And you sure as hell never reveal anything personal.

But Willy was the one asking favors here, and, training and paranoia aside, there wasn't much to be lost sharing a little with Nate.

"My ex-wife was found dead with that shit in her arm."

Useful or not, the effect of this admission was telling. Nate's eyes opened wide and he stared at Kunkle in amazement. "No wonder you're lookin' a little ragged. She live around here?"

"Lower East Side."

That surprised the older man. "Huh. It happens, but usually a home brew like that doesn't travel far from home. The local appetite's enough to keep the dealer happy."

"So, it is made nearby?"

Nate ignored the question, trying to step back a bit first. "Officer Kunkle, I know I owe you, so don't get me wrong, but is this something you want to do?" As Willy's face darkened, he quickly added, "Now, hold on, don't get me wrong. I'll help you out. I will. But see it from my side, too. That's all I'm askin'."

Willy's expression didn't soften, but he didn't say the harsh words that first came to mind. Instead, he asked, "What do you want?"

Nate waved both his hands at him. "Nope. That ain't it, either. I don't want a thing. But you come back after all this time, and you got one arm messed up and you say you're still a cop and then you show me the picture and say that dope killed your ex-wife. If you were me, you gotta ask yourself: What's goin' on here? You see what I'm saying?"

Once more, Willy fought the urge to react impulsively and tell him to mind his own business, and struggled instead to address Nate's concerns.

He took a swallow from his warm tonic water and then explained, hoping for the best, "I am a cop, but not from here anymore. I work in Vermont."

Nate's eyebrows shot up. "Vermont?"

Willy cut him off. "Yes, Vermont. I'm kind of a state cop up there, like a statewide detective. It doesn't matter, for Christ's sake. The point is, I got a phone call that my wife had died and I had to come down. They're writing it off as an accidental overdose—locked doors, needle in the arm, history of drug abuse. They just want to clear their books."

"They wrong?"

"I don't know for sure. I think they might be." Willy knew Nate would have liked more, but he was disinclined to hand it over. He also wasn't sure he wanted to actually air his misgivings, for fear they might lose credibility even to him.

Fortunately, Nate seemed comfortable working with that little. "I do know somethin' about this Diablo. That's why I was surprised you found it downtown. It don't really go there. She have a reason to come up here to get it?"

Willy thought of his brother, but he couldn't see how that fit. "Not that I know of. We've been apart a long time."

Nate stared at the tabletop thoughtfully. "Sounds kind of funny," he finally admitted, looking up. "Especially if it wasn't an accident. I don't know how much I can do, though. It's not like these people keep records, you dig?"

Willy opened his mouth to say something when they both heard a loud crash at the bar's entrance. The large bouncer was being propelled backward into the room by a flying wedge of men in uniform.

Willy responded first. "Shit. Cops."

Nate recognized them more specifically. "Vice," he said, and grabbed Willy's good arm as patrons and cops began falling over each other near the front. "Head out to the bathrooms and take the second door on the right."

Willy left his seat like a sprinter out of the blocks. "You coming?" he asked over his shoulder.

Nate merely flashed a smile and said, "Too old. Good luck."

Willy slammed through the "Outhouse" door and found himself in a short, dark corridor. With the noise escalating behind him, he pulled open the second door on his right and plunged through without hesitation, stumbling over a couple of steps and sprawling into the middle of a dimly lit landing with a staircase leading upward.

Scrambling back to his feet, he took the stairs two at a time, and had climbed two floors before he heard the door he'd used crash open and the sound of voices shouting.

"Upstairs, upstairs. I hear one of 'em headin' up."

Using his right hand on the banister to help propel himself, Willy increased his speed, peering into the gloom for some alternate way to what was looking like a straight shot to the roof. But every door he saw appeared shut tight, and he didn't have time to do more than look. He was pulling ahead of his slower, more heavily laden pursuers, however, so if the door to the roof was open, there might still be some way to escape.

He wasn't optimistic, though. New York was nothing if not a haven for the security-prone. Home of the fox lock, the LoJack, pepper spray, and more miles of razor wire than it took to tame the West, this city wasn't known for having rooftop doors left open.

Except when they'd been propped that way by a strategically placed brick. As soon as Willy made this discovery, now six floors above the speakeasy, he remembered from the old days how some drug runners would leave themselves a way out, just in case they needed an emergency back door.

Silently, he thanked this particular guardian angel's prescience, stepped through the door onto the gravel-covered roof, and shut the door behind him, hearing with satisfaction the spring-loaded lock snap to.

The roof was flat, bordered by a three-foot-high wall,

and pinned in place by an enormous, ancient, other-worldly water tank which stood in the center on lacy legs of steel and loomed overhead like a captured blimp. It was as symbolic of New York as that odd sound manhole covers seem to make only when taxicabs hit them at high speed, and was duplicated a thousandfold all across the five boroughs.

The light was better up here—the city's perpetual ocher glow a veritable sunshine compared to the darkness of the stairwell, and Willy took advantage of it to jog to the edge of the roof, step over it onto the neighboring building, and continue trying to distance himself from his starting point.

Just as he was beginning to think he might have pulled it off, however, he saw his luck begin to sour. Simultaneous to hearing a heavy ram repeatedly smashing into the door he'd locked behind him, Willy saw the beam of a flashlight clear the top of the distant fire escape he'd been aiming for, followed by the silhouette of a cop carrying a shotgun and rolling commando-style over the top of the low wall to vanish from view against the darkness of the roof's surface.

Willy began looking around for another way out, already knowing in his gut that he'd run out of options. He hadn't made five steps in a new direction before the door flew open and a voice from the fire escape yelled, "*Police, Don't move*. Get face down on the ground with your hands above your head. *Do it. Now.*"

Willy instead ducked briefly into the shadows cast by one of the water tower's legs, quickly removed his wallet, his shield, and his weapon, and slid them all under a flap of tarpaper he found extending from the footing of the tower leg.

"Get out into the light, you son-of-a-bitch, or I'll blow you away where you are."

Willy stepped out where they could see him, his right hand up. "Okay, okay. You got me. My left arm is paralyzed. I can't move it."

One of the cops, winded, adrenalized, and angry at having given chase in what should have been a routine bar sweep, came up behind him, threw him to the ground, wrenched his left hand free of where he parked it in his pocket, and kicked him in the ribs for good measure, frisking him roughly for weapons and contraband. Grunting with the pain, Willy also had to admit he would have done the same thing had the roles been reversed.

The cop finished his search by handcuffing Willy's wrists behind his back and rolling him over to shine a light in his face.

"What the hell did you think you were doing, asshole? You think we haven't done this before?"

He didn't wait for an answer. Instead, he looked up at someone Willy couldn't see and yelled, "We got him, Sarge. Any others up here?"

"Negative," came the distant reply. "Nuthin' with two legs, anyway. You got anything on that guy?"

The answer, Willy thought, was telling: "Nah, just looks like a cripple rummy. No ID, no nuthin'. Better search the area to make sure, though."

He was yanked to his feet and escorted back down the stairs, less troubled by the jam he was in, and more frustrated by the fact that his investigation has been put on hold.

# Chapter 10

The trip to the Tombs downtown, more formally known as the Manhattan Detention Complex, brought back memories to Willy of life in boot camp—lots of yelling, manhandling, shuffling together in groups, and a general sense that one's position in the human race had almost slipped from sight. That impression was driven home by his being cuffed and chained not just to a heavy belt around his waist, but to another man beside him. Fifteen of them, only a couple of whom he recognized from the bar, and certainly not Nathan Lee, were driven by guards like a small herd of clanking animals, first to a general processing center designed to handle large groups, then into a van with caged windows for transportation to the Tombs. The mechanisms involved in all this, and the clear point of it all, heightened a small tidal pool of dread Willy had been trying to ignore.

He'd hidden his badge and ID not solely from embarrassment, although that had been a factor. He'd also been keenly aware of what could happen to a cop in a prison environment. And the Tombs housed almost a thousand prisoners.

Years ago, just back from Vietnam, in an attempt to return to normalcy, Willy had gone out on a blind date with a college girl. They'd chosen a movie house in Greenwich Village, very trendy and filled with the sweet smog of marijuana, to see a black-and-white silent movie by some German pessimist. It had been about a future of brain-dead automatons, ruled by an unseen autocratic force, inhabiting a world of oversized, jagged, steel-and-stone structures, all designed with an indefinable but clearly industrial styling. The humans-as-cogs-in-a-machine point of the show hadn't suffered from any subtlety, but the image—unlike the name of the girl—had never left him.

As the guard from the van pounded on the roll-down steel door of the detention center's sally port off Baxter Street, sending up a rolling, clattering echo between the dark, high walls around them, the memories of that movie set, along with everything it implied, returned with the clarity of a prophecy come true.

Like the members of a chain gang, Willy and his co-prisoners were off-loaded from the van, paraded through the newly opened gap—actually a narrow alleyway between the two buildings constituting the Tombs—and told to stand still while the metal curtain rattled down behind them, cutting off the exterior world with a guillotine's finality. They were herded through a small door beyond a guard station, brought down a set of tiled concrete steps, and told to line up along a sterile, hard-surfaced, Lysol-smelling hallway whose only decorations were warnings of what they'd better not be doing, carrying, or even thinking about while they were there.

The most telling environmental detail for Willy, however, wasn't the harsh lighting or the antiseptic odors or the constant presence of mostly overweight people in uniform. It was the sounds of incarceration—the constant slamming of heavy metal doors, far and near, the harsh buzzing of electronic locks, and the nonstop chatter of people on portable radios, usually asking for some door or another to be sprung open on screeching hinges. That hard-edged, piercing, brain-grating symphony gnawed at him like a rat chewing a wire behind a wall, and was made all the more insidious by the steady, upbeat, dismissive laughter and bantering among the correctional officers.

For a man who didn't like being boxed in by people, routine, or impenetrable walls, the cumulative effect of all this began taking its toll. By the time it was his turn to be interviewed by the booking officer, Willy Kunkle's only thought was to keep his mouth shut.

"What's your name?"

Willy stared at the counter between them.

"What's you name, bud?"

Again, he kept silent.

The officer didn't react as the cop on the roof had. He simply sighed, looked over to his partner, said, "You deal with him," and beckoned to the next prisoner in line, reinforcing how little Willy's choices mattered to his eight-hour day.

And so it went throughout the entire procedure. Various people with various tasks asked him the questions assigned to them, got nothing for their pains, and simply passed him down the line. He was photographed, logged in as a John Doe, electronically fingerprinted on an AFIS machine, checked out for any injuries, strip-searched with a thoroughness even he found impressive, told to sit on a magnetic chair sensitized to any metal objects hidden in any body cavity, and finally relegated to a cell in the quarantine section reserved for the ill, the mad, the truly filthy, and the otherwise unclassifiable. For the time being, until the police could find out who he was, he would sit there, alone and thinking, trying to pitch the cool logic of the puzzle pieces he'd discovered so far against the personal demons that were nestling in the hard, bland, tiled walls of his cell.

Joe Gunther got the phone call the next day, sitting at his desk in Brattleboro. As soon as he recognized the nasal New York accent on the other line, he knew, if not the nature of the call, at least its subject.

"This is Officer Denise Williams of the New York City Department of Correction. We have a man in holding down here who seems to be one of your detectives."

"Is his name Kunkle?"

Williams's voice, which up to then had sounded half asleep, perked up with interest. "You know we got him?"

"I knew he was in New York. Not that he'd been locked up. What're the charges?"

"Disorderly conduct, obstructing governmental administration, and resisting arrest."

Gunther winced at the bureauspeak aspect of the second charge, thinking Willy had made a career out of that one. "Can you tell me what happened?"

"That's not my job, but from what I heard, he was in an after-hours bar."

"Drinking?" he asked in alarm.

There was a pause. "Well . . . it is a bar."

"He's a recovering alcoholic—hasn't touched a drop in years."

"Oh." There was a slight ruffling of papers in the background. "There's nothing about drunk and disorderly here, but if he was on police business, we don't know about it and he's not talking. Hasn't said a single word since we arrested him. We only found out about him 'cause the fingerprint machine kicked back his ID."

Gunther mulled that over for a moment before asking, "Why was he arrested in the first place?"

"It was a sweep. Looks like just a wrong-place, wrong-time kind of thing, but I don't really know. I was just told to contact you."

"What happens now?"

"Not much. As soon as we found out who he was, he was arraigned and moved upstairs. I'm not exactly sure, but he might be on Rikers already, waiting for his case to be heard. Anyhow, if he's not there now, he will be. You want to find out, here's the name and number you should contact." She rattled off the information in rapid fire, forcing Gunther to ask her to repeat it.

He hung up the phone and looked across the small room. Sammie Martens was staring at him, a piece of paper frozen in her hand.

"What's he done?" she asked.

"Nothing much. He was picked up in a sweep at an illegal bar. They're minor charges, but it doesn't sound like they're cutting him any slack. He's on Rikers right now, from what it sounds."

She put the paper down on her desk slowly, as if it were a thin sheet of ice. "A bar. What's it mean?"

"For his career? Don't know yet. Getting caught in a sweep is no big deal. He might have had a good excuse. It doesn't sound like he was drinking, so maybe he was running something down. But they mentioned flight and resisting arrest. Those might be problems. It wouldn't take much for our bosses to fire him, he's made himself so popular."

Sammie sensed a weariness in Gunther's voice, and understood—even if she wasn't much good at it herself—that there came a time when making allowances for someone wasn't in anyone's best interests any longer.

But she knew in her gut that this was not that time. Unfortunately, it also wasn't her choice to make.

Gunther was watching her with a small smile on his face.

"What?" she asked.

"Don't worry," he told her. "We'll make a quick field trip. Find out what he's been up to."


Willy Kunkle lay on his bed, his head propped up against a bunched-up pillow, staring at the ceiling. No longer alone in a small, dark cell, he was now someplace he considered far worse: in a huge barracks-style room, well lit with two opposing walls of windows, amid a serried legion of beds just like his own, each the tiny domain of an inmate just like himself. There were dozens and dozens of men here, bored, frustrated, restless, and full of the nervous need to talk, shout, throw things at one another, and get the ire of the few COs, or correctional officers, who watched them from a control booth at the head of the room.

He was on Rikers Island, which, with some nineteen thousand inmates, was touted as the largest penal colony in the world, depending on whom you believed. Mostly consisting of landfill, Rikers had over four hundred acres and hosted eleven different jails housing men, women, and juveniles. The facilities came in every conceivable shape, from open dorms like Willy's, for people accused of lesser crimes, to twenty-three-hour-per-day isolation cells designed for the truly out-of-control. All but a small percentage of these people were in fact inhabitants of a legal twilight zone, charged but not yet convicted of crimes that had yet to be adjudicated by New York's overworked, understaffed, around-the-clock court system. Some people had been living on the island for years, awaiting trial.

"Kunkle? You got a visitor."

He took his eyes off the ceiling and looked into the face of a tall, muscular Latino CO. "Who is it?"

The CO smiled broadly and quickly glanced over his shoulder. "Hey, Frank, he talks. English and everything."

Frank's distant voice floated overhead. "He tell you to get stuffed?"

The CO merely laughed and tapped Willy on his shoulder. "Come on. Get up."

Willy rose and turned to be cuffed, a gesture that had become second nature by now. He was then steered by the CO through a series of doors and long corridors, all ammonia-clean and shiny bright, feeling like a tiny particle in an industrialized intestinal tract, until he was finally delivered to a windowless beige room with a linoleum floor, filled with cramped glass-partitioned cubicles.

Sitting next to a man who was clearly a Legal Aid lawyer was Joe Gunther.

Freed of his cuffs at the door, Willy settled opposite them at the small table, his feet almost tangling with theirs, and addressed Gunther directly, ignoring the lawyer and his outstretched hand. "Now I know why I tried to stay anonymous."

Gunther didn't take offense. If anything, the attitude gave him hope that Willy was still functioning up to par. "Hi to you, too. And you almost got your wish. The AFIS took close to twenty-four hours to kick out your prints. You're a glitch wherever you go."

The lawyer tried asserting himself. "Mr. Kunkle, I thought you'd like to know our strategy in dealing with all this."

Willy barely glanced at him. "Just do what you got to do." He asked Gunther, "Is Sammie here, too?"

"You think I could keep her away?"

Willy scowled. "Shit. As if I didn't have enough on my plate already."

"She wants to help, Willy, and it's pretty obvious you need it."

"I need it from him"—Willy pointed at the lawyer— "not from you two."

"He's here because of us. I talked to the DA and the cops. Sammie was a character reference. Like it or not, we're helping you out. But I want something in exchange."

"Why? I didn't ask for any favors."

"You got 'em anyhow, and the biggest one is that you get to keep your job. The DA could've dropped the resisting arrest charge from the get-go, which is what's really hanging you up right now, but since the arresting cop was so pissed off, mostly because you put them all through a chase, the DA wants to do a little face-saving to appease the boys in blue. Your lawyer here will play his role, the DA'll do the same, and the judge'll have no other real choice but to kick you loose with time served.

From our side, if you tell me what you were doing there, which I'm guessing had nothing to do with drinking, then I'll be able to clean your slate entirely with our bosses back in Vermont, and that'll be an end to it."

Willy pressed his lips together and didn't answer.

"Why were you there?" Gunther repeated.

"I was meeting a guy."

"What about?"

Willy struggled with the frustration boiling up inside him. He just wanted to get out of here so he could pick up where he'd left off. He didn't give a damn about his job or the good graces of his superiors or fulfilling any deal with his Boy Scout boss.

"Joe," he finally said. "This is private, okay? I got busted on some chickenshit thing that doesn't have anything to do with anything. If my job's in trouble because of it, then the whole bunch of you are stupider than I thought. Just get me out and leave me alone. And tell Sammie to mind her own business."

"She feels she is."

Willy was beginning to feel hot, almost dizzy, the past twenty-four hours threatening to take him over by force. He pressed his hand against his forehead, fighting the urge to simply strike out in anger. "What is it with you people? You don't have the right to tell me what to do. Due process will get me out of this dump, and some excuse about vacation time or bereavement leave or whatever the hell will get me off with the pencil pushers in Vermont. Or not—I don't give a shit. Just leave me alone, okay?"

He shifted his attention to the lawyer at this point, fixing him with a furious stare. "Do your job. Don't feed me strategy. Just spring me out of here."

The lawyer looked from one of them to the other. Joe

Gunther nodded slowly and rose to his feet. "You two go ahead. Willy, you should be out by tomorrow morning, maybe the afternoon if things get jammed up downtown. If you don't act like a jerk and all goes as planned, Sammie and I'll see you afterward." He paused and leaned on the tabletop, putting his face close to Willy's. "I know what you're doing down here. I know you're not going to take Mary's death at face value till you can prove it to yourself." He quickly held up a hand to stop Willy from responding and added, "I'd do the same thing in your place. Just remember one thing, though, okay? You're not alone, much as you might think you are. And if Mary's death was anything other than what they're saying, you're also not the only one who wants to set that right." He straightened and finished by saying, "You know my pager number. I'm a phone call away."

He left the room, crossed the hallway, and exited the building through a double-doored vestibule where one door had to be locked before the other could be unlocked. At the other end, he retrieved the identity card he'd left with the CO there and went out to where he'd parked his car. There waiting for him was Sammie Martens.

"What happened?" she asked as soon as he'd slid in behind the wheel.

"For starters, you were right about not going in. He's wired so tight, his eyeballs are bulging. But I think he'll play ball with the DA. He is up to something, though—he didn't argue when I implied he was investigating Mary's death. I just don't know what he's got, if anything."

Gunther started the engine and put the car into gear. "One thing's for sure, though: As soon as he's out, he's going back on the trail, and I'd love to know exactly what that means."

# Chapter 11

Ward Ogden rounded the corner from the hallway, side-stepped a cardboard box, and bumped into two colleagues standing before the new coffee pool list, consisting of all those officers who pitched in to pay for the squad's current flow of caffeine. The coffee pool was an NYPD standard, since the department didn't supply this perk, and was frequently more often a topic of debate than the various reasons they all worked here. In fact, as Ogden stopped in order not to collide with them, he saw one of them finishing up a succinct piece of graffiti reading, "Martinez is a cheap fuck."

Ogden laughed. "Didn't pay again?"

The writer shook his head sourly. "Says he kicked the habit, 'cept I saw him drinking some an hour ago. Looked like a kid caught smoking in the john, for Christ's sake."

The other man jerked his thumb toward the squad room. "You got guests, by the way. Out-of-town fuzz."

Surprised, Ogden stepped past them and entered the room to see an older man and a much younger, wiry woman both sitting by his desk. The man rose as Ogden approached.

"Detective Ogden? Joe Gunther and Sammie Martens. We're from the Vermont Bureau of Investigation."

Ogden shook their hands. "Colleagues of Willy Kunkle?" he asked, waving them back to their seats and sitting down himself. "Didn't we speak on the phone?"

"Good memory," Gunther commented.

Ogden maintained a friendly, seemingly relaxed demeanor, but Gunther could see the guardedness in his eyes.

"We don't see too many people from Vermont, especially cops. Three of you must be a pretty big percentage of the total."

Gunther laughed. "Only a thousand of us—true enough."

Ogden nodded, looking amused. "Wow. We have over forty times that just in the five boroughs." After one of those miniature but detectably awkward pauses, he added, "So, what brings you down? Your guy find something?"

The phrasing caught Gunther's ear. "Was there something to find?"

Ogden smiled thinly, the look in his eyes spreading across most of his face. "We didn't think so."

He didn't say anything more, making his question about why they were there hang in the air between them.

Gunther was the first to address it. Sammie had obviously chosen to let the two old warhorses feel each other out on their own. "He's into a bit of trouble—got picked up in a sweep in an after-hours bar."

Ogden recalled Willy's admission to being an alcoholic. "Drinking?" he asked.

Gunther shook his head. "Not according to him, and not from what I just saw when I visited him at Rikers. He claims he was talking to someone, I think about how his wife died."

Ward Ogden returned to his original topic of interest. "So, you came down because he got busted, or because you think there's something we missed?"

Gunther could almost feel the thin ice under his feet. Ogden looked like a straight shooter, and from the little Gunther had been able to find out beforehand, he was a veritable legend in his own time. Gunther had already noticed the tiny gold brontosaurus on the other man's lapel, and knew of the weight it implied. To piss off one of these "dinosaurs" would be the end of whatever cooperation he might have been hoping for.

On the other hand, being a bit of a dinosaur himself, he also knew an alliance with one of them carried considerable weight.

As a result, he smiled at Ogden's loaded question and answered truthfully, "I don't think you missed anything. I'm not even sure Willy thinks so—he's carrying a lot of guilt about how his ex ended up—but one of the reasons I've lived with his attitude all these years is that he has instincts you don't see too often, and they're usually right. Right now, I'd say we're only down here to keep an eye on him."

"Unless something develops."

Gunther looked him straight in the eyes. "Stranger things have happened."

To his credit, Ogden returned the smile and nodded. "True enough. That having been said, though, I'm going to kick you upstairs before this conversation goes any further. We watch our backs in this department, and for good reason. I might have been willing to share a few details with Mr. Kunkle, cop-to-cop, but not with his brass, and not without a blessing from the Whip."

They looked at him blankly. He laughed. "Sorry. It's what we old-timers call the squad commander. You'll have to get used to some of that around here. Almost as bad as the Pentagon with all our jargon."

Gunther shook his head, amused. "It's okay, and if meeting the Whip means we get to work with you afterward, you got a deal."

Ward Ogden stood up and made a self-deprecating gesture. "We'll see what can be arranged. Follow me."

They didn't go far. At the back of the room was an office with one of those ubiquitous interior windows designed so the inhabitant can keep an eye on what's going on among the troops. With a quick knock on the open door, Ogden steered the two of them across the threshold to face a man in his mid-thirties with slicked-back black hair and a taste for expensive clothes.

"Boss, these are Special Agents Joe Gunther and Sammie Martens of the Vermont Bureau of Investigation. This is our squad commander, Lieutenant Miguel Torres. I should add that Mr. Gunther is also the Bureau's field force commander."

With a surprised look on his face, Torres rose from his feet and shook hands. "Vermont? Boy, you're a long way from home. Must be important. Have a seat. You want some coffee?"

When they both said yes, Ward Ogden moved to the door and purposefully motioned to one of the detectives he'd been chatting with earlier for two cups of coffee, fully cognizant of what he was setting in motion. As squad commander, Torres made a point of chipping into the coffee pool, but only for what he drank on his own.

Ogden knew the rest of them would soon be grousing that the lieutenant was overstepping his allotment—almost as big a sin as not paying at all. It was one of the trivialities of squad life Ogden could never resist toying with.

After seeing them all seated comfortably and equipped with their coffee, Torres leaned back in his chair and asked, predictably enough, "You just down here seeing how the other half lives?"

Ogden answered on their behalf, and Gunther noticed immediately the respectful way in which Torres paid attention to what his nominal subordinate had to say.

"Remember that overdose we had a few days ago? Woman with the needle still in her arm, all the windows and doors locked? Name was Kunkle?"

Torres was nodding, encouraging Ogden to continue.

"Turns out her ex-husband works for the VBI, and had to come down to identify the body, which he did a couple of nights ago. After that, he dropped by the precinct to ask me for more details. I gave him what I could, which wasn't much, and he went on his way. Now I've just been told we picked him up during a routine bar sweep and put him in Rikers."

Torres made a face. "Ouch. Sorry about that."

Gunther shrugged. "Wrong place, wrong time. He shouldn't have been there."

"The point is," Ogden resumed, "that he wasn't there getting a shot. We think he was interviewing someone about how his wife died."

"Who?" Torres asked, reasonably enough.

"We don't know," Joe Gunther answered. "I dropped by Rikers earlier to tell him I'd talked to the DA and to ask him the same question. He tends to be a little cagey when he's first digging into something, so I didn't get far, but it's pretty clear he's doing some checking."

Torres digested that for a moment, his expression showing no happiness. "Where was he when he got busted?"

There was a telling pause. "Washington Heights," Sammie answered quietly, causing everyone in the room to look at her. She smiled slightly and explained to Gunther, "I got out of the car when we were at Rikers. I guess having an out-of-town cop in jail was something to talk about, so I listened."

Torres turned to Ogden. "And I'm assuming his wife died in our precinct?"

His detective nodded wordlessly.

His elbows on the arms of his chair, Torres tapped his fingertips against his chin and stared into middle space. "I'm not really good at head games, Agent Gunther," he finally said.

"Call me Joe—makes me sound like a fed."

Torres fixed him with his gaze. "All right, but what I'm saying is, I think something's going on here that's not being owned up to."

"That may be," Gunther conceded, "but then it's Willy who's got the answers, not us."

Torres shook his head. "I'm not so sure. Look at it from my side: some cop gets his wife dead in the city, comes down to ID her, and then pokes around to find out why she died, even though we don't see the mystery. In the process, he gets tagged for a minor rap it looks like he'll recover from. Then, out of the blue, he gets not one but two fellow detectives, including a boss, to come to the rescue, even though, from what I understand, he doesn't like the attention. Is that about right?"

Gunther responded carefully. "From your vantage point, yes. What you wouldn't be expected to know is the nature of the people involved, and the past history we all share."

Torres sighed heavily. "Boy. I don't like this." He looked over to his trusted dinosaur for help. "Ward, this is your case. You're the one who put it to bed. Are we comfortable with this? I need to know if we maybe screwed up, or if we got some nutso grieving cop out there who won't accept reality and is going to cause us problems."

Ogden didn't seem the least perturbed that the case he'd signed off on might in fact have been closed prematurely. Impressing Gunther with his evenhandedness, he merely shrugged and said, "I'll take another look at it."

That seemed to be all Torres wanted to hear. "Show our guests the usual courtesies and let me know what you find."


Ward Ogden led Sammie Martens and Joe Gunther back to his desk and motioned them into the chairs they'd occupied earlier.

Gunther was once again feeling uneasy about their status. "Detective, I'm sorry if we've suddenly become a pain in the neck. I didn't know your whip was going to throw this back in your lap."

Ogden seemed unconcerned. "Call me Ward. And he's just covering his butt. If it is a ground ball, it'll pan out that way again pretty fast, and if your pal Willy is on to something, then we'll have him to thank later. It's not a big deal." He then smiled and added, "But come to think of it, since the two of you are sitting around with nothing to do except complicate my life, I might have you help me out. That way, you'll know I didn't blow you off, and I'll have two extra heads looking at this." He glanced over his shoulder at Torres's window. "But that's strictly unofficial, okay? Unless or until something crops up."

Both Sammie and Joe nodded without comment. Ogden rose to his feet, a thin file in his hand. "Take your coffee. We'll move this to the interview room."

The room in question actually looked like a catchall, with a rickety table in the middle, a small fridge and a microwave in one corner beside a narrow counter, the ubiquitous pile of more boxes lining one wall, and a bank of padlocked miniature metal lockers for the officers' personal property.

Ogden took a paper towel from above the counter and wiped the tabletop clean of some mysterious puddles. "Okay," he finally said, laying the folder on the table and pulling out two folding metal chairs. "That's the Mary Kunkle case file, from soup to nuts. Take a look and tell me what you think. I have to make a couple of phone calls, but I'll be right back."

Joe and Sammie sat side by side and scrutinized the contents of the file together, occasionally pointing out details to each other, generally just reading quietly or studying the many photographs. They were just finishing up when Ogden returned.

He sat opposite them. "What do you think?"

Sammie Martens was about to start up, but Gunther spoke first. "Sorry. I was wondering if we could add one last request to this. Could we go to the scene? See it for ourselves?"

Sammie looked at him, but Ogden simply smiled and began gathering up the paperwork. "No problem. I would've done the same in your shoes. We'll go in my car."

The drive to Mary's apartment took no more than ten minutes. Not bothering with a protracted search for an open spot, Ogden double-parked beside a car which was facing a fire hydrant zone, thereby allowing its driver a way to get out on his own. He laughed at Sammie's cool appraisal of the gesture and explained, "People think we can just throw a plate on the dash and get free parking wherever we want," Ogden explained. "That's true a lot of the time, but if we're blocking a hydrant or a bus zone, we get ticketed like everybody else, and we have to plead the summons with the boss and do all the usual paper-work. I even got towed once when I was inside a build-ing working a case. Took me all day to get the car out of hock."

They'd all three been walking while Ogden aired these woes, so as he finished, they were standing before the dreary, stained facade of Mary's apartment building. Ogden pushed the super's doorbell in the lobby and waited until José Rivera appeared, wiping his hands with a rag.

His face fell as he recognized who it was. "Oh, Detec-tive. Not again. I thought this thing was over."

Ogden smiled at him. "The fat lady hasn't sung yet, Mr. Rivera. Sorry. Could you let us in?"

Rivera turned heavily and plodded away into the gloom of the building's interior. "Follow me."

They climbed the stairs to Mary's floor and came to a halt before the taped door. Ogden reached out and touched the white warning label at the spot where Willy had sliced it earlier.

He hadn't said a word before Rivera cut in, "Don't

blame me. That was you guys. You too cheap to use new tape, it ain't my problem."

Ogden patted him on the back. "Relax, Mr. Rivera. Nobody's busting your chops here. Was this the guy with the bum arm?"

Rivera eyed him suspiciously, as if this were a trick question. "So?"

"So nothing. It's all right. I just wanted to know."

The super's expression softened. "Yeah. It was him. And tell him I appreciate whatever he did in there, too. That was a first. It went down good with the neighbors, too. I been through this routine before with you people, and he's the first to clean up after himself. I don't know why you can't make that policy, instead of letting a place smell like a sewer till nobody can live on the same floor. It's a sanitation thing, you know? You screw me over and then the health people're all over me for somethin' I can't do nuthin' about."

Ogden had already opened the door and waved the other two inside while Rivera was venting. Now he gave the super's shoulder one last pat, said, "It's okay. I'll let him know," and closed the door.

He smiled apologetically at his guests. "They don't see us face-to-face too often. I guess they have to get it off their chests when they can."

Sammie was looking perplexed. "What was he talking about, anyhow?"

Ogden tapped the side of his nose. "No stench. . . . In fact, it smells pretty good. The first time we were here, it was getting ripe. She'd been there awhile and she'd messed herself before dying." He moved past them as they stood in the tiny kitchen and glanced over the living room. "Yeah. Willy did a Spic and Span. Didn't do the scene much good, but, like the super said, made it more bearable. Sometimes a scene stays rank for months till some bureaucrat in our department clears the last of the paperwork."

He seemed to take Willy's violation in stride, removing a plastic jar from his overcoat pocket and holding it up. "At least, we won't have to use these."

Sammie reached out and took hold of the container.

"DOA crystals," Ogden explained. "That's what we call them. I think they look more like rabbit pellets. Open it and take a whiff."

She did so, made a face, and passed them on to Gunther, who did likewise. "Christ," he said, "talk about sweet."

Ogden laughed. "Might be worse than what it's supposed to hide. We usually spread them around the room in a few Styrofoam cups so they aren't that concentrated, but they do the job."

They all three moved into the living room, where Ogden once again opened the case file and spread it across the coffee table before them. "Okay, so you got your wish, Joe. This is it. You two see any problems with our conclusions?"

Ever wary, Gunther glanced at his face, but once more, all he could see was a helpful neutrality. Ogden, it was beginning to seem, was one of those rare birds: the ultimate professional. No matter the situation or the setback, he didn't take the job personally. It was all about quality control, not who was right or wrong.

Gunther began gently nevertheless, wandering through the apartment as he spoke. "To start with, because of Willy's neat-freak attack, I'm relying on the photographs for how the place looked before the search, but it seemed very clean and tidy for a junkie. Healthy food in the larder, a fully stocked and shiny bathroom."

Ogden nodded. "I noticed that. On the other hand, the premise we're working on—based on all her track marks being old except the lethal one—was that she'd been on the mend. She wasn't supposed to be down and out and living like a rat in a box."

Gunther paused by the TV set and picked up a small envelope. He handed it to Ogden with a wry smile. "It's addressed to you. It's Willy's handwriting."

Ogden opened the envelope and poured its contents out into his palm. There were the few crumpled receipts Willy had retrieved from the trash, and a thick wad of old Metro cards. An accompanying scrap of paper had the words, "Found this lying around. The Metro cards were wedged in the window. Figured you could put them to better use than me."

Ogden shook his head. "Interesting guy."

Gunther laughed. "That's one word for him."

"There was something else Sammie noticed from the photographs," he continued, returning to the kitchen and the front door. "The locks here: There's the regular one the super just opened to let us in, which I guess was locked when you first responded to the scene, and then the deadbolt, which can only be closed from inside." He snapped it to as a test, its sharp click sounding like a slap.

Ogden understood the implied question. "And it wasn't closed, as might be expected in the middle of the night."

He moved next to Gunther and opened the door entirely, checking the other lock's mechanism. "We really have three systems here," he said. "One's a spring lock, engaged when you just pull the door closed behind you.

Then there's a key-operated deadbolt, which Rivera opened at the same time he opened the spring lock. I noticed he turned the key twice. So, the keyless deadbolt's redundant."

He shut the door again and raised his eyebrows. "In the responding officer's UF-61, he makes special mention that both the spring lock and the keyed deadbolt were closed. Could be she felt that was enough and never did use the backup deadbolt."

To his own credit, Ogden followed his comment by bending over the keyless deadbolt to study it carefully. "On the other hand," he added, "the knob does look good and shiny from repeated use." He straightened. "Of course, I don't know how long she was living here, either. Might be her predecessor was less trusting."

He moved back to the living room, where Sammie was doing a thorough search, and retrieved a photograph from the open file. "I did find out something else, by the way," he confessed, holding the picture up. "While you were going over the file back at the office, I went next door to see the narcotics guys—our precinct is also headquarters for Manhattan South narcotics. I asked them if the devil symbol on the bag of heroin was local, and they said definitely not. It had to have come from outside the neighborhood." He replaced the photo. "May not mean anything, but I thought it was interesting."

"So's this," Gunther said from the kitchen. "Bring the file, would you?"

They both joined him, Sammie carrying what he'd requested. He pointed to the counter beside the sink. "You got a toaster oven and a microwave, right? One's plugged in, the other's not, freeing up the only easily accessible outlet in the room. Except, there's nothing else around that can be plugged in."

He answered the next obvious but unspoken question by plugging in the toaster oven and hitting the ON switch. It lit up and the metal coils inside slowly began to glow. No one said a word. He killed the toaster oven and removed the plug.

He reached out his hand. "Let me see."

Sammie handed the file over and he extracted a picture of the counter, taken from their vantage point. He held it up before the real thing, so they could see the before and after. In both the photograph and in reality, the one plug was unplugged. Also, there was a barely noticeable residue on the counter, near its edge.

"See that?" Gunther asked, tapping the spot in the picture. "It's still here."

He pointed at it as it lay before them. Ogden bent over and turned his head to better see it in the overhead light. "It glistens," he murmured. "Like gold dust."

"Remind you of anything?" Gunther asked.

Sammie and Ogden looked at each other.

"Think of a hardware store," Gunther prompted.

Ogden's face lit up and he studied the dust again with renewed interest. "It's like the shavings left over from a key-making jig."

"That's why the outlet needed to be freed up," Joe Gunther agreed.

# Chapter 12

Willy Kunkle sat in a corner of one of the holding pens tucked under the misdemeanor court at 100 Centre Street in Downtown Manhattan. The cell was about twenty-by-twenty and held some ten men who were waiting to be taken upstairs for their moment before the judge. One of them was sequestered in a small cubbyhole at the back, which had a barred window through which he could talk privately with his lawyer. Willy had been here two hours, watching his roommates intermingling in subtle hierarchical ways, and wondering if and when one of them might confront him to find out who he was and what he was in for. So far, no one had shown any interest in him.

He was a little nervous. After Joe and the lawyer had left him behind at Rikers, pending his court appearance the following day, Kunkle had been extracted from the general-population barracks where he'd been staying and put into isolation for his own protection, presumably because Gunther had confirmed that he was in fact a cop, and thus at risk among other prisoners who might be interested in moving up the food chain.

But right now was not the following day. It was only

three hours after that meeting with Gunther. To his surprise, Kunkle had been taken from his cell, driven to 100 Centre Street, and placed in this cell. Almost afraid of jinxing what looked like an early release, he'd nevertheless asked one of the commanding COs if Joe Gunther had pulled more strings to speed up his processing. The answer had been that the DA was behind it and that Gunther couldn't be located, despite their efforts to do so, presumably because his pager was malfunctioning.

On the surface, this was good news. Willy had been expecting Joe and Sammie to be at his hearing and to then do everything possible to stop his returning to the streets. This latest development implied he was about to sneak out before they found him. But that was just an assumption. This system, with which he was all too familiar by now, did not usually pride itself on working ahead of schedule. Thus, the possibility lurked that something was amiss, and that he was about to be handed a nasty surprise.

"Kunkle?" a CO asked from the hallway outside, a clipboard in hand.

Willy rose to his feet. "That's me."

"Step out."

Watched by the others, Willy rose and did as he'd been asked. The CO took him by the arm and escorted him down the narrow hallway, up a cramped flight of windowless stairs, and to a door at the top. There, he pushed open the door and gave Willy a gentle shove in the small of his back.

Ready for anything by now, Willy found himself in a huge, vaulted, wood-paneled room full of people and voices, as big as a train station, it seemed to him, especially in comparison to the reduced quarters he'd just left.

It was the misdemeanor court, in full action. Architecturally just like the staid and impressive place so popularly featured on TV and in the movies, complete with a raised platform and ornate carved bench for the judge, along with other latter-century touches of decorative excess, but in fact a place reminiscent of old Bedlam. It was jammed with people: spectators, lawyers, court officers, stenographers, newspeople, and, looming above them all, a black-robed, efficient, and calm woman judge, who looked as comfortable here as if she'd been supervising a family dinner at home.

Willy froze in place, causing the CO to bump into him from behind.

"Keep moving—over there." An index finger appeared over his shoulder and indicated the same lawyer Willy had met a few hours earlier.

It was only then that Willy Kunkle realized that no one besides his lawyer even knew who he was or cared anything about him. Everyone else was there on other business. As he walked hesitantly to where his attorney awaited him, Willy began to differentiate the various groups cluttering the room. Apparently, in order to keep things moving quickly, the system encouraged defendants to be processed by the judge as on a production line, each equipped with a legal representative, a prosecutor, and perhaps a few others, and each variously awaiting his or her turn, pleading the case, discussing some postjudgment deal with the appropriate bodies, or simply filling in paperwork at the court secretary's desk.

The lawyer quickly shook Willy's hand without making eye contact, his attention distracted by the contents of his open briefcase. "We're up in a few minutes. Like I explained at Rikers, this is an arraignment and a sentencing both. Just stay quiet, look at the judge, be respectful, and follow instructions. It'll be over before you know it."

It *was* over almost that fast. His name and case number were announced, the judge asked both sides what they wanted, the prosecution and Willy's Legal Aid rep traded facts about the circumstances, the character references, the otherwise clean record, and ended up presenting the one option they wanted the judge to take, which she did summarily. Before Willy had a chance to carefully study the faces of the people responsible for his fate, he was told he could go. The whole thing had taken mere minutes.

He was out on the street shortly thereafter, feeling like he'd just been teletransported there, the product of some weird commingling of *Star Trek* and *The Twilight Zone*.

Despite his surprise, however, he was certain of three things: He was once again a free man, he was in immediate need of his wallet, badge, and gun, and he wanted to finish his conversation with Nathan Lee.

He began looking around for a subway station.

"It was over here," Mrs. Goldblum said, gesturing to them to follow her.

Ogden, Gunther, and Sammie Martens crossed the modest room to where the elderly woman was now standing by the window.

"I was watering this plant when I saw the man working on the fire escape. He was right there, where the ladder swings down from that platform to the ground."

They were across the alley from Mary Kunkle's building, looking at its wall and her living room window on the third floor. There, they could clearly see the crime scene unit, or CSU, gathering what evidence they could. The CSU leader had made his unhappiness with his assignment crystal clear to Ogden, describing the apartment as "sloppy fourths" after EMS, the first police search, and finally Willy Kunkle had all raised havoc with it. But his was not to argue in the long run—he functioned at the investigator's pleasure. And he had confirmed that the shavings they'd found on the kitchen counter were consistent with a key cutter's.

Now Ogden, temporarily using his two unofficial tagalongs instead of an assigned partner, was conducting a canvass that would have been done long ago had Mary's death been deemed suspicious. They had just met their first ray of hope in Mrs. Goldblum, after two hours of knocking on doors and meeting with blank looks.

"That's great," Ward Ogden said soothingly. "Could you tell what he was doing?"

But the old lady shook her head. "I thought it must have been some maintenance work. They do that sometimes. I didn't think anything of it because he was wearing a uniform and had tools. What did he do?"

Ogden answered blandly, "As far as we know, he was working on the fire escape, like you said. We're just asking people if they saw anything at all. It doesn't mean it was anything bad, necessarily. Did you happen to get a look at him, by the way?"

Again, she disappointed them. "He was wearing one of those caps with the bill pulled down. All I could see was the top of his head."

Joe Gunther was still looking out the window, and softly asked, "Did the maintenance man ever go up the fire escape, or did he just stay by the ladder?"

"He just stayed there, moving it up and down."

\*     \*     \*

Ten minutes later, the three of them were standing at the
bottom of the alleyway, looking up. They'd come in from
the street, through a gate with a broken lock that Ogden
noted with interest, and now Joe Gunther reached out and
pulled the chain hanging down from the ladder suspended below the fire escape's second-floor platform. It
swung down to meet them without so much as a squeak.

The silence was telling. Without a word, Ogden led the
way up the ladder until they were clustered around the
hinge at the top. He touched it with his fingertip and examined the fresh, thick, greasy results. Then he cast his
gaze farther up the escape, obviously visualizing the
route one could take to Mary's window once this stan-
dardly noisy and attention-getting obstacle had been bypassed.

Sammie Martens voiced a counterargument to what
was clearly going through Ogden's mind. "But her window was locked from the inside."

"Worse than that," Ogden replied. "I checked the lock
earlier. It's old and stiff. You can't jimmy it from the outside without either leaving traces or waking up the neighborhood."

There was a long pause as they each digested that
point.

Ogden finally straightened and prepared to return to
ground level. "Well, let's see how the CSU people are
faring. I'm afraid that so far things aren't looking too
good."

Sammie flared at that. "What do you mean? What
about the key shavings?" She pointed at the hinge. "And
that?"

But both older detectives knew they needed more. And

they knew a little patience and some more time might give it to them. Gunther laid his hand on her shoulder as she reluctantly started down. "Don't get worked up yet, Sam. We're just beginning."

Back on the ground, Gunther paused as they began heading back toward the street. "What's the weather been like the last few nights?"

Ogden stopped. "On the cool side."

"So no reason for Mary to have her window open?"

"No. Cooler than that. Besides, that would call on co-incidence. Unless the guy lived within sight of her window, he'd want to be sure the window was open before he set out to visit her."

Gunther wandered the length of the alley, his eyes running along where the wall met the pavement. He found behind a Dumpster a basement window with a metal grate before it. He crouched down and gave it a shake. It was loose enough that he tried again with more force, and found that a grease- and dirt-covered wire was all that was keeping it closed. The padlock supposedly doing the same thing had been surgically bypassed with a pair of cutters.

Ogden had joined him and was looking over his shoulder as he discovered this. "You ever hear of a CUPPI?" he asked.

Gunther glanced up at him over his shoulder. "A CUPPI?"

"Yeah—stands for Circumstances Undetermined Pending Police Investigation. It basically means any dead body we get where we're not sure of the manner of death. Guy's found stone cold in the park. Did he fall and hit his head, or did someone hit his head with a rock and make him fall? That's a CUPPI until we find out he was a drunk prone to falling and was last seen stepping on a banana peel."

Gunther understood where Ogden was heading. "Mary Kunkle's become a CUPPI?"

Ogden straightened from where he'd been studying the grate over the basement window. "Officially, not yet." He tapped the side of his head. "But up here, absolutely. Let's take a tour of the basement."

They located José Rivera for this, who with growing irritation took them downstairs to near his own subterranean apartment, and there unlocked a door to the basement and utilities area.

Ogden asked him to lead them to the window off the alleyway, and Rivera took them to a long, dark room cluttered with an assortment of junk and discarded equipment, smelling dank and faintly evil. There was a general skittering sound when he hit the lights which made both Sammie and Gunther think about the safety of their ankles. Sammie let out a small, spontaneous, "Gross."

"Rats," Rivera explained simply. "They love this place. Was that the window? There're four of 'em."

Not needing to approach it, both Gunther and Ogden immediately agreed. It was the only one overlooking a crude staircase of piled wooden boxes.

"What's down here?" Ogden asked the super.

"Besides all this shit? Nuthin'. There's the usual service stuff—heating, water, electrical panels. There used to be a laundry, but that got messed up a long time ago."

"Where are the utilities?" Gunther asked.

Rivera picked his way down the middle of the room, turned left, and took them through an opening into a slightly less cluttered, windowless cavern whose walls and ceiling were interlaced with pipes, conduits, and a supporting trellis keeping it all in place.

The light was a dim glow from a couple of encrusted bare bulbs, so walking around inside the room felt like being surrounded by a black-and-white hologram. Ogden crossed to the wall housing most of the controls and tried deciphering its contents.

"Each apartment has its own panel?"

Rivera stayed rooted in the middle of the room. "Yeah. That way, one of them shits the bed, no one else loses out."

Ogden pointed at an assemblage of boxes, switches, and levers, all of which, like everything else in the place, looked like it had been built around the time of the *Titanic* and was now resting on the same sea bottom, complete with mysterious growths. "So, this is how you would control everything in Mary Kunkle's apartment on the third floor?"

"You got it."

This time it was Gunther's and Sammie's turn to sidle up next to Ogden and scrutinize what had caught his eye.

"Mr. Rivera, could you come here for a sec?"

The super reluctantly approached them. "What?"

Ogden pointed at what looked like a small steering wheel. "What's that for?"

"Heat."

Sammie looked at him in surprise. "The apartments don't have thermostats?"

Rivera laughed. "Not from around here, are you? You know what a bunch of junkies and drunks do when you give 'em a thermostat? They run you outta business, that's what. No way. We fix the temperature from down here. Even the fancier buildings do that. We keep 'em warm enough, even if they do bitch now and then."

Gunther could imagine the conversations there, and figured that "now and then" probably accounted for the entire winter.

"Which way do you turn the wheel to make things hotter upstairs?"

Rivera made to demonstrate the technique, but Ogden caught his hand in midmotion. "Don't touch anything, Mr. Rivera. Just tell me how it works."

"Clockwise. All the way. Makes the place hotter'n a bastard."

Ogden nodded. "Great. Thanks. Do me a favor, would you? Go upstairs and tell one of the police officers in that apartment that we need a detective down here."

Rivera scowled. "Look, I been real useful to you, but I got a job, you know? I can't—"

"You want us out of here as fast as possible, right?" Ogden asked.

Rivera shook his head angrily and moved toward the door. "All right, all right."

They heard him cursing under his breath as he picked his way back toward the basement door.

"What did you find?" Sammie asked the New York detective after Rivera had moved out of earshot.

Ogden motioned her closer to the hand wheel. "Take a look, and compare it to the others next to it."

She quickly saw what he had, that the surface of the metal, dusty and grimy everywhere else, had been wiped clean on this one, presumably to remove any fingerprints.

"The CSU people ought to be able to tell us which direction it was moved last."

She looked up at him questioningly, unable as yet to connect the dots as apparently he had.

Joe Gunther, however, was right up to speed. "It goes to the locked window and the key cutter's dust, Sam. How do you kill someone and make it look accidental? Best way I know is to make sure everything's locked from the inside. We're guessing whoever's been lurking around here made a key in the kitchen using Mary's original to lock the door behind him. The trick is to explain how he got in in the first place."

"He could have knocked on the door," Ogden picked up, "but in this town, that's risky. Too many nosy neighbors and too many thin walls. Plus, around here you don't let somebody in you don't know."

"We looked at the window," Gunther resumed, "and found it was too stiff to jimmy from the outside, so the only alternative, as unlikely as it seems, was to somehow get the occupant to open the window on her own."

The light went on over Sammie's head. "So, you crank up the heat and gain access up the pre-oiled fire escape and through the open window, any small sounds being masked by the fan she probably had running as well."

"Bingo," said Ogden with a smile. "Not that any of that happened, but it sure looks good."

"An official CUPPI?" Gunther asked him.

The smile faded from Ogden's face. "We'll need the lab to confirm all this." He waved his hand at the apartment utility controls. "And we'll have to run some interviews, but I think we're already beyond the CUPPI stage. My gut tells me we're into a murder investigation now—one I promise in particular to see through to the end."

# Chapter 13

**W**illy Kunkle looked around carefully before setting foot on the dark roof. Now that he was not being chased, he could better appreciate the view, and was surprised at how close Yankee Stadium appeared across the Harlem River, glowing like an oversized alien saucer waiting to pick up a spare load of discarded humans. What with the gloomy, featureless water tower looming overhead and the complete darkness of the roof before him, Willy felt he was taking in the stadium and the millions of surrounding city lights as from a black hole—that he could see the entire world, and that it had no idea he was even alive.

It was a feeling he'd known more than once in his life.

He walked cautiously toward the far foot of the tower, the one most lost in the shadows, his senses attuned to any unusual sounds or movements. He felt he was back in enemy country up here, as out of place as he'd been in 'Nam. There, he'd also spent many nights in close proximity to the unknown, sometimes so quietly that he hadn't dared to brush away mosquitoes that were drawing blood from his face. In those days, the enemy had often been so nearby, they had filled his nostrils. In his mind only, as a sort of meditation, he'd even imagined coordinating his heartbeat with theirs, not just to broaden the scope of his own silence, but perhaps—subconsciously—so that when he quietly stopped that other heart with his knife, his own could mimic its continuing beat.

There had been times, out there, lethal and alone, so isolated and removed from his feelings that he could barely feel pain, that he'd actually thought in those terms, of hearts beating in unison like those of lovers in poems.

Which had made stopping them as he had, time and again, a curious experience initially, and eventually a debilitating one. In the long run, he'd lost interest in thinking about such things. Or perhaps, given his own heart's condition, he'd lost the ability to match its beat to anyone else's.

He passed under the water tower, groping in the gloom, bent double and feeling the ground before him, when suddenly he heard a soft voice. He froze, waiting, his mouth half open to quiet his breathing, his eyes avoiding any bright pinpoints of light so his pupils could adjust to the darkest corners of the roof.

The voice continued, almost a whisper, close to an atonal chant. Now totally and instinctively back in combat mode, Willy moved forward, retrieved his belongings from under the tar-paper flap without a sound, and homed in on the source of the chanting. He found it after drifting like a shadow pushed by the breeze to the edge of the roof beyond the tower. There, he found a young man with his baseball cap turned backward, sitting atop the low parapet, his legs dangling over the side. Beside him was a plastic bag of powder and an assortment of drug paraphernalia. He was talking to himself in a low, regularly cadenced voice, as if reciting a mantra. Heartbeat-to-heartbeat once more, Willy Kunkle stood behind him, six inches away, and clearly heard that the young man was merely mouthing the lines from a rap song, without inflection or enthusiasm.

Willy looked down at the back of the head near his right hand, remembering the things he'd been capable of so long ago, the things both his hands had once done, virtually without thought, and willfully without self-reproach.

Half the rush from those situations, however, had nothing to do with the acts of violence terminating them. In some ways, Willy had seen the killing as a letdown—messy, occasionally smelly—a disappointment, given all the intensity leading up to it. The truly curious joy had come before, in the psychic dominance preceding the final act. It had come from the knowledge that while he could have dispatched his target, he hadn't quite yet, and had thus extended the man's life. Most importantly, he'd given himself the power to choose, if for only a moment.

Just like now.

He watched the man manipulate his lethal tools, preparing to give himself an injection, so close that his hands could have been Willy's own. Willy wondered about how many times Mary had done this same thing, quietly prepared herself as others might make a ham sandwich, her anticipation rising for the lift the drug would soon give her.

As the young addict tied the rubber tourniquet around his arm, his elbow almost struck Willy in the leg, and yet Willy still stood as quietly as the water tower over them, watching, absorbing, remembering, imagining.

Until the source of this scrutiny reached for the plastic baggy. As he moved it from its resting place, the dim light from the surrounding city glimmered off its surface, and revealed the crude stamped image of a smiling devil.

In one smooth move, as fast and silent as a snake's, Willy reached out with his one hand, pulled the man back from his perch, dropped him onto his back, put a knee into his chest, and shoved his gun up against his nostrils, so that both his crossed eyes could clearly see what was menacing him.

"Be very, very quiet," Willy said, his mouth three inches from the young man's face. "If I even feel you twitch the wrong way, I will pull the trigger. Do you have any doubts about that? Nod yes or no."

The man's eyes were huge and white. But he gave his head a slight shake.

"What's your name?"

"Dewey." His breathing was coming in short, shallow gasps.

"I need to know where you got the Diablo, Dewey. Give me the name of your source."

"Who are you?"

Willy moved slightly, increasing the pressure both on Dewey's chest and against his nose with the gun. Dewey's eyes began to water.

"Wrong answer. I am not someone you can deal with. I will kill you in a heartbeat if you don't make me happy. Where did you get the Diablo?"

Dewey started hyperventilating, his body shaking and his hands slowly stiffening.

Once more with startling speed, Willy put the gun aside, grabbed the other man by his shirtfront, and hauled him in one clean jerk up to the top of the parapet, so that he balanced there on his back, with one arm and one leg dangling over the deserted street far below.

"I'm getting tired of this. You talk, or I push. That simple enough?"

Dewey was raving by now, thrashing and babbling and crying. It was all Willy could do to keep him from falling off on his own. In fact, he was about to dump him back on the roof and abandon him when Dewey suddenly blurted out, "It's Marcus, it's Marcus."

Willy shoved his face up close again. "What's Marcus? He sold you this shit?"

"Yeah, yeah. It was Marcus, man."

"Marcus who? How do I find him?"

Dewey's fear notched up. "I don't know his last name. I swear it. I just know 'Marcus.' That's all. That's what they call him."

"Where's he hang?"

"Around 145th."

Willy made as if he were about to push him over. "Where, Dewey? That's a long street. Give me an address."

"There ain't no address, man. I swear. He's on the street."

"Meaning he doesn't make the stuff. I want to know who makes it, Dewey. You're being stupid here."

"Jesus Christ, man, how the fuck d'I know? I don't give a shit who makes it."

That much rang true, Willy thought. "Describe Marcus to me."

"He's real tall, and skinny."

Willy waited before asking, "That's it?" He shoved him slightly, making the young man flail out in terror. "Stop jerking me around."

"Okay, okay," Dewey stammered. "Let's see. He's . . . ah . . . tall. No, no. I mean, hold it. I said that. His hair. He's got spiky hair, and he wears a tight chain around his neck—silver, real shiny. And he's got a real bad scar down his right . . . no, wait . . . his left cheek. I think . . . no . . . I mean, that's all I can think of." He sounded on the verge of hysteria. "Is that okay? Please?"

Willy placed one foot on Dewey's chest to stabilize him, and leaned over to retrieve the baggy of heroin. He sprinkled its contents into the night air as Dewey softly moaned in consternation. Finally, he dropped the syringe onto the roof and crushed it underfoot.

He stepped back, retrieved his gun, and pocketed it. "A little advice from your fairy godmother. You got a real desire to live, Dewey. Think about that next time you want to shoot up."

Dewey merely covered his eyes with his hand.


Twenty minutes later, Willy Kunkle stepped into the small convenience store where he'd first met Nathan Lee. The large man he'd seen at the counter was still there, and gave him a blank-eyed stare as he entered. Willy recalled Lee's calling him Riley.

Willy checked both narrow aisles of the store for patrons. For the time being, they were alone.

"Seen Nate?" Willy asked.

"Nate who?"

Willy sighed. What a routine. New York, Vermont, it didn't seem to matter. Who? What? Don't know what you're talking about. Pain in the ass.

Tired, stressed, longing for some answers, Willy yielded to a fit of impatience, pulling his weapon and circling the counter to shove it into the big man's gut. As he did so, however, he walked right into the working end of a sawed off, double-barreled shotgun, solidly held in one of Riley Cox's meaty hands.

"We don't allow people back here," he said, almost apologetically.

Willy fell apart. He began laughing so hard, he had to put his gun on the counter to wipe the tears from his eyes. He laughed until his stomach hurt, flooded with images of Mary, of Dewey, and of the jungle flashbacks, of himself wedged into a corner of the holding cell, of a thousand images he'd spent years bottling up. Even in the middle of this bizarre and spontaneous release, he knew, as if he were standing outside of himself, that he was close to cracking up.

As if fully aware of this, Riley gently reached out and dropped a newspaper over Willy's exposed gun before stowing his own back under the counter.

He waited until Willy had recovered from the worst of his fit. "You okay?" he asked quietly, his eyes still watchful.

Willy held up a hand. "Yeah, yeah. Been an interesting day. Hell of a few days, for that matter."

Riley pointed at the limp arm. "You get that in country?"

Willy straightened, took a deep breath, and ran his hand across his face. "Nah. Got it later, back where it was safe. I never got a scratch over there."

Riley gave him a half smile. "I can see that."

Willy retrieved his gun and backed out from behind the counter. "Nate tell you about me?"

"Told me you cut him slack when he needed it. I didn't need telling you been in 'Nam."

"You, too, huh?"

Riley's response was a long, drawn-out, "Yeah."

Willy didn't bother going on. He sensed Riley was no more prone than he was to indulging in old stories and secret handshakes. Theirs was a shared nightmare that didn't need resurrecting.

"So, what about Nate? Last I saw him, we were both being busted at some bar."

Riley's expression didn't change. "He told me about that. Why'd they grab you?"

"Resisting." Willy patted his jacket pocket where he kept his gun. "Had to skip upstairs to hide a few things. They just let me out. He get off?"

Riley nodded. "Didn't have nuthin' on him."

Willy smiled. "Straight and narrow. He's probably the only good deed I ever did in my life. I need to finish a conversation we were having."

"That may be," Riley told him, "but I ain't seen him since right after that happened. What'd you tell him to do?"

"I didn't tell him anything. I just asked if he'd check something out for me."

"Like what?"

Willy didn't see what he had to lose, certainly with this man. "My ex-wife OD'd on some junk named Diablo, only she was downtown and that shit comes from up around here. Nate was going to look into why."

Riley looked suddenly very tired. His kind eyes turned old and his gaze dropped to the countertop. "Old Nate musta thought the world of you," he said, almost in a whisper.

A sick feeling rose up from Willy's stomach. Piece by

piece, he felt he was losing chunks of himself, one day at a time. "What's happened to him?"

"I don't know, man. But he shoulda been in touch by now. Most of the time, I could set my watch by Nate. I been worried about him all day."

Willy stepped over to the window and absentmindedly looked at the street outside, the passing pedestrians barely registering in his conscious mind.

After a long pause, he turned and asked Riley, "Ever hear of a dealer named Marcus? Works on 145th."

Riley made a face. "Along with a hundred others. You think he makes this Diablo?"

"Not according to my source. But he probably knows who does."

Riley knew what he was thinking. "So, the Great White Hope tracks the dude down and makes this a movie with a happy ending?"

"Up yours."

"Hey, I won't be the one paying the price. What you think you're going to accomplish finding this guy? What're you going to do then?"

"What do you care?"

"I don't, not about you. But Nate's my friend, and I'd like to find out where he is before you go shootin' up the neighborhood and maybe gettin' him killed."

Loner though he was, Willy was enough of a pragmatist to recognize the value of what Riley had just implied: He would be a local guide to the neighborhood and its residents, if only so far as determining Nathan Lee's whereabouts. On his own, Willy knew, a white, out-of-town, one-armed cop probably wasn't going to get far.

"You'll help me?" he asked.

"More like I'll keep an eye on you while I'm doin' what I need to do," Riley answered.

Willy looked at the man's size and steadiness, and remembered the way he'd handled that shotgun.

"Whatever," he agreed.

Joe Gunther glanced down at his pager. "Damn." He looked up at Ward Ogden. "Could I use your phone?"

Ogden gave him a questioning glance but pointed to the phone on the desk.

Gunther dialed the number given him by the Legal Aid lawyer that morning. It was now nightfall.

"This is Joe Gunther. Did you try calling my pager today?"

He waited while Sammie Martens watched him, her expression revealing she'd already sensed what had happened.

After listening for a few minutes, he said, "Thanks. Sorry. I didn't mean to leave you in the lurch," and hung up.

He tapped the pager clipped to his belt. "Batteries died. I just noticed it. There was a schedule change and Willy's hearing was moved to today. He's back on the street. So much for keeping tabs on him." He gave them both a resigned smile. "I guess Murphy's lurking as usual."

They were back in the precinct house, back in the interview room, away from everyone else. Over the intervening hours, the initial bond between the two older men had solidified, and it was clear that Ward Ogden, given his elite status, was going to exploit it by keeping Joe and Sammie inside the loop, even though standard department protocol decreed otherwise. It was a development the two Vermont cops weren't about to tamper with. Whatever Ogden suggested at this point, they would do if they wanted to stick around.

Not that he'd been in any way domineering. In fact, up to now, while they'd been waiting for confirmations from CSU, Ogden had been putting his house in order, changing the status of this erstwhile "groundball investigation" to a homicide, reorganizing his schedule, clearing up or delegating some of his cases, and otherwise giving himself more room to move. Sammie and Joe had used the opportunity to study Mary's file more carefully and to take notes on what obvious avenues of investigation to pursue.

Now, however, there was a knock on the door and a uniformed officer stepped in to hand Ogden an envelope. After waiting for the young man to leave, Ogden opened the envelope and consulted its contents.

"Fax from CSU," he said. "They agree with our scenario. The fire escape was recently oiled, the grate over the basement window tampered with, and the heating control was cranked way up within the last few days, they say here, 'enough to have caused considerable discomfort within the apartment,' and then returned to normal. They also confirm the metal shavings you found, Joe, are consistent with what a key cutter produces, but that's as far as they'll stick their necks out. Oh," he added, rereading the document before handing it over. "They also checked the window sash and found a recently killed spider along the groove, complete with torn web, indicating the window had been raised."

Joe Gunther tapped the case file with his finger. "We were going over the responding officer's report," he said, "and noticed that the old lady next door who called 911 mentioned how hot she'd been two nights previous to that. If you're right about how thin the walls are in that place, it could be Mary's apartment heat bled through to the neighbor's. That and the dated birth control pill dispenser give us a pretty good fix on the time of death."

Ogden glanced at the calendar on the wall. "Which would make it Tuesday night. By the way, I also called the morgue and told them to run a few extra tests on the body—fingernail scrapings, vaginal swabs, whatever they don't do for routine overdoses. Lucky thing Willy appeared when he did, or I would have released the body."

The dinosaur stood up and began pacing the tiny room, obviously building up steam. "Okay," he announced, "we're behind the eight ball on this, so some things'll be too cold to pursue. That still leaves us a ton to do. Some you can help with, others you'll have to stay away from. Most of the latter involves using the computers here, dealing with people like DMV, Social Security, Welfare, and others, or getting subpoenas for things like Mary's luds."

"What're those?" Sammie asked.

His answer came rapid-fire: "Her local phone calls, the ones that don't appear in the bill. Stands for 'local usage detail.'" He went back to thinking out loud. "Basically, we have three major areas of concentration: the technical, like forensics, those phone records, and the Metro cards; the internal, which means talking to the drug unit and combing through every nook and cranny in our files for any and all past arrests and whether anyone in Mary's building is on parole or has a record or ever filed a complaint with us; and the external, which covers everything from talking to her neighbors, friends, and co-workers, to dropping by local pawnshops in case something stolen was sold, to checking with the Homeless Outreach project to see what bums, if any, might have seen someone coming or going from the building that night. And that's just to begin with, unless something falls into our laps."

He snapped his fingers suddenly. "And we need to check the building's trash compactor. I noticed a trash chute on her floor. It should still be full—there's been a garbage strike all week."

"What can we do?" Joe asked.

Ogden stopped pacing. "Honestly? One of my biggest concerns is Kunkle. You know him, you know his style and habits. You could help me by finding him as fast as possible. I seriously doubt he's taking Circle Line tours or visiting the museums."

He placed his hands on the back of his chair to emphasize what he said next. "If he knows what we know, he's going to want to set things right. I don't blame him, but it could cause us all a world of hurt, including getting himself killed or screwing up the case so much that we can't nail the guy responsible."

Neither Joe nor Sammie doubted the likelihood of either possibility. They knew what Willy was like when he got his teeth into something.

"Get him off the street," Ogden reemphasized.

Gunther nodded once. "You got it."

# Chapter 14

Willy let Riley take the lead. They were in a high-rise—a cast-off, damaged monument to urban renewal, the likes of which dotted the city's landscape like smallpox. Cereal-box-shaped buildings with small windows often covered with plywood, overlooking abandoned concrete playgrounds that had only nestled children in the architect's imagination. The hard, open approaches to the building had been littered and devoid of life, with fragments of shattered glass that crunched underfoot. In the shadows beyond the harsh and sporadic lighting of the few still-functioning arc lamps, they'd heard people moving about, and the sounds of threatening murmurs. It had made Willy think of the jungle again, but not brought him back to it, for while this battlefield was just as ominous, it remained strange and remote—a wilderness cast in steel and brick, inhabited by warriors without hope or goal.

Riley had marched into it all with careful but confident familiarity, his long coat open, his hands empty and swinging by his sides, but exuding the message that Willy knew to be true, that he was carrying his shotgun in a sling under his arm. Riley was on familiar ground and accordingly prepared.

Now they were inside the building, surrounded by the turbulence of neglect and anger. The stench of urine and rot permeated the air, the walls and floor were scarred, broken, and stained, and as covered with scrawled insignia as the interior of a jail cell. Distant screams and shouting echoed down the sepia-lit hallways.

They took the stairs, Riley not even bothering to see if the elevator worked, not just because it probably didn't, but also because elevators were dead-end boxes from which escape in a crisis was highly unlikely.

Several flights up, in a corridor similar to the one they'd entered, Riley turned right and strode an enormous distance, still not reaching the end, but coming to a door that was open by just a crack.

Instinctively, Riley flattened himself against the wall to one side of the door, as Willy did opposite him. Both men had their weapons out, all pretense at discretion gone.

Riley tapped on the door with his shotgun barrel. "Yo, Nate. You in there? It's Riley."

The sounds around them continued. The silence from inside the apartment did the same. Willy saw down the hall another door open slightly and then immediately close, followed by the loud click of a lock falling to.

"Nate. Come to the door."

After another pause, Riley used his gun to push the door back on its hinges, but remained out of sight. A small amount of light fell out onto the floor.

Riley made eye contact with Willy, held up three fingers, motioned to the right and left, and then folded each finger back into his fist in an inaudible countdown. At zero, they both swung through the door, Willy cutting to the right and Riley to the left. There they froze, ready to fire from crouching positions, but confronted only with a single shabby, empty room that looked like a tornado had recently ripped through it.

Again, communicating with hand signals, the two men spread out and checked the closet, behind and beneath the furniture, and looked into the bathroom. Nate wasn't home.

Willy holstered his pistol and closed the front door for privacy's sake. "He always this tidy or are we supposed to read something here?" he asked.

Riley was standing in the middle of the room. "Nah. This has been tossed something good."

Out of habit, Willy began poking around, looking for anything that might clarify what had happened. "What else did Nate say to you last time you saw him?" he asked rhetorically.

But Riley wasn't interested. "Gee, he told me he was going to get killed and who was going to do it. Must've slipped my mind."

Willy stared at him. "What's your problem? We don't even know he's been hurt."

Riley looked at him contemptuously. "Oh, right. They're holding him for ransom—his life for the Rolls. What the fuck you think was going to happen, asking him to poke his nose into drug business? You might as well have pulled the trigger yourself, the way I see it."

Willy's instinctive, angry denial was entirely fueled by guilt. "The way you see it is your problem. I came to him asking advice. Is it my fault he thought he owed me?"

Riley clenched his fist in frustration, and for a split second Willy wasn't sure the big man might not take a swing at him, which Willy would not have ducked. But then he turned on his heel, walked to the cracked window, and stared out at the night sky, letting out a heavy sigh after a long hesitation.

"He saw you as a turning point," he said, speaking to his own reflection in the glass. "Used to call you his crossroads. I been hearing about you for years, like you were some goddamn saint."

He turned to face Willy. "Then you show up, some half-nuts, scrawny cripple, and you get him screwed to the wall in no time flat. If that's what saints do, I'd just as soon pass."

Willy had nothing to say.

Riley seemed to pick up on the emotional riot occurring behind the silence, though, and reluctantly tried easing him off the hook. "I guess you're right," he admitted. "Nate was a big boy, and he knew how to stay out of trouble. You're just the only one I can blame."

Willy was looking at the floor, lost in thought. At that, he glanced up. "I'm good for it," he said.

But Riley wasn't having that, either. He slipped his shotgun back under his coat and turned on a few more lights. "Wallow all you want. I'd just as soon nail the ass-hole who did this. And if we're lucky, there's something around here that might give us a lead."


Joe Gunther stepped off the commuter train onto the platform and looked around. Across the parking lot, the village of Mount Kisco, New York, spread out to the right and left, a bustling, upscale, redbrick town with a seemingly bullet-proof look of security about it. Most of the cars he saw going past were the rolling equivalent of a year's salary.

"Wow," Sammie muttered. "Suburbia."

"High-end suburbia. Big distinction."

"And Bob Kunkle can afford to live here? Must be doing all right."

"He doesn't live here, Sam. He works here."

"Ah, right," she said. "Big distinction number two."

They crossed the parking lot, squinting against the bright morning sun. The train trip north had been leisurely and pleasant, since they'd been running against the commuter flow, and the village seemed equally peaceful, temporarily empty of most of its high-power residents. Gunther was struck with how, even in these modern times, most of the people he saw shopping or strolling along the street were wealthy-looking women, the only men being shopkeepers, a road crew, or the odd man in uniform, from a cop to a UPS driver. It was like taking a trip back to the fifties, albeit accompanied by a herd of modern SUVs.

"His store's on the main drag," Gunther explained, heading that way. "When I phoned him last night, he said to look for a London wannabe."

"I take it from that he's not the owner," Sammie commented.

"Manager," Joe explained briefly.

They found it easily enough, not just from the sign, but in fact from its faux-Brit aspirations. Crossing the threshold, he and Sammie were embraced by the smell of wood oil, rich wool, and the faint odor of pipe tobacco, although Gunther couldn't swear that last part wasn't his imagination.

"How are you?" asked a young man in an immaculate pin-stripe suit, silk tie, and a shirt with French cuffs.

"We're fine. We're here to see Bob Kunkle."

"Of course. Please wait here a moment. I'll go fetch him. Whom shall I say is calling?"

"Joe Gunther."

"I'll be right back," he announced unctuously, and slid soundlessly off toward the rear of the store.

"There's an eligible man for you, Sam," Joe said. "Once you were done with him, you could park him in the closet till next time."

Sammie was already wandering around the place, giving the fabric a feel and ogling the price tags. "Can you believe this stuff?"

A shadow emerged from the gloom at the back and another perfectly dressed man, older than the first, stepped forward, looking like a modern-day English butler, complete with vest and elegantly rounded stomach.

"Mr. Gunther? I'm Robert Kunkle."

With the younger salesman lurking in the distance, Joe introduced Sammie by name alone.

But Kunkle caught his meaning and suggested, "Why don't we talk somewhere more private?"

He led them down the length of the store, but not to his office. He'd taken his brother back there years before when he'd dropped by for a visit, and Bob had never forgotten the look in Willy's eyes at the contrast between the ancient, feudal glow of the sales area and the fluorescent-lit concrete gulag where Bob tallied the books. It had revealed more to Bob about the discomfort between the siblings than words ever could have, and wasn't something he wanted to repeat, even with total strangers.

He ushered them instead into a changing area designed to make his customers feel like English lords. Along with the standard dais surrounded by mirrors, there were leather armchairs, side tables, reading material, a wall of unread books with fancy leather bindings, and a silver tea set on a sideboard. The lighting was tasteful and intimate, and the rug deep enough to tickle your ankles.

Bob invited them to sit, which they all did, before asking, "Is Willy all right?"

"We think so," Gunther answered matter-of-factly. "That's one of the reasons we're here. Have you heard from him?"

Bob nodded. "A few days ago. We met near where our mom lives. He told me about Mary. What a shock."

Sammie was comfortable enough being away from the city and the odd kind of diplomacy they'd been practicing there to speak up as she might have back home. "What was the reason for your meeting? You two aren't all that close, are you?"

Gunther looked at her in surprise, thinking her approach had been overly direct, but it had the right effect on Bob. He laughed sadly. "Yeah, you could say that. I've had enemies I spend more time with." He paused briefly and then answered the question. "He wanted to know what I could tell him about Mary."

"Why would you know about her?" she asked.

"She started calling about six months ago. I don't know how Willy knew that, but he wanted to know why. I told him I thought she was just reaching out after cleaning herself up—and wanting to know how he was doing. I wasn't very helpful, I'm afraid. After he told me she'd died, I got angry at him and the conversation sort of ended."

"As brother's go," Joe Gunther commented, "he must be a little high-maintenance."

Again, Bob let out a short laugh. "You kidding? He's no maintenance at all. It's his way or the highway, and you get to do all the lifting." He ran his palm across his bald pate in exasperation. "I can't blame him, though. When it came time to hand out the bad luck, Willy was first in line. I don't know that I could've dealt with half the shit he has. I mean, I know he's a pain and a bully, but he's a real straight shooter, you know? Mary's dead by her own hand, from what he told me, but he's still going to find out why. It's just his way."

"Is that what he told you?" Sammie asked.

Bob looked over at her but didn't seem to have heard. "He hasn't talked to our mom in years, he's insulting to my wife, and he's never even met my kids, but if I were in a jam, he's the one I'd want to come after me. He's like a bulldog that way."

Sammie smiled at the description. Over the last several days, she'd done her best to keep her own emotions to one side, being Joe's faithful sidekick and Willy's steady colleague. But she loved Willy Kunkle, and was being torn apart by what he was going through, and it was all she could do not to cross the room and give his brother a hug. He'd fallen under Willy's truly bizarre charm just as she and Joe Gunther had. Either that or only they had recognized the value of not heeding his tremendous ability to reject people. In point of fact, Bob's sketch of Willy's stubborn tenacity alone might as well have been used on Joe Gunther, and, now that she thought of it, herself as well.

"Did he say anything at all that might help us find him?" she asked.

He gave her a hapless expression.

Gunther cleared his throat softly. "Bob, you said Willy questioned you about Mary. What *had* she been up to?"

"Basically putting her life back together. She got a job

at a drug rehab place near her home called the Re-Coop and she was trying to put some money away."

"She was taking birth control pills," Sammie said. "You know why?"

Bob flushed red. "I didn't ask her things like that."

"What about right after she and Willy broke up?" Gunther asked. "Were you in touch with her then?"

"A little bit, at first. She was hurt and confused, and pretty frightened. Willy really went over the top with her, I guess. She told me he'd hit her, just once, but that was enough. He was in a pretty bad way back then, drinking hard and acting strange. I heard later it might've been posttraumatic stress disorder or something—maybe had to do with what he did in Vietnam. But he never talked about that, and I was always too scared to ask."

Sammie understood what he meant. The Willy she knew was further from the edge, but that particular topic was still hypersensitive. "What was she up to down here?" she asked him.

"Escaping, I guess is the best way to describe it, although I had my doubts she knew what she was doing. If I was in her condition, the last place I'd come to start over would be New York. Unless you have someone to turn to, it can be the loneliest place on earth."

"Was there a someone?"

"Eventually, yeah. His name was Andy Liptak—an old war buddy of Willy's. I only met him once, and he seemed nice enough, but I guess he had other things on his mind than taking care of Mary. He was out to make a buck, and I think she kind of drifted off, in a way. You know, got into things she shouldn't have."

"You mean the drugs?"

"Well, yeah. Once she started with them, it was like

Willy had been with the booze. Kind of ironic, when you think about it. That she ended up like he'd been. Anyhow, she and Andy broke up. No surprise there."

Joe Gunther was picking up something in his voice, just a hint of evasiveness, as when someone moves solely to avoid becoming a target.

"Bob," he asked, "you told us Mary called you right after she and Willy broke up, and about six months before she died. Both times in which she was going through a quantum change. Were you and she good friends when she was married to Willy?"

Bob looked at him nervously. "We were friendly, the few times we met. I mean, she was up there in Vermont, and they only came down one time so she could see the city. She always struck me as a nice person."

"A person who could have done better than your brother when it came to husbands?"

Bob was fidgeting with his fingers, intertwining them in various ways. He flashed a false smile and said, "Well, that's probably true for any woman who'd marry Willy. Not that he's a bad man, of course. But he's tough to live with. I sure know that much."

"So, you sympathized with Mary."

"Well, yeah. Who wouldn't?"

"Which is why you visited her when she called you after the breakup."

Bob glanced at Sammie and then back at Joe. "I . . . ah . . . gosh, I might have. I forget. Long time ago. I remember the phone calls, although, like I said, she talked to Junie more than me. You know, girl stuff, I guess."

"Junie's your wife?"

His eyes widened. "My wife? I told you—"

Gunther hardened his tone, driving a wedge into the

gap he'd opened by pure chance. "You didn't mention Junie to us, Bob. Maybe you used that line on Willy. Do they get along—Willy and Junie?"

"No."

"Then it's unlikely they'd compare notes. How many times did you go to see Mary, Bob?"

Bob's voice was thin and tight. "I told you. I don't remember."

"First it was never, then once, now so many times you can't remember."

"You're twisting my words."

Sammie ganged up on him from her side, now fully aware of what Gunther was after. "Bob, it's not a crime what you did, not that we can't treat it like one—check your phone records, look for witnesses who saw you together, talk to your wife about any unexplained trips."

Bob stared at them for a moment of absolute silence, and then burst into tears, covering his face with his hands.

Gunther got up and handed him a handkerchief from his back pocket, making Sammie wonder incongruously how many men still carried such items.

"Bob," Gunther said kindly, "it might help to get it off your chest. Chances are it won't go any further than this room."

Bob didn't seem to have heard the equivocal nature of the phrase. Through his hands, he confessed. "I didn't know what was happening at first. She was so lost, so unhappy. What Willy had done to her, casting her off. It was so cruel. I know he had it tough over there, but lots of people went through that without making everyone around them miserable, too. It's like Willy has to dominate every person he meets."

"What about Mary?" Gunther asked gently.

"She was a mess when she came to the city. She didn't know what to do, who to turn to, had no idea how to get a job. She was too shy to call Liptak right off. I just helped her out at first, got her an apartment, stuff like that."

"But without telling Junie."

He shuddered, took his hands away, and straightened slightly in his seat, looking at them in a hangdog way. "I told her about the first call, but not about afterward. Not that anything happened at first. Neither one of us was looking to do anything wrong, but things had been rough at home for me, and Mary was totally at loose ends." His voice trailed off and then he added weakly, "I guess we just sort of found comfort in each other's company for a while."

"How long did it last?"

He wiped his eyes with the borrowed handkerchief. "Not long. Maybe a couple of months. I wasn't the kind of man she was after, and I was too torn up with guilt to let it last much longer. It wasn't even that good while it lasted."

"Does your brother know anything about it?"

Bob sighed heavily. "I'm alive, aren't I?"

Joe Gunther thought that was a little melodramatic, but supposed Bob had to cling to a few misconceptions to maintain his dignity. "Well," he said, "since all that's out of the bag, maybe you can tell us a little more about Mary."

But Bob still wasn't so sure, and answered vaguely, "It didn't take her long to get comfortable in the city. She was thirsty for a change and angry at her life up till then—told me just before we split up that Willy had done her a favor. I guess that didn't turn out to be so true, after all."

"You implied there were other men," Sammie suggested.

He nodded sadly. "Even before we were finished. She was like a starving man at a feast. It made her very exciting to be with—for a while."

"So, you lived with the infidelities."

"Sure. What choice does a guy like me have? It was a miracle I got a part of her at all. Christ, I was grateful. I told myself it added to her sexiness." He slumped forward again, his elbows on his knees. "After it was over, I couldn't believe what I'd done. Junie must've thought I'd lost my mind, I spent so much attention on her. I suppose, in that way, Mary helped save my marriage."

"What about just recently?" Gunther asked. "Who made the first move to get in touch?"

Bob straightened, suddenly on surer footing. "She did, and this time Junie did know about it. There was nothing romantic there, anyhow. Mary just seemed to want to contact the people from her past she could trust. She even apologized for what had happened between us. It was like she was going back in time, repairing bridges."

Now his sorrow seemed genuinely about her, instead of inwardly focused. He added, "I just can't believe she died of an overdose. She sounded so sure of herself. So happy to be free."

"Including the very last time you spoke?" Sammie asked.

"Yes," he said incredulously. "That's what I'm saying. I really thought she'd licked it."

"I'd like to back up a little," Joe Gunther said. "When

the two of you were together and she was beginning to act differently, was she already into drugs?"

"She'd smoke a joint. Said it relaxed her."

"Anything more serious?"

"She talked about it. Said she wondered what it would be like to get high on coke or heroin, but I don't think she ever tried it while I was around."

"Who supplied her with the joints?" Sammie asked.

"I assumed it was one of her boyfriends."

"You ever get to meet any of them?"

He shook his head. "Only Liptak. Once. It was at a party Mary threw at her apartment. But he was the only one I know of for sure. And it took a while before they actually did set up house."

"Tell us about Liptak," Gunther suggested.

"I don't know much except that he and Willy served together. That's how Mary met him. Willy introduced them on a trip to New York right after they were married. That's what I meant about Willy's bad luck, see?"

Gunther decided to leave that one alone. "Was Andy into drugs?"

"I think so. She called me a few times after they started living together," Bob said. "She sounded like she was on cloud nine, but sort of detached, too, you know what I mean? Like the reason she was having so much fun was so she wouldn't have to ask questions she didn't want answered."

In the silence that followed that statement, he added, "I can't swear to it, but it seemed like they were a matched pair."

"What happened with this Andy Liptak?"

"That's what Willy wanted to know. I told him: Nothing. Far as I know, he's making a lot of money being a wheeler-dealer in Brooklyn. He and Mary broke up after a few years."

"When was that?"

"I don't know dates, but it's not like she left him and then started calling me right after. In fact, I think it was after they broke up that she really hit bottom."

"You have an address on Liptak?"

Bob shook his head. "No. Never did. He shouldn't be hard to find, though. I think he's pretty rich. He called me," he added almost as an afterthought. "Just recently."

Sammie and Joe glanced at one another. "What about?" Gunther asked nonchalantly.

"He wanted to know how she was doing. Said he was married now and just got to thinking one day, sort of reliving old times."

"You tell him about her?"

"What little I knew, sure. He was happy she was bouncing back."

"Did he ask where she was living?" Sammie asked.

Bob thought back. "I don't think so. I couldn't have told him anyway."

"How 'bout Willy, Bob?" Gunther asked after a pause. "If you don't know where he is, can you think where he might be? Friends he had when he lived here, old haunts?"

Totally recovered now from his emotional breakdown, Bob gave them a chastened, war-weary look. "I don't know how long you've known my brother, but I wouldn't go looking for any old friends. He didn't make friends, and if for some reason someone tried it with him instead, he made sure it wouldn't last."

Gunther glanced at Sammie at that, but she was staring at the carpeted floor.

He rose to his feet. "Thanks, Bob. You've been a big help. And for what it's worth, I think having you in his life has helped Willy a lot, even if he'd never admit it."

Bob smiled weakly. "I guess that's good to hear."

# Chapter 15

It was so dark in the alley that Willy Kunkle couldn't even see Riley Cox, although they were standing just four feet apart.

"That Marcus?" asked Riley in a disembodied whisper.

"According to my source, it is," said Willy. "From spiky hair to silver necklace—too far off to see the scar on his face. And I guess we're at the right address."

Willy watched Marcus cross the street, carefully check up and down the block, and then vanish into the entryway of a beaten-up building with the first two floors of windows covered in metal and a row of dented trash cans out front. Willy quickly trained his small telescope on the site, as he'd been doing throughout, steadying it against a drainpipe running down the wall beside him. They'd been standing here for several hours, waiting for some indication that their information was accurate. Not finding any clues at Nate Lee's apartment to Nate's whereabouts, Riley had taken them on a round of personal contacts to make inquiries. It hadn't taken long to find someone who claimed to know where Diablo was reportedly packaged for distribution. They'd also been told that there was good reason this brand had been around for a long time. The man in charge—nicknamed La Culebra, or the Snake—was known for his ruthlessness and a penchant for security. Riley's informant had described the address they were now looking at as a fortress. If it was, however, it didn't include the entire building. The traffic in and out up to now had been strictly mundane: moms with kids, old people, a few couples. And the windows of the upper floors had revealed the kind of normal activity one might expect in a regular apartment house. La Culebra might have been a tough nut, but he apparently wasn't well heeled or paranoid enough to claim the whole place as his own.

Willy lowered the telescope. "He hit the second-floor buzzer."

There was a small moment of silence before Riley murmured, "Okay, we seen day-to-day stuff on the third and fourth floors, and who knows about the first and second."

"First's probably the factory," Willy ventured, "with several exits besides the front door. And the second's where he lives. At least that's the way I'd lay it out."

Riley didn't disagree, but his focus was on something more pragmatic. "So, what now? We don't even know what La Culebra looks like, much less how to get at him."

Willy looked thoughtfully across the street. "The trick," he said, "is to come at them some way they don't expect."

"And they expect cops and the competition," Riley added, "meaning a big show of force."

Willy admitted with grudging admiration, "I bet that's why half this place looks normal. Fill a potential combat zone with civilians and you screw up the other guy's attack plan. No free-fire zones, no Philadelphia-style bombings from helicopters. We can't even burn them out with a Molotov cocktail."

"Too bad we don't have more time to recon this," Riley mused.

"Well," Willy answered, "we don't, so we'll just have to improvise. Maybe we can underwhelm them, instead." He reached into his pocket, extracted his gun, and held it out to where Riley was standing in the inky darkness, nudging him in the shoulder. "Here."

"What're you doin'?" Riley asked in surprise.

"Going in there," Willy said simply, and stepped out into the open.

"Wait," Riley whispered from his hiding place. "You'll get your ass shot off."

"Whatever," Willy said without looking back. "Stay put and keep an ear out."

He crossed the street, climbed the front steps, and rang the same bell he'd seen Marcus hit earlier.

"What?" came the reply through the small loudspeaker above the door.

"Police. Open up."

The speaker went dead. Willy waited for several minutes, aware of the conversation that must be taking place overhead.

Finally, the disembodied voice came back with the most standard of inquiries. "You got a warrant?"

"Not necessary. La Culebra needs what I have."

"What d'you mean?"

"I'll tell that to him."

"The fuck you will."

"You'll be fucked if I don't."

There was another prolonged silence. Willy let out a small puff of air. Despite the stakes, there was an element of formal, almost boring protocol to this, as if all of them were locked into a pattern of behavior none could escape.

Without further comment from the loudspeaker, the door lock buzzed noisily and Willy turned the knob. He stepped into an empty, dimly lit lobby with a staircase and an elevator door against the far wall.

"Step into the middle of the room and put your hands up," said a voice.

Willy looked around. There were several doors to each side, one of which was barely open. He moved forward. "My left arm is paralyzed. I can't lift it."

"I suppose to believe that?"

"You don't have much choice."

The door swung wide, revealing a young man pointing a small machine gun at Willy's chest. He smiled as Willy watched him. "I got a choice, dummy, and this is it."

"What? You kill me and then La Culebra kills you because he learned what I got too late to save his butt? Sharp thinking."

"Fuck you."

Willy smiled. What would these guys do without that word?

The gunman hesitated, thrown by Willy's seeming lack of concern. "Open your coat, then," he finally ordered.

Willy did so slowly, revealing the badge he had clipped to his belt.

"Okay. Go over there and lean against the wall with your legs spread out."

Half amused at the irony of the request, Willy did as he'd ordered countless others to do in the past. The other man emerged from his refuge, crossed the lobby, and patted Willy down, looking for weapons or hidden wires.

Satisfied, he stepped back. "Okay. Go upstairs."

Willy took the steps slowly, his right hand held slightly away from his body so the gunman could see it at all times. One flight up was a landing with three doors, two of which had been welded shut with steel plates, and the third heavily beefed up against forced entry. A camera was perched over this last door, surveying the entire landing.

The gunman pounded on the door. "Rico. Open up."

A mechanical chorus of bolts and locks snapping to was followed by the door opening onto another man with a similar weapon.

"He clean?" this one asked the first.

"No, asshole. I made sure he was carrying hand grenades."

"Fuck you, Manny. Who made you the big man?"

Willy shook his head. "Boys, boys."

Manny poked him in the back with the barrel of his gun. "Fuck you, cop. Maybe I don't care what you got and I kill you right here."

Willy looked at him. "Maybe you do. So what?"

Manny's eyes narrowed. "You fuckin' with me?"

Willy considered commenting on his limited vocabulary, but said instead, "Take me to La Culebra. Let him figure this out."

Manny pressed his lips together angrily before spitting out, "I don't like you, man."

Willy knew he should be a nervous wreck by now, bearding the lion in his den, bluffing all the way. But fear was an instinct he'd lost long ago. Once, during a similar confrontation when he'd been taken by surprise by a Viet

Cong guerrilla, the man had threatened to shoot him on the spot. Willy had merely opened his shirt and exposed his bare chest in a moment of stark self-revelation, all concern for survival gone. During the stunned hesitation that had followed, one of Willy's companions had appeared from the foliage behind them and shot the young man dead. In that moment, Willy had both mourned his passing and the service he'd been about to provide.

"Join the crowd," he told Manny.

They took him down a hallway, past rooms with other men loitering inside, some watching TV, others talking, a couple cleaning more guns. It reminded him of a base camp between operations. Willy noticed all the windows were equipped with closed steel shutters.

They reached what might have once been a dining room, now converted into a hodgepodge of den and office and general storage area. There, sitting at a badly abused metal desk covered with an assortment of weapons, paperwork, wads of money, and a couple of powder-filled baggies, was a man in his late thirties sporting a trim beard and mustache, his hair swept back and held in a ponytail, incongruously wearing a pair of half glasses on the end of his nose. He was reading something in a folder, much as any businessman might.

He looked up as Willy entered with his escort.

"He's clean," Manny announced unnecessarily. "He's got a crippled arm, too."

The man with the beard gave Manny a careful look, but didn't say anything to him. Instead, he motioned to an empty folding chair and told Willy, "Sit."

Manny and Rico fanned out to either side.

"You Culebra?" Willy asked.

"La Culebra, yes."

"What I got is for your ears only."

The Snake pushed out his lips thoughtfully, taking in the man opposite him. He then gave his two lieutenants a rapid order in Spanish and sent them off.

He waited until the door had closed behind them. "So," he asked, removing his glasses, "what do you want to tell me?"

"Nothing," Willy admitted. "I wanted to ask you a question."

La Culebra sat back in his chair, his face slightly flushed. He sensed he'd been taken advantage of, but knew the value of staying cool. "All this trouble just for that? You are a strange man. Are you really a policeman?"

Willy flipped open his jacket again, revealing the badge. "Vermont Bureau of Investigation."

La Culebra broke into a broad grin. "Vermont? What the hell is that? You the ski police or something?"

Willy smiled back. "Close. I'm looking for a friend of mine—Nathan Lee."

The bearded man touched his forehead with his fingertips, as if trying to locate something he'd misplaced there. "A cop from Vermont lies his way in here to ask me about a man I never heard of. If I kill you right now, will anybody care?"

"Nobody that matters to you."

"You're not going to tell me you have backup?"

"Nope."

"Why do you care about Nathan Lee?"

"He was doing me a favor. I think it got him in trouble."

"What favor?"

"I asked him to find out who was making Diablo. I wanted to ask that person a question."

Clearly fascinated, La Culebra now sat forward and rested his elbows on the desk. "Meaning the question is not where is Nathan Lee. Has anyone ever told you you're a very strange man?"

"All the time. And this is a different question."

He nodded. "Very good. What is it?"

"A friend of mine died from an overdose of Diablo on the Lower East Side. I wanted to know how she got hold of it."

La Culebra laughed incredulously. "How she got hold of it? You're kidding, right?" He pretended to shuffle through the papers before him. "Let's see . . . what was the serial number on the bag? I'm sure I have it cross-referenced here somewhere. She did mail in her warranty card, didn't she?"

He laughed some more, only quieting down once he saw no reaction from Willy. "Okay, this is where you tell me I am a monster, a peddler of death, worse than the shit on your shoes—the person who killed your friend."

Willy shook his head. "You are worse than the shit on my shoes, but you didn't kill her. You were just the delivery boy. If anyone's responsible, it's me."

La Culebra looked at him with renewed interest. "You made this woman unhappy?"

"I married her."

The drug dealer remained silent for a moment before saying, "I don't know how your wife got hold of Diablo. I am sorry she did. I have no retailers outside this neighborhood. Either she bought it up here or someone else did and then gave it to her. I could ask my people if she was the buyer, though. Do you have a picture?"

Willy reached into an inner pocket and removed the photograph he'd taken from her apartment. He hesitated before handing it over, however.

La Culebra set him at ease. "I have a Xerox machine in the other room. You can have that back."

Willy dropped it on the desk between them. "She's the one right in the middle."

The other man picked it up and considered it for a while. When he spoke next, he seemed to be addressing the picture directly. "My name is Carlos Barzún."

Willy watched his face carefully, wondering at this spontaneous admission. "And you tell me that so I'll know who to credit for this act of grace?"

Barzún smiled. "I am a Catholic. I have memories of such things."

Willy smiled slightly. "My name is Willy Kunkle."

"You are not the only person interested in Nathan Lee," Barzún admitted. "I am to report anyone asking about this batch of Diablo."

"Report to who?"

"A customer who paid me a lot of money."

"Did he say to watch for a one-armed cop?"

Barzún paused. The muted sounds all around them slowly filled the silence. "Yes," he finally said.

"And you told him about Lee?"

"Yes, after I heard Lee had been asking about me."

"But you won't tell me this man's name."

"I have to think about that," Barzún confessed. "I am not sure how generous I should be with you. I worry I have already made a big mistake."

He rose from his chair and picked up the photograph. "You are a bad influence, Willy Kunkle."

"I've heard that before."

"Wait here."

Barzún left the room. Willy stayed absolutely still, knowing the fragility of the slender string keeping him alive—a ruthless man's quirky yielding to a tiny spark of sentimentality, as inexplicable as a hungry shark forgoing an easy meal.

Barzún returned and gave the photo back. "If I hear about your wife, how do I tell you?"

Willy gave him the name and address of Riley's store.

Barzún then picked up a small portable radio and spoke into it in Spanish. Moments later, Manny entered the room, still carrying his squat, ugly gun.

Barzún gestured to Willy and told Manny, "Make sure he gets safely to the street."

With Manny walking warily behind him, Willy retraced his steps out of the apartment, down the stairs, and into the lobby. As they both neared the door, the radio attached to Manny's belt uttered a single short sentence, which Manny briefly acknowledged.

As he held the door open for him, Manny said to Willy, "The boss told me to give you the name Ron Cashman."

"Thanks," Willy replied, and stepped back outside.

# Chapter 16

Joe Gunther and Sammie Martens paused on the sidewalk before a newly renovated brownstone on a quiet, leafy residential street on the edge of Brooklyn Heights. The block was essentially empty of people aside from one woman walking a pair of greyhounds in the distance. They could just see the water down one of the side streets behind them, and a bit of Manhattan Island's southernmost tip, now oddly antique-looking with the absence of the World Trade Center twin towers. The air was still and quiet, the perpetual background hum of the city's vitality almost lost to the slight rustling of the branches overhead.

"Fancy neighborhood," Sammie commented.

"Very," Joe agreed, climbing the stoop to better read the discreet brass plaque mounted to the wall beside the heavy, glass-fronted entrance. It read, "Liptak Associates, Ltd."

He glanced back at Sammie. "Shall we?"

"You think he'll be there?"

"I'd be, if I had an office here. Besides, even if he's not, I wouldn't mind finding out something about him. That's why I didn't call ahead."

They stepped into an expensively appointed, neutrally colored reception room, staffed by an attractive young woman sitting behind a round maple table.

"May I help you?" she asked.

"Hi." Gunther smiled broadly, glancing around for signs of Liptak Associates' function in life, and finding only nondescript artwork on the walls. "Is Mr. Liptak in?"

She punched a couple of keys on the laptop computer situated slightly to one side of her, placed as if to indicate that she didn't actually type into the thing on any regular basis. "Do you have an appointment?"

"No, we don't. We're here on personal business."

"Is Mr. Liptak expecting you?" she asked, her expression blatantly skeptical.

"No, but I think he'd be sorry to miss us. Tell him we're friends of Willy Kunkle's."

A furrow had appeared between her carefully plucked eyebrows. This was not an approach she approved of. "And you are?"

"Do you have an envelope?" Gunther asked her.

"What?"

"An envelope. I'd like for you to take something in to Mr. Liptak. It'll make things clearer to him."

Irritation replaced by confusion, she opened a drawer at her lap and extracted a single envelope, handing it over without comment.

Gunther took it, placed one of his business cards inside, sealed it, and returned it. "Joe Gunther and Sammie Martens are our names."

Rising slowly, watching them as if they might try to steal the paintings during her absence, she moved over to a closed door on the wall behind her. "I'll be right back."

Sammie waited until the door had closed behind her before asking, "Why didn't you just tell her we're cops?"

"Discretion, for both Liptak and us. It might make him chattier if he knows we didn't fly the flag in front of her highness, plus, I don't doubt she would've given us flak for having the wrong badges."

Sammie accepted that without judgment and made a small tour of the reception area instead. "What do you think they do here?"

"I think if you have to ask, they don't want you on the premises. That would be my guess."

The door behind the desk opened, and the regal young woman reappeared, accompanied by a man who looked downright plain by comparison, although with careful, watchful eyes.

He circled the desk and approached them with hand held out. "Hi. Mr. Gunther, Ms. Martens. I'm Andy Liptak. Why don't you come back to the conference room with me? Much more comfortable there."

Sammie smiled at the neutral phrasing of his greeting. Joe had read the character of the place correctly. As they fell into line behind their host, she also noted with satisfaction the pissed-off expression of the beauty queen.

Like most brownstones, this one was tall and narrow, so the conference room right off the lobby had a single window overlooking the street and ran long and thin toward the back of the building. There was just enough room in it for the table down its length and the thickly upholstered chairs lined up around it. Liptak took a seat just off the parental head of the table and motioned to his guests to make themselves comfortable. Gunther sat where he imagined Liptak normally did, with his back to the window and a full view down the middle. It made him think of what it might be like having a small family meal at the Rockefellers'.

Except that Andy Liptak didn't look like any blue blood. With his square, blunt body, stubby hands, and thick neck, he reminded Gunther more of a longshoreman than a man of means and leisure.

Liptak started things off. "I wanted to thank you for your under-the-radar approach," he said. "It's going to drive Casey nuts for the next week."

Casey, Sammie thought. Of course.

Gunther laughed pleasantly. "Actually, that was for us as much as for you. We thought she might accuse us of impersonating police officers otherwise."

"She might have at that. Very protective woman. I'm guessing you're here about Willy?"

"Not entirely. Our interest is more Mary Kunkle."

Liptak looked crestfallen. "Christ. I couldn't believe it when Willy told me. I mean, I knew she'd hit the skids. It's one of the reasons we broke up. But it's hard to imagine anyone you once loved could die that way. Really knocked the wind out of me. And, not to get personal, but Willy wasn't too subtle about breaking the news. I guess he told you I got a little pissed off at him."

Sammie waited for Gunther to take the lead, which he did by admitting blandly, "Well, it's an emotional issue for him, and we all know how lacking in subtlety he can be. That's actually one of the reasons we wanted to meet with you on our own. I want to make sure his report wasn't colored by his own view of things."

"His view of things?" Liptak echoed. "What's that mean? I thought she was an accidental overdose. He didn't tell me otherwise."

Gunther was purposefully vague, although curious

about the other man's reaction. "Oh, that's a possibility, sure. We're also looking to rule out something a little more complicated."

Liptak's surprise seemed genuine. He sat forward in his chair, his eyes widening. "You're kidding. That's why Willy was being so cagey."

"How do you mean?"

"Well, he basically sandbagged me. We had dinner together and he spent the whole time letting me go on and on about the old days, milking me about how things had gone between Mary and me, and only at the end did he admit she was dead. I figured it was because he was still pissed off she'd moved in with me after dumping him, but now I guess he was fishing, seeing if I might've had something to do with killing her. That son-of-a-bitch. I accused him of being a cop even off duty—little did I know."

"Did he have any reason to think you wished her ill?" Gunther asked.

Liptak became agitated. "No. It was over between Mary and me. I didn't even know where she lived or what she was doing. To be honest, she could've died two years ago and I wouldn't have known it. It's not that I disliked her, but we'd broken up. It was over. I'd moved on."

"Why did you break up?" Sammie asked quietly.

Liptak looked both sad and angry. "I wasn't going to tell Willy this, but it wasn't just the drugs. She was screwing around, too. He might be pissed at me right now, but back then, I didn't think too highly of him, either. I thought he'd messed her up big time, and that I was the unintended victim."

He shook his head apologetically. "I know how that sounds. I also know it's dead wrong. We all bring a bit of ourselves to these messes, right? I can admit now that I was as much a part of her problem as Willy was, or her mom, or herself, for that matter." He rubbed his cheek with his open palm. "Christ, when he told me about her, it hit me like a ton of bricks. All the denial I'd piled up inside—the way I'd told myself she was just self-destructive, and there was nothing anyone could do to save her. I mean, that might've been true, but when he broke the news, I couldn't stop feeling guilty."

Gunther was impressed by the big man's candor. How many times had he, too, been caught in a similar web of guilt and self-delusion, and had struggled later to save face?

"Mr. Liptak," he asked, "were you able to tell Willy anything at all about who Mary might have been entangled with after you two broke up? Her drug dealer or dealers, for example?"

He shook his head. "He asked me the same thing. Mary's and my parting was pretty friendly. I didn't know and didn't ask who she was seeing."

Gunther was beginning to run out of questions. The guy appeared so candid about his shortcomings that there weren't many obvious cracks to pry open.

Except for one point of interest. Looking around at the muted but expensive decor surrounding them, Gunther asked, "What exactly do you do, by the way? You seem pretty well off."

Liptak gave an embarrassed smile. "Yeah, well, there're a lot of smoke and mirrors here. I mean, I do okay—it's mostly real estate, to answer your question, and a few businesses—but appearances play a big role. It costs me a fortune to have this office and that debutante outside, but you know what they say about spending money to make money."

"Were you making this kind of income when you were living with Mary?"

Liptak burst out laughing. "No way. I was clueless then, trying to find my footing. Wasn't till after she left that I started to get serious." He paused and added, "Too bad, too. If I'd gotten my act together sooner, maybe I could've saved her."

Gunther pushed himself away from the table, encouraging Sammie to do the same. "Okay, Mr. Liptak. We'll get out of your hair. We might want to talk again at some point, if that's all right."

Liptak got up and ushered them back out into the lobby. "No problem. Call me anytime. If I'm not around, Casey'll know where to find me."

Casey didn't bother looking up from the document she appeared to be reading.

They shook hands on the stoop and Sammie and Gunther returned to the sidewalk.

"What d'you think?" Gunther asked his sidekick.

Sammie thought a moment before saying, "I think it was interesting he didn't ask about the investigation."

For some reason, they found a parking place barely half a block away from the Seventh Precinct house. Gunther got out and scrutinized every sign he could see along the street, looking for the one that would explain this anomaly and make moving the car a necessity. But while several signs were contradictory, none made it clear that he was in violation.

Yielding to the evidence, he walked with Sammie the short distance to their destination. Immediately to their left, the trash-clotted stone base of the noisy, graffiti-laden Williamsburg Bridge loomed overhead on its way to Brooklyn across the river. In his admitted limited experience, Joe Gunther had never been to a New York precinct house that wasn't located within similarly bleak environs. As one wizened cop had once put it to him, that way the commute to round up business was kept at a minimum.

The lobby was quieter than during their first visit, but the scrutiny they received upon entering was just as cursory. They mentioned to the receptionist that they were headed up to the detective bureau, and without looking up, she said fine and once again gave them directions.

They found Ward Ogden at his desk, on the phone and taking notes on a piece of paper, a file folder open before him. He caught sight of them standing in the doorway and motioned them toward the interview room they'd used before. Beyond him, behind the inward-facing glass window, his Whip, the lieutenant they'd met on their first visit, was hard at work stabbing at the keys on a computer. They quickly and quietly tucked into their hiding place.

Ogden joined them several minutes later, holding the same piece of paper in his hand, along with the file folder. "That was the medical examiner's office," he announced. "There was definitely something organic under her nails—they think skin—and they're guessing she scratched somebody shortly before she died. They walk the straight and narrow over there, so they won't commit themselves to a connection between her death and that finding, but as far as I'm concerned, this clinches it as a murder case. They'll be running what they found for a DNA sample, in case we get lucky with a suspect. You find your friend Kunkle?"

He asked this as he sat down at the small, battle-scarred table with them.

"Nope," Gunther admitted. "Went up to Mount Kisco to see his brother, and just got back from Brooklyn, where we talked to a friend of his named Andy Liptak. Both of them had seen him recently, but neither knows where he is now. Until he calls us or draws attention to himself again, we're at a dead end. How 'bout you?"

"Andy Liptak, huh?" Ogden asked, raising his eyebrows and writing the name down. "Small world. . . . As for us, it's too early to say anything for sure," he said, glancing at the contents of the folder before him. "But this is what we've got so far." He interrupted himself briefly and looked up. "By the way, I brought in a partner on this—standard procedure and something I would've done from the start if I hadn't had you two around. His name is Jim Berhle. He's downstairs right now digging through some files. He's up to date about you two, so you don't need to tiptoe around him, and he knows not to brag about you in front of the brass. Just so you know."

He returned to scrutinizing his file, adding as he read, "Told you about the scrapings. They also did a vaginal swab—that came up negative. Nothing to add about the injection site, but they did find subcutaneous bruising to her upper arms where she may have been held down. She died too soon for a bruising to surface. Jim's been working the computer like a dog, checking all the data banks from Social Security to Welfare to Parole and Probation to anyone else he can think of. Mary Kunkle managed to duck all the relevant ones of those, as far as we can find, which is incredibly unusual, and therefore a negative finding of note—"

"Telling you what?" Gunther quickly asked before he moved on.

Ogden placed his finger on the page he'd been consulting and glanced up. "On the surface? That she was never busted, never hit bottom so she had to ask for assistance, was never stopped for a motor vehicle violation, never entered a methadone clinic. Under the surface, it tells me that she had some kind of support system in place, even during the rough times. What do you think of the two gentlemen you interviewed today?"

"Both could qualify," Joe admitted.

Sammie agreed. "Willy's brother has the emotional wherewithal and Liptak's got the money. Neither one of them fessed up, though. Now that she's dead and we're asking why, they both may be acting dumb."

"Or covering their tracks," Ogden murmured, returning to his paperwork. "We talked to her neighbors in the building and next door," he continued, "and couldn't add anything to what we already knew. The pawnshops I haven't done yet, since we don't know what might be missing. I did call our Homeless Outreach people and got a few names, but the only bum I actually talked to didn't see anything notable. I had the trash compactor in her building torn apart and found a pair of coveralls that I ran by Mrs. Goldblum from across the alley. She said they looked right for the guy she saw working on the fire escape, so I'm having them checked by the crime lab. If we're lucky, the guy sweated and left us some DNA in the armpits. But I didn't find a key cutter or any tools.

"That," he added, straightening up and rubbing his eyes, "suggests to me that he left the building dressed differently but still carrying the stuff he entered with, so I had Jim go up and down the block to see if any stores or buildings had surveillance cameras overlooking the street, maybe aimed through the display window beyond the cash register or something. The best one he found was an ATM video that took a shot of every customer. That still ain't much, though—leaves a lot of gaps. He's still checking it, but nothing yet."

"What about Mary's phone records?" Sammie asked.

Ogden nodded agreeably. "Yup. Just getting there. We got a subpoena for them. That's some of what Jim's doing right now, running reverse checks on the numbers she called. We found Willy's brother right off, of course, it being long-distance—she called him a few times. I tried contacting you about that, but your pager's on the blink. Not that it mattered, since you found him anyway. It should all make interesting reading once Jim's done.

"Until then," he went on, extracting a sheet of paper from the file and laying it face up between them, "we have this, which may be nothing at all."

It was a subway map of the five boroughs, with several of the stations circled in red, accompanied by red numbers running anywhere from one to fifteen.

"Her Metro cards?" Gunther asked.

"Yeah. As Willy figured, our technical people had fun with them. When you run one of these cards through the entrance gate, it marks the date and the station. Course, we have no idea where each trip ended, but it still sets up a pattern of sorts."

Sammie pointed at the one station with a fifteen written next to it. "This the one closest to her home?"

"Right."

Joe saw one that immediately caught his eye. "Look. Four times at 135th Street, not all that far from where Bob goes to see his mother every week."

"It gets better," Ogden commented. "I ran that bag of heroin by the narcotics folks here. It's called Diablo, and 135th is near where it's circulated most. It's supposedly the trademark of some guy calling himself La Culebra, which means The Snake."

"Cute," Joe muttered. "I don't guess Mr. Snake would be too interested in a chat."

"I doubt it," Ogden agreed wryly, "but it's a big coincidence to overlook. On the other hand, that same subway stop also services a City College campus up there. It may be a stretch, but I've asked one of the local detectives to check the enrollment files, just for what-the-hell."

"You talk with her co-workers and friends?" Sammie asked.

Ogden laughed. "Several of them, and found that Willy had been there already. He goes right after it, doesn't he?"

Neither one of them could argue the point, but Gunther asked, "Did he say anything to them that might tell us what he's up to?"

"Mary's old boss thought he was having a hard time accepting the accidental overdose scenario, but she didn't think he had any evidence proving otherwise. The other one—a friend and colleague of Mary's—was almost too pissed off at him to even talk about it. Apparently he didn't fess up to being the infamous ex, and she didn't find that out till she talked with her boss later.

"But," he added, holding a finger up in the air, "there were a couple of things that came out of that conversation we should look into. And if they pan out, I want the NYPD to get full credit for having trained your guy to be as good as he is."

"You want the credit," Gunther replied, laughing, "we

might give you the guy, too, if my bosses get sick enough of him. What were the couple of things?"

"First, he asked about boyfriends, specifically mentioned someone named Andy, which is why I lit up just then when you mentioned Liptak. Mary's girlfriend, Louisa Obregon, drew a blank there, but she did say Mary had been a bit of a party girl and that Obregon even met a couple of her dates. She couldn't remember their names, but they were ordinary-sounding like Bill or Dave."

"Or Bob," Joe said quietly.

Ogden smiled. "Thought you'd find this part interesting. I couldn't get any worthwhile descriptions, but flying a mug shot of Bob Kunkle under her nose couldn't hurt. The other two things she told me were just as interesting: One, she swore Mary was a speedball shooter when she last used. She'd shot heroin in the old days, but had moved to speedballs exclusively and wouldn't have touched straight heroin with a pole, supposedly. Two, she said that Willy really got after her about the Re-Coop—asking who owned it, how was it financed, what was its real story—stuff like that."

"Interesting," Gunther said. "You look into any of that yet?"

Ogden shook his head. "Nope. We've already jammed a lot into a short time. I just haven't gotten to it."

"Maybe we can help. Some of this just requires breaking down data—noncomputer stuff—matching Metro stops to phone call addresses or credit card and sales receipts to various dates we have on hand, or even chasing down the incorporation records on the Re-Coop. Couldn't Sam and I do that while you and your partner do the street cop and computer work?"

Ogden didn't take two seconds to react. "Sure. I'll tuck you away somewhere upstairs. More than one case has been made that way. After losing so much time, we should be that lucky."

He stood up and began collecting his paperwork. Smiling at them as he did so, he added, "But I'm an optimist at heart. Ask anybody."

There was a knock on the door and one of Odgen's colleagues poked his head into the room. "Call for you, Ward. Guy named Willy Kunkle."

"Thanks, Freddy." Ogden waggled his eyebrows at the two Vermonters. "See?"

# Chapter 17

The subway dropped Willy Kunkle off at the Essex Street station, just shy of where Delancey begins ramping up to meet the Williamsburg Bridge on its leap across the East River. It's an impressive view and a true monument to engineering, especially superimposed over the Lower East Side backdrop. It's also a visual testament to the cars-over-people mentality born in the twentieth century's first half, when the already downtrodden, rough-and-tumble neighborhood was furrowed up to make room for what, even at the time, was deemed a remarkably ugly bridge. It made of the whole area a fractious orchestra of brick and steel, poverty and history, mixed in with the bridge's contradictory, even incongruous promise of a way out. It had forever been a picture Willy could appreciate.

He continued walking toward the river on the northern sidewalk, intending to cut under the bridge at Ridge Street to the precinct house below. But the route had an extra benefit, offering up yet another telling symbol of the neighborhood—one reflecting the locals' ability to rally against the sheer weight of the city around them. It was an enclosed chicken ranch, complete with wire racks jammed with hundreds of red hens strutting around and pecking out of feed trays, all tucked behind the broad plate-glass windows of an otherwise conventional store. Willy pondered an ad that might accompany such counterintuitive offerings: "Manhatten Free-Range Chickens." This was definitely a town for the innovative.

It was dark by now, and Willy paused in the shadows under the bridge to look at the redbrick station house and consider his actions one last time. He and Riley Cox had wasted hours fruitlessly chasing down a match for the name Carlos Barzún had given him: Ron Cashman. They'd even tried calling every Cashman in the phone book. But in a town of so many millions, a good many of whom were less than eager to be located, they hadn't held out much hope. And along those lines, they hadn't been disappointed.

Willy's working out in the cold had just hit its first distinct disadvantage. He didn't have the resources, the equipment, or the manpower to conduct a search like the one he needed done.

The challenge, therefore, was to locate Ron Cashman using police help without losing control of the case, something his recent incarceration and attending mistrust was going to make that much more difficult.

Which is why he'd phoned Ogden a half hour ago.

He broke cover and headed for the Seventh, vowing to make it up as he went along, and hoping to get lucky.

As soon as he entered the detective bureau upstairs, he knew this might be more difficult then he'd thought—certainly more complicated. Both Joe Gunther and Sammie Martens were clustered around Ward Ogden's desk, drinking cups of sacrosanct coffee.

"Hey, Willy," Gunther said affably enough.

"Hey, yourself," he answered, watching Sammie.

Sammie merely looked at him, her expression closed.

"Pull up a chair, Mr. Kunkle," Ogden suggested, "and let's compare notes."

Willy instead parked one hip on the edge of an adjacent desk, so he was sitting with a slight height advantage over them all. "I doubt I have much to offer," he said, "seeing that I've spent most of my time in town behind bars." He suddenly gave his two colleagues closer scrutiny. "Why are you two still here, anyway?"

"I called the boss," Gunther explained. "Sam had vacation time coming, and I told him I was taking emergency grief leave—death in the family with complications. Not too far off."

"And he bought that?"

"I told him the death was the result of a murder."

In the sudden stillness, Willy heard the background clatter of a couple of old-fashioned typewriters and the ceaseless ringing of the phones slowly yield to a buzzing in his ears.

"Is that true?" he asked, his own words sounding distant.

"You surprised?" Gunther inquired doubtfully.

Willy felt a numbness spread throughout his body. Despite his dogged efforts of the past few days and his own nagging doubts verging on conviction, he suddenly realized that he'd still been holding out hope that Mary had perhaps died simply of the despair for which he so pointedly took responsibility. To think that she'd also been murdered compounded his loss, and, as unreasonable as he knew it to be, made him feel somehow doubly responsible for her death.

"I suspected as much," he said quietly, settling into the chair beside him. "I just wasn't a hundred percent sure."

"What made you suspicious?" Ogden asked, obviously keen to know anything he might have missed.

"I don't know," Willy answered vaguely. "It felt wrong. She'd been happy, planning ahead—looking to go back to school. And there were things at her apartment—a missing date book, no address book. She always had those, and they weren't in your file."

He was finding it helpful to talk. "You also have three letters. That may be all there was, but she used to be a pack rat with those, and the birth control pills and her girlfriend both told me she had men in her life. I got the feeling someone had sanitized things, probably one of them."

"Was the girlfriend Louisa Obregon?"

"Yeah. The Re-Coop director gave me her name."

"And she told you about Mary wanting to go to school?"

"Yeah. Why?"

Ogden chose his words carefully, still unsure of Willy's trustworthiness. "We heard she might've visited the CCNY campus in Harlem."

Willy shrugged. "Maybe. Obregon didn't say." The proximity of that campus to La Culebra's neighborhood wasn't lost on him. But he, like Ogden, was keeping his own counsel for the moment.

A couple of detectives entered the squad room, laughing. Ogden rose without fanfare and quietly suggested the four of them retreat to their familiar, more private lair.

Once the door was closed behind them, and they'd settled into new seats, Joe Gunther commented to Willy, "Obregon mentioned you'd asked her about the Re-

Coop—how it's run, funded, who's behind it. What made you so curious? You smell something there?"

Willy answered truthfully. "Not particularly. It just seemed pretty ritzy to me, given where it is, and I was surprised Mary could just walk in off the street and get in. Most of these places have waiting lists a mile long. Made me wonder, is all. I never checked it out."

He was by now fully recovered from his earlier shock, and returned to the topic that had stimulated it, asking the New York detective, "Since we're playing twenty questions, why're you so convinced she was murdered, 'specially after you almost shelved the case?"

It hadn't been diplomatically worded, but Ogden apparently had Joe Gunther's talent for forbearance. "Thank your fearless leader. He saw what we missed."

For the next twenty minutes, Ogden and Gunther briefed Willy on their theories, with Gunther going beyond the dinosaur's reluctance and telling Willy exactly what they were investigating. Gunther knew as Ogden didn't the extent of his renegade colleague's abilities and dedication, but he was also fully aware that had it not been for Ogden's status and the fact that they'd hit it off, none of the Vermont team would have stayed in this building, much less become an integral part of the investigation.

Willy, for his part, didn't press for details. In fact, he was more interested in extracting information they wouldn't know anything about.

"So basically," he said once he'd been brought up to date, "you're crunching numbers and pounding the pavement, hoping to get lucky."

"You know how it goes," Gunther agreed, having noticed that Sammie Martens hadn't said a word so far.

"Sure," Willy conceded, and played the card he'd arrived with. "Then maybe you should add the name Ron Cashman to the list. I heard he might know something, and I can't get a location on him."

Both old-timers studied him carefully. "What's his story?" Gunther asked.

Willy looked nonchalant, willing to share information, within limits. "I was chasing down the drug angle—Diablo?"

Ogden nodded. "Right, the uptown stuff. What'd you find out?"

"Nothing. My options were to poke around generally or ask the manufacturer directly if he knew Mary. The last approach seemed a little suicidal."

"That's what we were thinking earlier," Ogden admitted. "Did you find out who makes it?"

Willy feigned surprise. "You don't know that? I only heard the street name, La Culebra. Cashman's name came up as someone who'd done business with him from this part of the city. I thought it was both unusual and an interesting coincidence."

Ogden nodded and wrote the name down in his notepad.

Willy was suddenly struck by a thought. "Add Nathan Lee to that list, too, would you?"

"Why?"

Here he felt freer to be honest. "He's a friend of mine. Been helping me out—in fact, he was the one I was with in that bar—but he disappeared. I've been looking all over for him. I'm worried he got into a jam. I checked his apartment, his friends. He's vanished. Black guy, mid-sixties—maybe older—small and wiry."

Ogden watched him carefully. "What kind of business is he in?"

"Hustling. Nothing big time. He makes ends meet. I met him when I was on the beat and cut him some slack. He never forgot it."

Ogden got to his feet. "Let me add these to Jim's list. He's already staring at a computer. I'll be right back."

He left the room. There was an uncomfortable silence before Gunther rose, too, and said, "I gotta go to the bathroom," and followed Ogden's example.

After he'd left, the silence remained. Willy stared at his shoes. Sammie stared at him.

"How've you been?" she finally asked.

He spoke to his toes. "Okay."

Her cheeks flushed. "I'm not asking about your health."

His jaw clenched. He'd been dreading this ever since Gunther told him she'd come along. "I'm trying to set things right," he said.

"I know that. How's it going?"

Something in her voice made him look up. It was the strength he heard—familiar, natural, welcome. In his own emotional gyrations, he'd begun to blend his memories of Mary with those of Sammie, making the latter weaker and less reliable than she was. Sammie was high-strung, and he knew that he'd occasionally put her through the wringer, but she wasn't Mary. She'd be someone who would throw him out when the time came, not run to get away from him. And she certainly wouldn't seek out male companionship for security or drugs for escape. Sammie was a fighter—passionate and emotional, definitely, but tough as nails when it counted.

The way she'd just voiced that short sentence reminded him of that, and helped reestablish one of the few tethers he had to a world he felt he was only orbiting at the moment.

"Pretty shitty right now," he admitted.

"Nathan Lee?" she asked.

His face registered his surprise.

She smiled, which came as a relief. "The sphinx you're not—not with me, anyhow."

He sighed in concession. "I hadn't thought about him in years. Only did now because I needed his help. I saw it as calling in a marker, but he treated me like a friend. And now I think maybe I got him killed, like I've been doing all my life."

Sammie cupped her cheek in her hand and studied him. "Your whole adult life you've been either a soldier or a cop, same as me . . . except you're a whole lot older."

"Hey," he said, smiling despite himself.

"And you've been in combat," she continued. "What did you expect? That your friends wouldn't get banged up or killed? It's a dangerous life."

He frowned at the seeming banality of the comment until she added, "You should ask yourself why you chose those lines of work."

That stopped him. He actually never had, and only now wondered why not. He shared a contempt for self-analysis that many did who needed it most, using those who overindulged in it as the reason why. Except that now, in a virtual flash, he saw that his might have been like an anorexic's view of a glutton, with no acknowledgment that the majority of humans inhabit neither extreme.

But this was a passing thought only. Willy wasn't given to clarifying epiphanies, and he answered Sammie instead with a defensive, "You saying I like this? That I do it on purpose?"

She didn't back down. "That's for you to find out, Willy. And while you're at it, ask yourself why you shut out the people who aren't likely to get killed, like your mother, or Bob, or your friends."

Willy stood up angrily, making his chair skitter across the floor. "Speaking of mothers, who elected you, all of a sudden?"

But he stopped his ineffective outburst almost as quickly as he'd started it, stalled by her simply rolling her eyes. For a moment he just stood there, breathing hard, his face red, fighting for some of the dignity she seemed to possess without effort. It was a side of her he hadn't seen in a long time, and the fact that it had resurfaced told him something he couldn't yet clearly define.

The door opened and Ward Ogden stopped on the threshold, his eyes moving between the two of them. "Everything okay in here?"

Willy retrieved his chair and sat back down. "Yeah."

Sammie let out a silent breath of air. Her show of strength notwithstanding, her heart had been pounding all through that last exchange. She was sick and tired of feeling anxious and manipulated. All it did was remind her of her poor history with men. Except that this one, she believed fundamentally, was not to be grouped with any of those preceding him. While still probably one of the worst choices for a lifelong companion, Willy had stamina and courage and a strong sense of righteousness, and the potential of being someone extraordinary, if he could beat back his own personal Mr. Hyde.

The trick for her was to figure out how to disconnect

his fate from her own self-regard, and it was there, just lately, that she felt she'd been making inroads.

She had no idea if this was actually true, of course, but it made her feel better about herself, and for the moment that was enough.

Slightly warily, Ogden stepped farther into the room and placed a photograph on the table. Gunther was watching from the doorway.

"That the guy you were looking for?" Ogden asked gently.

Willy gazed down onto the obviously lifeless face of Nate Lee. "What happened to him?"

"He was found under the 145th Street Bridge, dressed like a bum. The assumption was he'd fallen and hit his head. He had no ID, nobody in the area knew who he was, so they declared him an accidental and took him to the potter's field on Hart Island yesterday. We're lucky they started photographing these folks a while back and cataloguing where they're buried. We can have him exhumed first thing tomorrow morning."

Willy pursed his lips, drawing connections in his head. "Anything on the other one—Ron Cashman?"

"No, sorry. We only came up with this 'cause of a habit of mine. Anytime somebody living hand-to-mouth goes missing, even if he fancies himself an independent businessman, as I'm sure Mr. Lee did, I check the Hart Island index. I figured this was him. They've only had four this past week, and he was the only one fitting the description."

Willy nodded. "Well, I appreciate it."

Ogden checked his watch. "It's getting late. I got a couple of people keeping the search engines running on some of our inquiries. I suggest we get a good night's sleep and meet at Bellevue after they bring the body back from Hart Island."

"I'd like to be with him," Willy said softly.

Ogden gave him a surprised look, but instantly grasped his meaning. "At the exhumation?"

Willy simply nodded, not making eye contact.

Ogden immediately defused any possible debate. "Sure. We'll all go—make it a field trip. It's a beautiful spot. How 'bout the dock on City Island at eight A.M.? You need directions?"

"I know where it is," Willy said, turning to Gunther and Sammie. "Where're you two staying? I'll pick you up."

Joe gave him the name and address of an inexpensive hotel, followed by, "You want to have dinner together?"

But predictably he shook his head. "No. I better pay somebody a visit I haven't seen in a while." He smiled sadly at Sammie and added, "Maybe make amends. I'll see you seven-forty-five."

It wasn't all that late when Willy reached Washington Heights by subway and began walking toward the street where he'd spent his entire youth. If she was keeping to her old habits, which he had no reason to doubt, his mother would be lost in whatever television was beaming out after suppertime, and would probably stay there until eleven. She'd always been a night owl.

He wasn't making this journey with any great conviction, or holding out much hope. In fact, he wasn't sure he fully understood his own motives, aside from the fact that Sammie had indirectly made him feel he should make some sort of gesture—that and Nate's death being confirmed right afterward. Sammie's comment about his abandoning people who didn't do him the service of either abandoning him or dying first had struck a chord. Despite all that had befallen him, Willy had never seen himself as one of life's victims. However insensitive, clumsy, and even brutal his ways of fighting back, he had never considered quitting. So, while the cynical pessimist in him was gearing up for a disappointment, he was nevertheless going to show Sammie that he was at least sometimes capable of making the first move.

As he approached its perimeter, the old neighborhood seemed to echo similar contradictions to the ones he was struggling with. The buildings and streets were familiar, the roll of the terrain underfoot like an old and comforting home movie, but the foreground of language, people, and general spirit was utterly foreign, as if the old hometown had been completely taken over by a busload of tourists.

Gone were the sausage shops and beer parlors and the guttural shouts of angry hausfraus yelling at children running in the streets. Gone, too, were the synagogues and kosher delis and serious men all dressed in black that had been as much part of the landscape as trees were to Vermont. The Irish Catholics, whose presence here had wobbled between the entertaining and the threatening, depending on who you were and what the alcohol intake had been that evening, were also just figments of memory. Now, nearly everywhere he looked, Willy saw a world almost completely become Hispanic.

As a result, he noticed with some amusement, the old stomping grounds had been blessed with a lot more life and color. He knew the area had suffered hard times, including violence, drugs, and civil unrest, but there was also an exuberance now that he didn't recall from before. The music spilling into the streets, the effervescence of the neon store lights, even the swagger of the people loitering on the sidewalks, laughing, catcalling, and having a good time after work, were all things he wished had been there when he'd been young. Admittedly tainted by retrospection, his memories were of a dour place of Germanic discipline and disappointment, and of traditions he'd longed to escape.

He continued walking up St. Nicholas Avenue, to where Washington Heights becomes Fort George. Here were the remnants of his youthful experience, surviving like an outpost on foreign soil, and sure enough, the old familiar restlessness began welling up inside him like an instinct.

He turned the corner onto 187th Street, now just a few blocks away from his mother's apartment, the smell of some familiar German meal drifting by on the cool night air, when he heard a tired, slightly querulous voice say behind him, "Hey, mister, gimme a buck?"

The question wasn't directed at Willy. He was already too far past the spot for that to be the case. It was also nothing he hadn't heard before, especially given the streets he'd been walking recently. But there was something about the plea that made him turn around. Later, he thought it might have been the utter silence following the request, instead of the usual muttered evasion. But whatever the cause, when he looked back, he saw not the bum propped up against the wall, but the man who'd stirred him to speak.

And as soon as he saw him, a tall, angular man with a large, flesh-colored bandage incongruously plastered across the bridge of his nose, Willy knew he was looking at someone wishing him harm.

He didn't hesitate, as an innocent might have. Nor did he wait for this perceived threat to announce itself, as cops are trained to do. He simply reached under his coat and pulled out his gun.

The other man reacted with equal instinctiveness. Producing his own weapon, he ducked and sidestepped, dropping behind the bum, using him as a barrier behind which to draw a bead. Willy fired once at a spot just beside them to make his pursuer tuck in, and then made for the nearest alley at a dead run, his eyes still smarting from the brightness of the muzzle flash.

The ploy worked. The one return round sang harmlessly by like a wasp on adrenaline.

Willy ran down the alley to where an oversized metal Dumpster lay as large as a sleeping buffalo. He swung around behind it, using its bulk as a shield and its side to steady his arm, but even as he waited for his follower's shadow to fill the opening of the alleyway, he knew it was over as quickly as it had begun.

As if in confirmation, the bum's thin voice drifted down to meet him. "Help, police. Somebody call the cops. There's shootin' goin' on."

Willy straightened, pocketed his gun, and returned to the street, cautiously peering around the corner. The bum was on all fours, crawling around, uselessly wailing and trying to collect his scattered belongings. The rest of the block was empty, but he could already hear the sounds of startled voices asking one another if they'd heard what they thought they had.

Willy continued in the direction he'd been headed, his casual pace belying his vigilance.

But the family reunion wouldn't happen tonight. He was not going home. He was confident he hadn't been followed here. He'd been keeping an eye out instinctively. Which meant the shooter had known of his mother's address, and had selected it as the perfect site for an ambush, and the perfect way to make Willy Kunkle join Nate Lee in the hereafter.

For Willy was pretty sure he'd just met Ron Cashman.

# Chapter 18

Ward Ogden was already at the dock when the three of
them drove up and parked near the small shed the ferry
crew used as an office and lunchroom. He was pacing the
top of the ramp, watching the early morning sun flash off
the mirror-smooth water of Long Island Sound. Below
him, nestled into the boat slip like a foot in an open-back
shoe, was the *Michael Cosgrove,* a small, steel-decked
ferry with a wheelhouse and an engine room mounted
like long, narrow bookends on the starboard and port
sides of what otherwise would have looked like a raft.

On the horizon, as flat as an airstrip except for a low
growth of trees, was Hart Island, site of the largest potter's field in the United States.

Ogden turned as they approached. "Good morning.
Everyone sleep well?"

Gunther and Sammie answered in the affirmative.
Willy, typically, asked, "When do we leave?"

Ogden was unfazed. "Soon as the truck from Rikers
arrives."

Sammie looked at him quizzically.

"A detail of volunteers from Rikers comes here every

day," he explained, "along with a truck of unclaimed bodies. It helps the city cut costs and it gives the prisoners a little time outside the walls. They're very respectful," he added without being prompted. "Probably more so than if they were just city workers. Could be some of them appreciate the fine line between them and the people in the boxes."

"There's a truckload every day?" Sammie asked.

Ogden smiled reassuringly. "No, no. Not a load, just a truck. Sometimes it only has a box or two on board. It does mount up, though." He pointed at the island. "Since that opened up right after the Civil War, three-quarters of a million people have been buried out there." He glanced at his watch. "The ME's office is sending a vehicle later for Nathan Lee's body, after it's been exhumed."

They all turned at the sound of a large white box truck trundling down the feeder road toward them. Its sides were labeled, "Queens Health Network" over the names of two hospitals. Behind it was a Department of Correction bus.

They stood back while the correction officers and the ferry crew went through the formalized routine of loading all vehicles on board, including Ogden's car. Once that was done, Joe, Willy, and Sammie stepped onto the steel deck themselves and watched while the ferry's engine kicked to life, belched a cloud of diesel smoke from its stack, and began plowing a line through the cold, smooth water toward Hart Island, just over three thousand feet away.

There was a mystical sensation to the trip. Intermingled with the trees, crumbling, decrepit buildings slowly began emerging into view as the boat neared the shore, lending a feeling of a lost civilization to the already known quantity of just under a million lost souls.

Ogden continued acting as tour guide, standing at the chain closing off the ferry's bow ramp and pointing at the various landmarks. "Lot of history to this place, beyond the potter's field. There was a prison out here once, a shoe factory, a psychiatric hospital and drug rehab center. There's a peace monument they put up after World War Two, and, as ironies would have it, the remnants of a missile launching pad within sight of it."

"Hold it," Gunther said. "They had missiles out here?"

"During the Cold War, yeah." Ogden gestured to the left. "On the island's northern end. It was one of those ramp-mounted things, lay covered up in a shallow trench till needed. Gone now, of course, but the hatches are still there, along with what I guess is a command center—all you can see is a manhole with a huge rock on top of it. I always wondered what was inside. Far as I know, nobody's ever looked."

They were drawing near and the crew was getting ready to dock. Through the windows of the bus, Gunther could see the dozen or so prisoners enjoying the early sunshine.

They drove in a caravan to the island's southern end along a rutted gravel road that cut between the shore and what looked like not just an assemblage of buildings—as it had appeared from the water—but an entire village, complete with hospital, church, power plant, greenhouse, and homes, all laid out along a grid of paved streets, and all choked by a junglelike growth of young hardwood saplings, which made the whole thing resemble a bizarre northern version of some Mayan ruin.

"It's sort of a shame, really," Ogden said as he drove

last in line. "It's a beautiful setting, inhabited solely by the dead. Seems like somebody could find a way to get something up and running again out here."

They rounded the island's largely treeless southern tip, observing the faint impressions left by several long, narrow, parallel trenches in the sod, and parked near a backhoe situated beside a utility shed. There, everybody got out, the prisoners to unload and stack the wooden coffins, the others to wait and watch.

"I think it's about a hundred and fifty coffins per trench," Ogden continued. "Different for the children's area, of course. They stack the adults three deep and two across, end to end. You'll notice, as they off-load each box, that one of the prisoners will number it with a router, so they can be cross-indexed with a location map later on in case they need to be retrieved. That's how they'll find Mr. Lee."

As he spoke, that's exactly what was happening. The box truck's back was opened and several orange-clad prisoners began dragging out the contents to where each one could be branded with a number. In the meantime, deep in the open trench, another party was getting ready to receive and stack the boxes in regimented fashion. As Ogden had said, they were quiet and respectful of their duties, working with peaceful decision.

The New York detective turned toward a long rectangular patch of raw earth immediately adjacent to the open hole. "As luck would have it, they filled in that last trench yesterday. Otherwise, we could've just shoveled out a little dirt and found the box we're after. Not to worry, though, these guys are pretty good at what they do.

"They'll be at it awhile, though," he said. "Afterward, the prisoners will be taken to a small, secure compound near the missile pad for lunch. The exhumation will happen just before then. So, if you want to walk around a bit, feel free. It's pretty interesting. The really old graves are to the north—lots of slightly sunken troughs—and a ton of geese that live there."

Willy tentatively touched Sammie's forearm with the back of his hand. "Go for a walk?" he asked.

Surprised by the unusual offer, she fell into step beside him as he headed north toward the abandoned settlement.

"I'm sorry I blew up yesterday," he said after several minutes of walking in silence.

"You're in a tough spot," she answered, figuring she'd let him lead the conversation.

"Still . . ."

She kept quiet.

They came to the outskirts of the empty, ghostly, mostly brick-built buildings, almost every door and window of which was open to the casual onlooker. It was like touring a long-forgotten movie set.

"I reach a point, sometimes," he continued, "where all I got left is my anger. It's the only thing keeping me together."

"Anger at who?"

As if proving the point, he sneered. "Oh, right. This where I say, 'My mother'?"

But Sammie didn't miss a beat. "How would I know?"

She watched him compress his lips, struggling to keep track. To his credit, he returned to what he'd been saying.

"I've always had it," he admitted. "From as far back as I can remember. Maybe I was just born pissed off."

She sensed some of this had been running around his head when they'd parted ways earlier, so she asked, "Is that where you were going last night? To find out? You said you were off to make amends."

He sounded wistful. "Yeah. That was the idea. I figured I'd go visit my mother. I wasn't holding out much hope after all this time. From what Bob told me, she's pretty much a basket case anyhow. It's just . . . I don't know . . . that maybe if somebody has an idea of what went wrong, it might be her. I mean, I'm not stupid. I know there aren't any violin sections out there, waiting to help me see the light. But I keep hoping I can find some way to get on the right track."

Sammie was a little confused. "What happened? She wasn't home?"

It was an obvious question, given the conversation. But he knew with a slight jolt that he wasn't about to answer it. It would have been like opening the shutters from around a candle and allowing the wind to blow it out. And having abruptly realized how committed he was to seeing this investigation through alone, like the pursuit of the Holy Grail, he also saw that his entire supposed confession was probably corrupt. If he was truly interested in opening up and addressing his problems, being straight with this person above all others would have been the reasonable place to start. But apparently he wasn't ready. The complex, ephemeral issue of settling emotional past dues held sway. "Something came up."

They stopped before a large building with a central circular room just beyond the open double doors. The light filtering through the windowed cupola high overhead fell upon row after row of disheveled, disemboweled, and rusting metal filing cabinets, their massive paperwork contents spilling all over the floor in disastrous quantities. God only knows what files these were, whose lives they documented, and what void they'd created by being discarded here to rot.

Watching the cabinets lined up like disorderly, drunken, speechless soldiers, Sammie had to wonder about the similar repositories that everybody carried around in their heads, either ignored and neglected or simply inaccessible. In Willy's terse answer, it was as if she'd overhead him struggling in vain with this very dilemma and realized the best she could expect right now was that this conversation might be just the first of more to come.

Nevertheless, a little disappointed, she tried another angle. "Joe says that despite all the shit you hand out, you've got a lot to offer."

"Good for Joe. He's fed me that line."

"Maybe good for you. This is the first time I've ever heard you talk about why you are the way you are. That can't be all bad."

He turned away and resumed walking up the street. "I'm not so sure."

"You've tried ignoring it," she pressed him, her own frustration and irritation welling up. "You tried drowning it with booze. For all I know, you're down here trying to get yourself killed avenging a dead woman you think you wronged. How can talking about it be worse than any of that?"

She heard the words tumbling out of her the way a bystander might watch a car hit a bicyclist—unbelieving and a little fearful. Nevertheless, she did have some control, and that part of her now suddenly felt relieved. The inner strength she'd experienced the night before had been suddenly reinforced with the realization that she had nothing to lose by challenging him.

And in his own way, he rose to that challenge now. Instead of bursting out as he usually did, deflecting an assault with a response of greater magnitude, he stopped dead in his tracks.

Sammie almost bumped into him from behind. "What?" she asked.

There was a drawn-out moment of silence before he said, staring at the ground before him, "You're right. And so's Joe. He told me a while ago I should just be straight with you—to honor you by taking the risk, was what he really said. Such a crap artist. You want to know the great thing about anger?" he asked, looking up at her. "It's that you don't have to worry about anything else—not the other guy, not what's going to happen to you. There're no consequences. You just fire both barrels and walk away if you're lucky."

"What about after the smoke clears?"

"It doesn't matter. You don't think about it. And if it gets to be a problem again, and you're still alive, you reload and fire off another round."

She thought about that before saying, "You're not firing now. If you're not angry, what are you feeling?"

He pursed his lips and smiled ruefully. "Confused. That's why I don't like talking. It just screws me up."

"I think that's bullshit," she told him flatly. "I think you're sick of being mad all the time, but you don't know what to replace it with."

He laughed bitterly, recalling what had happened to him since getting that phone call in Brattleboro a few short days ago. "Yeah . . . maybe I'll try love, peace, and harmony. That would really fit."

"You can't tell till you try it," she suggested.

But they both knew that was pushing things. He rolled

his eyes and resumed walking. "Can we talk about something else?"

She smiled. "Yeah, for the moment. We're going to circle this hydrant again, though. Count on it."

He shook his head, curious as to why that didn't sound as bad as it should have. "Good image."

By the time they returned to the burial site, the boxes they'd arrived with had been covered with dirt, leaving the rest of the trench open, and the backhoe was scratching at the ground next to the previous hole. All but four of the prisoners were back in the bus with the driver and one of the COs. The remainder waited patiently, leaning on shovels, while the backhoe's blade picked at the earth's raw surface with surprising dexterity and tenderness.

Slowly, a hole slightly longer than a coffin began to grow as the operator dug straight down into the fresh, previously untouched ground.

"What're they doing?" Sammie asked. "He's not in the trench."

"He doesn't want to hit the boxes," Willy guessed as they approached Joe Gunther and Ward Ogden.

"They exhume from the side," the latter explained, "like an archaeology dig."

Sure enough, after going down some ten feet, the backhoe backed off and the four prisoners jumped in and began cutting into the side wall, quickly revealing the stacked boxes, their pine sides still pale and unstained by the dirt.

"Good thing we got after this so fast," Ogden said.

"They don't embalm these folks. Doesn't take long for them to get pretty messy."

The team in the hole removed the uppermost box and lifted it to the edge. The CO above them then gestured to a waiting medical examiner's hearse to come pick it up.

Ogden began walking toward his own car. "Okay. It's a wrap. We go to Bellevue now so they can take a closer look at your friend. And I hate to do this to you," he said to Willy, "but it looks like you're going to have to play next-of-kin again in identifying the body, if that's all right."

"Fine," Willy said, feeling like the sole conduit to society's late discards. "And thanks for letting me come out here."

When the time came, of course, and Willy was looking down onto Nathan Lee's dead face, he no longer felt like a pinch hitter for corpses. He truly mourned the loss of this person whose life he'd changed for the better so long ago. Maybe it was because he saw Nate as his only success along those lines, or maybe because, despite that, the end result turned out to be the same, but whatever the truth, he missed the man he'd rediscovered so recently, who seemed to bear only good memories of Willy, and who'd traveled the last mile to help him out.

"That him?" Ward Ogden asked quietly.

"Yeah."

They weren't in the formal and neutrally supportive environment where Willy had viewed Mary's remains. This was the ME's more functional part of the building, and everything around them spoke of the emotionally detached curiosity the inhabitants applied to their silent patients. It was starkly lit and equipped for one purpose, all of which made it easier for Willy to focus.

He looked up at the doctor, who'd already given Nate a thorough going-over. "What d'you think?"

The doctor was a woman wearing a mask, goggles, and gloves, the mask, he suspected, mostly to ward off the odor that Nate's body was already exuding.

"Massive trauma, for sure," she said. "Consistent with a fall from a bridge. He could have been killed and then pitched over. It would be pretty hard to tell, especially if his heart was still beating when he hit. There're no signs of anything else, though. No bullet holes or stab wounds. But that's not to say I don't have a few questions."

She moved to the body's right hand and held it up to the light. "He's got two skinned knuckles and a broken finger, for instance. Again, that might've happened in the fall, but it's more consistent with a fistfight, especially if he was right-handed, which his musculature suggests."

"Also," she added, moving up to the head, "I found something really curious. See this small smear of blood just under his ear? Where did it come from?"

Sammie pointed at a gash on the dead man's leg. "Is it too stupid to think there?"

The woman shook her head. "That would make us both stupid, 'cause that's what I thought—at first. But then I wondered how it was transferred. There's no laceration except for the leg. It's not a splatter mark, so it didn't splash there when the body hit the ground, and aside from the skinned knuckles, which didn't bleed, there's no blood on his hands. So, what's the explanation?"

"It's not his," Joe Gunther suggested.

Her eyes widened behind the plastic glasses. "That's

what I'm thinking. Two men in close combat, one with maybe a bloody nose. This one here lands a punch in the other one's stomach, let's say. That guy doubles over, and his face connects with the dead man's neck and shoulder area, depositing a smear. Too bad the clothes weren't kept. They might've given us a clearer picture."

But Willy didn't need a clearer picture. He'd seen that broken nose.

Ogden gestured toward the blood smear. "You got enough to work with there?"

"Oh, sure," she answered. "We'll compare it with the deceased's. If I'm right, they won't match. That won't tell you who it does belong to, of course, but maybe it'll come in handy later if and when you line somebody up."

Ogden nodded his satisfaction. "Okay. Another piece for the puzzle. Things're beginning to move along." He looked at the doctor. "You'll call me as soon as you get the autopsy results? I'd love to hear what else you find out about Mr. Lee."

She nodded without comment, writing a note to herself on her clipboard.

Ogden waved his arms at the others like a nanny shooing his small charges out of the room. "Then I guess we'll go back to hitting the bricks."

Out in the hallway, the cell phone rang in his pocket. He pulled it out, listened to what the caller had to say for several minutes, thanked him briefly, and hung up. "That was Jim," he explained as they all continued walking. "He spoke with someone at CCNY in Harlem. Turns out Mary Kunkle had just enrolled there for a course in psychology and drug counseling—one of their community outreach programs. According to them, she visited several times to set up the enrollment and payment schedule, so that gives us at least the most obvious explanation for her subway trips there. He also got something on Ron Cashman. Turns out he has quite a history. How was it again that you heard about him?"

The question was asked genially enough, but given his own lack of forthrightness on the subject, Willy couldn't help hearing a note of suspicion in Ogden's voice.

"I was trying to find out about La Culebra," he said. "Cashman's name came up as a possible associate who hung out near the Lower East Side. That made me curious. Does he live down there?"

Willy made an effort to sound only marginally interested, but in fact it was a struggle. This was the sole reason he'd broken cover, after all, and since then, the man he thought was Ron Cashman had not only taken a shot at him, but had just now been all but nailed as Nate Lee's killer.

But Ogden wasn't going to just blurt out an address and wish Willy happy hunting. Unlike Sammie and Joe, Ward Ogden didn't know Willy, and what little he'd discovered hadn't filled him with confidence. He also had serious doubts that Willy had asked to have Cashman's name run through the computers for the reason he'd just stated.

"No," he answered vaguely. "He's more of a Brooklyn boy. Was it drug dealing he was supposed to be doing, or what?"

Willy sensed what was going on, or was paranoid enough to imagine it. The question was designed to draw him out, and possibly to reveal that he knew more than he was admitting. So, instead of answering in the affirmative, he merely looked confused.

"That was the weird part. I asked the same thing, and

got nowhere. But it wasn't just the Lower East Side connection that caught my attention. I mean, the guy's not Hispanic, he's not from the neighborhood, and nobody I talked to knew what the hell his angle was. It was the whole package that made me wonder. Why do you ask? What kind of bad boy is he? Did I fall over something hot?"

That put the shoe on the other foot. Now Sammie and Gunther were looking at Ogden expectantly, and Willy interpreted Ogden's frown as a sign that he was feeling slightly outmaneuvered.

"Good lord, I don't know," he said lightly, ducking the question. "All I got was a synopsis of the man's rap sheet. We'll have to put him under a bigger microscope back at the office."

"What part of Brooklyn?" Gunther asked, making Willy suddenly feel kindlier toward him.

Ogden hedged his reply. "Sort of Greenpoint to Red Hook area—ten to twelve square miles. Jim said it looked like he moved around."

"Does he work for anyone or is he a freelancer?" Gunther persisted naturally enough.

At that point, Ward Ogden changed tactics. Being a realist, he weighed the chances of locating the killer of a dead junkie and an all-but-homeless black man in two completely different parts of the city. Time was against him, his own caseload wasn't getting any smaller, and his boss would soon start wondering just how much effort all this warranted.

He didn't like the idea, but he was coming to terms with having to deal with this one-armed bird dog in any case, which meant he might as well put him to work.

Maybe the man would prove as professional, if unconventional, as his colleagues seemed to believe.

"My partner told me," he therefore admitted, "that years back, Cashman was connected to Lenny Manotti. Manotti ain't what he used to be, but in his day, he worked the Brooklyn docks a fair bit. What the movies call the 'import-export' business. I don't know what Cashman did for him—that's where the microscope'll come in—but his record implies enforcement. Weapons and assault charges, mostly. The drug stuff was minor— a couple of small possession raps."

He stopped there and watched Willy's expression as he added, "Looks like an interesting angle to chase down if we get the chance."

Willy kept walking down the long hallway, his eyes on the floor ahead of him. The last thing he wanted to do now was tip his hand.

# Chapter 19

Willy Kunkle excused himself from Ward Ogden and the others as quickly and innocuously as possible—never wondering why Ogden seemed so amenable to this—and was back in Riley Cox's store in Washington Heights just as night was beginning to fall.

He found the big man as he had before, holding the fort behind his elevated counter by the door, his hand within reach of the shotgun, and his eyes looking half asleep.

"Hey," Willy greeted him.

"Hey, yourself," Riley said, barely moving his lips.

Willy glanced down the two aisles, saw a kid studying comic books in a distant rack and two women picking out items from the glass-walled fridge against the back wall.

"I got bad news," he said in an undertone.

Riley's expression didn't so much change as imperceptibly soften, as if its underlying scaffolding had collapsed. "Nate's dead," he said without inflection.

It wasn't a question.

"Yeah. I'm sorry."

Riley watched Willy's face, struck by his tone of voice, and saw that this enigmatic hard-ass was being neither considerate nor compassionate. He was feeling his own loss with Nate's death, putting it in a special category in his brain as a collector might add a priceless addition to a vault.

"You know who?" Riley asked.

Willy paused as one of the women approached the counter, laid her few items down, and paid for them in crumpled dollar bills pulled from her coat pocket.

"Pretty sure it was Ron Cashman," Willy answered after she'd left. "Same guy who took a shot at me last night, uptown."

"You saw him?"

"I shot at him first."

Riley produced a hint of a smile. "Why doesn't that surprise me?"

Willy ignored the comment. "Who do you know in Brooklyn, both sides of the old Navy Yard?"

"A few people," Riley answered vaguely.

This time, it was Willy's turn to smile. "I thought you might. Cashman used to work for an old crook named Lenny Manotti. That ring any bells?"

Riley thought about that for a moment. "He Mobbed up?"

"I didn't know you were so prejudiced. Not that I heard."

"What does 'old' mean?"

"From what I got, semi- to fully retired."

Riley grunted, straightened, stretched his thick, muscled arms out to both sides of him, and arched his back. "Good," he said. "Then he won't have too many people around him."

Which was exactly what Willy wanted to hear.

*    *    *

Several hours later, Willy Kunkle and Riley Cox entered a restaurant/bar on Bedford Avenue in the Northside section of Brooklyn. The Waldorf Astoria it wasn't, but it did have the relaxed, well-used feel of a popular neighborhood dive. Thankfully, it was also not a place so wholly given over to one race, creed, or sex that their sudden appearance caused any notice.

Riley led them to the bar and to two stools either side of a heavyset, bearded man nursing a half-empty beer.

"Hey, Zeke," Riley said softly.

Zeke looked up at the row of bottles against the wall opposite him, as if he'd just heard a distant alarm bell that made him only mildly curious. "Who's your friend?"

His voice was gravelly and low-pitched, somewhere in the suburbs of Louis Armstrong, except that he was white.

"He's shy," Riley answered. "You got what I'm after?"

"Sure." Zeke took a long pull on his beer and wiped his mouth with the back of his hand. "What d'you want with an old dog like Manotti? He's barely breathin' anymore."

The bartender approached. Riley ordered a beer, Willy a black coffee. Riley slid two twenties in front of Zeke, who had them enveloped in his fist almost before they touched the bar top.

Zeke, still staring at the bottles before him, said, "He's the one in the corner booth, facing the door like anyone cared about him anymore. Fat guy with the three hairs combed over the top."

Willy glanced at the man as he reached for some pretzels. Manotti was eating alone, and seemed almost done with his meal.

"He in a car or on foot?" he asked.

The bearded man slowly swung his head around to look at him and raised his eyebrows. "Wow. It talks."

"It can also shove that bottle up your ass."

Zeke returned to his earlier, meditative posture. "I liked you better before. He's on foot."

"What's his address?" Riley asked.

"My, my, you boys are demanding," he said, but he gave them an address nearby.

"Now leave," Willy ordered.

From his body language, Zeke looked ready to protest, or at least proffer up some face-saving witticism, but he apparently thought better of it, and muttered, "Next time you're shoppin', don't call me, okay?" as he slid off the stool.

Riley waited until he'd left the bar, and then told Willy, "That was useful. Thanks."

Willy drank from his coffee. "Too goddamned chatty," he said, and as if to set an example, stopped at that.

Riley smiled and shook his head slightly. "You always this much fun?"

Willy didn't answer.

"There was a guy like you in the neighborhood when I was a kid," Riley told him. "Real sour, never had anything good to say. We stayed out of his way or we cranked him up, depending on how many there were of us. My grandmother used to let me have it when she heard me criticizing him, though. They weren't friends or anything, but she said anyone like that had to have had things a lot tougher than we did, 'cause nobody gets born that way."

Willy kept at his coffee. He'd thought about that, of course, blaming his father for abandoning them, his mother for never owning up to it. And, in fact, it had been a little weird—one day the old man had been in the house, the next he wasn't, not a single person anywhere saying a word about it. Not once. The last communication Willy remembered—the night before his father left—was being slapped across the face by him because Willy had dropped his spoon at the table.

But lots of kids lost their fathers, or were turned into punching bags, or who knew what else. Willy hadn't suffered as much as most of them.

What people didn't understand was that it was kind of liberating to speak his mind when he felt like it, to live with his curmudgeon's reputation. It disentangled him from other people, and he'd come to see that as a blessing.

Willy put his cup down and rubbed his eyes with his hand, pushing hard enough to cause stars.

"Looks like he's on the move," Riley said, breaking into Willy's meditations.

Willy turned discreetly to see Lenny Manotti settling his bill.

So much for deep thinking.

They let Manotti get halfway down the block before leaving the bar and tailing him. If there ever had been a period when the old man had shoved his weight around and needed protection, it was apparently a long time back. Now he sauntered along nonchalantly, one hand working a toothpick, the other buried in a pocket, occasionally waving to some acquaintance on the street. Another retiree enjoying the twilight years.

They'd discussed what approach to take, the most obvious being the one Willy had used on Carlos Barzún. Riley's information was that despite Manotti's current inoffensiveness, he hadn't been a gentle player when he'd been in the game. But he was toothless now, unlike La Culebra, and capable of striking a time-wasting tough-guy pose from pure nostalgia.

As a result, Willy had decided not to give him the option.

Riley hadn't argued the point. Odd as it appeared, he'd discovered in Willy a man whose combat sense he could trust. It had been for him the rediscovery of one Vietnam experience he hadn't expected to ever feel again: a bonding not based on shared backgrounds or cultures, but on the other guy's proven ability to get the job done. Riley had no delusions about Willy's survival skills—the latter seemed devoted to his own self-destruction in a loopy, roundabout way—but Riley did believe that following his lead might well result in avenging Nate's death, while leaving his own skin intact.

Any further sentiment didn't apply, and clearly wasn't asked for.

Manotti lived in a bland apartment building of no architectural merit—merely one of those square brick blocks with dozens of windows, reminiscent of a child's drawing. Willy picked up his pace, leaving Riley behind, and reached the lobby just as Manotti was digging into his pocket for his keys. Willy was holding his dead pager up to his ear as if it were a cell phone.

"Look," he said in a slightly argumentative tone as he came up behind the old man, "I don't care what he told you. We settled on that price a week ago. He can't expect me to move this kind of deal and then have all the numbers change. . . . Hang on a sec. I gotta get my door key."

He made a show of trying to keep the fake phone wedged against his cheek while fumbling deep in his pocket for the fictional keys. Manotti noticed the effort as he unlocked the door, correctly interpreting Willy's pleading expression, and held the door open for him to pass through.

"Thanks, man," Willy murmured with a quick smile. "It's been a hell of a day."

He regained control of the pager and said, "No, I was talking to somebody else. Harry, tell me exactly what he told you. I wanna hear if maybe I missed something the first time around, like maybe what a crook this guy is."

Together, Manotti and Willy walked the length of the building's inner foyer and arrived at the waiting elevator around the corner.

"He said what?" Willy said eventually, his voice rising. "That doesn't sound even vaguely right. I got the contract upstairs, unless he sent me something new in the meantime. . . . Shit." He held the pager against his chest as Manotti pushed the button for the third floor. "Mister," he explained, "I hate to be a pain, especially after you helped me out, but I forgot to check my mail and I gotta get to my apartment fast. Could you hold the door?"

After a pleasant dinner out, and being flattered for his courtesy, Manotti wasn't inclined to turn him down. He nodded, said, "Sure," and placed his hand against the doorjamb.

Willy jogged back the way they'd come, opened the door for the waiting Riley, gave him the floor number, and retraced his steps, pretending as he rounded the corner to be stuffing something into his inner pocket. "Hang on, Harry. I'm doing two things at once." He rejoined the old man, nodded his thanks, and said, "Four. I really appreciate it," as Manotti waved inquiringly at the elevator's control panel. Willy then spoke into his fake phone,

"No. Just junk mail and a bill. All right, tell me exactly what he said."

For the rest of the trip up, all Willy had to do was make facial expressions and an occasional comment to fulfill what remained of his charade. On the third floor, he raised his eyebrows in grateful parting to Manotti, who waved back, and waited for the doors to close before replacing the pager on his belt. On the next floor, he ran down the hallway, found the stairwell, and double-stepped down one flight.

He carefully poked his head into the hallway, looking both ways, and saw Riley leaning against the wall to the left, out of breath from his quick climb up three stories.

Riley met him halfway. "Number 340," he said in an undertone. "Lucky for me he doesn't live on the top floor. No dog met him at the door and all the lights were out when he opened the door. He's gotta live alone. You want to hit him now?"

Willy shrugged. "No reason not to."

They quietly returned to Manotti's apartment door. Willy stood directly opposite the peephole. Riley flattened against the wall near the doorknob.

Willy rang the buzzer.

They heard a man's heavy tread approach. "Yeah?"

"It's Randy," Willy said brightly. "Remember? From the elevator just now. You dropped this just as you stepped out. At least it has your address on it." He held a checkbook up too close to the peephole for anyone to see what it was.

It didn't matter in any case. The lock was already being snapped open. As the door swung back, Riley whipped around from where he'd been hiding and charged through the opening, his shoulder leading, with

Willy close behind. They were both inside, the door closed behind them, before Lenny Manotti had stopped sliding across the floor on his back.

Riley was down on one knee beside him, one large hand clamped across his mouth, before he'd been able to utter a sound. Willy stood at his feet, pointing a gun at him.

"Hi, Lenny," he said in a quiet voice. "We're the ghosts from Christmas past. You wanna play ball, or should I shoot you right now? Nod if it's the first."

Manotti nodded once. Slowly, Riley removed his hand. At that, Manotti narrowed his eyes. "Who are you fuckin' assholes? I don't know you."

Willy put on a disappointed look. "You hear what he called us? Guess we better turn up the heat."

Riley grabbed Manotti by the scruff of the neck and yanked him up like a mannequin. He dragged him into the living room beyond the entrance hall and slammed him down into a chair. He then pulled some duct tape from his coat pocket and began strapping the older man down.

Manotti licked his lips. "What the hell d'you want? Maybe we can make a deal."

Willy smiled, moving a chair opposite his victim and sitting in it so they were virtually knee to knee. "I like that. We're not after much. Problem is, I want it to be the truth. You could tell us anything you wanted to get us out of your hair, and by the time we found that out, you'd have rounded up some of your old buddies."

"I'm retired," Manotti protested. "What do I give a fuck about that shit anymore? What d'ya wanna know, fer Christ's sake? This is stupid."

Willy laughed. "Makes me wonder how many times

*you* did the same thing in your prime. Or did Cashman do it for you?"

Manotti scowled. "You friends with that bum? I shoulda guessed. Couple of fuckin' leg breakers. No style."

"Right. So says the artist. Spare me, Lenny. Actually, we're not friends of Cashman. Haven't seen him in a long time. What's he up to?"

"Who cares?"

Willy leaned forward, suddenly menacing. A switchblade had appeared in his hand and was now resting on Manotti's upper lip, forcing him to cross his eyes as he stared at it.

"What the—"

Willy interrupted him with a tiny jab. "That's the question, Lenny. Truth or consequences. Where do we find Cashman?"

The other man's eyes widened. "That's what this is about? That asshole? Shit. You coulda asked me that in the elevator, I woulda told you. You guys're crazy. Fuckin' boneheads."

Willy was losing patience. The knife tip eased into one of Manotti's nostrils.

"Hey, hey," he said, careful not to move.

"Don't give me etiquette," Willy said menacingly. "Give me what I want."

"All right, all right. Jesus Christ. Last I knew, he was hanging around the Carroll Gardens area, either on Clinton or Henry. I don't keep in touch."

Willy laughed at the cliché. "Doesn't mean you won't drop a dime and let him know we came asking."

Despite his precarious position, Manotti flared, "What's with you? You dumb and ugly both? I told you I think the guy's an asshole. You wanna take him out, be my frigging guest." He leaned forward slightly, making his nose bleed, and yelled, *"I don't give a fuck."*

Willy sat back and glanced at Riley. "You believe him, Reuben?"

Riley was standing out of Manotti's view and rolled his eyes at the name. He spoke for the first time since entering the apartment. "Sure."

"I guess I do, too. Who's Cashman working for nowadays?"

"He's a freelance," Manotti answered, calmer now that he felt he'd made his point. "That's the biggest reason we split up. I thought he was ripping me off; he thought I was too much the big boss. It's not like I miss him, the guy was a thug."

Willy stood up and moved the chair he'd been sitting on. "Wild guess: You wouldn't want us coming back. Am I right?"

Riley had removed enough duct tape so Manotti could bring his hand up to his nose and touch it gingerly.

"No shit."

"You got anything to add, then? Some way we could find Cashman extra fast?"

Manotti examined his fingertips for blood, finding only a drop. "Go to that neighborhood and ask for a cold gun. That oughtta flush him out. He's into guns big time."

Willy pocketed his knife and stuck out his hand. "Thanks, Lenny. You're a stand-up guy."

Manotti shook his head, but he also took Willy's hand in grudging respect. "And you're an asshole. Close the door on the way out."

# Chapter 20

Sammie Martens intoned, "Nancy Hidalgo," and gave an address.

Jim Berhle, Ward Ogden's young partner, typed the name into the computer and waited a few moments for it to respond. "A shoplifting rap six years ago. Otherwise clean," he read back to her.

"Anthony Mallon," Sammie said next, and followed it with another address. She was reading from a list in her hand.

Berhle repeated his part of the exercise.

"Wonder if that's one of the boyfriends," Joe Gunther said, standing by the coffee machine they'd smuggled into the room. The three of them were upstairs in the precinct house, far from the Whip's prying eyes, or anyone else from the detective squad. Ogden was where he was supposed to be, satisfying the powers by catching up on some of his other cases. He'd been taken "off the chart" for any new cases, but Mary Kunkle hadn't been declared worthy of undivided attention.

"Clean as a whistle," Berhle reported.

"Last one," Sammie announced. "Michael Annunzio."

Jim Berhle waited for the address and typed in the name. After the usual pause, he said, "Little more interesting: Mr. Annunzio's been busted for possession twice, disorderly twice, and once for domestic assault. He might stand a friendly chat."

They'd been closeted for hours, Sammie and Gunther scrounging through all the Metro cards, bills, sales receipts, and credit card slips, building what they could of a timeline and linking it to a geographical chart on one hand—where Mary had been each time she'd generated one of these mundane documents—and to a list of names and addresses of everyone she'd phoned over the past six months on the other.

Berhle shoved his chair away from the computer, pushed his glasses up high on his forehead, and rubbed his eyes vigorously. "Man, I can't imagine doing this all day, every day." He stood up and paced the floor briefly, stretching his legs, before coming to a stop behind where Sammie was sitting so he could look over her shoulder at the complicated, hand-scribbled chart.

"So, we have anything after all that?" he asked.

Joe Gunther by now understood why Ogden had chosen this particular partner for this case. Like the dinosaur, Berhle was calm, thoughtful, smart, and not driven by ego. He'd also proved to be as happy as his senior colleague to work with a couple of complete outsiders, at least when it came to pure grunt work.

Sammie tried to decipher her own handwriting, not to mention the arrows and scratch-outs that also covered her notes. "One thing's for sure," she told him. "Mary had a whole different lifestyle than we thought. I'd pictured some walking wounded dragging herself toward employ-

ment and education through guts and determination.
She's a whole lot more complicated than that."

She tapped one of the sheets with her pencil eraser.
"Like with these phone contacts. Besides the usual co-
workers and friends is an inordinate bunch of social mis-
fits. Michael Annunzio is the sixth man with a violent
criminal record, all of which include domestic assault
raps. That's either a weird coincidence or she wasn't able
to break the cycle. Did you cross-check to see if any of
their victims was Mary?"

"I tried," Berhle admitted. "But I only scratched the
surface, and some of that information isn't in our data
bank, either. We're getting better, but the idea of one
computer terminal doing everything is still a ways off.
Anyhow, she didn't surface in anything I checked, to answer your question. What else did you find out?"

Sammie turned to the Metro card map. "First time we
saw this, the big thing that jumped out was how many
times she went to Harlem, which we're now figuring was
to sign up for those classes. This map shows only three
Brooklyn locations, in three different neighborhoods. No
big deal on the face of it. Except"—and here she pulled
together several more scraps of paper—"for when you
start superimposing a bunch of these."

She placed her finger on the map. "Here, for instance.
We've got a subway stop one day, a thrown-out receipt
for a fast-food lunch on another, and the address of one
of the men she called, all happening within the same
three-block area." She moved to another section. "Same
thing for here. No subway stop, but another receipt, a
credit card charge for some store item, and again, a
nearby phone number of some creep. In fact, each of the
three subway stops corresponds to one of these kinds of

men. She was definitely up to something. I can feel it in my gut."

"It also brings back what Ogden said," Gunther added. "That she never surfaced where most junkies do, on the welfare rolls, or unemployment, or parole and probation. Like she had a secret nest egg."

Jim Berhle had finally worked out the kinks enough to sit down again. "I also wondered about that credit card. I know she didn't use it much, and the limit's low, but I was surprised she had one at all. Most junkies aren't that organized."

"What was the name of her primary girlfriend?" Gunther asked.

Sammie looked it up. "Louisa Obregon, nicknamed Loui."

"She said she'd seen a couple of boyfriends. Maybe we should get mug shots of these gentlemen and run them by her."

"Yeah," Sammie agreed, "add them to Bob Kunkle's picture."

The phone rang beside Berhle's elbow. He picked it up, muttered a few monosyllables, and hung up.

"That was Ogden," he told them. "Sounds like your loose cannon is at it again. Ogden told Kunkle on purpose that Ron Cashman used to work for an old hood named Manotti, but didn't tell him Manotti and Ogden are old acquaintances. Apparently Willy and another guy just finished giving Manotti the third degree, looking for Cashman. It wasn't a casual interest."

Crestfallen, Sammie stared at the floor. "Damn him."

*     *     *

"Christ," Riley Cox murmured. "I thought I was out of this kind of thing."

Willy didn't comment, but he knew the feeling. They were in Brooklyn's Red Hook district, a thumb-shaped appendage jutting into New York Bay below Governors Island. It was late at night and they were approaching a very large, very dark warehouse that sat at the end of an enormous concrete pier surrounded by cold jet-black water. The surrounding light show of distant buildings, twinkling like Christmas lights, and the muffled, far-off rumblings of the urban sprawl around them only enhanced their isolation. Falling back on their separate memories, neither one could shake a sense of foreboding.

They had made contact with Ron Cashman—or at least someone they hoped would turn out to be he. Buying illegal guns, unlike scoring drugs, was a tangled and cautious affair. Guns were expensive, high-profile with law enforcement, and easily traceable through serial numbers and federally mandated recordkeeping. Not only that, but the gun laws in New York specifically were among the harshest in the nation. No one with any survival skills was going to do business with the first joker into a neighborhood asking to buy a gun.

So, at Willy's urging, Riley had sent inquiries through his contacts about making a buy. After a lot of talk and negotiation, he'd eventually been told to come alone to the Red Hook warehouse and to bring six hundred dollars in cash. The deal was to purchase a new Glock .40, and ammunition, with an option to buy many more if the deal proved satisfactory. From what they'd been told, and as they'd been hoping, the discussions had piqued Cashman's interest. He was going to be there himself to check out this new, potentially big buyer.

The two men stopped in the darkness several hundred yards shy of their target.

"You got everything you need?" Willy asked.

"I got everything I got," Riley answered him. "I'll only know what I need when I find out I don't have it, like a missile launcher."

Their plan wasn't very sophisticated. It hadn't been allowed to be. Cashman's people had only told them to be near a particular pay phone at a certain time in order to find out the location of the meet. That call had occurred just twenty minutes before, precluding any chance of getting to the place first to check it out.

More than anything, that's why they'd both been nurturing memories of Vietnam: As they'd chronically had to do over there, they were going in blind.

And, as everybody knew, the worst time in these deals was when the product met the money.

Their choices were rudimentary: Either Willy went in first covertly and found a place to hide and observe, from which he could quickly move in as backup, or Riley went in first as the buyer—since Cashman knew Willy by sight—hoping that most of Cashman's team would then be focused on him and pay less attention to any additional company. They knew the opposition would keep an eye out for the cops, but that didn't preclude a single, trained man from slipping through.

They'd chosen the latter course of action, and after a few whispered exchanges to coordinate what little they could, they parted company, Riley slowly, carefully, and in plain view, walking down the rest of the pier toward the warehouse's primary entrance.

He wasn't armed, despite his rocket launcher comment and their assumption that the sellers would be. The core problem in these deals was that the guns allowed either party to try taking the other guy's offerings by force. In fact, there was a growing trend demanding that all weapons be left behind. Riley had chosen to do so even though the subject had never come up.

He reached the huge, partially open sliding metal door and sidled inside, stopping to let his eyes adjust to the gloom. The only light was the city's reflected glow coming through a string of skylights high above. Slowly, what emerged before him was a long, towering central hall extending the length of the building, with girders overhead equipped with traveling winches and catwalks, metal grid-floored galleries on either side about twenty feet up, and a series of large doors, some open, some closed, lining the walls on the first floor. Massive steel pillars stood like regimented redwood trees, two by two, all the way to the end.

The whole enormous place was as still as a tomb.

Riley proceeded to the distant far wall, as he'd been told, discerning as he went a small glimmering of light in the distance. There was moisture on the concrete floor—occasional small puddles of water or oil as black as onyx—and his footsteps, no matter how soft his tread, echoed off the walls to either side of him. He wondered how in hell Willy was going to enter undetected and, not for the first time, why it was he'd stuck his neck out for a dead friend and a complete stranger. Not that he didn't know in his heart. For all that he might have denied it, he hadn't felt this alive since returning from 'Nam.

"Stop."

The voice had come as from some celestial height, without an identifiable point of origin. Riley stopped, keeping his hands open and within plain view.

With a startlingly loud metallic snap, a light suddenly burst alive and surrounded him in a blinding white cone, making him squint in pain. He considered ducking away, to dispel their advantage, but knew that might be the last move he ever made.

"Why are you here?" asked the voice in a dispassionate, almost bored tone.

"Same reason you are."

"No games. Answer the question."

"I want to buy a gun."

There was no response from beyond the light.

A couple of minutes passed before Riley clearly heard the sounds of approaching footsteps, although he still couldn't see a thing. The voice spoke again, but this time from just beyond his vision, a mere few feet away, startling him.

"What's your name?"

"Waldo Upshriner. What's yours?"

The voice laughed. "Very good. You bring the money?"

"Turn the light off or you'll never find out."

Whether because of his tone of voice or the fact that his request had already been anticipated—which was far more likely—the light died as abruptly as it had appeared. The man with the voice waited patiently as Riley blinked and slowly got used to the softer glow of a battery-powered camp lantern atop a nearby fifty-five-gallon drum. Beside it stood two rough-looking men dressed in dark clothing, with guns stuffed into their belts. Whatever this was, it wasn't the romantic claptrap of the movies, where everyone wears fancy suits and pulls up in limos with ten bodyguards. This was a street-level business deal, as gritty as the surroundings in which it was occurring.

High above and nearer the front entrance, Willy Kunkle silently stepped onto one of the grid-decked galleries overlooking the vast room. He had located the one sentry outside, equipped with a walkie-talkie to give the alarm, and had knocked him unconscious without a sound. Then, not trusting to follow Riley's path, he'd opted instead to climb an exterior ladder and enter through a broken office window. Which had led him to where he was now, just in time to see the bright light replaced by the weaker one.

He could hear the voices of the three men, although not what they were saying, and hoped to hell things would continue smoothly, at least until he got closer. He removed his rubber-soled shoes and shoved them into his coat pocket, to be sure that the metal grating beneath his feet would not issue a betraying sound at the wrong moment.

Moving slowly, crouched low from instinct, his gun in his hand, Willy placed one foot before the other, as carefully as if he'd been treading razor-thin ice.

Below him, Riley was negotiating: "You said on the phone it was six hundred for the one piece. I can live with that this time, to show good faith, but I got to have a break if we're going to be dealing in quantity."

Ron Cashman—whom Riley recognized from Willy's description of the bandage especially—shook his head. "You think the risk goes down with more guns? It's just the opposite. Besides, I don't know you. Why should I cut you any breaks?"

Riley smiled. "'Cause you're goin' to want to know me. I got what you need. And don't feed me that crap about higher risk. I'm offering to buy fifteen pieces off you in one shot. What d'you think is riskier? One deal for good money, or fifteen deals where you got fifteen chances of selling to a cop?"

Willy was getting closer, had almost gotten to where he had the advantage over both Cashman and his henchman.

Cashman pulled his gun from his waistband. "What tells me you're not a cop?"

This time Riley actually laughed. "You knew me, you wouldn't ask." He turned and began walking away, adding, "You also ain't the only guy sellin' guns."

Cashman hesitated, either thinking things over or waiting for Riley to stop.

But Riley kept on walking, out of the lantern's immediate reach.

"Wait. Hold on. We got off on the wrong foot here," Cashman said, replacing his gun.

Riley turned to face him, but stayed where he was. "We stopping the dick-around dance, then? We gonna do business?"

Cashman let out a forced laugh. "Yeah, yeah. You show me yours, I'll show you mine." He reached into his pocket and removed a rag-wrapped bundle the size of a hardback book. He laid it onto the barrel's top with a deep, echoing clang.

Which was repeated by Willy as he brushed past a piece of unseen rebar leaning up against the wall and knocked it over with a startling, reverberating, heart-stopping rattle.

The reactions below him were simultaneous and immediate. The sidekick pulled out his gun and stared up at the gallery, partially blinded by the light near his head.

Cashman pointed his gun at Riley. And Riley dove for cover farther into the darkness around him.

Three gun flashes filled the air like a triple burst from a fireworks display—the sidekick shooting in Willy's direction, Willy shooting back, hitting the man in the chest, and Cashman firing at Riley Cox, who let out a grunt, spun around, and landed like a dead tree, bouncing without a twitch.

After that, it was a running firefight between Willy and Ron Cashman, with the latter sprinting toward the back of the building, shooting wildly over his shoulder, and the former keeping pace twenty feet above him, firing through the steel grate at his feet and sending up a row of sparks from the fragmenting bullets.

At the end of the gallery there was a staircase leading down to the ground floor. Willy took it three steps at a time as Cashman slammed through a door on the far wall and disappeared from view.

Breathing hard, his feet hurting from running on the grating, Willy didn't even hesitate at the door. Seeing Riley drop amid a nightmarish flashback that commingled with images of Mary and Nate somehow finalized a cycle in his head. As he had so long ago, opening his shirt to the enemy soldier for a clean ending to it all, so now did he go after Ron Cashman with suicidal intensity, exchanging self-protection for a longing to stop the guilt and confusion.

There was a hallway beyond the door, leading down a row of abandoned offices. Ahead of him, visible in the harsh light cutting in through a shattered window from a security lamp outside, Cashman leaped over a pile of debris, dove to the ground to use it as cover, and twisted around to kill Willy Kunkle.

But Willy didn't care. He continued running at full tilt, the bullets singing by his ears as Cashman fired in a panic, methodically squeezing off his own shots, making them count, until he stopped on top of the debris pile and was staring straight down at Cashman's crumpled, bleeding body.

The dying man looked up at Willy, his gun now beyond his reach, his eyes wide and white in the artificial light. "Don't shoot," he said. "Help me."

Given his fatalistic passion of moments earlier, Willy felt suddenly totally remote, Riley's inert body blending with countless other killed and mangled corpses, to be filed in a part of his brain he both cherished and loathed.

He used the trick he had earlier of pretending his dead pager was a cell phone, holding it up, half hidden in his hand, and saying, "I'll call 911 right now if you tell me what I want to know."

Cashman groaned, tried to move, and rolled his eyes. "Oh, Jesus."

"You killed my wife?"

"Yes."

"With dope you bought from La Culebra?"

"Yes."

"You killed Nate Lee?"

"Yes."

"You tortured him first to get the goods on me?"

"Yes. Please call."

Cashman closed his eyes briefly, like a man fighting off sleep. Willy knew he was running out of time.

"Why did you kill Mary?"

Cashman's breathing was becoming erratic, his fingers flitting against the filthy floor as if trying to escape their dying host.

"Why?" Willy repeated.

The eyes half opened. The answer came as a whisper. "She was . . . greedy."

The last word was an exhalation, and after it had drifted away, Willy felt utterly alone.

# Chapter 21

Ward Ogden's voice on the phone was lacking its usual friendliness. "Something's up you better see. A car'll be downstairs in fifteen minutes to pick both of you up."

Gunther groped in the dark to replace the phone in its cradle and peered groggily at the red numbers on the hotel's radio alarm clock. It wasn't quite three in the morning. He swung his legs out of bed, padded over to the double door separating his room from Sammie's, and pounded on it with his fist.

"Sam. Rise and shine. Gotta hit the bricks."

The door was yanked open with surprising speed and Sammie's face hovered before him, looking both haggard and anxious. "Is it Willy?"

"I don't know. Ogden just called. Told us to be downstairs in fifteen minutes."

Her face contorted with anger. "Shit, he's done it again," she burst out, and slammed the door, just missing Gunther's fingers.

They were downstairs in time to greet a patrol car as it pulled up to the curb of their marginally solvent hotel. The two men in the front were polite but claimed ignorance on the reason for the trip, admitting only that they were headed for Red Hook on detective Ogden's orders.

The found Ogden at the back of the empty warehouse, beyond a huge central room rigged with halogen lamps and a team of crime scene investigators. Outlined on the floor was the bloodstained drawing of a man, not far from another stain at least as big, along with a dusting of empty shell casings as thick as sprinkles on a doughnut.

Where Ogden was awaiting them, a second human outline lay sprawled behind a random pile of smashed-up office furniture. A gun rested just beyond the reach of one of the outline's extended arms.

Ogden did not look happy. "Two dead: Ron Cashman with three slugs in him, and a man named Franco Silva, hit once in the heart."

"I noticed a third stain," Gunther commented, keeping his voice neutral. He was very aware of Sammie's tension as she stood beside him, prepared for the worst.

"Man named Riley Cox," Ogden explained. "Badly wounded, but apparently not lethally. He's also refusing to talk. We checked his hands for gunpowder residue. He didn't have a weapon we can find, and right now it doesn't look like he fired at anyone, either."

"Which presumably leaves Willy as the missing party," Gunther filled in the blanks.

Ogden's response was terse. "Right. Not that we have any proof—yet."

"Have you come up with a likely scenario?" Sammie asked, her tone purposefully strong and professional.

"We've come up with a scenario, whether it's likely or not." He jerked his thumb toward the huge room behind them. "Some of it's from Cashman's lookout. We found him gagged and handcuffed to a chain-link fence outside.

His boss was supposed to sell a gun to someone, we think Riley, although the gun in question is missing. It was a one-gun deal, with the option of a bigger buy if everybody got along. We think your boy took care of the sentry while Riley played the front man. Then he snuck along the gallery to nail the other two. After that, who knows? Riley was found near the middle of the room. The paramedics were phoned by an anonymous caller, probably Kunkle. As for him"—Ogden nodded his chin in the direction of Cashman's last resting place—"it's anybody's guess how he died."

"You think he might have crawled here after the shootout?" Sammie asked hopefully.

"Not with all these shell casings. He was probably wounded, though. We found him face up and he had one bullet hole in the back. One possibility is that he and Kunkle shot it out western-style. There's a trail of shells all along the hallway."

"What's the other possibility?" Gunther asked, already knowing the answer.

Ogden looked at him grimly. "That Kunkle shot him where he lay. At this point, from what I've seen, I wouldn't put it past him."

Speechless because he knew it could be true, Gunther returned his gaze to the outline, wishing there was some way he could get it to talk.

"It's only fair to tell you," Ogden told him quietly, even gently. "I would seriously like to have a sit-down with Willy."

The dawn was just paling when Willy Kunkle drove into the ghostly quiet community of Broad Channel. One of the city's most unusual neighborhoods, Broad Channel was built on an ironing-board-flat island in Jamaica Bay, hemmed in by a few dozen other, uninhabited islands, and located midway between Kennedy Airport and the Rockaway Peninsula, all tucked under the sheltering arm of Brooklyn and Queens combined.

Despite the airport's proximity, it seemed as if Broad Channel should play host to the Fort Lauderdale set. So sliced into by parallel boat slips, it looked like a chunky comb on a map, and with its wildlife refuge neighbors and proximity to Lower New York Bay beyond Rockaway Point, it seemed perfect for those mega-rich who like both their banks and their recreation within arm's reach. In fact, as he glanced west across the water, Willy could just make out Manhattan's prickly skyline beginning to emerge from the night's tendrils.

But Broad Channel was no rich man's retreat. Surprisingly, it better resembled a forgotten Florida backwater for seasonal workers. The buildings were extremely modest, middle-class, mostly one-story wooden structures, packed together like mixed spare parts from a variety of construction sets, and lorded over by a congestion of sagging, heavy utility wires crisscrossing the main road from a forest of light, telephone, and power poles.

This wasn't a total surprise to Willy. He'd heard about Broad Channel, and its reputation as a pretty conservative enclave, suspicious of outsiders and any enlightenment they might bear. He'd also heard, deserved or not, that it was an aggressively all-white neighborhood, and that any and all strangers, regardless of race, were checked out pretty thoroughly.

If one could not afford to live in a gated community, but wished to leave most of the world at the door, this sounded like a fair compromise, assuming the locals let you in to begin with.

Willy slowed down and looked again at the address on the driver's license he'd stolen off Ron Cashman's body, along with his wallet and keys, and later his car, which he'd found parked just outside the warehouse. Broad Channel wasn't on any subway route, and Willy had known that he didn't have much time before the cops were called in to investigate the firefight in Red Hook. Stealing a car seemed the least of his problems now. Also, he comforted himself with the fact that the license, while equipped with Cashman's photograph, was in the name of John Smith, which he hoped would buy him some additional time. He hadn't ruled out that the address might also be fictional, of course, but it would have been foolish to simply make that assumption.

Craning over the wheel, he tried to read the street numbers unfolding in the half-light.

He knew he'd stepped over the line by now. Certainly the Ward Ogdens of the world would want him back in jail for the moment, and out of a job at the very least. And it was possible even Joe Gunther had reached the same point. Lord knows, Willy hadn't done much to encourage the poor guy to do otherwise.

But Willy was back in overdrive mode now. He'd survived his charge through Cashman's hail of bullets, he'd discovered that Riley was probably going to live and had done what he could to guarantee it with a 911 call, and he'd been given just enough through Cashman's last words to propel him once more toward resolving Mary's death. Never the best of long-range thinkers, Willy was once more consumed with a need to know and heedless of what it might cost him.

He finally found the street he was after, the equivalent of a wide alley lined by more squeezed-together homes, and drove down half the block before parking in front of one of the humbler residences.

He stayed put for a few minutes, with the engine and lights off, watching the street for signs of life. Three or four houses had lights on, perhaps in a bathroom or kitchen, but otherwise things still seemed acceptably dormant. Willy got out of the car, walked quietly and quickly to Cashman's front door, and slipped the key into the lock, hoping to hell the dead man didn't have a fondness for pit bull housepets.

He didn't. The place was absolutely silent.

By the dawn's strengthening light, Willy took rapid inventory of the small house, deciding how to maximize his time. He figured half an hour overall would be risky but acceptable.

The home's interior made its shabby outside look good by comparison. Cashman had been clearly uninterested in decor, or cleanliness, or even eating more than cereal, Spam, and/or bread. The whole place felt like a temporary lodging, which in fact it might have been. Given the phony license and his erstwhile livelihood, Cashman quite possibly had several home addresses. Willy could only hope that this one had more in it than dirty clothes, broken furniture, and dying food in the fridge.

He finally found the one exception in a small cubbyhole off the living room, which shared with it a large window overlooking the boat slip.

The desk in this tiny office was a hollow-core door laid across two filing cabinets and covered with bills, newspapers, several phone books from far-off states, three empty beer cans, a calendar with cryptic notations, an assortment of survivalist and weapon catalogues, a legal pad covered with doodles, arrows, boxes, and seemingly unconnected words, and a phone.

Willy didn't stop to read any of it at first. He was still in the reconnoitering phase, and eager to explore the contents of the filing cabinets.

A loud knock on the front door stopped him cold.

He froze in place, trying to imagine who might be outside.

"John? You in there? It's Budd."

Willy remained silent.

The knock came again, slightly heavier. "John. I didn't see you drive up. You okay?"

Willy very slowly rose from the chair he'd just sat in, careful not to make the slightest sound.

He clearly heard the door latch open and the front door swing back on its hinges. He'd forgotten to turn the lock behind him.

"John?" Now the voice was more tentative, betraying the first inklings of concern.

Willy realized his hoped-for half hour had just evaporated. Trying his best to sound vaguely like Cashman, he growled, "Yeah," and stepped behind the office door.

Heavy steps approached with renewed confidence, along with Budd's commentary. "Jesus, man. I thought you were dead or something. Why didn't you speak up the first time?"

Through the crack in the door, Willy saw a tall fat man flash by, sporting a tight T-shirt, a beard, and tattoos on both arms.

The sheer bulk of the guy dictated Willy's course of action.

As soon as Budd stepped into the room, Willy threw his

weight against the door, smashing it against the big man and sending him staggering into the far wall, where he hit his head. Not letting him recover from the impact, Willy reached him in two steps, grabbed his hair from the back, and smacked the front of his face into the wall a second time.

Budd collapsed like a felled ox, crumpling to his knees and coming to rest like a drunk taking a quick rest between swigs.

Cursing his bad luck, Willy returned to the desk, grabbed the calendar and the legal pad, and ran for the exit. Whether it was Budd waking up, another neighbor dropping by, or the police suddenly appearing, Willy knew his survival time here was now being measured in seconds.

He reached the car just in time to see a woman appear on the porch next door, squinting against the rising sun's first glare, trying to see who was at the wheel.

"John?" she called out. "Is Budd with you?"

Willy fired up the engine, did a squealing U-turn, and retreated the way he'd come.

The four of them were back in the interview room adjacent to the detective bureau—Joe, Sammie, Ward Ogden, and Jim Berhle. The mood, once enhanced by a camaraderie cutting across state and department lines, had chilled to where Joe Gunther was thinking he and Sammie might be asked to disappear at any moment.

It was midmorning of the day following the shootout and they were all living on a steady diet of coffee.

Ogden was the only one standing, pacing back and forth across the small room as he spoke. His tone of voice, however, while a little more concentrated, retained much of its familiar calm friendliness. If he did have problems with the Vermonters, he was keeping them to himself.

"Okay," he said. "Things are getting messy. I've got someone baby-sitting Riley Cox. He's definitely out of the woods, but still refusing to talk, and there's not a hell of a lot we can do about that. He didn't have a weapon when we found him, there were no drugs or contraband at the scene, so he knows all he has to do is keep quiet and this'll go away without a murmur.

"A crime scene unit was sent to Cashman's legal address in Sunset Park," he continued. "So far, they haven't found anything of interest that we didn't already know, but records search has revealed he had a car, which apparently now is missing."

"What about the lookout who was hooked up to the chain-link fence?" Sammie asked.

"Vinny West. Nothing there, either," he told her. "He lawyered up almost as soon as they took the gag off. What he did say was that he never saw who nailed him. He's got a similar background to the other dead man at the scene—Franco Silva—but nothing with either one of them seems to connect to our case."

"Actually," Jim Berhle interrupted in a surprised voice, "maybe we do have something." He hadn't been at the crime scene that morning, but now pulled a sheet of paper from one of the several files before him and studied its contents briefly before handing it over to his partner. "That's Mary Kunkle's luds and tolls. Look at the seventh number down. I wrote who it belongs to in pencil: Franco Silva. She called him twice in the past month and a half."

Ogden looked at the list with renewed interest. "No kidding? That's great. Any cross-reference to his address and her metro stops or receipts?"

Berhle immediately started pawing through the pile at his fingertips, eventually locating the map they'd all worked on earlier. "Right there," he said, tapping a marked spot with his fingertip. "Both a Metro stop and a receipt, not three blocks away. Sorry. I should have read your pink on the shootout. I would've caught Silva's name earlier."

Ogden waved that away and studied the map over his younger colleague's shoulder. Since Ogden had been working on other matters while the three of them had been collecting most of this, he was less familiar than they were with its particulars, which was one of the reasons for this meeting now. "Huh," he commented, "looks like we're getting a cluster in Brooklyn. Silva lived there, Cashman, Lenny Manotti . . . who's Michael Annunzio?"

"Right," Berhle said. "Hold it. That's another connection. I just remembered." He repeated his search and extracted a document, scanned it quickly, and smiled. "Known associates," he quoted, "Franco Silva. Small world."

Ogden tapped him on the shoulder with two fingers. "Nice catch, James." He straightened and peered down at them all. "What else? Did you run a picture of Bob Kunkle by Mary's girlfriend, what's her name?"

Sammie spoke up, although it wasn't really her place. She'd been feeling out on a limb ever since this morning, acutely aware that the one thing they'd studiously avoided so far was much mention of Willy. "Loui Obregon. She didn't know him."

"Right," Berhle added. "I went back and questioned

her and several other Re-Coop workers on Mary's habits. Now that we've got our suspicions about her, I was able to lead the discussion a little. I can't say I got much, but there was definitely a private part to Mary's life that she didn't share with any of them."

Ogden was back to pacing, his eyes running along the ceiling. "Okay. What about the Re-Coop? There were questions earlier about how it could operate the way it does."

Gunther took this one. "I did some digging around in whatever incorporation records were publicly available. It's a little hard to tell, and this not being my patch, I probably missed some resources you would've known to hit, but it looks like the primary backer of what's called the Re-Coop Foundation is a nonprofit charitable outfit named the Seabee Group. There're other supporters, of course, but Seabee was by far the heavy hitter. I ran out of time before I could chase that down, though."

Ogden pointed at Berhle. "See what you can do about that, okay? Almost sounds like the name of a boat. What's the timing on the DNA from the overalls we recovered from Mary's building trash compactor and the blood from Nate Lee's head?"

Jim Berhle shook his head. "We're still weeks away from that, or the samples the ME collected from under her nails. She did confirm that the blood wasn't Lee's."

Ogden picked up Mary's phone record again and peered at it. "What about John Smith? That sounds bogus."

Berhle shrugged. "For all I could find, it could've been a wrong number. It's way out in Broad Channel, the call lasted less than a minute, only happened once, and the

John Smith cross-indexed with that address is clean as a whistle. I even called it, but got no answer."

"Well," Ogden announced, "since the local Brooklyn precinct guys are working on the shooting scene, I think I'll go out and knock on John Smith's door. I gotta do something. This standing around is driving me nuts." He looked at Sammie and Joe. "You two can either stay with Jim and keep beating on the computer or grab some shut-eye. I'll kidnap whoever's sitting around the squad room to keep me company."

"I'd like to ride along, if that's all right," Gunther said.

There was a momentary silence. They all knew Ogden's generosity was wearing thin, and that this could only further erode it, but the veteran detective finally smiled, if faintly, and granted the concession. "Okay."

Sammie quickly played the team card. "I'll stay here and help Jim."

Berhle looked happy with that, so Ogden said, "Whatever," and headed out into the larger room to recruit someone from his own department to ride shotgun with him.

On the face of it, the trip to Broad Channel didn't make much sense. There was no probable cause to request a search warrant of the John Smith residence, Jim Berhle had gotten no answer when he'd called the number, and there was no reason to suspect that the number's appearance on Mary's phone record was anything other than an anomaly. But anomalies were what interested Ward Ogden most in cases like this, where he was being faced with an otherwise solid wall of nothing.

As things turned out, it was a fortunate impulse. As

soon as he, Joe Gunther, and the junior detective Ogden had tapped to come along emerged from their car at the Smith address and began approaching the front stoop, a large, bearded, tattooed man with a bandage on his head and an ugly expression on his face appeared on the next-door porch and shouted at them, "Who the hell're you guys?"

Ogden displayed his badge. "Police."

"We didn't call for you. Take a hike."

Ogden's face broke into a smile. "Well, we're here anyway. The head feeling better?"

The man touched the bandage by reflex, his eyebrows knitting. "How'd you know about that?"

"Lucky guess," Ogden answered him. "How'd it happen?"

Whether confused by Ogden's affable response to his own hostility or simply wishing he could get things clarified in his own mind, the big man came off his porch and crossed the five feet of lawn to join them, his tone softening as he drew near.

"Damned if I know. I went in there to shoot the shit with John a little, and the next thing I knew, the son-of-a-bitch coldcocked me."

"You had a fight?"

He looked contemptuous. "No, we didn't have a fight. I would've killed him if we had. I told you: He snakebit me. Hit me from behind."

"Damn," Ogden commiserated. "That's pretty weird. The two of you been having problems? What's your name, by the way?"

"Budd Wilcox. And we're really good friends. I saw him drive up around dawn—he's got crazy hours—and I went in to talk, like we do sometimes before I go to work.

I shouted for him a couple of times and he finally answered me from his office, so I went back there and that's when he hit me, first with the door, and then by smashing my head against the wall. Bastard turned my lights out, and I never did a damn thing to him. I had to call in sick because of this. Really pisses me off."

"I bet," Ogden said, eyeing the house with renewed interest. "So you never got a look at him. Did you actually see him walk from the car to the house?"

Wilcox stared at him dumbly. "What d'you . . . ? It was his car. I looked out once, it wasn't there, then it was. He'd just gotten home."

"You didn't actually see him."

"You saying it wasn't him?" he asked incredulously.

Ogden looked surprised. "Me? How would I know?"

Budd scowled and whipped around to face his own house. "Judy," he yelled, "get out here."

His wife appeared moments later, her face flushed and her expression ready for battle. She stopped dead when she saw her husband had company.

"You saw John this morning, right? When he drove away? This is the cops."

She nodded. "I called out to him. Asked him if he knew where Budd was, 'cause I thought they were together."

"You saw his face?" Ogden asked.

She gave him the same blank look Budd had earlier. "Yeah . . . well, sort of. He was in his car, pulling out."

"But you saw his face clearly?"

"No, but it was him," she answered belligerently. "Who the hell else would it be?"

Ogden murmured to himself, "Who indeed?"

Judy Wilcox studied them for a moment, shook her

head, and muttering, "Goddamn cops—frigging useless," turned and retreated into her house.

Budd faced them again, now totally perplexed. "Why're you here anyway?"

Ogden gave him a slow smile, as if a ray of sunlight had just slipped into a dark recess of his brain. He reached into his pocket and removed a photograph of Ron Cashman, which he showed to the burly Wilcox.

"You ever seen this man?"

Wilcox stared at it, stared at Ogden, and began to look angry again. "You jerking me around?"

"Not on purpose."

Ogden looked so ingenuous, Wilcox had no choice but to set him straight. "That's John Smith."

Ogden handed the picture to his sidekick, along with his cell phone. "Get us a search warrant for this place."

# Chapter 22

Sammie Martens unclipped the quietly vibrating pager from her belt and looked at the call-back number. She wasn't surprised she didn't recognize it. A stranger here, all she knew was that it wasn't a Vermont exchange. Probably Joe on one of a billion phones outside the building. She glanced around the small room she was sharing with Jim Berhle. "There a phone in here?" she asked.

He looked up from the computer screen before him. "No. Use one of the ones outside. Just dial nine to get out."

She stepped outside and crossed to an empty desk and punched in the number, reading it carefully from the pager.

Willy Kunkle answered after the first ring. "Meet me at the Greenwood Cemetery. Boss Tweed's tombstone."

The phone went dead.

Greenwood Cemetery was commissioned in 1838 and occupied almost five hundred acres in Brooklyn, just a few blocks inland from the Red Hook warehouse where

Ron Cashman had breathed his last. The primary inspiration for the much more famous Central Park in Manhattan twenty years later, Greenwood had many of that spot's sylvan touches, but being both a cemetery and reflective of a gaudier era, it was enhanced with some truly over-the-top flourishes. Pavilions, gatehouses, ornate shelters, fountains, reflecting pools, streams, lakes, and dozens of other oversized wedding cake accoutrements were scattered among the half million graves, monuments, mansion-sized mausoleums, and hundreds of statues to display a Gothic/Victorian vision of what heaven was thought—or hoped—to be like.

Sammie drove through a gatehouse that looked as if it had been stolen off the front of a thousand-year-old French cathedral, and after asking directions from a bored guard, meandered along a narrow half mile of curving, forested, paved hill-and-dale roadway, aware of the fact that the higher she got, the more spectacular became the view facing west, overlooking New York Bay and the rigid, serried ranks of stalwart Manhattan skyscrapers. The contrast between the two impressions—the cemetery's contrived Valhalla and the city's concrete commercialism—made Sammie feel she was part of neither, like a fly crawling across two overlapping photographs.

She slowed among a copse of trees near the top of an incline and pulled over on the outside of a gentle curve, having finally discovered William Tweed's headstone, downright demure given the setting and his own flamboyant reputation.

Sammie killed the engine and got out of the car, enjoying the sense, however artificial, of being in the countryside once more. She hadn't fully admitted it yet, but

New York's unremitting geometric solidity—its hard angles, lack of earth, and the peculiar way everything seemed to either run up and down or left and right, but rarely in nature's random way—was getting to her.

As if to communicate that fact to a kindred spirit, she crossed over to a nearby tree—large, old, and supporting a broad, comforting canopy—and laid her palm against its rough surface.

"Hey, Sam."

She turned to see Willy cautiously emerge from behind a statue-topped monument. He looked tired and worn.

She went to him, put her arms around him, and kissed his cheek, feeling his one arm loop around her waist and a shudder run through his body.

"I forgot how good this feels," he said, barely above a whisper.

"You should practice more," she suggested, rubbing his back.

"Along with a lot of other things."

She pulled away enough to look him in the face, struck by the total absence of his usual edginess. "You going to survive all this?"

He gazed at her with a sudden wave of tenderness. In its utter simplicity, it was a wonderful question: caring, supportive, and pertinent, all while being discreet. She wasn't asking for what he couldn't tell her. She'd neatly sidestepped the fact that they were both police officers and avoided asking him anything that might force him to either lie or admit to a malfeasance.

All she'd posed was the single core question. And all it had done was to render him speechless.

He buried his face in her neck and shut his eyes, feeling for the first time something other than the slow buildup of an indefinable, all-consuming heat that had been kindling inside him for longer than he could remember, and threatening to explode for the last several days.

"Come over here," she finally said, leading him to the low stone wall surrounding one of the lots. "Sit down."

They sat side by side for a long time, watching the gentle breeze barely ruffle the nearby branches, enjoying the smell of grass and the sound of water running, even superimposed as it was over the low, steady thrumming around them.

"Why do you stay with me?" he finally asked.

She'd asked herself the same question so many times, she didn't hesitate to answer, "Because your trying so hard has made it worthwhile. So far."

He smiled bitterly. "A man on the road to redemption?"

But she shook her head, well used to his deflecting cynicism. "I don't know where you're headed, especially now, but you've never taken the easy way."

His voice betrayed his skepticism. "And that's good, the way you see it?"

She took her eyes off the scenery to look at him. "Think about it, Willy. The people we deal with every day, most of them didn't start any worse than you, or suffer more than you have. They just quit."

He looked over the past few days, not just at what had happened recently, but at what he'd been forced to confront from years before, all the way back to his childhood.

"I don't know about that. Feels like I quit a bunch of times."

"Stopped, maybe. For a while. Like you're doing now, I hope."

She'd gone back to gazing at the trees before saying this, and he studied her profile with a sudden sense of revelation. What was it that made some people see things the way they did? He was so self-absorbed most of the time, he never paid much attention to such philosophical musings, finding it easier to simply ignore them. He was a pretty good student of human nature, funnily enough, smelling out people's inner motivations and often getting them to reveal what they didn't want others to see. But that was when they were opposed to him, like another hockey player in a face-off. He wasn't as good when it came to his own teammates. The effort expended on his behalf by people like Sammie or Joe confused him, since it wasn't something he ever practiced himself.

Looking at this woman whom he'd never bothered understanding, he was struck by her thoughtfulness, and embarrassed by his own lack of depth. When they'd become lovers, he'd been in turn stunned by his good fortune and dismissive of her common sense, but in both guises, he hadn't chosen to consider her view of that decision. It had merely been something he figured she'd soon see as a giant mistake.

Now, as stupid as it seemed, he realized she hadn't come to him on the rebound or out of pity or simply because she wanted someone to hold. She'd made a conscious choice.

And there was something else, something that harked back to an earlier situation that had baffled and angered him. During a case the previous winter, Sammie had gone undercover as a ski instructor, dying her hair blond and sporting the tight jeans and high-waisted parka she thought suitable for the job. He'd been furious with her for that, for looking so good, for making the role seem natural. He'd seen how everyone had appreciated her in purely physical terms, and had realized how easily he could lose her. Then, of course, that fear had only made him lash out as usual.

Not that this sudden revelation would necessarily help now. For his newfound respect for Sammie came saddled with an equally powerful conviction that he'd never be able to express it. Even as he watched her, filled with this sudden knowledge, he was at a loss for what to do.

As if realizing this, she stood up and looked down at him. "Do you know why you wanted to meet?" she asked, looking faintly surprised at how the words had come out. She corrected herself. "I mean, why did you want to meet?"

He considered both questions, and knew neither one could be given an honest answer, the first because of his own emotional inability, and the second for legal reasons.

He therefore chose the latter's more familiar terrain— he'd certainly skirted the law's finer points before.

"I was wondering how the case was going," he stated neutrally, hoping she'd work with him in tiptoeing through a metaphorically mine-laden conversation.

She did. Avoiding the shootout and the wounding of— and silence of—Riley Cox, she answered, "We found out Ron Cashman had two apartments, one clean and listed under his name, the other somewhere over near Kennedy Airport. They're going over that one right now. Joe called in with an update about a half hour ago."

"Find anything yet?"

She paused and rubbed her lower lip with her thumbnail. She was in a real quandary here. There was strong circumstantial evidence linking Willy to the shootout, although no actual witnesses who would talk, and certainly it made sense that he was the one who assaulted John Smith's neighbor in Broad Channel, possibly stealing something in the process. Not only did that make him someone whom the local authorities would love to put in an interview room, if not worse, it also certainly meant she shouldn't be discussing details of the case with him. Just being with him now put her in professional jeopardy.

Not that any of this was all that relevant, of course. Willy was going to motor on regardless of what she did or didn't tell him, and maybe her judicious release of some information might help him go where he needed to without getting killed or jailed. She wouldn't violate the black letter of the law, but she would tell him what she could because in her heart she knew it might be his only route to salvation.

"I don't know what they've found at the covert address. I only heard that Cashman was using the name John Smith, and that Mary called him there once from her home phone."

"She did?" he asked, surprised.

"Not only him, but other people connected to him. From her receipts and Metro cards and whatnot, we found out she was going regularly to Brooklyn and maybe meeting with several of these guys. Ogden has people knocking on those doors right now, too. I don't know what or how, but something's definitely starting to break with this case. For example, we think now that even though she wasn't rolling in dough, she had access to some secret assets. It would explain why she never went the traditional welfare and assistance route."

He absorbed that for a moment, remembering Cashman's last words about Mary becoming greedy. "What else?" he asked.

"Not much. We took your suggestion to look into the Re-Coop a little closer. Turns out some nonprofit named the Seabee Group is their major backer, but that's all we've got right now. I think Joe was going to study that more, but he and I are almost on the outs now. We've outlived our welcome."

She didn't explain why. She didn't need to.

There was an awkward pause. Now that they'd moved from their personal feelings to discussing the case, each of them was anxious about the other's welfare. The first topic made them yearn to stay here longer, the second almost guaranteed that any more time together endangered them both.

Willy ended the unspoken debate by getting to his feet. "Thanks, Sam. I better go."

She stood next to him and laid her hand on his forearm. "I can't ask what I want to. Maybe that's the way it'll always be—"

He interrupted her. "If you want to know have I stepped over the line, the answer is no. Enough to get me fired, maybe. But not the way you're worried about."

He looked ready to say more, to tell her things that seemed to be brimming up inside him, but he pressed his lips together tightly, as if physically biting the urge back.

She made the choice easier for him, kissing him and stepping away. "Will you at least try to come back in one piece?"

He smiled at her, again struck by how much she seemed to know of his inner struggles. "I will now."

He watched while she retreated across the narrow roadway, got back into her car, and drove away with a small wave of her hand. Then he stepped in among the surrounding headstones and extracted from his pocket the top sheet of the calendar he'd stolen off Ron Cashman's desk. Circled several times in blue ink on a date just following Mary's death were the initials "CB," followed by a phone number. The face of Carlos Barzún—La Culebra—rose up in his mind like a specter.

Ward Ogden sat back in Ron Cashman's rickety office chair and stretched his arms high above his head. The setting sun was angling in through the dirty window overlooking the boat slip, filling the dingy room with a greasy yellow light. He and a search team including Jim Berhle and the young detective he'd brought with him hours earlier had been combing through the contents of Cashman's two filing cabinets, deciphering what they could of the dead man's arcane and half-encrypted notes. What they had made for interesting if frustrating reading, detailing a range of activities far beyond what Ogden would have guessed from these modest surroundings. It was true that Cashman had also maintained that other apartment, as clean and respectable as the proverbial hound's tooth, but if his records were any reflection of his income, he could have afforded twice that and much more. Whether it was a credit to his discretion or simply because he had no love of material possessions was anyone's guess.

Ogden lowered his arms and studied the scene out the window. Joe Gunther was sitting on the edge of one of the docks overhanging the narrow, slightly mired boat slip, staring out over the view as if he were taking in the Grand Canyon. He liked Gunther, respected his low-key, hardworking style. The man gave credit where it was due, shared what he found, didn't put on airs, and nurtured his younger colleagues. In short, a cop without swagger or self-righteousness. Ogden could only rue that such a creature was so rare.

Which made his own predicament all the more unfortunate, since he was gong to have to tell Gunther that regardless of what Willy Kunkle might or might not have done—and the lack of any hard evidence so far was galling—the Vermont contingent was no longer welcome. The case was simply becoming too big and too complex, and it involved too many unanswered questions about both Kunkles, Mary and Willy.

It was a shame, and meant the loss of two good extra brains, but even Ogden could only skirt the rules for so long and by so far. The NYPD held its own fully accountable, often unfairly and sometimes with a vengeance. The dinosaur wasn't going to trade on his hard-won reputation and seniority for a bunch of outsiders, especially when one of them was running the risk of landing some serious jail time. In fact, Ogden was feeling a little uncomfortable that, having stretched this alliance out for as long as he had, he'd not only been carried away by a combination of intrigue, mutual respect, and cooperation, but had fallen prey to a pinch of old-timer's arrogance. He was still not above thumbing his nose at authority now and then, but in the past he'd usually been a little less obvious about it.

Until they all returned to the office, however, where he would finally lower the boom, he didn't mind passing along the interesting bits he'd collected. He felt he owed Joe Gunther at least that much, if only as a kindred spirit.

He leaned forward over the top of the ramshackle desk and rapped his knuckles against the glass.

He met Gunther at the front door as the Vermonter was rounding the corner of the house. "Go for a walk?" he suggested. "I need to stretch my legs."

They fell into step side-by-side and headed west, where the street ran straight to the water at the far end of the block.

"I'm sorry I've had to park you on the sidelines," Ogden apologized. "I think I've abused the system all I can on this one."

Gunther was already waving his hand dismissively. "I appreciate all you did. I know everything past the first five minutes has been pure courtesy. I thank you for that. Not many people would've been that generous."

Ogden laughed. "I wouldn't overdo it. I think I was more curious than anything, not to say a little embarrassed at having dropped the ball with the initial investigation. If you hadn't come knocking, we wouldn't be where we are right now."

"Which is where, if that's okay to ask?"

Ogden immediately set him at ease. "Of course. That's why we're taking this walk. I didn't want to push my luck back there with so many people around. It's starting to look like Ron Cashman was a high-ranking lieutenant in a major car theft ring, among other things. He ran guns and drugs to a lesser extent, I think mostly to keep his options open and maintain a sense of independence, but the big money was cars."

"Did you know anything about this ring before now?" Gunther asked.

"I didn't," Ogden admitted, "but Customs did. They have a task force with some of our people and they've been trying to get a handle on this bunch for a couple of years. Berhle's been on the phone with them for a half hour or more and they're about to show up, which'll pretty much bring our involvement to an end—another reason I'm going to have to cut you folks loose."

"Sort of frustrating, isn't it?"

Ogden shrugged. "Yes and no. They need something for all their efforts, too, and it's not like I don't have other things to do. Besides, we cracked it for them. I can rub that in if I get in the mood."

They continued walking a little farther before Ogden added, "It's not all altruism, either, so don't go thinking I'm plain old Mister Nice Guy. I didn't have Jim call the feds till now 'cause I wanted a long look at all that stuff first." He tapped the side of his head. "The old brain cells may not be what they used to be, but I love filing little factoids up there. You never know when they might come in handy."

Joe Gunther wasn't sure if this conversation allowed him to ask questions. He sympathized with Ogden's position, and while he didn't want to abuse that, he still had a big investment in reaching the truth.

"You find any reference to Mary Kunkle?" he asked with intentional vagueness.

Ogden smiled. "One thing we did find was a small electric key-cutting jig. Also, a lot of the names on her phone records match what we found in Cashman's files. Does that make you wonder what her role was."

"What do you know of the setup?"

"I'm no expert," Ogden cautioned, "but it looks like Cashman ran a whole crew of spotters, thieves, drivers, choppers, money handlers, and whatever else he needed to identify, steal, and get rid of high-end cars, mostly SUVs. From what I could see, he was shipping them right out of New York to places like Russia, the Dominican Republic, South America, you name it."

"How did that stay under wraps for so long?"

"He had a cell system. Old trick: You make sure none of your people knows anybody else inside the organization. That way, one of them gets busted, he's all the cops end up with. Pretty neat, really, but it takes brains and a flair for organization."

"Which explains why you think Cashman was a lieutenant and not the boss?"

"No doubt in my mind," Ogden agreed. "The problem with that kind of structure is that sooner or later, one guy is going to have more knowledge than the top man is happy with, unless, of course, that boss is running the whole show, which is pretty unlikely."

"Why?"

"Skill levels. The real brains with the international contacts is probably not going to be the same man who knows where to find and control the local worker bees. It's just asking too much of a single individual. Besides, it's clear from Cashman's files that he had someone he reported to."

"And that is?"

Ogden shook his head. "Dunno yet. That'll probably be up to the task force to figure out. Cashman just used a cipher name. It won't be hard to figure out, though, not with everything we found. We—or they—just need to turn over that one last rock. Then maybe we'll all get what we want, including you."

They'd turned back now in the ebbing light and had almost retraced their steps. Coming up even to Budd Wilcox's place, they were stopped by the oversized man coming out onto his porch and saying to them in a quiet voice, "I just heard John was killed."

Ogden reacted without emotion. "Where'd you hear that?"

"One of your patrol people."

Ogden frowned slightly, glancing at the group of uniforms gathered up the street. Gunther sympathized. No matter how professional the department, people liked to talk.

But Ward Ogden apparently saw no reason to deny it. "Yeah. Sorry you had to find out like that."

Wilcox stepped off his porch. He was carrying a large envelope in his huge hands. "That's okay. I guess he knew it might happen."

"How so?"

"He gave me this," Wilcox said, tearing open the envelope and spilling its contents out into his opposite palm.

"Whoa," Ogden burst out, startled at the big man's initiative. "Let me do that."

He relieved him of the documents and asked, "You know what this is?"

"Nope. He said to hand it over to the cops in the event of his death."

The phrase was said formally, and it was clear Budd Wilcox felt he'd just relieved himself of a chore directed from the netherworld. Without further ado, he turned on his heel, retreated to his porch, and said, just before closing the front door behind him, "It's all yours now."

Ogden leafed through the contents of the envelope in the light cast by a nearby streetlamp. He chuckled slightly and showed Gunther what he had. It looked like a date book, several letters, an address book, and a sheaf of documents. "Remember that last rock I was talking about? Well, here he is, and proof that Mary Kunkle was blackmailing him. No wonder she never showed up on the welfare rolls and was such a shoo-in to get into the Re-Coop. I guess Cashman was saving up for a rainy day."

# Chapter 23

Willy Kunkle stood in the darkness, as he had so often in years past, watching, waiting, one half of him alert and utterly tuned in to what was happening around him, and the other drifting, almost meditative, like a bird on the wing simply enjoying whatever breeze happened by. It was the part of his spirit that he usually put to sketching on a pad he routinely carried in his stakeout car, clipped to the steering wheel as an impromptu easel.

That struck him now as a quaint self-indulgence, like a combat soldier's daydreaming about mowing the lawn back home—mundane, incidental, and completely without meaning anymore.

It was close to midnight. He'd been standing outside Casey Ballantine's upscale brownstone in Brooklyn's increasingly trendy Cobble Hill district for hours, ever since he'd backtracked her address, rather than Carlos Barzún's, from the "CB" initials and the phone number on Ron Cashman's calendar.

Sammie's passing mention of the Seabee Group had been a lifesaver there, if a little misleading initially. Both the calendar and the legal pad that Willy had stolen from the Broad Channel house had proved confusing, cryptic, and largely counterproductive. Whether cautious or careless, Cashman had apparently been incapable of simply writing something down. Instead, he'd doodled, drawn arrows, circles, and boxes, and filled or connected them with initials and abbreviations whose sense was known only to him. There were dozens of these hieroglyphics covering many pages. Only Sammie saying "Seabee" had supplied the key.

Willy still wasn't sure what he was in the midst of tracking, though, having never heard of Casey Ballantine, but it was something, and given his growing impatience and his increasingly precarious position, he wasn't about to let the opportunity slip by. And there had been signs of life inside the brownstone: curtains being drawn and lights going on and off throughout his surveillance, as if someone had been moving around pursuing an evening's normal pattern.

Nevertheless, as the majority of these lights began to stay off, he started wondering about the benefit of standing there much longer.

Which was exactly when the last two lights died on the first floor.

Willy sighed, wondering what to do next. He'd known when he'd found this address that it was at best a long shot. Still, he thought, might as well wait another half hour.

It didn't take that long. Not two minutes later, the front door opened and a tall, blond, aristocratic young woman stepped out.

Willy readied his slender pocket telescope to get a closer look.

Keeping the door open with a small case she unhooked

from her shoulder, the woman, presumably Casey Ballantine, began ferrying in and out of the house a small
mountain of matching suitcases and several bags of what
looked like canned and boxed groceries. As she neared
completion, replacing the small case on her shoulder and
slamming the door shut, an upscale, oversized silver
SUV with New Hampshire plates appeared around the
nearest corner and came purring to a stop before the piled
luggage, followed moments later by a dark, very new
BMW with tinted windows.

No one got out of the BMW, but from the driver's side
of the first car, reminiscent of some doting hubby cater-
ing to an impatient mate, Andy Liptak emerged, apolo-
gizing with hand gestures and virtually leaping to move
the woman's possessions into the back of the larger vehicle. As he did so, however, throwing open the rear door
right in front of the other car's hood, he angrily but in-
audibly summoned the driver to help him out. Then, all
smiles once more, he went from lugging things himself to
directing this second man—large, slow-moving, and
transparently a bodyguard—in doing it for him. In the
meantime, he chatted with the young woman, pecked her
on the cheek, placed her case on the front passenger seat,
and generally fussed about.

After all the bags had been put away and the bodyguard had returned to his vehicle, Liptak gave his girlfriend a squeeze and a kiss, helped her into the huge SUV,
and waved good-bye as she drove off.

Then, clearly visible through the lens, his expression
metamorphosed once more, turning hard and purposeful,
and he walked back toward the BMW. Willy quickly
memorized its New York plate number, as he had the
New Hampshire one, and faded back into the shadows to

retrieve his own vehicle, which he'd exchanged for Cashman's stolen one hours earlier.

He turned on the ignition, but not the headlights, and pulled into the street about a half block behind Liptak's car.

This final revelation linking Liptak to Cashman was less the emotional jolt it should have been and more the settling of the keystone into an archway of time and events dating back to when Willy had introduced his wife to his erstwhile best friend years ago.

Even in Vietnam, Andy Liptak had been a user. Not of drugs, although he'd certainly indulged there as well, but of people, and of any situation that allowed for the smallest abuse of trust. He'd called it working the system back then, of course, using the age-old cliché of the morally corrupt, and in the context of Vietnam, it had in fact appeared just shy of a virtue. He wasn't killing anyone, at least, just lying, stealing, and enriching himself—something he almost had to stand in line to do. Willy—the Sniper—immersed as he'd been in far darker exploits of his own, had barely given it a second thought. Andy had been a welcome source of normalcy to him: a drinking buddy, someone who didn't ask questions and to whom the war had seemed almost a lark.

Only later, when they'd met up in New York, had Willy wondered about those details, if only fleetingly, sidetracked as he'd been by his own demons and poor judgment.

Now, of course, it all came clear to him, like an unnecessary epilogue at the end of a bad play, supplied to those spectators too slow or self-absorbed to have understood the obvious.

As a result, instead of the satisfaction such discoveries

usually gave him at the end of his knottier cases, here Willy just felt stupid and used—the last guy in the room to realize that the joke had been on him.

Depressed and distracted as he was by this realization, he didn't see a third car, its lights out like his own, pull into line down the street far behind him.

They were still in Ron Cashman's small, weather-beaten bungalow in Broad Channel, so many of them now that it looked like a dentist's waiting room for short-haired, type-A overachievers. Cars clotted the narrow, dark street outside, and murmured cell phone conversations and the muted squawk and hiss of portable radios supplied a steady backdrop to the inner sanctum meeting in the living room between Ogden and his bunch, and a whole new group from the Customs/NYPD task force that Ogden had mentioned to Gunther. Joe Gunther himself, taking advantage of the comings and goings and the fact that he'd become an unknown but familiar face over the last few days, had tucked himself into a corner, hoping to milk his interloper's status for all it was worth. After they left this place, as Ogden had told him, his ties to the investigation would finally be severed.

Phil Panatello, a small, intense, dark-haired man from Customs, was in charge of the task force and was occupying the center of the discussion with Ward Ogden.

"Do you have a record on Casey Ballantine?" he was asking.

"Not a thing," Ogden explained. "Which is obviously why he used her. Having no rap sheet and being the buffer between Cashman's operations half of the business and Liptak's management half, she basically became a fire wall. If it hadn't been for Mary Kunkle knowing both sides, we might still be wandering about in the dark."

Panatello picked up the contents of the envelope Budd Wilcox had handed over hours earlier. It was now getting close to midnight. "Right. So, what was her story?"

"Kunkle used to be Andy Liptak's girlfriend. From what we pieced together, after they split up and she got totally hooked on dope, the guilt kicked in and he began covering her basic financial needs, if just barely. That's obviously something he'd see now as a big mistake. 'Cause while she might've been grateful enough when she was scraping bottom—assuming she could think that clearly—after she cleaned up, she decided she was due some compensation."

"Is that where the Re-Coop comes in?" Phil Panatello asked, consulting another file.

"Maybe in part. Who knows if that was an incredibly ironic money-laundering device, or a deal Mary forced him to set up? There's a lot more digging to do yet. It's clear Mary's life took an upturn about six months ago— the rehab, the enrolling in school, the talk of future plans—which is also when she began contacting Cashman's people, presumably as a conduit to Liptak and his financing. But there's a ton of hypothetical thinking in there. We may never know all the details. We think we have a line on a secret bank account of hers that we were hoping might tell us more." Ogden paused to smile affably before adding, "All yours now, of course.

"You have to admit, though" he continued, "if she did force Andy to finance the Re-Coop, it would show off how complicated the psychology became in all this. It not only got her out of a jam, but a lot of people who'd been in her shoes, as well. 'Cause the Re-Coop deal is a good thing. It's not a con. They really do what they say they're doing, which makes Mary the person they should thank. I'm not saying she was just being altruistic, necessarily— another thing that bank account might show—and I don't guess we'll ever know what her ultimate plans were for Andy. But, considering her modest lifestyle and what we know she forced Andy to do, it doesn't look like she was such a bad egg. It might turn out she was blackmailing a crook not just for a little payback, but to be useful, too."

"Until Ron Cashman killed her, stole what she was holding over Andy, and then kept it for himself. That is what happened, right?" Panatello asked.

Ogden shrugged. "Probably wanted it for a rainy day. I'd almost bet he told Andy he couldn't find it anywhere. You have a location on Liptak yet?"

The Customs agent glanced over his shoulder at one of his men, who shook his head. "No. We think he's on the move. We hit his office an hour ago and found the place sanitized. Combining what you found with what we've been putting together, we have a pretty good picture of his operation, but not where he is. He has a wife out in Long Island. We've been grilling her ever since you called us, but she's clueless—had no idea what he did for a living, legit or otherwise, much less where he might be hanging out."

He handed Ogden a file and opened it to what looked like a flow chart to Joe Gunther, who was craning to see from his corner. "That's a breakdown of what we know so far. Liptak, through Cashman, grabbed cars from wherever he could get them—car dealerships, off the street, airport parking lots, even from way out of town— decided which ones would get top dollar either as parts cars or complete models, and then sent them to chop shops or to overseas and Latin American receivers, shipped right out of New York. Incredibly well organized. One of his people's favorite hunting grounds, by the way, was on both sides of the GW Bridge, which not only provides a quick getaway to New Jersey or New York when the heat's on, but where there're a bunch of limo storage yards to pick through for extra cars. That would explain how Cashman got friendly with La Culebra and how and why he bought the junk that killed Mary Kunkle. And you may be right about the Seabee Group. We found no mention of it anywhere—it was a totally separate deal."

"How did he keep the stolen cars under wraps?" Ogden asked.

"Empty eighteen-wheeler boxes," Panatello answered. "You see them in vacant lots all over the city. Some of those are as abandoned as they look, but most are put there by legitimate shipping container brokers. They get a call for a forty-footer, for example, and they spot it at whatever location they're given, no questions asked, for maybe thirty-six hundred bucks per. From there, the bad guys can either move it or fill it with a couple of cars, rig a dummy shipping document, and put it on a boat. Unless we tear into every big box in every port every day of the week, there's no way we can separate the stolen goods from the legit stuff. What we do find is almost nothing."

Ogden returned the file and waved his hand at all the documents and cell phones littering the table between them. "Is any of this going to help?" he asked reasonably enough. "Sounds like you're still at a loss."

But there, Phil Panatello looked more optimistic. "No. With Mary's facts and figures, we'll be able to shut him down, even if he splits the country. That's what we're doing now—using what you found to send people knocking on doors, checking warehouses, and rounding up peons. When the banks open in the morning, we'll hit him there, too. Guaranteed he knows we're after him by now, so we don't want to lose time."

The cell phone in Joe Gunther's pocket began chirping, making everyone in the room stare at him.

His face flushing, he removed it and held it up to his ear. He listened briefly, asked for a couple of clarifying details, and snapped it shut, looking directly at Ward Ogden. "I think we've got a fix on Andy Liptak."

The Bush Terminals line the Brooklyn shore below Red Hook like an endless row of abandoned, pre–World War Two beached tankers, lined up nose first to the uneven, broken-backed wide expanse of First Avenue. Dark, quiet, vast, and cavernous, they speak both of an earlier industrial might and of a changing world in which urban powerhouses like New York have yielded to an evolving national identity, leaving in its wake aging remnants, largely empty, in which only the occasional bare bulb advertises the rare, usually short-term tenant.

Willy followed the black BMW from farther and farther away as the midnight traffic thinned to near nonexistence at the north end of First Avenue. Even with his headlamps out, there was the odd security light that threatened to reveal his presence, so he played a game of hit or miss, sometimes letting the lead car get so far ahead that he risked losing it altogether.

It was with some relief, therefore, that he saw the car's brake lights blaze brightly one last time before suddenly swinging to the right and disappearing into the yawning mouth of one of the pitch-dark pier buildings.

Driving very slowly, he closed the gap by only a few hundred feet and then killed his engine to continue on foot. It was an odd sensation, leaving the cloistered security of the car. The huge buildings were so far apart and the spaces between them, once home to vast fleets of container trucks, so wide open that he felt as exposed as if he'd been the only man standing in the middle of a prairie. The vast, flat void of the water beyond didn't help, of course, introducing its own image of a cold and hostile hole in which the far-distant New Jersey shore lights vanished without reflection.

The building Andy Liptak's car had entered was far different from the dilapidated warehouse where Ron Cashman had died. This place was a shipping transfer station, designed to handle thousands of tons of material coming off cargo ships and headed for trucks aimed toward the nation's interior, and vice versa. An erstwhile maze of mammoth corridors, loading docks, and storage areas, it was now compartmentalized to serve a new hoped-for clientele of small manufacturers or people needing extra space for their excess inventory. Once a layout for maximum traffic flow, it had been cut up, diverted, and otherwise thwarted so that as Willy stepped gingerly into its midst, he was hard put to know in which direction to turn. Only by staying very still and listening carefully could he get some sense of activity off to one end of the building.

Slowly, watching for lookouts or warning devices, he began working his way toward the muffled sounds of voices, guided only by the crepuscular light seeping through the occasional broken window. It was like he was wandering through the heart of a gigantic tomb or the base of an ancient pyramid. The night before, in the warehouse with Riley, he'd felt more the way he had when he'd operated behind enemy lines. The familiar sense of calm focus had lent him an inner stillness from which to make decisions based on training and experience. Even when all hell had broken loose, he'd kept on task and gotten the job done.

Here, he was out of sorts, neither in combat nor police mode, thrown by circumstance to act alone and by instinct from a purely emotional basis. Cashman, like opponents before him, had been the enemy, a faceless target. Andy Liptak, by contrast, was wholly other. An old friend, a drinking buddy, a keeper of mutual experiences, the one person who'd known Willy as the Sniper, but who'd chosen not to treat him as such. Andy probably wouldn't have been accepted as a friend in normal circumstances. He came from a different world, even while being a fellow New Yorker. But in Vietnam, he'd filled a need that fate had chosen to prolong beyond the war, up to and including sharing time with the same woman. Given those facts, the memories attending them, and the sense of betrayal that had finally subsumed them all, Willy was left without much rational latitude. As too often in the past when his boldness had bordered on the suicidal, he was tempted to merely run screaming through these funereal, gloomy spaces, and have it out with Andy Liptak and all the metaphorical baggage he carried, once and for all.

A sudden outburst of sound snapped him out of his dark reverie, making him flatten against the wall as a shaft of light shot down the long, broad passageway he'd been traveling.

"No, Al, this is it for a while. I'm closing up. Things're getting hot. Cashman's dead and the cops are starting to swarm. If I were you, I'd lay low or pull up stakes. That's what I'm doing."

In the light, Kunkle now saw that the BMW was parked in the gloom just ahead of him, much as it might have been in an alleyway, except that here everything was under a single roof. Andy Liptak was stepping out of a side room, looking back over his shoulder and talking to someone Willy couldn't see.

"I wouldn't, not if I were in your shoes," Andy was saying to some comment Willy hadn't heard. "Take the money and run. That's why I gave it to you. You get greedy now, you'll just get caught. That's how the cops get most of the people they're after. Me, I burned my bridges or settled my debts, just like now. Lay low. It'll be a piece of cake."

He laughed at whatever he heard in response to that and moved completely outside the room, waving a hand. "Whatever, Al. It's been real."

Tired of the waiting, of trying to keep his thoughts in balance, of putting his hopes on a future free of the past, tired even of thinking at all anymore, Willy drifted into the light, his gun in his hand, and said, "Hey, Andy. Got time for one last debt?"

Liptak reacted as though he'd been splashed with scalding water. He spun around, his arms flung out, his mouth open in surprise, making Willy think of a bug flattened against a windshield.

"Jesus Christ. Sniper. What the hell?"

Willy leveled his gun at him, so tired it felt like lifting a cinderblock brick. "It's over. That's what. For all of us."

Liptak gave him a broad, strained smile. "Hold it, hold it. What's going on? What're you talking about?"

The man Andy had been speaking with appeared in the doorway. "You okay?" He paused, freezing in midmotion. "Oh, oh. Sorry, guys."

"Leave," Willy ordered.

The man named Al was instantly accommodating. "Sure thing. This way?" He pointed down the dark corridor.

"I don't care."

Al slid down and away from them both without further ado, adding over his shoulder, "Good luck, Andy. Sorry."

Liptak blinked once, slowly, no doubt impressed by his friend's loyalty. "You got a problem with me?" he asked warily.

"I don't have the energy," Willy answered. "I know you had Cashman kill Mary. I probably can't prove it, but that doesn't matter anymore."

Andy took a step toward him, his face showing how fast and hard he was thinking. "I'm going into my pocket for a cell phone, okay? Just two fingers, super slow. One call and I make you a rich man. You have any idea how much money I have? I give you three million bucks, I won't even feel it. Four, if you want."

"You really are a piece of work."

Liptak removed a phone from his pocket with his fingertips. Willy had never felt so exhausted.

Liptak moved the phone in front of him and took hold of it with his other hand so he could punch the buttons of the keypad. He was holding the phone awkwardly, pointing it at Willy. "Maybe I am. You have no idea what Mary had turned into. I supported her for years, giving her enough to survive but not so much she could buy a lot of dope. I took care of her, Willy, and it wasn't easy. She hated me for it—you know how crazy junkies get. And then after she got clean—again, thanks to me—she threatened to destroy me. She'd become a monster, man."

As he uttered this last statement, he fine-tuned the way he was holding the phone.

*"Willy. Dive."*

The shout was Sammie's, coming from the darkness behind him. Willy did as she ordered without thought, on pure reflex, just as a white-hot lick of flame appeared out of the cell phone's front end, accompanied by the sharp report of a small-caliber cartridge. As he bounced off the wall and fell to his knees, his left cheek stinging from the slug barely kissing him, Willy smacked his hand, lost his gun, and saw it skitter across the floor, vanishing from sight.

Andy Liptak didn't hesitate. Swinging the phone gun in Sammie's direction, he fired twice more into the dark, using her one muzzle flash as a guide. Her shot went wide, but one of his hit her in the leg, making her cry out and spin around. He then ran up to her, kicked her gun away, and grabbed her by the scruff of the neck, half throwing her toward his car. In pain, off balance, and surprised by his desperate violence, Sammie staggered and fell against the car's fender, where Liptak finally struck her cross the back of the head with the phone, further stunning her.

Willy was almost back on his feet by now, unarmed but intent on charging Liptak, when the latter fired wildly once more in his direction—a haphazard, almost incidental shot—and hit him in the heel of his shoe, knocking his leg out from under him.

Before Willy could get up a second time, Liptak had

tossed Sammie into the back of his car and slid behind the wheel. As Willy launched himself at the driver's door, Liptak gunned the engine and squealed away, careening down the enormous corridor toward the entrance bay he'd used not fifteen minutes earlier.

Willy was left on his knees, his one good hand supporting him, looking like a three-legged dog.

With a sound wedged between a shout of rage and a strangled sob, he staggered back to his feet and began running toward his car.

# Chapter 24

It was a fruitless effort. By the time Willy reached his car, Andy Liptak's BMW was long gone. Nevertheless, trusting to instinct, Willy took off in the direction he'd seen Liptak use, flooring the accelerator and paying no attention to any obstacle that couldn't either be ignored or defeated by the weight of his vehicle. He rammed trash cans, destroyed parking meters, creased several parked cars, and burned through every red light he encountered in his effort to catch some glimpse of the black German car.

Beneath all this frenzy, though, his instincts were still at work, for in short order he found himself within sight of an on ramp to the Gowanus Expressway, one of his tires flat from hitting a curb, but in time to see the BMW heading north at high speed.

As frustrating as that should have been—his quarry within reach but his car out of service—Willy was instead seized with a cold, calm confidence. He knew, as surely as if he'd been left a detailed map, where Liptak was headed. All he'd needed to see was the direction and the fact that Andy had chosen a freeway to take.

Twenty minutes later, his tire changed and his spare gun moved from his glove box to his pocket, Willy was driving north toward Portsmouth, New Hampshire.

It was a long drive, propelled by anxiety and self-recrim-ination, but accompanied, too, by the realization that the city had slipped behind him like a bad dream after an abrupt awakening. Willy drove automatically, steady and very fast, trusting to luck that he wouldn't be pulled over, feeling with each passing mile a sharpening sense of pur-pose. This was his third hasty departure from New York—once to go to war, once in an attempt to escape his past. This time, the most precipitate, also found him the most resolved. With his own fate as tenuous as ever, he felt the job at hand had never been clearer. There would be no second-guessing now. No walks along the road or procrastinating at a diner, as there'd been when he'd left Vermont to find Mary in the morgue. New York, in its confusing, contradictory, all-enveloping way, had finally seen fit to set him free.

He stopped once at a pay phone to call a friend of his in the New Hampshire State Police, telling him he was on a case and needed the address for the license plate he'd memorized off of Casey Ballantine's SUV. He was given an address in exclusive Castle Island, New Hampshire, located in the mouth of Portsmouth Harbor. He felt no elation or sense of luck turning. He'd remembered Andy mentioning a house in Portsmouth. All this information did was specify his target.

Besides, self-congratulation, never his strong suit, was now as remote as his ability to grow a new arm. All his thoughts through this long, sleepless night were on Sammie, on her miraculous appearance at the last moment, on the fact that she'd tailed him from their meeting at the cemetery, against his wishes. It had been a rare show of willful independence, shown not only for his benefit, but in defiance of the caution that cops especially were supposed to honor.

It wasn't just her recklessness that so moved him, however, although that was certainly impressive. It was that she'd acted instinctively. Much was made of the fellowship among cops—how they stuck up for each other, created the ballyhooed "thin blue line"—and Willy himself, though he never used the term, had demonstrated that same loyalty.

But rarely had it ever been extended toward him.

It had come time to pay homage, regardless of the confusion that might cause in a man so supposedly committed to solitude and hostility.

Joe Gunther, Ward Ogden, Jim Berhle, Phil Panatello of the Customs/NYPD car theft task force, and a host of others all showed up at the Bush Terminals building shortly after Willy had left in pursuit of Andy Liptak. Responding to Sammie Martens' call to Joe that she'd followed Willy here and was about to enter the building, what they found instead were Willy's service weapon, a .40-caliber shell casing, fresh tire marks, a small amount of blood, and, eventually, a rental car in Sammie's name parked up the street.

Feelings were running high. Officers were missing, along with the primary suspect, and evidence of gunplay was clear to see, as was the fact that it had all transpired without any knowledge or sanction. In a department well known for lopping off the heads of people found responsible for screwups, even Ward Ogden's lofty perch was beginning to look assailable. It was only he and Gunther working together as a choir that convinced the doubters—including Ogden's Whip—that without these supposed Vermont renegades, the case would never have progressed this far. Things were looking a little chaotic, fair enough, but in chaos there was still movement, and it was pretty obvious *something* was definitely in motion now.

That indefinable something was a major help to Gunther's and Ogden's cause. Rather than going head-hunting to lay blame, everyone knew the order of the day was to find the two missing officers and to help them if possible.

In that pursuit, the previous plan of waiting until the banks opened in order to peruse Andy Liptak's finances was scrapped in favor of a far more aggressive strategy. Now they would round up every known associate from the information they'd gathered, and grill them until something surfaced. Also, alerts were put out on Willy Kunkle's car and on anyone resembling him, Sammie, or Andy Liptak.

Joe Gunther at last found himself out in the cold. Ward Ogden told him privately to go back to his hotel room and wait by the phone.

For Gunther, a company man, the request was hardly news. Nevertheless, it would result in one of the most anxious nights of his career.

Willy Kunkle arrived at the Castle Island address just as the dawn was defining the ruler-straight line where the

Atlantic Ocean met the sky. The house was a traditional New England monstrosity with a huge wraparound porch, a castle's worth of dormers, turrets, and stained-glass windows, and a lawn running down to the water and deserving of a Kennedy touch football game.

It was also as dark as a tomb. The high-end silver SUV was parked alone at the end of the drive, tucked under a broad portico to keep it safe from the elements.

Willy drove by the place and killed his engine on the edge of the road, knowing it wouldn't be long before either some rental cop or the real McCoy would notice it and call it in. While not literally a closed compound, Castle Island had all the trappings of one.

Not that he cared. He knew he hadn't passed the BMW on the drive north, which implied that Liptak had ended up somewhere other than this address. The time factor that had pushed Willy this far at breakneck speed was narrowing fast, he sensed. Liptak's grabbing of Sammie had been purely impulsive, the spontaneous slipping of an extra card up his sleeve. But now that he'd had time to reflect, he knew that in fact the reverse was true: Kidnapping a cop could only bring him more trouble.

He'd have to kill her or dump her as quickly as possible, so Willy didn't have time to worry that his own activities might be flagrantly illegal.

He ran across the broad lawn in a crouch, although aside from the possibility of a dog's coming at him, he wasn't much concerned with being spotted. In fact, as his reckless momentum took over, he sprang up the porch steps two at a time, shifted his alignment to favor his good shoulder, and simply continued right on through the glass front door, half falling into the lobby amid a galaxy of flying shards. Staggering, he pulled his backup gun out as he continued up the oversized staircase ahead of him, figuring that wherever Andy's blond girlfriend might be, it was probably in an upstairs bedroom overlooking the water.

His choice of doors at the top proved only half right, however, but it was the half that turned out to be a life-saver. He burst into an empty bedroom, cut through an adjoining bathroom, and into the master bedroom beyond, just as the disheveled, half-dressed woman on the bed fired a wild, preemptive round with a shotgun at the room's front door. Willy saw her in profile in the enormous muzzle flash, covered the distance between them in four long strides, and simply took her out from the side like a linebacker, sending them both flying off the far end of the king-sized bed.

Willy rolled as he landed, taking the woman with him, and ended up on top of her, his knees pinning her arms, staring down into her startled wide-eyed face.

He slapped her once, hard. "Where's Andy?"

She screamed out in pain. "Oh, please. Please. Don't hurt me. If you want money, I'll show you where it is. But—"

He slapped her again, hoping to build on her panic to get what he was after. "Listen to me. I want to know where Andy is."

She was still trying to hide her face from his attacks. "Oh, please don't. Please—"

He shoved his face to within inches of hers and repeated slowly, "Tell me where Andy is and I disappear. Right now."

She blinked a couple of times. "Andy? He's coming up. He'll be here soon . . . with a lot of men," she added as an afterthought.

Willy raised his hand and she cowered, her legs scrabbling beneath him as if that might help her escape.

"He's not in New York," Willy said, "he's not coming here, and he's running for cover. Where would he go?"

Her answer was startling: "The prison."

Willy stared at her. "What?"

"The prison at the Portsmouth Navy Yard. He's renovating it. Took it over from a developer who ran out of money. He spends a lot of time there. He called me on my car phone a few hours ago and told me he'd be going there first. I don't know why, but that's why he said he'd be late. He told me not to go there."

Willy straightened and took his knees off her arms. "Roll over."

Her face crumpled up in fear once again. "Oh, no. What're you going to do?"

Willy scowled at her. "Jesus, lady. Put it in park. Roll over. Hands behind your back. *Now.*"

She did as she'd been told. He pulled off the silk belt she had looped around her pajama shorts and tied her hands together. He then looped the free end several times around the bed's foot and secured it there to keep her from crawling to where she might cut herself free.

"Thanks," he then said, and left her lying on her face.


Back in New York, Joe Gunther got the phone call he'd been waiting for all night.

"Joe, it's Ward. We're taking a Customs chopper up to Portsmouth, New Hampshire. Liptak's got a place near there—someplace named Castle Island."

"I know it. Very fancy neighborhood. What makes you think he's there?"

"I'm not sure we do, but your boy Willy does. His car was spotted abandoned near the house. You want to come along? This being your people, Phil Panatello has no problem with it."

"Of course I do," Gunther answered. "You have local liaison up there?"

Ogden hesitated. "Not yet. I don't think so."

"Contact Janet Scott of the Portsmouth PD. She'll do what needs to be done. One of the good guys."

"Got it. Here are the directions for getting to the chopper."

# Chapter 25

The Portsmouth naval prison is one of the region's oddest landmarks. Located on the eastern edge of the large island housing the Navy Yard, the now-empty prison dominates most inland vistas like a cross between an ancient fortress and a gigantic, Stalinist apartment block. It is at once stately and hideous, alluring and repellent. Built at the turn of the twentieth century and nicknamed the Castle, it was designed as the Navy's premier high-security facility and made to the then-popular template of Leavenworth and comparable hellholes, complete with stacked and terraced jail cells, electrically controlled sliding doors, and shooting galleries for the guards—a James Cagney movie hauntingly frozen in concrete and steel.

Unaware his car had been identified and was now under surveillance, Willy drove to Seavey's Island, showed his badge to the guard at the gate, and was waved through without further effort. Once a beehive of Eisenhower's "military/industrial complex," the Navy Yard was thinly manned now, enough that periodically it had to justify its existence before congressional subcommittees—an unheard-of humiliation in the old days. As a result, while parts of the island were still closely guarded, a good chunk of it was virtually open to the public, an aspect some initial investors had hoped to bank on by transforming the prison into a business condo with some of the best views in town. Until their funding crumbled with only a few rooms gutted and refitted with new windows.

Willy had no idea what Andy Liptak's plans were when he bought the lease from those disappointed visionaries, but he suspected money-laundering probably played a role.

The day had fully arrived by the time he parked nearby. There was a modern bachelor-officer's housing unit within twenty yards of the prison's west wall, so the presence of vehicles went without notice, and it was already late enough that the owners of those cars were at work elsewhere on the island.

Willy took his bearings. The building lay along a roughly north-south axis. It had a central portion resembling a castle keep—ergo the nickname—complete with four looming, crenellated corner turrets, and two asymmetrical wings, both shorter and narrower and equipped with smaller, evenly spaced turrets of their own. The whole was utterly massive, if neglected and weatherbeaten, and seemed well endowed with windows, until closer scrutiny revealed that all of them had been tightly boarded up, lending to the place the look of a medieval Playmobil toy hormonally run amok.

Architectural integrity, however, had been altered long before the windows had been sealed. The "new" section, also called the Fortress, had been tacked onto the tail end of the southern wing to handle World War Two's excess population. Its axis was east-west, it was as tall and massive as the central Castle, but while it tipped a hat to the

Castle's architecture with a single turret and some arched windows, the turret was square and the windows were graceless, and the overall aspect was so bland, white, and blockish, it ended up looking like a Montgomery Ward warehouse in need of repair.

But it was also where Willy saw his best hope for gaining entry. The Fortress had been where the developers had done their truncated remodeling and in the process had both breached the exterior walls and punched holes in some of the rusty chain-link fencing designed to keep out trespassers.

Willy cautiously crossed to the foot of the Fortress's walls and cut around to the south wall to get a feel for his surroundings. Before entering this abandoned behemoth, he wanted to know how the ground lay around it.

In fact, it was remarkably desolate. Despite its location in the middle of a major city's harbor and on the edge of a military base, the prison had a distinctly lonely feeling to it. Virtually surrounded by water on three sides and at the farthest distance possible from the island's busiest spot, the building seemed shunted aside, as if not just history but geography had decided its usefulness was firmly in the past.

This isolation became an advantage on the other side, however, and helped explain the eagerness with which those long-vanished developers had eyed the property. The harbor; the city of Portsmouth; the string of bridges spanning the Piscataqua River; Kittery, Maine; and Castle Island, all stretched before it like a peaceful, unblemished maritime panorama. And as if in poignant and ironic contrast to the building he was about to enter, Willy was startled to see the ancient, tumbledown Wentworth-by-the-Sea Hotel just across the water, once host to moneyed visitors from Boston and elsewhere, standing in stark contrast to the far harsher quarters behind him. What feelings those jailed sailors must have had a half century ago, watching the rich and famous being liveried to and from this monumental watering hole, and listening to the laughter and music that once must have emanated from its open windows on a summer night.

Now, both abandoned, empty, and falling apart, they stood as mute witnesses to bygone times, as anachronistic and retrospectively romantic as the contrast between Sing Sing and Jay Gatsby.

Willy, however, saw all this only in passing. What caught his eye and heightened his anticipation was the black BMW parked out of the way, under a tree, as discreetly as possible. Running the risk of being seen, he trotted over to the car and glanced inside, finding what he thought he might—a smear of blood across the back-seat—but which still didn't look as bad as he'd been fearing. From that scant evidence alone, he took heart that Sammie was still alive.

He returned to the most likely breach in the prison's exterior wall and slipped inside.

Joe Gunther pointed to the tall, blond, athletically built woman in uniform who was standing by the edge of the helicopter landing pad.

"That's Janet Scott," he told Phil Panatello, shouting over the sound of the rotors.

They waited until the crew chief gave them the thumbs-up before jumping out of the aircraft, instinctively ducking as they jogged over to where Scott was waiting.

She gave Gunther a smile as he drew near. "Hey, Joe. Long time. You're traveling in style. I didn't know you were a part of this."

"More of an outrigger than a real part," he admitted, and made introductions all around.

She directed them away from the prop wash into a small concrete building that doubled as a waiting room.

"This is what we've got so far: Your Willy Kunkle apparently broke into the Liptak house—smashed the door down—smacked her around a little and forced her to tell him that Liptak might be holding out in the old naval prison on Seavey's Island." She cast a glance at Gunther. "He really one of yours?"

"As is the one who's missing."

"Granted." She held her hand up as Panatello opened his mouth to say something. "Anyway, that was her story, and it's true that we found her hog-tied on the bedroom floor. But we also found a twelve-gauge hole in the bedroom door where she tried to kill Kunkle as he entered, except that he came in through a different door."

"What about Kunkle?" Panatello asked.

"He went straight to the prison. He was seen scoping it out, including the beemer parked on the far side, and then he ducked inside." She checked her watch. "That was about twenty minutes ago. I've since assembled a multidepartmental tac team and parked them out of sight all around the place, on the water as well. There is blood, by the way, covering the car's backseat."

That introduced a pause in the conversation.

"And there's been nothing since?" Joe Gunther finally asked.

"Not a peep."

Gunther stepped away and absentmindedly watched

the chopper crew through the window as they secured their craft to the helipad. Behind him, Scott and Panatello coordinated how to get to the prison without attracting undue attention.

"Worried about your people?"

Gunther turned at Ward Ogden's quiet, resonant voice.

"Willy especially," he admitted. "Mostly because of what he might do. I mean, Sam could be dead by now, which would damn near kill me, but Christ only knows about Willy. He's already in enough hot water—but that'll probably be nothing compared to what he comes up with next."

Ogden smiled enigmatically. "Water may not be that hot."

Gunther's eye narrowed. "Meaning what?"

"Panatello and I were talking during the flight. If he agrees to play along, Wild Willy might just duck this bullet—for the most part, at least. Roughing up Casey Ballantine'll need a closer look by the locals, but right now, from a legal standpoint, what he did in New York might not even surface."

"He shot Cashman, for God's sake."

Ogden shook his head. "Somebody did, but we don't have any evidence and Riley's not talking. Same thing with the assault on Budd Wilcox—he never saw who hit him—thought it was Cashman. And Lenny Manotti's never going to say he was pushed around by a one-armed man. Panatello's bunch are going to be busy enough without dragging Willy into it.

"And," he added, "the Casey Ballantine thing up here'll probably end up in the same place. She'll be way too busy trying to stay out of jail to be pointing fingers at Willy Kunkle."

The voices behind them rose up as people began crowding the exit. Ogden laid a hand on Gunther's shoulder. "I'm not saying I'm right, and I'm not saying it won't all be moot depending on how crazy he gets today, but if I were you, I wouldn't worry about his legal problems too much.

"Of course," he put in almost as an afterthought, "I'm also not sure I'd let him out of Vermont for ten to twenty years, either."

The first floor of the Fortress looked like the aftermath of an earthquake. As Willy picked his way carefully through the debris left by the remodelers, he was impressed by both their ambitions and their destructiveness. Walls had been sledgehammered through, holes chopped into ceilings, and massive piles of glass block windows had been gathered where more conventional windows had replaced them. The logic of their plans was just barely discernible through the rubble, and he had to admit, what with the open spaces and the generous views, it did look like a potentially attractive workplace.

But it was also empty of any signs of life. If Liptak was here, he'd apparently tucked himself away inside the building's older, so-called Castle section.

Willy found a single door connecting the addition to the mother ship: a narrow hallway on the ground floor, a concrete tunnel with a gaping, open steel-barred gate, leading into a void so dark, he felt he was stepping into pure space.

His already cautious progress slowed to a tentative creeping, and he placed each foot carefully before the other, gently pushing aside any trash and rubble on the floor to avoid crunching it underfoot. He even opened his mouth to breathe so that he could better hear whatever might be awaiting him.

By the time he reached the end of the connecting tunnel, he was walking blind. He extracted from his pocket a small flashlight he always kept on hand, and, after listening carefully, held it as far away from himself as possible, in case it was used as a target, and switched it on.

What appeared before him was like a still from a black-and-white movie: a long, constricted, towering slit of a corridor, with a wall of boarded-up windows on one side and a stacked tier of rusty caged-in galleries on the other. Both the ceiling and the end of this long room extended beyond the reach of the tiny flashlight, and in the silence he could imagine the voices of thousands of confined men, their hands gripping the bars, or playing cards on the floor between cells. In the still dampness of the air, he could all but smell the sweat, the bland food, and the stink of hundreds of toilets. Willy had visited old, overcrowded prisons before, some almost as decrepit as this one, and knew too well what was missing from the picture now before him.

Satisfied that his light hadn't given him away, Willy took his bearings and found a staircase leading up, walled with more bars. Still moving gingerly, he climbed to the next level, which also took him to the building's west side. There, he came to a balcony inside the second-floor gallery, a row of cells on the right, and instead of a conventional railing to the left, a wall of open vertical bars as far as he could see. The same gloomy silence prevailed, but the sense of vastness was reduced. Now he felt truly entombed, wrapped up by darkness, silence, and aging steel. Everything was made of metal, from floor to overhead canopy, and from everything hung large flakes of peeling gray paint, making him feel he was brushing alongside an endless length of stretched-out alligator skin. As he walked as softly as possible across the debris-strewn floor, past cell after devastated cell, each with its own rusty bedsprings, toilet, and sink, and each choked with the small, accumulated rubble of the ages, he felt himself being swallowed whole.

The trip felt interminable, but eventually he came to the end of the gallery, to another set of stairs, and finally to a passageway leading to the prison's central administrative area—the heart of the Castle proper.

There he found himself on a balcony with an ornate wrought-iron, mahogany-topped railing, overlooking an immense, three-story-high reception area with an enclosed section in the middle, much like a teller's cage, and several grand staircases more suitable to a European-style hotel. It was like stepping from Devil's Island into the lobby of the Ritz, albeit right after a bombing run.

Now he was at a loss. The mezzanine he was standing on split in two directions, surrounding the great hall below him, and he also had a choice between the stairs leading both up and down to the ground floor, all with nothing to indicate which direction to follow. Instinctively, he killed his small flashlight to help himself rely solely on his hearing.

A faint scraping sound drew his attention toward the northwest. Turning the light back on, he took the left branch.

This led him to another door, a second slightly smaller room with erstwhile offices lining the walls, and the first trickle of daylight presumably from an unboarded up window.

He pocketed his flashlight and replaced it with his gun. The scraping he'd just barely heard earlier was now loud, rhythmic, and definitely coming from one of the offices ahead.

Barely breathing at all now, Willy sidled up to the entrance, aware of the tiniest sound from beneath his shoes, and very slowly peered around the corner.

Sammie Martens, bound, gagged, and with a large bloodstain on her right leg, lay propped up against the wall, under the open window where the marks on the floor indicated she'd dragged herself with considerable effort, digging her heels into the floor and pushing again and again.

Willy swung rapidly into the room and crouched to one side of the door, his gun covering the area before him. The room was otherwise empty.

He straightened and crossed over to her, immediately slipping the gag from her mouth.

"Jesus," she said in a whisper. "You're a sight for sore eyes."

"You, too," he admitted, putting his gun down so he could work on the knot binding her hands behind her back. "How bad are you hit?"

"Hurts like a son-of-a-bitch, but I can walk. Bullet's still in there, though."

Willy thought back to the cell phone gun Liptak had used on her. "What the hell was that, anyway? How'd you know it was a gun?"

"We got an alert on them a few weeks ago. Something you threw out, probably. They're the latest rage. I thought of it when I saw how he was holding it."

He gave her a quick, almost embarrassed kiss. "Yeah, well, you saved my butt. Where is he now?"

She shook her head. "Somewhere around. He has a real cell phone he's been trying to use. It didn't work down here, so I think he went up."

Willy glanced over his shoulder at the door. "Which way?"

"Turn right. You got anyone with you?"

He looked at her without comment as she began rubbing her chafed wrists and rolled her eyes. "I should've known."

"Stay put," he said, and quickly left the office.

Turning the way she'd indicated, he saw a small door in the far corner of the central room, and beyond it, barely visible in the gloom, a spiral staircase. He realized he was looking at the interior of one of the Castle's four large central turrets he'd seen from the outside.

His gun ready once more, he'd barely started walking in that direction when a figure appeared in the doorway with the suddenness of an apparition.

*"Don't move,"* Willy shouted, leveling his gun.

But Andy Liptak was having none of it. As quickly as he'd appeared, he backed into the stairwell and vanished, accompanied by the sound of footsteps pounding on hollow metal stairs.

Willy ran to the door, paused, and quickly stuck his head past the doorjamb. As in a turret of ancient times, the staircase was a tight spiral, hugging the round walls around the center of a sheer drop, and lit solely by the feeble daylight seeping through the occasional firing slit. The sounds of Liptak's retreat came from above.

Willy gave chase without hesitation.

He ran, taking the steps two at a time, fueled by the same adrenaline that a marathoner uses to make it to the finish line. And finishing is what Willy had solely in mind by now, now as so often in the past—a near-pathological drive to reach some kind of resolution, which, since he couldn't locate it in his day-to-day life, he kept trying to find in the face of lethal danger. Discovering Sammie alive had come as a huge relief, but it had made him think, if only in this brief flash of a moment, that he'd come as close to balancing the books as ever he might. That coming to Sammie's aid had in some way counterbalanced his failure to help Mary.

He heard footsteps above him slow down, falter several times as Liptak neared exhaustion, and finally stop altogether.

Willy charged on regardless.

He saw Liptak sprawled on his back, his mouth hanging open, one hand clinging to the banister as if it were a lifeline, just seconds before he was on top of him. Liptak had a gun out, too, but Willy slapped it aside with a swipe from his own, causing the other man to cry out in pain as the gun went hurtling down the narrow, empty stairwell, some eighty feet straight down.

Willy dropped his pistol on the steps and grabbed Liptak by the shirtfront in his powerful right hand, hauling him up and throwing him across the railing so that he balanced there over the long, empty hole below them. Willy was barely breathing hard.

"Hey, you little turd," he said softly, his face inches from Andy's. "You done yet?"

Liptak's body was as still and stiff as a board. His hands were clenched to Willy's shoulders in a fierce grip. "Put me down, Sniper. For Christ's sake."

Willy felt the fear coming off him like an electrical current. He watched Liptak's dilated pupils and thought he could see in their depth the darkness of the jungle, of the blackouts he'd suffered as a drunk, and of the pure inky well of his own despair, on the edge of which he balanced every day. He shifted his gaze to the gloomy, bottomless funnel of the stairwell just past Liptak's left ear, and found there the same image—and perhaps as well, a solution. The nagging thought tugging at the corner of his mind loomed into something more tangible, a synergy combining good timing, pure and brutal justice, and with it, relief.

"What d'you say we go for a little flight?" he suggested.

Liptak's mouth opened, but it was Sammie's voice he heard.

"Willy? You all right? Where are you?"

He paused, his muscles tensed for the leap. Liptak's breathing was now coming in short gasps.

"Willy?" she called again from far below, her voice almost breaking. "Goddamn it, you bastard. Answer me."

Her anger worked its way through the tangle of his mind, drawing his attention away from the task at hand, if just for a moment.

"I'm up here. With our mutual friend," he answered finally, reluctantly.

Whether it was something she heard in his voice or just simple dumb luck, she answered, "Well, don't screw it up doing something stupid, okay? Bring him down here so I can beat the crap out of him."

Her words echoed up the hollow shaft of the turret, reverberating off the walls. Slowly, he smiled, straightened slightly, and refocused on Andy Liptak's face.

"You may not believe it, but today's your lucky day," he said, and pulled him off the railing and back onto the steps.

\*     \*     \*

"There's movement by the chain-link fence, southwest wall."

Gunther, Ogden, Panatello, and Janet Scott all turned to look at the spot indicated by the sharpshooter through their radio earpieces.

"Roger that," Janet responded. "Do you have a visual?"

"That's affirmative. Two men and a woman. She's limping and one of the men looks like he has his hands cuffed behind his back."

Gunther whispered into her other ear.

"Does it look like the other guy has a useless left arm, probably with the hand stuffed into his pants pocket?"

There was a startled pause. "Hang on."

Despite the tension, Scott smiled. "That got him."

"Affirmative," came the report at last, the tone of voice betraying the speaker's confusion.

She reassured him. "That's good news. Hold your positions and wait till they're out in the open."

Slowly, awkwardly, three figures emerged from the jagged hole at the prison's base and picked their way across the rubble and through the torn fencing.

"It's okay," Joe Gunther said.

Janet Scott radioed everybody to stand down and ordered in the ambulance hidden nearby as the four of them broke cover and walked to meet Andy Liptak and his escort in the middle of the parking lot.

Gunther's first concern was for the wounded Sammie Martens.

"You okay?" he asked her as they drew near.

Her smile gave him what he needed to know. "Flesh wound," she answered. "I've always wanted to say that. Just didn't know it would hurt so much."

Panatello and his people grabbed Liptak away from Willy and whisked him off toward a waiting car.

Willy shook his head at her. "Such a wimp."

Ward Ogden gave him an appraising look. "We weren't sure we hadn't lost you."

"Wishful thinking," Willy told him, but then looked straight at Joe Gunther. "I figured I hadn't been a big enough pain in the butt yet."

Gunther studied his face, and seemed to read there the debate that Willy had just barely survived. "Practice makes perfect, Willy," he finally said.

More
Archer Mayor!

Please turn this page
for a preview of

# GATEKEEPER

a new hardcover available
wherever books are sold.

"That's five dollars even."

Arnie Weller looked over the shoulder of the balding man holding out a ten-dollar bill and checked on the whereabouts of the young woman he'd seen entering a few minutes earlier.

"Out of ten," he automatically chanted, not bothering to meet his customer's eyes. Where was she? He turned briefly to the cash register, his fingers dancing across the keyboard in a blur. He caught the spring-loaded drawer against his hip as it opened, quickly made change, and proffered it to the man.

"Want a bag?" he asked, back to surveilling the rear of the store.

There was a telling pause from the customer, forcing Arnie to reluctanty focus on him. "What?"

The man smiled. "I bought gas."

Arnie stared at him, briefly at a total loss. "Sorry. Have a nice night."

Shaking his head slightly, the man slipped from Arnie's line of vision, through the double glass doors to the right, and into the night where his pickup was parked beside one of the gas pumps.

Arnie saw what he thought was the top of the girl's head pass behind a row of stacked boxes and six-packs near the bank of fridges along the far wall. *Hardest place to see anyone,* he thought angrily, still nursing a grudge. Two weeks ago, he'd asked a so-called security expert for an estimate on rigging the place with cameras. One week later, he'd bought a gun instead. For a whole lot less.

Bastard.

Arnie Weller ran a clean store, paid his taxes, took care of his employees, most of whom were worthless. He dealt with the chiseling gas company, the wholesale suppliers who screwed him out of habit, and the endless state forms issued monthly to make his life difficult. He paid his insurance, although they never settled his claims, donated to charitable causes he didn't agree with, and belonged to a chamber of commerce he thought was as useless as tits on a bull. He even cleaned the bathrooms twice a day, despite and not because of the disgusting condition he found them in, each and every time. If his customers were pigs, it didn't mean he'd join them.

And he put up with the disrespect, the surliness, the petty thefts, and the general offensiveness of the young people and trailer trash who supplied most of his retail business.

All in all, Arnie believed, he was a model businessman, employer, and patriotic citizen.

And he despised every aspect of it.

Three times, he'd been robbed in the past two months, once by a man with a hammer, and twice by people carrying guns. Arnie had known the kid with the hammer and had told the cops right off. They'd caught him hours later buying drugs with the till money. The little jerk had ended up with barely a scratch, being underage. No record, no jail time, just a few weeks in rehab. To Arnie's thinking, hardly the penalty for threatening a man's life. This was Vermont, after all, famously one of the best states in which to break any law you liked.

But Arnie had suffered nightmares for weeks, envisioning that hammer coming down on his skull. And that was before the two guys with guns. They had really scared him.

The first had been so nervous, Arnie had worried more about the gun going off accidentally—the ultimate irony. The kid had worn a ski mask, dark with sweat, and his hand had trembled as if he'd been sick. Even his voice had cracked. If the barrel of the gun hadn't been so real, Arnie might've even felt sorry for the poor bastard. But the gun had been real, and the son-of-a-bitch had hit Arnie across the head with it just before he left, for no reason at all.

They'd caught that one, too—a drug user like the first—and him at least they'd put away. But Arnie still had the scar, and the flash of realization that had accompanied its acquisition that one of these days, he might actually be killed for running this marginal, ball-busting convenience store.

Then the latest one had shown up.

Not a kid. Not nervous. An out-and-out bad man.

The gun had been bigger, the hand hadn't shaken, and he'd worn the hood of his sweatshirt pulled down over half his face, giving him an almost demonic appearance. And he'd clearly enjoyed his work. He'd come around the counter, forced Arnie to the floor, face down, and had emptied the cash drawer himself. He'd even stuffed some

Slim Jims into his pocket as an afterthought. Then he'd knelt next to Arnie's head, had shoved the barrel of his gun into Arnie's ear, and had cocked the hammer, chuckling all the while.

"Tell me where you live, little man," the man had whispered.

Arnie had told him, the dread rising up in him, making it hard to breathe.

"Now we both know. You might want to remember that if you're planning on calling the cops."

After which he'd reached with his gloved hand between Arnie's legs and had given his testicles a hard, painful squeeze. "I got you here, little man. Never forget it. Keep your mouth shut or this'll be nothing compared to what's next."

Arnie hadn't told anyone about him. Not the cops, not his wife, not his buddies. He'd swallowed the loss, had struggled with the fear, had consulted with the security man.

And had bought the gun.

That hadn't turned out too well. Instead of supplying him the comfort he'd hoped for, the gun had nestled under Arnie's untucked shirt like a tumor threatening his life. He started judging everyone who entered the place in relationship to the gun—would they force him to use it or not? The anger he'd channeled into visions of shooting the hooded man, were he to dare to show his face again, was gradually replaced by the fear that he really might return—and that Arnie would die for having presumed a cold-bloodedness he knew he didn't possess.

Tentatively, as he'd done a hundred times since buying the damn thing, Arnie touched the butt of the gun through his shirt with his fingertips, as if the bulk of it against his stomach weren't enough to confirm its presence.

They were alone in the store, the girl and he, and he knew goddamned well she was hiding back there, biding her time to step forward.

He'd recognized the type, of course, as soon as he'd caught sight of her—underfed, dirty hair, her clothes a mess and probably not her own. Her body language upon entering hadn't met the two standards of legitimacy—either looking around to get a bearing or heading straight for a known product. Instead, it had been like a rat's running for cover—from the door to the aisle offering the most cover from Arnie's view. He'd seen that in shoplifters before. And with both the hammer kid and the nervous man with the ski mask. Although not the last guy.

Still, she was only a girl.

"Miss?" he finally called out, doubtful of the authority he tried to inject into his voice. "Is there something I can help you find?"

"The money," she answered from a totally different direction. And very nearby.

He swung around, startled, stumbling slightly as his feet tangled. She hadn't stayed by the fridges. Somehow, she'd circled around, coming at him from behind his own counter, slipping through the narrow gap beyond the hot-dog machine at the far end. She was ghostly pale, her red, sunken eyes resting on dark pouches of swollen skin. She looked barely able to stand, much less resist an attack by him.

But in her hand she held a knife, large and glinting in the light, and the gun against his abdomen suddenly felt like an ice cube, sending a deep wave of cold from his stomach out to his extremities.

"Take it easy," he said.

"Give me the money," she ordered, her voice barely a whisper.

"You need a doctor."

She stepped closer and gestured with the knife. What strength she had was clearly being routed to that hand. He had no doubt whatsoever she could harm him if necessary.

And yet, inexplicably to him, staring at another weapon in still another loser's fist suddenly reversed the coldness he'd just experienced, flushing his face with rage and making him at least think of some heroic counteraction.

But that's where it stayed—in the thought process. The impotence remained, compounding his anger. He turned toward the cash register, humiliated, presenting her with his back. "You fucking bastards."

The sound of the till springing open matched the electronic ding of someone crossing the threshold of the store's far entrance—the one near the hot-dog machine behind the girl.

Despite it being summertime, the man entering had the hood of his sweatshirt pulled partly over his face.

They were a team.

Seeing his nightmare brought back to life threw Arnie into a second reversal. Yielding to fear and fury combined, he pulled his gun from under his shirt, swiveled to face the girl, who was looking over her shoulder at the man in the hood, and fired.

The explosion was huge, deafening Arnie, reverberating off the walls, dropping the girl like a pile of clothes to the floor, and sending the hooded man staggering back in alarm against the door behind him.

His hood slipped from his head as his head smacked against the glass and Arnie, his gun now trained on him, his finger tight on the trigger, saw a wide-eyed, pimply teenager he knew well from past transactions.

They stared at each other for a long, very quiet moment before the teenager finally managed to stammer, "Oh, shit. Please don't."

Arnie saw him raise his empty hands in surrender and finally lowered the gun, the realization of what he'd just done slowly settling on him like a fog.

Crumpled and silent on the floor, the girl began leaking a dark puddle of blood.


Joe Gunther didn't bother showing his badge to the Brattleboro patrolman guarding the convenience store entrance. They knew one another. Gunther had once been his superior.

"Hey, Larry. Who's running this?"

"The detective's inside. How'd you hear about it? We barely got here."

Gunther smiled. "Scanner. Hard to break old habits."

The patrolman opened the door for him and Gunther stepped from a cool summer darkness filled with flashing red and blue strobes into the store's harsh fluorescent lighting, suggestive of an operating room.

Or a morgue.

A tall young man with an oddly hesitant manner rose from behind the counter. His face broke into a broad smile as he recognized the new arrival.

"Lieutenant. Good to see you. God, it's been a while. I didn't think the VBI went in for things like this."

He stuck out a hand, realized it was sheathed in a latex glove, and began struggling to remove it.

Joe Gunther quickly grasped him by the forearm in

greeting. "It's okay, Ron. It's not worth the hassle to put it back on."

He didn't bother correcting the other man on his outdated rank. Gunther hadn't been a lieutenant in several years. It was "Special Agent" now, a burdensome title he still found absurd, but which the political birth mothers of the new Vermont Bureau of Investigation had chosen in a typical effort to impose profundity where it could only be earned over time. "And I'm not here officially—just offering help if it's needed. You okay with my dropping by?"

Ron Klesczewski shook his head in amazement. "You kidding? Just like old times. Not that we need help. This is more like the inevitable finally happening."

"I just heard it was a shooting."

Klesczewski invited Gunther to look over the far edge of the counter at the wide pool of drying blood now spread from one edge of the narrow space to the other. It was smeared and covered with lug-soled boot prints, he presumed from the ambulance crew he'd also heard summoned on the scanner. If not for the slaughterhouse color, it might have looked like the aftermath of a playful struggle in a mud bath.

"Storekeeper shot a nineteen-year-old woman. She's still alive—barely. He used a .357. Real cannon. I don't think he had any idea what he was doing."

Gunther tilted his chin toward a carving knife lying at the edge of the crimson mess. "That hers?"

Klesczewski nodded and quickly glanced at the small notepad in his hand. "Arnold Weller's the owner. He's been robbed twice recently, once at gunpoint, once by a guy with a hammer. He bought the gun out of frustration.

Said he wouldn't have shot her if he hadn't thought the other guy was involved, but I'm not so sure."

Gunther looked at him briefly without comment. Klesczewski quickly answered the implied question. "Some teenage kid walked in just as these two were facing off. He had his sweatshirt hood down low over his face—it's a fad right now, plus it's a little on the cool side. Arnie swore he thought he was a bad guy."

"The kid was clueless?" Gunther asked.

"Oh, yeah. Went to the hospital, too. He could barely talk, he was so shaken up. Like I said, the whole thing was just waiting to happen—more and more dopers doing more and more rip-offs. Storekeepers getting cranked by the week. Matter of time before somebody killed somebody. Maybe this one was itching for an opportunity, maybe he was just frazzled to the limit."

Despite the nature of the conversation, Gunther suppressed a smile at his young colleague's seasoned attitude. Ron Klesczewski had been a fresh-faced detective when Gunther had run the Brattleboro squad a few years back. He'd been given command of it upon Joe's departure only because Gunther had taken the most obvious successor along with him to his new job. A natural with paperwork and computers, Klesczewski had been slow gaining self-confidence otherwise. Although things had obviously improved now that he was top dog. Gunther's amusement was in adjusting the new to his memories of the old.

"She was on drugs?" he asked.

Klesczewski shrugged. "Blood tests'll probably tell us before she will—assuming she survives. But she has the look, all the way down to the fresh track marks in her arm."

Gunther gazed once more at the gore covering the linoleum behind the counter—a body's life blood diluted with the root cause of its own destruction. Ron Klesczewski was perfectly correct about the inevitability of Brattleboro's increasing dilemma, but he could just as easily have extended it to include the entire state. While bent on pushing the same old romantic, fuzzy image of cows and maple syrup and grizzled farmers muttering "Ah-yup," Vermont was in fact facing a heroin epidemic. Almost one hundred fatal overdoses had been racked up in the past ten years, and countless more reversed in hospitals and ambulances. Small potatoes compared to Boston or New York, but not so negligible on a per capita basis, in a state of a half million residents. And it was climbing fast. The state police drug task force, which used to count heroin busts in the single digits five years back, was now spending fifty percent of its time on these cases alone.

"What's her name?" he asked, almost as an afterthought.

Klesczewsi again consulted his notes. "Laurie Davis."

Gunther became very still, catching his younger colleague's attention. "You okay? You know her?"

"She a blonde?" Gunther asked.

Klesczewski began rummaging around in a box he'd placed on the counter. "Hang on. I think I can do better than that."

He extracted a plastic evidence envelope with a driver's license captured within it. Gunther held it at an angle under the bleak lighting to better see the small photo.

"And this was definitely her?" he asked.

Klesczewski nodded. "She's got more meat on her there. I have crime-scene photos in the digital camera if you don't mind the small screen."

Gunther shook his head and returned the envelope to

him, feeling tired and mournful. "Doesn't matter. I know her."

Two hours later, Joe was staring at the coffee machine in a hallway off the waiting room at Brattleboro's Memorial Hospital, wondering if more coffee at this time of night would qualify as suicide by insomnia.

"Don't do it," came a woman's voice from behind him, as if his thoughts had been blinking on and off above his head.

He turned to see an equally tired-looking Gail Zigman approaching from the doors of the intensive care unit. She gave him a half-hearted smile and slipped her arm through his. "We both need some sleep," she finished.

"How's she doing?" he asked her.

"She's alive. They did what they could, but the blood loss was huge. Basically, she's in a coma and they have no idea if she'll come out of it." She rested her head against his shoulder and sighed. "At least they're getting some brain activity—whatever that means."

In books written a hundred years earlier, Gail was what might have been called Joe's "particular friend." She was all of that, certainly—his sounding board, the echo of his conscience, his love of many years—but she was not his wife. Perhaps because they'd met later in life, or were in many ways too independent, or simply were loners drawn together by instinct, they'd formed an eccentric partnership as solid as that found in a good marriage, but in which they sometimes didn't see each other for weeks at a time. In fact, for half of each year, Gail lived and worked as a lobbyist in the state capital of Montpelier, which under normal conditions was a two-hour drive away.

Not that these conditions applied. Gail had driven

down at warp speed following Joe's phone call to her, and had been monitoring Laurie Davis's progress from just outside the operating room ever since.

Laurie Davis was ner niece—her sister Rachel's daughter.

Gunther kissed the top of her head. "She might get lucky. Sometimes, the brain just needs a little nap before waking up, good as new."

They began walking down the empty, bland hallway toward the elevators at the far end.

"You're talking about a previously healthy body," Gail responded. "Not someone already half dead from drugs."

He thought about saying something comforting, as he would have with anyone else, but that wasn't their way. Plus, they'd both seen the girl, or what was left of her. There was little point pretending she wasn't a train wreck before Arnie Weller's bullet had torn into her skinny chest.

Gail shook her head, her voice hardening as she stared at the floor. "What the hell was she thinking?"

Joe felt uncomfortable. Laurie wasn't his relation. He'd only met her a couple of times. But she'd lived in Brattleboro, having moved up from suburban Connecticut at Gail's urging, and he was wondering now if he shouldn't have known that she'd fallen on hard times. He wasn't on the PD any longer, but he stayed connected. It would have been easy to keep tabs on her. Cops did that for one another's families, even extended ones.

"Thinking probably isn't a huge prerequisite," he suggested vaguely instead. "Seems like it's usually more about dulling the pain."

She looked up at him sharply, and he realized he'd unintentionally turned the tables on her, causing her to question her own responsibilities here.

"Sorry," he added quickly. "I didn't mean it to come out that way."

But Gail wasn't looking for a way out. "You're right," she admitted. "If she had been feeling any pain, I wouldn't have known about it. I didn't keep in touch— barely paid attention to her."

She paused to sigh. "My sister's going to flip out."

"You haven't reached her yet?" he asked.

She shook her head. "Got the answering machine. They're probably on the town. They do that a lot. It was one of the issues between them and Laurie." She paused and then added, "Everyone thought coming to Vermont would give them all a break."

# RIVETING, ACTION-PACKED DETECTIVE ADVENTURES by ARCHER MAYOR

☐ **BORDERLINES**
(0-446-40-443-8)

☐ **FRUITS OF THE POISONOUS TREE**
(0-446-40-374-1)

☐ **OPEN SEASON**
(0-446-40-414-4)

☐ **THE SKELETON'S KNEE**
(0-446-40-099-8)

☐ **SCENT OF EVIL**
(0-446-40-335-0)

☐ **THE DARK ROOT**
(0-446-40-376-8)

☐ **THE RAGMAN'S MEMORY**
(0-446-60-590-5)

☐ **BELLOWS FALLS**
(0-446-60-630-8)

AVAILABLE AT A BOOKSTORE NEAR YOU FROM

# WARNER BOOKS

1044b

# VISIT US ONLINE @ WWW.TWBOOKMARK.COM

## AT THE TIME WARNER BOOKMARK WEB SITE YOU'LL FIND:

- CHAPTER EXCERPTS FROM SELECTED NEW RELEASES

- ORIGINAL AUTHOR AND EDITOR ARTICLES

- AUDIO EXCERPTS

- BESTSELLER NEWS

- ELECTRONIC NEWSLETTERS

- AUTHOR TOUR INFORMATION

- CONTESTS, QUIZZES, AND POLLS

- FUN, QUIRKY RECOMMENDATION CENTER

- PLUS MUCH MORE!

Bookmark A Time Warner Book Group @ www.twbookmark.com